About the author

After leaving the regular army of the Federation of Rhodesia and Nyasaland, Jeremy Mallinson joined the staff of Gerald Durrell's newly formed zoological park in Jersey. During his forty-two year career in zoos and conservation he has studied animals in Africa, Asia and South America. He served as Gerald Durrell's Deputy and Zoological Director and, after his mentor's death in 1995, he was appointed Director of the renamed Durrell Wildlife Conservation Trust. He has written more than two hundred papers and articles, addressed conferences in over twenty different countries, and is the author of ten books. He has received many awards for his service to animal conservation worldwide, including a DSc (Hon) from The University of Kent and the OBE in 1997. Jeremy Mallinson lives in Jersey.

By the same author

Okavango Adventure – In Search of Animals in Southern Africa (David & Charles, 1973)
Earning Your Living with Animals (David & Charles, 1975)
Modern Classic Animal Stories, Editor (David & Charles, 1977)
The Shadow of Extinction – Europe's Threatened Wild Mammals (Macmillan, 1978)
The Facts about a Zoo (G. Whizzard, 1980)
Travels in Search of Endangered Species (David & Charles, 1989)
'Durrelliania' – An Illustrated Checklist (Bigwoods, 1999)
The Count's Cats (Llumina Press, 2004)
The Touch of Durrell – A Passion for Animals (Book Guild, 2009)
Les Minquiers – Jersey's Southern Outpost (Seaflower Books, 2011)

SOMEONE WISHES TO SPEAK TO YOU

Jeremy Mallinson

Book Guild Publishing
Sussex, England

First published in Great Britain in 2014 by
The Book Guild Ltd
The Werks
45 Church Road
Hove, BN3 2BE

Copyright © Jeremy Mallinson 2014

The right of Jeremy Mallinson to be identified as the author of this work has been asserted by him in accordance with the Copyright, Designs and Patents Act 1988.

All rights reserved. No part of this publication may be reproduced, transmitted, or stored in a retrieval system, in any form or by any means, without permission in writing from the publisher, nor be otherwise circulated in any form of binding or cover other than that in which it is published and without a similar condition being imposed on the subsequent purchaser.

While this book is set amid real events, it is a work of fiction.

Typesetting in Sabon by
Keyboard Services, Luton, Bedfordshire

Printed in Great Britain by
CPI Group (UK) Ltd, Croydon, CR0 4YY

A catalogue record for this book is available from
The British Library.

ISBN 978 1 909984 39 4

*In memory of two of the greatest of friends,
Colin C. Jones and Jay M. Duncan*

Contents

Acknowledgements	ix
Part One In Pursuance of a Doctorate; 1965–1973	1
1 Adventurous Ambitions	3
2 Mount Kahuzi's Kingdom of Gorillas	20
3 Conflicting Sentiments	51
4 A Moral Dilemma	80
Part Two A Return to Africa; 1974–1979	117
5 Leopard's Rock	119
6 Chief Chidzikwee	145
7 Spirit of Rhodesia	174
8 Change of Direction	198
9 An Imire Rendezvous	223
10 A Diversity of Decisions	249
11 The Reluctant Informer	276
12 A Paradox of Valour	301

Postscript; 'A Sadness to Behold' 331

A Selected Chronology of African Events 335

Glossary 347

Bibliography 349

Acknowledgements

The book, which merges fact with fiction, has greatly benefited from advice and conversations with the following persons:

A director general of MI5; a British ambassador; a British honorary consul; a lieutenant general (Rhodesian); a major general (British); an assistant commissioner (Colonial Police); a major (Household Brigade); an RAF pilot officer (Aden, 1965); an officer of the Psychological Warfare Action Group (Rhodesian); an international airline captain and flight lieutenant Rhodesian Air Force (Territorial); an equestrian expert; two American college and university graduates (Dickinson and Duke); the director/founder of Marwell Zoological Park; a director of Edinburgh Zoo; and an international primatologist.

Finally, the author is greatly indebted to Imogen Palmer (editor on behalf of Book Guild Publishing), who greatly developed the book's dialogue, fixed inconsistencies, and helped to more directly involve the reader with its main characters.

Part One

In Pursuance of a Doctorate; 1965–1973

1

Adventurous Ambitions

'Captain Lumumba and his crew welcome you aboard – and we hope you enjoy your flight with us!' said the tall, attractive flight stewardess as she showed Mathew Duncan to his window seat. He was one of the first passengers to board the Boeing 737 on its flight from Lubumbashi to Bukavu. The stewardess wore a long, green *pagne* with the head of President Mobutu Sésé Seko emblazoned prominently on the front of it, her hair combed with immense care and ingenuity into a series of neat rows, each with tightly plaited spike-like tufts erupting from the top. Soon the plane was seemingly at bursting point and the paraphernalia associated with such African travel appeared to block all access to emergency exits and even, in some places, to the aisle itself.

Just after noon the plane landed at Kalémi, about half way up the west coast of the long sausage-like form of Lake Tanganyika. A couple of poorly camouflaged armoured cars were parked near the eastern edge of the airfield, close to a disorderly collection of khaki tents. A group of dishevelled-looking military personnel were lounging or standing about like a small flock of perplexed sheep. During the plane's two-hour refuelling stop at Kalémi, the passengers had been allowed to disembark under the watchful eyes of a couple of soldiers in full battle dress, casually brandishing their lethal-looking AK-47s. In order to escape from the intense heat of the midday sun, the passengers were guided to an airless, corrugated-roofed reception area where an Air Congo ground staff member served lukewarm Coca Cola, packets of stale crisps and over-ripe bananas.

On the plane's onward flight to Bukavu, in order not to stray across an international border, it clung to Lake Tanganyika's western shoreline casting its streamlined dolphin-like shadow on the water. Forming the central basin of the Rift Valley, the lake marks the boundary between Zaire and Tanzania and in the northern region, between Zaire and Rwanda Burundi. This was Mathew's first visit to Africa, although he had read a great deal about the European scramble to colonise central Africa in the mid-nineteenth century.

'Where to, Bwana?' After a scramble at the airport, Mathew had managed to secure a battered diesel Mercedes 504 taxi, driven by a jovial middle-aged man called Alfonse who fortunately spoke fluent English as well as the local Bemba dialect. 'The Hotel Metropole in Bukavu,' Mathew replied. 'Do you know it?' After a brief haggle over the fare – Mathew was too tired to put up much of an argument – the taxi started to wind its way along the potholed tarmac road as the rays of the sun were just starting to melt behind the sombre forested slopes of Mount Kahuzi. First, some neat and lush-looking coffee estates could be seen on either side of the road, prior to such order of cultivation being disrupted by clusters of thatched-plumed mud-built dwellings, their female occupants starting the evening chore of preparing fires to cook upon. Other womenfolk walked in single file at the side of the road, returning to their huts with old oil cans filled with water balanced miraculously on top of their heads. Small groups of goats were nibbling at everything within their reach, while the ubiquitous poultry pecked incessantly at the ground, with some of their number narrowly missing being run over as the driver scattered them, speeding past with a degree of cavalier abandon.

ADVENTUROUS AMBITIONS

'So ... what brings you to Bukavu?' asked Alfonse, looking at his passenger in the rear-view mirror. 'I'm here to visit the Kahuzi-Biega National Park,' replied Mathew. 'The gorillas...' 'This is it!' interrupted Alfonse before Mathew had a chance to elaborate. The taxi had reached the attractive township, picking its way through a generous rash of market vendors and past the small port into the main street before drawing up in front of the Hotel Metropole. Mathew paid the fare and paused to take in the faded grandeur of the hotel's exterior for a few moments before entering.

Mathew had been given a letter of introduction to the Chairman of the Metropole Hotel Group in Lubumbashi by the Managing Director of Amiza, a major Belgian company that had been trading in the Congo for many decades prior to the country's independence in 1960. Such an introduction had come by way of the Belgian CEO of Amiza having been on a number of grouse shoots on Mathew's father's estate in the Yorkshire Dales. For after having heard that one of Sir Colin Duncan's sons was about to undertake some field work in Zaire he had arranged, through his Amiza headquarters in Kinshasa, to sponsor Mathew's accommodation in Bukavu. This generous gesture provided Mathew with a spacious room, complete with a dramatic view over Lake Kivu, nestling comfortably within the embrace of the surrounding mountains. The scene reminded Mathew of the Alpine environments around the Italian lakes of Maggiore and Como. However, although the hotel must have been quite luxurious in its pre-independence prime, he was soon to find that in keeping with the majority of manmade structures in this region, it had seen better days.

In contrast with the beauty of the view from the window, the room itself was stark. The walls were bare, the mattress was thin with some uncomfortable-looking springs protruding and the bedding itself was rather threadbare – but all appeared to be reasonably clean and provided a perfectly serviceable base. He kicked off his shoes and lay down, grateful to have reached his destination.

Mathew was the second son of Sir Colin and Lady Sally Duncan. Sir Colin's father, Reginald Duncan, had been a wealthy Bradford land and mill owner who had purchased his baronetcy in 1914 at the start of the First World War. Sir Colin (and later, his two sons) had been brought up on the family's 1,800-acre estate at Hartington Hall. The majority of Mathew's formative years had been occupied by attending a preparatory boarding school on a large estate in Northumberland; horse riding, fox hunting, beagling and grouse shooting – all experiences which had led him to develop a fascination with natural history.

Mathew was just over six feet in height, with a mop of blond hair, pale blue eyes, a Duke of Wellington nose (which no doubt highlighted his family's Viking ancestry) and the overall bearing of an athlete. During his teenage years he was inclined to be rather shy with a self-effacing disposition, but possessed that detached, distinguished-looking presence which in certain company set him apart from the usual rank and file of society. In spite of his initial shyness, he had inherited an adventurous spirit and had always thrived on unexpected challenges in atmospheres of uncertainty. Also, whenever he had set his sights on achieving a particular objective, more often than not he would be successful in seeing it through. Although Mathew had been brought up in the traditional manner for an English gentleman, while studying for 'A' levels at Wellington College, a prestigious public school in Berkshire, he had decided that instead of going to either Oxford or Cambridge he wanted to go to a university in the USA to further his academic career. For he was very much of the opinion that such a course of action and change of social environment would provide him with a wider cultural awareness, in turn further stimulating his ever-inquisitive mind and spirit of adventure.

So it had been during Mathew's early days at Scaife University, an exclusive liberal arts college in Tupelo, Mississippi, that his liberal views on segregation had been tested to the extreme. In particular, when he had learned about George Corley Wallace's inaugural speech as Governor of Alabama with his foretelling: 'In the name of the greatest people that have ever trod this earth, I draw the line in the dust and toss the gauntlet before the feet of tyranny, and I say segregation now, segregation tomorrow, segregation forever', and how in September 1963 Governor Wallace attempted to stop four black students from enrolling in four separate elementary schools in Huntsville.

In spite of public segregation officially ending in the USA in 1964 with the Civil Rights Act, Mathew had been sensitive to the fact that there remained formidable forces resisting change in the Deep South and that, even among some of his Scaife University colleagues, there were some who were finding it difficult to come to terms with the act. The assassination of Dr Martin Luther King Jr in Memphis, Tennessee, in April 1968, which had occurred during Mathew's final year at Scaife, had prompted him to join Tupelo's local Civil Rights Movement and to participate in one of its protest marches. As a result of his support for the Civil Rights Movement, Mathew had been disappointed to sense how he had been, to a degree, socially ostracised by some of the university's more hard-line students, who still considered that socially enforced segregation of African-Americans from other races should continue.

It had been at Scaife University that Mathew had studied under a renowned Professor of Psychology and Animal Behavior, Professor Ralph Candland, and on the completion of his BA he had been awarded the highly coveted Emerson D. Miller Prize for Academic Achievement in Animal Behavior. As a result of this success, Mathew decided to go directly into a PhD programme and due to his academic prowess, was readily accepted by the Zoology Department at Emory University, Georgia. It had been at Emory that he had been able to carry out his doctorate studies with some of his coursework being directly involved with the captive gorilla population at the Yerkes Regional Primate Research Center in Atlanta, which had its main research building located on a 25-acre tract of land on the Emory University campus. The Yerkes Center was one of the world's oldest scientific institutes for the study of primates; in 1929 its founders Robert and Ada Yerkes had published *The Great Apes*, in which they brought together all available knowledge about the gorilla and other apes.

During Mathew's initial behavioural research on the centre's gorilla population, he had worked within the department overseen by Professor W.C. Osman Hill, the Associate Director. It had been the professor who had guided Mathew in his selection of a specific dissertation topic and had advised him that his future academic studies should have as their main tenet to carry out comparative work between captive and wild populations of gorillas. Also, on behalf of Emory University, Osman Hill as a 'major professor' had agreed to be responsible overall for the supervision of Mathew's academic programme, and it was decided that once Mathew had completed his initial studies at the Yerkes Center, he would be given the opportunity to go to Africa to study gorillas in the wild. With this in mind, Mathew took the opportunity to read as much as possible about the African travels of some of the great nineteenth-century explorers. These included books by David Livingstone, Samuel Baker, Richard Burton, John Speke, Henry Morton Stanley and Paul du Chaillu, all of whom had provided him with a longing to travel to Africa at the earliest opportunity. For, as far as his academic work was concerned, he could not help feeling that the natural social interactions of captive gorillas would be significantly different from those living in the wild state.

ADVENTUROUS AMBITIONS

Through the Yerkes Research Center's many contacts and, in one particular case, as a result of Emory University's support for a specific *in situ* conservation programme, Osman Hill was confident that he would be able to arrange for Mathew to go to Zaire to spend several months studying the social interactions of a habituated group of eastern lowland gorillas on the western shores of Lake Kivu, as the university had been a significant donor to the conservation work being carried out at the newly created Kahuzi-Biega National Park. So it had been this much-desired goal that had provided Mathew with an additional stimulus to concentrate the first year of his studies on the captive population at the primate centre, as well making some comparative observations on the gorillas at the Atlanta Zoo.

Prior to flying to Zaire, Mathew had completed the initial writing-up of his research work, which Osman Hill had been most complimentary about. Now that Mathew had arrived in Africa, he could not have been more delighted to leave behind the intense clamour of Atlanta's traffic-congested streets and the jostle of overcrowded pavements, to have escaped the overall claustrophobic effect of city life. In spite of Mathew's concern about the attitudes towards racial segregation he had witnessed from some of his peers at Scaife University, he had found the majority of his time in the Deep South to be most stimulating and enjoyable. However, there could hardly be more of a contrast between the environment of an American metropolis and that of Bukavu in Central Africa – a contrast that appealed greatly to Mathew's curiosity for the unknown. He would soon be embarking upon the challenges involved with his field research work in furthering the methodology he had been working on at Yerkes; studies which he hoped would usefully contribute by more clearly defining the cognitive skills of the gorilla kingdom and their relevance to human communication.

Osman Hill had provided Mathew with a letter of

SOMEONE WISHES TO SPEAK TO YOU

introduction to Adrien Deschryver, Director of the Kahuzi-Biega National Park, who had agreed to cooperate with Mathew and to allow him to study his habituated group of eastern lowland gorillas, *Gorilla g. graueri*. Such assistance had resulted from the sizeable grant that Emory University had made in support of Deschryver's long-term conservation activities in the park, as well supporting their anti-poaching patrols.

So it had been soon after breakfast on the day after his arrival in Bukavu that Mathew, armed with his professor's letter of introduction, had with the enthusiasm of a young man-about-town about to meet a debutante on a first date, taken a taxi to the National Park's headquarters.

'Oh! So pleased to meet you – do come in,' said the strikingly attractive girl who answered the door of the small whitewashed bungalow. 'My name is Lucienne Luzembo. I'm afraid the *Conservateur*, Adrien Deschryver, will be away from Bukavu for the next four days – his plane has developed some mechanical problems that need to be fixed in Nairobi. He's very sorry not to be here but I can tell you more about our work. Can I get you a cup of coffee?'

'I must say that would be very welcome, yes please,' replied Mathew, disappointed that he would not be meeting Adrien Deschryver that morning but eagerly looking forward to making Lucienne's aquaintance.

'I came to Bukavu from Lubumbashi with a Belgian-based television crew,' explained Lucienne over a cup of locally-grown Kivu coffee. 'We were filming Adrien with his habituated group of eastern lowland gorillas in Kahuzi-Biega. I was the crew's translator.'

'That sounds interesting... What led you into that line of work?' asked Mathew, keen to find out everything he could about Lucienne. 'Well, I majored in French and English at the University of Congo in Lubumbashi and also speak Bemba, the local tribal language, so when the film company approached the university to ask if they could suggest anyone to translate, they put my name forward. It was luck, really, as these things often are. But as we were filming, I realised that what I was really interested in was the gorillas – I wanted to learn about their environment, their conservation, everything about them. I suppose because Adrien could see how much it meant to me, how much I shared his enthusiasm for the future welfare of the gorillas, he offered me a job here as his office manager, with scope to act as a translator in the future for tourists. So here I am!'

Mathew was quick to observe that Lucienne possessed the self-assured poise and body of a model and whenever she spoke in her French-accented English about the park's gorillas, her dark brown eyes flashed with excitement. Her profile was further enhanced by the attractiveness of the dimples in her cheeks and the twitching of her button-sized nose, which all blended perfectly with the smoothness of her caramel-coloured complexion. However, although Mathew was quick to recognise that Lucienne's appearance would be sure to set any male pulse racing, he knew only too well that in this particular situation his priority was to retain his usual degree of British formality and decorum.

Keen to carry on the conversation, Mathew delved further into Lucienne's background. 'Was Lubumbashi your hometown?'

'I was born in Katanga, twelve years before the Congo's independence from Belgium in 1960. My parents chose to privately educate me at the Mission de Sacré Coeur at Ankoro, a small town on the Lualaba River to the north of Lubumbashi. My father was African, Dr Gaston Luzembo – my mother Karen was European. She was a nurse ... they married while he was studying medicine in Antwerp. The difference in their cultures never seemed to bother them, they have always been very close.'

On the strength of the letter of introduction from Osman

SOMEONE WISHES TO SPEAK TO YOU

Hill, and Lucienne having recalled the correspondence with Mathew and the financial aid that had come from Emory University, she promised to make radio contact with Deschryver that same evening. 'You must have the *Conservateur*'s permission for your first visit to the park, as he can't be here himself. I should have his reply by tomorrow morning – why don't you come back then? Let me give you a lift back to the hotel for now, it will be much quicker than a taxi.' They jumped into the Park Department's open mud-encrusted Brazilian-manufactured jeep and continued an animated conversation until Lucienne dropped Mathew at the doors of the Hotel Metropole.

From the literature that Lucienne had given Mathew about the history of the Kahuzi-Biega National Park, which included the background of Adrien Deschryver's involvement with the conservation of its gorillas, he noted that it had been given its park status in 1970, only one year previously. Prior to this, since 1937, Mount Kahuzi had been classified as a Zoological and Forest Reserve and during the colonial days of the Belgian Congo, Deschryver's family had owned extensive tea and coffee plantations on the twin mountains of Kahuzi and Biega. As Deschryver had been brought up in the region, he knew the mountainous environments extremely well and, when he had been old enough to carry a gun, he had hunted antelope, wild pig and even elephants in the surrounding forests. However, during the mid 1960s the area had suffered from serious depredations; many trees had been cut down on land cleared for cultivation and a great deal of hunting had taken place. What had made this particularly deplorable was that the eastern lowland gorillas had been among the chief victims.

It had been in 1965 when Deschryver had first reported that the gorillas were being hunted systematically by the

ADVENTUROUS AMBITIONS

Pygmies with the aid of dogs, nets and spears. He had also recorded how old silverback males had tried to defend their families but had been massacred with spears. Females that had taken flight became entangled in nets, while the sub-adults and juveniles that had climbed into the trees for safety became a fine target for the poachers' poisoned arrows. Due to such an uncontrolled onslaught on this remnant population of the eastern lowland gorilla species, it was not long before almost all the young gorillas of Kahuzi had been exterminated, and the remaining adults had become fragmented, aggressive and uncharacteristically dangerous. It was as a result of such carnage that Deschryver had made it his personal crusade to do as much as possible to preserve this isolated wild population, as well as to conserve the mountains' important ecosystems on the south-west shores of Lake Kivu.

As ex-poachers frequently made the best gamekeepers, Deschryver first set about converting the Pygmies from poachers into guides. Once the national park had been established, some of the gorillas that he had managed to habituate began to realise that not all members of the human race represented danger and a number of paying visitors were permitted to see gorillas in the wild for the first time. Even more rewarding for Deschryver, it had not taken too long before nature had started to make amends and the population of gorillas had started to increase.

That evening, Mathew received a call from Lucienne. 'I hope you're not disappointed, Mathew – Adrien would like you to wait as he considers it essential to introduce you personally to his family of gorillas. Also, he would like to take you to the area that he considers would be best for your behavioural studies and to show you from the start the type of contact that he would happy for you to have.'

'No, I'm not disappointed, Lucienne. That makes perfect

sense. I'm happy to wait for Adrien – I would hate to offend him unintentionally.'

'When I arrived in Bukavu with the Belgian television crew, Adrien was initially rather wary about our presence, he was worried about taking newcomers to Kahuzi-Biega and allowing them to interact with and film his precious gorillas. When you meet him for the first time, tread carefully ... it's a bit like being interviewed by a university entry board and being assessed thoroughly in the process. It might help if you show as much enthusiasm as you can about the science that could result from your behavioural studies and the financial benefits that could well result from future funding sources for the park. One more thing – it would be a good idea to tell Adrien how fortunate you consider yourself to be in having such a wonderful opportunity to study the endangered eastern lowland gorilla and that you recognise fully that this is only possible thanks to him – the *Conservateur* – having spent so much time in habituating them to the presence of human beings.'

'That's excellent advice; I shall do a little preparation before I meet him. I can quite understand why he's so protective, I would be exactly the same, but rest assured I will abide by his guidance – I share his aims completely.'

'As you have some free time, you could take the early morning *vedette* to Goma, on the far northern tip of Lake Kivu. The Virunga volcanoes are nearby – they span the borders of Zaire, Rwanda and Uganda – and there you will find the fragmented montane forest habitats of the remnant populations of the endangered mountain gorilla, *Gorilla g. beringei*. You may be able to visit their habitat if you go to the tourist office in Goma to see whether a guide is available. Virunga Park call them their "Tourist family groups", it could be worth a try.'

So it had been at 7.30 the following morning that Mathew had taken Lucienne's advice and had climbed on board the overcrowded *vedette*. He had found himself to be the only European on the daily ferry to Goma. Lake Kivu's eastern coastline represented Zaire's international border with Rwanda and, during the boat's six-hour voyage to the top of the lake, it chugged its way past and between numerous islands, the majority of which sadly had been shaved of their blankets of forest and provided little refuge for the lake's wildlife. It was while taking some photographs of the attractive Rwandan landfall that Mathew was tapped on the shoulder by an aggressive-looking African who snatched the camera from his grip, gesticulating that in Zaire it was forbidden to take photographs of an international border. It was only after several minutes of Mathew's protestations in his smattering of French, repeating that he was a research scientist at the '*Parc National du Kahuzi-Biega − Sanctuaire des Gorilles*', that his camera was returned by the security official who was to address him as 'comrade', squeeze his hand, and to pat him forcibly on the back before returning to a bottle of beer that he had left nearby.

Prior to the boat docking at Goma, Mathew was afforded the dramatic view of the most westerly of the group of eight Virunga volcanoes, and could see the smoke issuing forth from the summit of one of the two still-active younger ones. If time had been on his side, and permits had allowed, Mathew would have loved to visit the Albert National Park, the history of which he had recently read about. How Carl Akeley, the famous naturalist and sculptor, had shot five gorillas at the Virunga volcanoes in 1921 for the American Museum of Natural History, and had subsequently become so impressed with his quarry and the mountains in which the gorillas lived that he urged the Belgian government to set aside a permanent sanctuary for the animals where they could exist in peace and be studied by scientists. The Albert National Park was established in April 1925, and in July 1929 was enlarged to include the whole chain of volcanoes, which undoubtedly represented a fitting tribute not only to Carl Akeley but also to King Albert of Belgium, after whom the park was named. However, it was not until the 1950s and 1960s that the two doyens of long-term field research, George Schaller and later Dian Fossey, arrived to study the mountain gorillas of the Virunga volcanoes.

Lucienne had advised Mathew to stay at the Hotel de Grand Lacs during his three days in Goma. Like so many other buildings in the region, it very much resembled a mere apology to its former glory – in some places a series of shrapnel scars could be seen on the walls. She had also suggested that during his time there he should go to the Nyiragongo lava lake, as it was a dramatic moonscape spectacle not to be missed. But Mathew had made it his priority to do everything possible to see the mountain gorillas, even if it meant having to visit them with a group of sightseers, so he walked to Goma's small tourist office only to find its heavy green wooden window shutters firmly closed, and its front door securely locked and bolted.

At the nearby police station a burly and surly, suspicious-looking sergeant, who had a sizeable scar on his left cheek, meticulously studied Mathew's passport and visa, at one stage even holding it up to the light as if looking for some evidence of forgery.

'I'm sorry, Sir, but it is impossible to go into gorilla country without first crossing the Zaire/Rwandan border – and there are political problems at present. It could be dangerous for you, so I cannot grant you permission to do so. Also, if you were to go into Rwanda, you would not be allowed to re-enter Zaire as your visa clearly states that you can only enter the country at Kinshasa or Lubumbashi.'

Mathew contemplated offering the policeman a $US 100 bribe to secure a visa to record an additional place of entry into the country, as well as a letter of 'free passage', and to receive the sergeant's advice as to the safest way to travel without encountering any problems. But due to the policeman's increased hostility, Mathew had the feeling that for some reason or other he didn't care for Europeans and that he had therefore taken a dislike to him, preferring to be left alone in his office at the earliest opportunity. He decided it was best to thank the policeman for his time and beat a hasty retreat.

Back at the Hotel de Grand Lacs, Mathew described the encounter to the hotel's Indian manager. 'He was nothing short of hostile, to tell you the truth. I don't know what I'd done to offend him but he just refused point blank to help in any way.'

'Don't take it personally. There was terrible fighting in this region during the upheavals ten years ago, at the time of the country's independence from Belgium. A group of heavily armed European mercenaries arrived in Goma, shot dead some of the townspeople then caught and tied the policeman to a chair. As he wouldn't help them find the men they were looking for, the mercenaries gave him a severe beating – you may have noticed the wound on his face.'

After their conversation, Mathew recalled how he had read similar accounts of beatings of African-Americans in some of the prisons in the Deep South. He could well understand the degree of racial animosity that he had just experienced at Goma's police station.

So, with Mathew's ambition to have at least a brief encounter with the mountain gorillas being so conclusively thwarted, he decided to return to Bukavu the following morning and to await Deschryver's arrival from Nairobi. He would also see whether Lucienne would have time to accept an invitation to join him for Sunday lunch in order to try to gain her confidence, as well as to learn as much as possible about Adrien Decshryver and the eastern lowland gorillas of Kahuzi-Biega that he had done so much to protect.

* * *

SOMEONE WISHES TO SPEAK TO YOU

Bistro Zanzibar was situated on the south-eastern shores of Lake Kivu. It offered a sizeable shaded veranda dining area that extended out over the water, supported by some irregular-looking wooden stilts. In this way, the bistro's guests were able to benefit from the comfortable gentle breeze that came down the rift valley from the mountains to the north-east of the lake.

Mathew had arrived at his rendezvous with Lucienne a good fifteen minutes early. This was not only to select the best table, but also to follow his mother's advice that whenever entertaining a lady guest to always be sure to arrive in good time to welcome her, and to position a chair at the table to provide her with the most commanding view of other diners and of the overall environment.

Lucienne's arrival was heralded by a warm welcome from the bistro's manager, and admiring glances from some of the other customers. She was wearing a colourful, loose-fitting blouse with a floral pattern, her hair tied back in a ponytail with a ribbon of the same material. Her pale sky-blue slacks and matching sandals completed the outfit, which perfectly suited her ebullient personality. 'Mathew! How nice to see you again – you must tell me all about your trip ... so sorry it didn't go quite according to plan,' said Lucienne as she approached the table. Mathew wanted to welcome her with a kiss on both cheeks, but decided to deflect such a spontaneous temptation by just formally shaking her hand. 'There's not much to tell!' laughed Mathew as the waiter drew out Lucienne's chair for her to take a seat. 'Is this table all right for you? I thought it would give you a good view of the lake. Now, let's order some wine... Sauvignon Blanc?'

To any onlooker observing this young couple during the course of the meal, enjoying a dish of freshly caught lake fish and with the wine having started to dilute their inhibitions, it would be fair to assume there was a degree of intimacy. One would suppose from the way they were speaking to one another that they were either close relatives nostalgically recalling past experiences, or perhaps even a couple on their first date, such was the apparent degree of familiarity and the strength of like-minded thinking between them.

With the lunch over, which Mathew could not have been more pleased to have hosted, Lucienne drove along the lake's picturesque shoreline, past small stands of the ubiquitous eucalyptus and clusters of the slender-shaped fishing boats, back to the Hotel Metropole. As Deschryver had now returned to Bukavu, he had asked Lucienne to arrange to pick Mathew up from his hotel at 6 a.m. the following morning and to collect him from his home on the slopes of Mount Kahuzi, so that they could all go on together to the national park. Once preparations had been made, and after a goodbye that felt rather awkward on Mathew's part, Lucienne sped away in the Park Department's open jeep with a flourish of farewell waves and the happiest of smiles.

2

Mount Kahuzi's Kingdom of Gorillas

It had been just after 7 a.m. the following day that Deschryver had picked up the two Pygmy trackers by the entrance to the Kahuzi-Biega National Park. They joined Lucienne in the back of the four-wheel drive vehicle, while Mathew sat in the front passenger seat as they drove on for twenty minutes or so, until turning off onto a small track and parking under the shade of a sizeable stand of bamboos.

Lucienne seemed quiet in comparison to her high spirits during their lunch the day before but during the journey, Mathew was relieved that she was directing secretive smiles and glances towards him when the opportunity arose. Deschryver's opinion was so important to Lucienne that she didn't want him to think that anything – or anyone – was distracting her from their mission.

'OK, now we'll follow the trackers into the forest,' said Deschryver in a hushed voice. 'Just remember to keep vigilant, silent and calm. They know exactly what they're doing.' The three of them followed the trackers along a well-worn trail into the denser foliage of the montane rain forest of Mount Kahuzi, where the trackers kept stopping to examine food remnants, faecal deposits and gorilla spoor that looked comparatively recent. As they had picked up such a recent trail, they became as alert as a brace of tracker dogs having just caught scent of their quarry – although in contrast to a pack of hounds they now remained silent, only communicating with each other by way of hand signals. As they continued to deftly cut their way through the thick blankets of bamboo with their menacing-looking metal pangas, laying each bundle neatly to one side, they continued searching for every telltale sign of the direction that the gorilla family had taken.

The small party negotiated their way through the density of the vegetation – in some places it was impossible for them to even walk upright. They had on a number of occasions to either crouch, or even crawl, through the undergrowth in order to follow the gorillas' spoor. Some of the mature stands of bamboo measured up to 8-10 cm in diameter and their lush feather-like branches reached almost 20 m into the light mountain air. After almost an hour there had become increasing evidence that a group of gorillas had only recently traversed the trail that the guides were following. Small piles of sheaths of bamboo shoots, deposits of light-coloured faeces, broken branches and varied sizes of foot and knuckle prints could be seen in the forest's sponge-like peaty ground, which all provided additional evidence that a gorilla family was close by.

'Have you seen piles of shoots like these before?' whispered Deschryver to Mathew during one of their brief pauses for rest. Mathew shook his head. 'At this time of the year, between September and February, bamboo shoots are in season around here – the gorillas take full advantage. They gather a handful, settle down in a favourite spot and enjoy the delicacy of the hearts of the shoots. Once they've eaten what they want, instead of discarding the leftovers like a troop of baboons would, the gorillas arrange them in neat little piles of between four and twelve.'

As they progressed further, Mathew's nostrils detected the familiar effluvium musk odour of the gorilla, an aroma that he had been first exposed to in the late 1960s while viewing the solitary male lowland gorilla (Willie B.) in his original Victorian-style cage at the Atlantic Zoo, and later while observing some of the gorillas at the Yerkes Primate Research Center. The guides soon became more hesitant, stopping to listen carefully, before using their pangas to hack at some of the sturdier ringed stems of a nearby bamboo stand to create as much noise as possible among the vegetation, in order to alert the gorillas as to their presence. Within no more than thirty seconds of the disturbance, the tranquility of the forest was broken by the deep-bellied roar of an adult male silverback that had been in quite close proximity to them. This was soon to be followed by a further roar, the noise of breaking branches and the crushing of nearby bamboo stems.

With a gorilla so nearby, Deschryver had taken over the lead position; the Pygmies immediately looked more at ease as they smiled at each other in seeming relief and gratitude. Then, after the party moved on a little further, through a gap in the heavy foliage Mathew gained his first sight of a magnificent eastern lowland gorilla in the wild. The young silverback was sitting on the far side of a fallen tree; his jet-black head, sparsely haired chest and the long hairs on his arms and stomach contrasted significantly with the light grayness of his silver back. As soon as Deschryver had seen the gorilla he had taken some leaves to chew, and by not looking directly at the silverback, he kept making the soft, rumbling noise of a gorilla welcome and repeating in an equally soft voice, 'com-com', 'com-com', 'com-com'. The silverback responded to this by giving a deep yawn, throwing his head back and displaying a fine array of ivory-white teeth, which were set within an oasis of pinkish gums. He then shifted his position slightly and suddenly stood up, executed with his cupped hands the familiar gorilla chest-beat display of 'pok-a-pok', 'pok-a-pok', 'pok-a-pok', 'pok-a-pok', then turned his back on them and disappeared out of view into a small valley beneath where they had been standing.

'I believe that the young silverback has come into the area from a nearby small group of bachelors to try to lure some females away from Casimir,' whispered Deschryver. Casimir was the leader of a family group, an elderly silverbacked male that Deschryver had befriended some five years previously. 'With all the chest-beating and vocalisations of this young male, Casimir's family will be very unsettled – I very much doubt we'll see anything more today, we may as well retrace our tracks.'

About half an hour later, Deschryver heard a branch being snapped about 25 m to the right and, within two minutes, they came upon the large bulk of Casimir lying down with his back towards them, with six members of his family relaxing to the rear of him. Another large male, whom Deschryver had named Hannibal, sat in a restful position to the right of his younger family members, with his broad back leaning against a massive tree trunk. Hannibal's attention appeared to be divided between the casual regarding of the knuckles of his right hand, and seemingly contemplating what to do next; although at the same time glancing good-naturedly in Deschryver's direction. Three of the younger gorillas were tussling together like friendly wrestlers, with two adult females grooming and picking through the thick black hairs of Casimir's shoulders and arms, while two juveniles peered inquisitively from behind them, as if seeking some type of reassurance that this small group of humans were not a threat to their well-being.

While the gorilla family relaxed during the mid-morning period, it was customary for Deschryver to always do likewise; to just stand or lie down on the peaty soil and to take notes of his observations and, as if sharing his lunchtime with the gorillas, to continuously chew some leaves. Mathew noticed that Lucienne often acted in a similar fashion, and he could see by her keen sense of alertness and constant excitement when following the Pygmies and Deschryver that she was in her element. Whenever Lucienne had stopped to peer through the foliage at the gorillas and Mathew had been able to look at her more closely, he could appreciate what a stunningly attractive woman she was. He found that her considerable enthusiasm for what she was observing was utterly contagious, and he felt quite humble in having been in the presence of such a seemingly contented family group of one of man's closest relatives.

After Casimir had been almost motionless for some twenty minutes, he had rolled onto his side, propped himself up on his right elbow, and then gathered his massive body up into a sitting position as if to better acknowledge the presence of Deschryver, his benefactor and guardian. Only then could Mathew fully appreciate Casimir's size and true magnificence. He had been fascinated by the way that Deschryver had mimicked the silverback's welcoming noise, and how two or three of the group had joined Casimir with their rumblings of greetings. During this time it had been obvious to Mathew just how enthralled Lucienne had been in watching the gentle playful interactions of the family group. After a further fifteen minutes of seemingly mutual admiration between Deschryver and Casimir, the silverback made a series of soft rumbling stomach sounds that brought a chain of similar responses from the other members of his group. This heralded Casimir's tight-knit family reverently following him down a slope through the giant bamboos to a further foraging site prior to dusk, and the making of their respective sleeping nests for the night.

During the next hour, they followed the gorilla family, keeping as close to them as possible without wishing to disturb their afternoon foraging. At times, the three sub-adults climbed high up into the trees, feeding on the red berries of a species of stinkwood. (On a later occasion, Deschryver told Mathew that the eastern lowland gorillas of Kahuzi-Biega had been observed to feed on over 200 vegetable food plants, as well as on a variety of small invertebrates.) Three-quarters of an hour before dusk, the party left the gorillas to settle down for the night. 'The females and their young will make their

MOUNT KAHUZI'S KINGDOM OF GORILLAS

nests in the trees,' explained Deschryver to Mathew, 'while the senior males and Casimir will stay on the ground – they will sleep but they will also keep guard.'

Just as the daylight was finding it difficult to filter its way through the forest's thick canopy to the peaty substratum of the soft ground, with Mathew finding it quite a challenge to keep up with the rest of the party, it seemed to him almost like a miracle that the Pygmy trackers were able to guide them back to where they had left the vehicle, taking them by the 'white man's route' through this mountain of Eden. In this respect, Mathew had found that it was rather as if the Pygmies had been empowered by the same navigational skills as migratory birds when they return annually to their original nesting sites. Deschryver dropped off the two now jovial and very talkative trackers at the small thatched and mud-built dwellings just outside the park's entrance, which he had constructed for their families. On the journey back to Bukavu, Mathew found the lifeless span of the tarmac road to be in sharp contrast to the delights of the lush tropical foliage that they had just spent over nine hours negotiating.

During the remaining part of their return journey, hardly a word had been exchanged between Mathew, Deschryver and Lucienne for they were each thinking about the time they had spent with Casimir and his family. Mathew was amazed that on this, his first visit to the park, he had experienced such a close and lengthy encounter with the gorillas. 'That sort of lengthy viewing is by no means the norm,' Deschryver had later told him. 'Although it's quite common to hear chest-beatings and those screaming roars, I've had many trips into the forest where I completely fail to catch a glimpse of them.' Also, due to Lucienne's responsibilities in running the office, it was rare that she had the opportunity to visit the park, let alone to have had such an excellent face-to-face encounter with these doyens of the kingdom of anthropoid apes. Mathew well recognised how

SOMEONE WISHES TO SPEAK TO YOU

much the day's experience had represented one of the highlights and most memorable occasions of his life so far, made even better by having been in the company of two such remarkable people.

'Could you come to the office at 8.30 tomorrow morning?' Deschryver asked Mathew prior to dropping him off at Hotel Metropole. 'It'll give us a chance to discuss the details of your forthcoming field work... I'd like to hear some more about the main objectives of your observations.'

'Good idea,' replied Mathew enthusiastically. 'Now I've seen the park itself, I have a much clearer picture of the conditions and the environment I'll be studying in.' Mathew was keen to establish with Deschryver exactly what restrictions would be placed on him, but was aware that he must tread carefully. 'I would like to thank you for what has truly been one of the greatest experiences of my life... I'll never forget what I've seen today,' said Mathew as he got out, at the same time reaching over from the front seat and lightly squeezing Lucienne's right hand, as if to express his gratitude to her for having paved the way to such a satisfactory introduction to Deschryver, and for arranging such an unforgettable day.

As Lucienne had previously inferred, Mathew's initial meeting with Deschryver had been similar to appearing in front of an examiner. He recognised that the many questions he was asked about the way he wished to undertake his field observations amounted to a thorough assessment. He would have to pass the test if he was to receive Deschryver's full cooperation. Also, Mathew had been aware that Deschryver had kept a very close eye on him, particularly during the time they had spent in close proximity to the gorillas. It had become obvious that Deschryver had wanted to see just how he reacted to being confronted for the first time by gorillas in the wild state. However, on this first meeting, Mathew had come to recognise what a reserved and self-contained

26

MOUNT KAHUZI'S KINGDOM OF GORILLAS

disposition he possessed but, at the same time, how this athletic, clean-shaven man in his mid-forties radiated a similar degree of authority to that of one of his treasured silverbacks.

'Whenever you're close to gorillas in the wild,' emphasised Deschryver at the meeting the following morning, 'you must remain as calm and peaceful as possible. Let me give you an example. I once took a group of Belgian tourists to visit the gorillas. One lady was so alarmed to see a silverback close to her that she screamed, setting off a whole chain-reaction among the gorilla group. The silverback in question, Hannibal, was obviously alarmed and gave out a loud, deep-throated roar of defiance, together with a mock-charge at the tourists. As you can imagine, the whole party were in a state of considerable panic and disorder and retraced their steps as quickly as possible to take refuge in the undergrowth. It took quite a while for some of them to extricate themselves and join up with the rest of the party, before we whisked them back to the safety of their vehicles and their hotel in Bukavu. It certainly taught me a lesson.'

'Of course, Mr Deschryver. I am the first to admit I'm inexperienced with gorillas in the wild, but I have spent some time observing them in captivity so I feel confident I can keep my head, whatever happens. Yesterday's encounter with Casimir's family was an incredible experience for me, I can't quite believe I was so fortunate on my first visit.'

'We were lucky, such a prolonged experience is quite rare.'

'So I understand, but now I've had that introduction to Casimir and his family, now I know the type of environment I'll be working in, I would like to express my gratitude to you for being given this opportunity to undertake comparative observations between the gorilla colony at the Yerkes Centre and your habituated group.'

'Your observations should help us in our work, in the long

term.' Deschryver was, as expected, guarded in his response to Mathew's enthusiasm.

'I'm hoping that while I'm writing up my dissertation, I can get an article accepted in a major popular title which will highlight the significance of your conservation work at Kahuzi-Biega, which could perhaps promote further funding opportunities for your national park. The methodology I've been working on with the captive gorillas combined with these studies of gorillas in their natural environment should help to identify the cognitive skills of gorilla families and their relevance to human communication. It's a fascinating area, it deserves to get some coverage.'

'Once you've completed your field observations and written up the dissertation, I must ask that you submit a bound copy of it to the government's Minister of National Parks in Kinshasa, as well as a copy for the park's library in Bukavu. Also, your article for a popular title – could you let me see the manuscript prior to publication? If there's anything in it that I believe could be considered in Zaire to be politically counter-productive to future financial support from the government, I will have to ask you to edit it accordingly.'

'Of course, Mr Deschryver. I can supply the two bound copies and you would be most welcome to see a copy of the article. You are no doubt far more in tune with the attitude of the authorities than I, so it would be most beneficial if you could give me your opinion.'

'Good,' concluded Deschryver. 'In that case I think we've covered everything for the time being. I will arrange for two guides to take you into the park for your field studies and sort out the other arrangements. In the meantime, I wish you luck.'

Lucienne told Mathew later that Deschryver had been guardedly impressed by the way he had handled himself in the forest, and had been encouraged by the degree of apparent genuine enthusiasm he had shown. Although Deschryver had been slightly apprehensive as to how Mathew would be able to cope by himself in the company of two Pygmy guides (who would have to be carefully chosen), their meeting had facilitated the mapping out of a provisional *modus operandi* to cover his first four weeks of study, as well as the agreement that he should occupy one of the small wooden huts close to the eastern entrance to the park.

Prior to Mathew arranging to gather together the stores he would require for his semi-isolation, as a matter of local diplomacy and the potential of gaining additional knowledge and assistance Deschryver had arranged for Lucienne to drive Mathew to the nearby headquarters at Lwiro of the Institut pour la Reserche Scientifique en Afrique Central (IRSAC), to meet its director and some of its scientific staff. On the way to Lwiro, Lucienne briefed Mathew of the current status of the research centre.

'It's really quite a place – you'll be surprised. The centre was built by the Belgians in 1951, with the original decree stating that the objectives of the institute were to undertake scientific research concerned with man and nature. Five research centres were initially developed, each under the supervision of permanent European staff and specialising in a variety of disciplines. After all the post-independence upheavals of the 1960s, the majority of the institute's research work ground to a halt.

'When I visited with the Belgian film crew, I was introduced to Dr Peter Kunkel – we found that we had both studied at the same university. Dr Kunkel told me how he had joined the zoology section of the Lwiro research centre straight from university in the early 1960s, so he has been there throughout the troubled times, and how he had been only recently appointed Director General. He is developing as many of the scientific research programmes as possible, in particular the ethnographic studies of the peoples around Lake Kivu, the problems of combating malnutrition and a study of tropical rain forest ecology – ecological studies on the Pygmies of the forest as well as on many animal and plant species, including the mountain gorilla. I think he could be a very useful contact for your research.'

On arrival at the research institute's impressive headquarters, Lucienne and Mathew passed through its covered entrance way and into a courtyard with two large ponds, overspilling with an abundance of tropical water plants and with a carapace of colourful butterflies flitting to and fro, providing a welcome coolness to the heat of the mid-morning sun.

'Lucienne! How good to see you again – and you must be Mathew Duncan.' Dr Kunkel greeted Lucienne warmly like a long-lost university friend and shook Mathew's hand with vigour. 'Come, have a look around and meet some of our people.' He immediately proceeded to give them a conducted tour of the well-equipped research laboratories, spacious conference room, library and offices, as well as introducing them to a cross-section of scientists and technicians from a range of nationalities: Rwandese, South African, Belgians, Germans, French, Japanese and local Zairians from Lubumbashi. They took tea in his spacious office, where light streamed in through the windows to counteract the formality of the dark wood panelling of the walls. Mathew was impressed by Dr Kunkel's dedication and enthusiasm for the centre's research work. He was interested to learn that Lieutenant General Mobutu Sésé Seko becoming president in November 1965 had brought stability to the country; that IRSAC itself had been placed under the direct responsibility of the President of the Republic of the Congo and was thereby assured of government support.

'I've been carrying out research on a captive population of

gorillas at the Yerkes Primate Research Center,' explained Mathew, 'and hope to spend three months carrying out comparative work on Adrien Deschryver's habituated family group of eastern lowland gorillas in Kahuzi-Biega.' Dr Kunkel listened to Mathew's description of his previous research with considerable interest and after discussing the nature of the methodology that he intended to use during his field investigations, said that he would be only too happy to help by providing any of the institute's resources, both human and technical, that could be of assistance.

He dialled a number and asked Patrice Daman, a postgraduate from Brussels, to come to his office.

Patrice Daman was in his early twenties, five feet eight, thick-set and of a ruddy complexion. His heavy dark eyebrows were half hidden under a mop of unruly black hair, which somewhat shadowed the intensity of his deep-set eyes.

'Patrice, meet Mathew Duncan – he is carrying out some primate research at Kahuzi-Biega – I have suggested that you should be Mathew's main conduit with the institute as you frequently visit the area.'

'Pleased to meet you, Mathew,' said Patrice in a heavy Belgian accent, stepping forward to shake his hand. 'I'm carrying out ethnological studies of the Pygmy populations in the environs of the national park – I look forward to working with you.' His dark eyes didn't reveal much enthusiasm, but Patrice was very helpful in discussing the potential for Mathew to utilise some of the institute's resources. Patrice suggested that his technicians would be able to help identify the type of vegetable matter that the gorillas had been observed feeding upon, as well as for the institute's laboratory to analyse the contents of their faecal matter. He offered to collect the samples weekly from Mathew's hut.

'Once you've completed your studies,' said Dr Kunkel, 'yourself and Lucienne must come to see me again. I would be very interested in receiving a summary of your research findings – and I would be delighted if you would both join me for dinner. My home is up in the hills over there, not far from here.'

'I will be certainly be in touch once the field studies are complete and would be delighted to accept your invitation. In the meantime, my sincere thanks, Dr Kunkel, for all the assistance you have offered. Your help will be invaluable.'

Patrice accompanied them both back to their vehicle, during which time Mathew could not help feeling a little jealous of the amount of attention Patrice was paying Lucienne and the way he was directing the majority of his conversation toward her. He felt excluded as they chatted away enthusiastically in Flemish, while Lucienne appeared to be very much enjoying such a degree of masculine attention.

On their return journey to Bukavu, Mathew was more reserved than usual – perhaps it was his self-conscious way of beginning to experience a degree of possessiveness toward Lucienne. On her part, Lucienne had greatly enjoyed her time at the institute and had been fascinated by the variety of research activities being carried out there, as well as in meeting Patrice Daman for the first time. She had been very pleased by the amount of cooperation that Dr Kunkel had offered Mathew and so as she drove, she was as happy and high spirited as ever. After skillfully negotiating around some of the potholes on the tarmac road, and no doubt as a consequence of her female intuition in recognising that Mathew was not acting in his normal relaxed manner, Lucienne suddenly swerved the jeep up a corrugated earthen track. She drove to a vantage point that commanded a dramatic view of Lake Kivu, through a valley of lush tropical vegetation.

As soon as they got out of the jeep, Lucienne took Mathew's hand and pulled him towards her to confront him directly, with a bewitching sparkle in her deep brown eyes. 'What's the matter with you? Why have you gone so quiet all of a sudden? Have I done something to upset you?'

Mathew spontaneously responded to these uninhibited questions by momentarily dropping his guard, gently cupping his hands on either side of her soft cheeks and planting a brief kiss on both of them, although one of these had been through a thin curtain of her long, silken hair. Then, slightly blushing, he gave her hand a gentle squeeze.

'Yes, I've been very fortunate to receive such offers of assistance from Dr Kunkel ... and all the help of the institute's scientific staff. What a marvellous view of the lake one gets from here...'

Lucienne, recognising that Mathew was embarrassed by his sudden unexpected display of affection towards her (one which she had so much appreciated), decided to diplomatically share his conversation as if nothing had happened between them. 'Yes, it's been a productive day, Mathew. I'm so glad you like the view – this is one of my favourite places...'

The following morning, in preparation for Mathew's forthcoming semi-isolation, Lucienne willingly helped him to gather together the week's required provisions which, apart from food items, included a case of red wine, a supply of local beer, soap, shampoo, sterile plastic sample bags from a chemist, and a box full of candles.

Back at the Hotel Metropole, these stores were combined with the assortment of equipment that Mathew had brought with him from Atlanta or had purchased with Lucienne's help, which included waterproof clothing, a pair of US Marine canvas army boots, a sleeping bag, mosquito net, medical supplies, binoculars, camera, films, note books and a small library of research literature. Lucienne drove Mathew to a rendezvous with Deschryver, who had arranged to be with him during his first few days of exposure to Casimir and his family. Deschryver was very pleased with the success of the meeting with Dr Kunkel. He wanted to select two of his

SOMEONE WISHES TO SPEAK TO YOU

most trusted Pygmy trackers to accompany Mathew in the forest, as well as to appoint a suitable house boy to cook for him. It was important for Deschryver to feel as confident as possible that Mathew would not take any liberties with his very precious habituated family group of gorillas, as well as to see just how he would react in an emergency.

'Well, I wish you success for your first week – goodbye for now.' Lucienne bade Mathew a rather formal farewell, but once out of Deschryver's sight, she blew him a kiss, whispering with an engaging smile that at the end of the week, she would drive out to see him with some further supplies. Finally, all of Mathew's equipment and stores were safely stowed in Deschryver's mud-encrusted VW Kombi and he was ready to go.

On the journey, Mathew was keen to ask Deschryver as many questions as possible. What did he consider the estimated population of gorillas to be in the park? How many gorillas were now familiar to him? Now that Kahuzi-Biega had gained the status of a national park, what were the chief threats to the gorilla population? How much erosion of the habitat was currently being inflicted by human encroachment? What other mammal species would he be likely to encounter, etc. etc? It had been fortunate for Deschryver, for on the whole he was not by nature known to be a very talkative person, that there had been little traffic on the road so that he had been able to make the journey in almost record time.

On arrival, Deschryver introduced Mathew to a jovial-looking Pygmy called Tilli-Tilli, who had been waiting for them next to a wooden hut under a thick canopy of lush foliage, just behind the park's main entrance. With Tilli-Tilli were a small group of fellow villagers and two Zaire army soldiers who had immediately sprung to attention in the presence of the park's *Conservateur*; it was obvious that when Deschryver addressed them, he was regarded very much as their '*Bwana Mkubwa*' (big chief). After a brief inspection

MOUNT KAHUZI'S KINGDOM OF GORILLAS

of the soldiers' .303 rifles, Deschryver turned his attention to Tilli-Tilli and those who had accompanied him, and asked them in their local tongue to bring him up-to-date with the whereabouts of his two habituated gorilla groups. He had then, on Tilli-Tilli's recommendation, selected two additional trackers and a houseboy/cook to care for Mathew. In the same way as the soldiers showed obvious respect to Deschryver, Mathew could sense as he talked to the Pygmies that a deep bond of trust existed between them.

Mathew found the next four months to be the most thought-provoking, challenging and stimulating period of his life. How humble he had felt himself, after having been on so many occasions in close proximity to Casimir's group, as well as with the second sub-group led by Hannibal, by the way he had been accepted by them. Also, how much he had admired the social interactions within the gorilla family, especially during their resting periods, which he frequently found to last up to 40 per cent of their day. During these times how delighted he had been to witness the mother-infant relationships, with mothers having to regularly put up with their offspring jumping up and down on their heads and backs.

Mathew's numerous note books were overfilled with his observations which had included the jubilant play-jostling of the juveniles; the boisterous exchange of chest-beating between blackbacks and silverbacks; the way group members sought closeness to the silverbacks during day-resting periods, which further promoted mutual grooming; the way the sexually mature females mainly always solicited matings with the more mature silverbacks; and how Mathew had so much respected the extremes that silverbacks would go to in order to avoid physical clashes. How very much he wished that their human counterparts would emulate this enlightened and pragmatic behaviour.

35

SOMEONE WISHES TO SPEAK TO YOU

As quite an accomplished artist, Mathew had accumulated a comprehensive set of 'mug' sketches of the majority of the gorillas he had encountered in an attempt to determine whether there was any underlying geometry of facial signals between them. As a result of his drawings of an individual's eye flashes and facial patterns, he had been able to clearly identify each member of the family group he had been studying. Also, during his time with the gorillas he had been able to well imitate their chest-beating and vocalisations, from the soft belly noise of 'Uh-uh-u' to their screams and roars; as well as to appreciate a gorilla's 'pig-grunt' as a sign of discipline within the group or perhaps a signal he had come too close to one of the sub-adults who was not too familiar with his presence. During the writing up of his daily log reports, he had been particularly keen to document how mutual grooming served both a socially binding and a functional purpose, as well as noting how there had always been a degree of competition in the grooming of the group's dominant silverback, and how silverbacks seldom groom others for they have no need to reinforce their dominance.

Some days, the heavy mists and fog that frequently rolled into the saddle area of the lush, gently rolling hagenia forested slopes of Mount Kahuzi prevented Mathew from making direct visual contact with Casimir's group. On such occasions he was able to collect samples of some of the vegetation that he had observed gorillas feeding upon, including some of the roots that he had seen them digging for. The plant life included a variety of mosses, lichens, ferns, orchids, vines, nettles, thistles, wild celery, blackberries, bracket fungi, red-flowering parasitical plants belonging to the mistletoe family, worms, grubs and some samples of the epiphytes supported by the limbs of the hagenia. Mathew was able to give these, as well as some of the fresh faecal samples he had collected from the gorillas, to Patrice Daman on his weekly scheduled meeting with him.

Although elephant and buffalo were still to be found in the park, and Mathew had seen some signs of the destruction to the habitat that the elephants had caused during their foraging, he was relieved not to have encountered either species. While carrying out field work in such a densely vegetated environment, the last thing an observer wishes is to suddenly come across and alarm an animal the size of an elephant or a buffalo, and as a result to cause a panic charge by them. However, during his months in the forest he had seen a cross-section of animal species ranging from blue monkey (which he wished he had time to carry out a specific study on), bushbuck, duiker, bush pig and within some of the older and partly hollow hagenia tree trunks, he had caught glimpses of hyrax, genet, mongoose, dormouse and tree squirrel. Also, always present, was a diversity of bird species feeding upon the berries among the foliage, although due to the thickness of the vegetation he had found that, apart from the touracos they had been difficult to identify. Mathew had also observed a variety of lizards inhabiting the peat-like substrate of the forest floor, which he had occasionally seen being caught by a gorilla, pulled in half, and eaten in a similar fashion to the way they devoured earthworms. Safari ants, mice and rats were frequently observed, but perhaps the most ubiquitous were the clouds of midges that accompanied the gorillas wherever they went. During resting periods, these were frequently interlaced with the fluttering of a diversity of colourful butterflies.

Throughout his field studies, which usually took place from soon after sunrise to when the light began to fade, Mathew had always found himself to be totally preoccupied with his observations and note-taking. Prior to sunset each day he would return to his forest hut which he had named 'Chatsworth' and his cook, whom he had christened 'James', would present him with the regular meal of goat meat, rice and black beans, followed by a banana dish and a pot of strong Kivu coffee.

SOMEONE WISHES TO SPEAK TO YOU

It was only after Mathew had written up his daily observations at an old wooden table under the hut's solitary hurricane lamp, only during the following hours of solitude, that he experienced a degree of isolation and loneliness until the first light of the following day. Also, and somewhat to his annoyance, he had found it difficult to prevent his thoughts from drifting towards Lucienne and his desire to be in her company.

Mathew had found it necessary to hang his hammock well above the planks of the wooden floor, for as soon as the hurricane lamp had been extinguished a nocturnal invasion took place by what appeared to represent the majority of the local rodent population, and animal life that was not scampering over the wooden floor would be either flying or hovering around the hut's cobweb-festooned rafters. However, each evening, prior to climbing into his hammock and zipping up the mosquito net which was stitched into either side of it, Mathew would do as much reading as possible in order to keep his mind occupied, as well as to help distract him from Lucienne.

In one of his books, he had been fascinated to read a letter dated April 24, 1847 written by a Dr Thomas S. Savage when he stayed at a mission house on the Gabon River, West Africa, while *en route* to the USA. He had written: 'I have found the existence of an animal of an extraordinary character in this locality, which I have reason to believe is unknown to the naturalist. As yet, I have been unable to obtain more than a part of a skeleton.' He also read how eight months later, a Captain George Wagstaff, master of a ship trading between West Africa and Bristol, obtained three skulls from the Gabon River which were presented to Samuel Stutchbury, Curator of the Museum of the British Institution for the Advancement of Science, Literature and the Arts. These skulls had formed the basis for the first descriptions of a member of the genus *Gorilla*, the western lowland gorilla *Gorilla g. gorilla* (Savage and Whyman, 1847), which were subsequently published by Richard Owen.

MOUNT KAHUZI'S KINGDOM OF GORILLAS

Mathew also had the opportunity to read Paul du Chaillu's 1861 dramatic account of his first meeting with a gorilla in his book *Explorations & Adventures in Equatorial Africa*, in which he claimed to have been fortunate enough to be the first white man to see gorillas in Africa. How disparagingly du Chaillu had maligned the character of the gorilla species when he recorded: 'I can vouch that no description can exceed the horror of its appearance, the ferocity of its attack, or the impish malignity of its nature' – a 'King Kong' legacy that regrettably remained with the gorilla species for almost a further hundred years.

However, now that Mathew had experienced and so much relished the introverted company of members of the gorilla kingdom and had never much appreciated his exposure to the more bombastic extroverted characters of chimpanzees, he had enjoyed reading a 1896 account by a Dr A.E. Brehm, quoting von Hermes, which had highlighted: 'GORILLA – it seems as if he was born with a patent of nobility among apes... In comparison to a Chimpanzee, holds its head higher, producing the impression that he belongs to a better class of society.'

Mathew had seen Lucienne on the majority of Sundays during his months of study at Kahuzi-Biega, when Tilli-Tilli and his Pygmy compatriots were given a day of leisure. On the Sundays that Lucienne had been unable to visit with his weekly supplies and to spend time with him, she had dispatched the provisions by taxi with a note to explain how she had very reluctantly stayed away to attend to her national park office responsibilities. On these occasions, Mathew had been surprised just how despondent he was made by her absence.

During Mathew's time at Kahuzi-Biega, Deschryver had visited him at irregular intervals, although never giving him any advance notice of when he was going to appear. At times, he would follow their tracks into the forest and, when coming quite close to where they were, would either stand or crouch and just watch them for a while unobserved, before deciding to make Mathew and the Pygmy guides aware of his presence. As soon as the gorillas saw Deschryver, they would respond to his soft rumbling noise of 'Uh-uh-u', the gorilla's welcome, followed by his familiar 'com-com', 'com-com', 'com-com'. Tilli-Tilli and the other two Pygmies would immediately become more relaxed now that their *Bwana Mkubra* had joined them. On each of these visits, Deschryver would stay to return to the park's main entrance with them, and prior to returning to Bukavu would share some beers in front of Mathew's hut and receive an update on the highlights of his observations. Although during these discussions Deschryver never mentioned how much he had been impressed by Mathew's diligence and dedication to his field studies, and the comprehensiveness of his written recordings, he had conveyed such sentiments to Lucienne, for in all probability he was well aware that she would in turn pass them onto him.

With Lucienne's almost weekly visit to Mathew, their relationship had developed into a deep friendship and mutual affection for each other, although their intimacy was confined to a quick hug and a kiss on both cheeks on both their meetings and farewells, and sometimes to holding hands when they walked through some of the more negotiable parts of the forest. But in spite of Mathew's ever-increasing desire to be in Lucienne's company, he had to keep reminding himself that as a consequence of their very different backgrounds and heritages, he was unable to see just how his strong emotional feelings and admiration for her could possibly lead to any sustainable long-term relationship.

It had been during Mathew's attempt to reconcile the complexities of his emotional turmoil regarding Lucienne that he reminded himself how his professor at Scaife University would have dealt with such sentiments. In his analysis of this type of scenario, he had highlighted how mankind was merely an evolutionary self-domesticated animal – a mammal, an ape, a social anthropoid ape, a human anthropoid in which the difference between male and female stemmed from a past, when the man hunted and the woman gathered. Also, how his professor had reflected that falling in love was mysteriously cerebral and highly selective, with sexual interactions being merely a genetic joint venture resulting from a degree of self-assurance and the priority for the male to perpetuate his genes. While Mathew reflected on his professor's dispassionate scientific approach to such a state of mind, he attempted to pull himself together and be more realistic as to any future long-term involvement with the person he had now considered that he had fallen in love with.

It had been during their many discussions about primate behaviour that Lucienne had mentioned to Mathew that through her desire to increase her knowledge and, in particular, to learn as much as possible about the comparative psychology of anthropoids, she would very much like to embark on a university degree course. With this in mind, she had asked Mathew whether his mentor Dr W.C. Osman Hill would be willing to help her gain a place at Emory University and to undertake some behavioural research work with the gorilla colony at the Yerkes Primate Research Center. Although contrary to Mathew's intended attempt to try to distance himself from Lucienne, the thought of having her in Atlanta during his final months of writing up his dissertation appealed to him greatly. He promised to write to his professor and to do as much as possible to promote her cause. At the same time, he suggested that she should tell Deschryver and ask him to write a letter of recommendation and reference on her behalf, which would be sure to carry a great deal of weight with Emory University's Board of Admission.

During Mathew's final ten days at the Hotel Metropole, prior to his departure from Bukavu, he found that his intention to separate his life from Lucienne had totally failed and he was therefore to be seen in her company almost on a daily basis. Deschryver had written an excellent supportive 'To Whom It May Concern' to add to Mathew's letter to Osman Hill, requesting his help with Lucienne's application. As Mathew was anxious to receive his professor's reaction prior to his departure from Zaire, the correspondence was cabled to Osman Hill with the original top copies sent by airmail.

Now that Mathew had completed his field studies he had been able to get to know Deschryver on a more informal basis; although he had seemed to be rather reserved and outwardly self-effacing, the more he got to know him, the more relaxed and outgoing he became.

Deschryver's home was situated high up above the township, with a spectacular view of Lake Kivu in the distance. The house, with its spacious veranda, was surrounded by well-manicured lawns, studded at intervals by impressive beds of the scarlet-flowered, purple-leafed, hybrid cannas, which were shaded from the heat of the midday sun by small groups of acacia trees. On several occasions they had talked here into the early hours of the morning about the constant political upheavals that had occurred in this eastern region of Zaire since the Congo's independence from the Belgians, twelve years previously. Also about the increased human pressures that were currently being exerted on one of the eastern lowland gorillas most important remaining sanctuaries at Kahuzi-Biega. Mathew had concluded from his many conversations with him that if it had not been for Deschryver's personal drive, dedication and hard work during the last seven years, it would have been unlikely that the national park would have been established, thereby giving the eastern lowland gorillas who lived there the opportunity to survive.

Prior to his departure from Bukavu, Mathew was anxious to take up Dr Peter Kunkel's invitation for Lucienne and him to have dinner at his home near the IRSAC headquarters. Also, to have the opportunity to thank the botanists and the staff of the institute's pathology laboratory for the painstakingly detailed analysis they had carried out, all of which had established some important new data about the gorilla's varied diet and aspects of their digestive systems.

After Mathew and Lucienne had spent almost two hours at the research institute thanking all those involved, they followed Dr Kunkel's VW Kombi several kilometres over a winding, rough earth road to his home at Tshibati, a sizeable white-painted villa with a courtyard at its rear. A large well-kept lawn to the front of the house sloped downhill with a view to some of the institute buildings. However, in the far distance was the dramatic backdrop of the magnificent mountains of the rift valley, with the sparkling waters of Lake Kivu nestled comfortably between them.

The dinner party guests included a number of the institute's staff: the South African pathologist, Dr Kurt Jorgensen; the Rwandan botanist, Annette Sausman; and Patrice Daman. When Mathew had been told that Patrice was going to be one of the dinner guests, he had been quick to reassure Lucienne that his initial jealousy had been due to the enthusiastic attention his potential rival had shown her, but that as a result of their weekly meetings they had become good friends.

On learning about this friendship, Lucienne considered it prudent to inform Mathew that while he was undertaking his field research in Kahuzi-Biega, she had accepted an invitation from Patrice to have dinner with him at a small nightclub in Bukavu.

'It started pleasantly enough,' she explained, 'but by halfway through the evening, he had drunk a lot of wine and he kept trying to touch me... It was getting very embarrassing. I shouldn't say it, but what made the whole thing unbearable was that he absolutely reeked of garlic and was smoking Gitanes – the fumes were all over me – so I pretended to have a stomach bug and called a taxi to take me home as soon as possible!'

'Well, friends or not, I'm very relieved to hear that you

didn't enjoy your evening with Patrice... Long may he continue to eat excessive garlic, smoke Gitanes and touch his dinner guests inappropriately.'

'He still wanted to come back to my flat and tuck me into bed,' Lucienne gently teased, 'but of course I didn't let him. The next day, once Patrice had sobered up and carried out a post-mortem on his behaviour, he sent me a beautiful bunch of white lilies with the sweetest note of apology. All is forgiven, but I haven't seen or spoken to him since.'

Despite Lucienne's regrettable encounter with Patrice, the dinner party was a thoroughly amicable and enjoyable evening. Dr Kunkel was the perfect host; the conversation and the wine flowed freely and Mathew and Lucienne ended the evening feeling very glad to have made the acquaintance of the IRSAC scientists.

A week prior to Mathew's departure from Bukavu, he received a response to the cable to Osman Hill.

> Dear Mathew,
> I read your cable with great interest. I will certainly do what I can to help your friend Lucienne Luzembo gain entry to a degree course at Emory University, and also to assist her in carrying out some of her course work at the Yerkes Center. It sounds as though she already possesses a good deal of experience in the field and I look forward to having someone so enthusiastic on our team. I'm sure if she has gained your recommendation and that of Adrien Deschryver, she will possess the qualities needed to succeed as a student here.
> I have some funds available for a student to help with my literary research in connection with the next volume of my monograph on the comparative anatomy and taxonomy of primates. Lucienne may be particularly

interested in this as Vol. 9 is going to cover Hylobatidae (Gibbons & Siamangs) and Pongidae (Orang Utans, Chimpanzees & Gorillas). If she would like it, the position is hers.
Warm regards,
Osman Hill

'Oh Mathew! I can't believe it – it couldn't be better. Not only is he going to help me get a place, but he's giving me a chance to help with research that is so closely connected to my interest in anthropoids ... and he's going to pay me for the pleasure of doing it! This is a godsend, an unbelievable opportunity. I can't thank you enough for making it happen.' Lucienne could not stop herself from throwing her arms around Mathew's neck and kissing his cheek in gratitude.

Lucienne's overflowing enthusiasm and joy was obvious to everyone as she talked excitedly about her future in the USA, rushing to and fro in a concerted attempt to keep her mind on her office duties. On Lucienne's insistence, Mathew cabled Osman Hill back immediately in appreciation of his help and to say on her behalf that she would love to help him with the research for his primate monograph.

Lucienne had arranged with Deschryver to take the last few days of Mathew's time in Bukavu away from the office in order to be with him as much as possible. In particular, she wanted to talk about her forthcoming time in Atlanta for she well recognised that she would require help to settle into such a new and alien environment. Mathew had already told her that he would be first returning to the UK for four to five months to be with his parents in Yorkshire, and to take the opportunity to embark on the writing up of his dissertation in the peaceful surroundings of the Yorkshire Dales. His return to Atlanta could well be after she had arrived.

* * *

SOMEONE WISHES TO SPEAK TO YOU

Lunches at the Bistro Zanzibar had been full of joyous harmony on the one hand, and a degree of apprehension on the other. During some gaps in their conversation they had both sensed a degree of trepidation; their separation was imminent and their future relationship was uncertain. On the Saturday evening they had decided to visit the typically African nightspot of Le Tropicana, where the soft lights, the enthusiastic beating of the drums, small tables lit by flickering candles, all added to the intimacy of the place. In the centre of the room, the bodies, arms and legs of those who had succumbed to the seductive beat of the drums swayed in total harmony.

After a dish of lake fish and greasy fries, accompanied by some agreeable glasses of South African Sauvignon, Lucienne had suggested that they should take the opportunity to dance to the intoxicating music. Although Mathew had warned her that he was unable to jive and could only do ballroom dancing, he had taken her hand and led her onto the crowded dance floor. Thanks to not being able to follow the example of the other dancers, he had placed his arm around Lucienne's waist and, as their dancing progressed, he had held her body close to him. As they swayed to and fro to the beat of the drums, she had rested her head on his shoulder so that some of her long, soft hair draped loosely over it. He gently ran his fingers through the silky curls.

As they returned to their table, a wine glass reflected the flickering of the candle that danced on Lucienne's left cheek. Mathew could just detect a few small dew-drops of tears gathering beneath her now rather soulful-looking dark brown eyes. At the same time, he found himself experiencing some pangs of breathlessness and emptiness of spirit. However, after holding hands across the table, and being both aware of their respective emotional dilemmas, they soon pulled themselves out of despondency and happily danced with each other into the early hours of the morning.

'As tomorrow is my last day here,' ventured Mathew as

they were leaving, 'I was wondering if you would like to come on a picnic with me? Maybe somewhere on the shore of Lake Kivu... Somewhere quiet and beautiful.'

'What a lovely idea!' smiled Lucienne. 'I know just the place, a little bay on the south-east coast. Why don't I pick you up just after 12?'

After they had made arrangements, Mathew found a taxi to take Lucienne back to her flat and, after an emotional embrace during which he managed to maintain his customary disciplined 'mind over matter', he dutifully returned to his room at the Hotel Metropole.

By Sunday morning, Mathew had completed the majority of his packing and had made sure that all of his valuable field notes and photographic records had been securely placed into his hand luggage, ready for the following day's early morning flight to Lubumbashi and onwards to Kinshasa. Lucienne had arrived at the hotel in her open jeep just after midday, and appeared to be in the highest of spirits. She was determined not to put any damper on the last afternoon that they would be together for so many months.

As they drove along the lakeside they passed a number of well-manicured tea gardens, within which the bushes were gently shaded from the strong rays of the sun by slender groves of tall trees. As Lucienne turned up a narrow track towards a small, isolated beach, they reminisced about the wonderful times they had shared together in Bukavu and at Kahuzi-Biega.

'Mathew, I can't tell you how much I've enjoyed your company here... It's been a very special time and one I will remember for the rest of my life. But it may be six months until we see each other again and when we do, we'll be in Atlanta – it will be completely different from our lives here. What I want to say is ... well ... let's enjoy this afternoon for what it is, and face the future when it comes to us... Let's not spend today worrying about what lies ahead.'

SOMEONE WISHES TO SPEAK TO YOU

Mathew sighed. 'You're quite right, as usual. I don't want anything to spoil this afternoon. Oh Lucienne, you've chosen the perfect spot – just look at that! And not another person in sight. I have you completely to myself.'

After admiring the view, they selected the top of a large, smooth boulder on which to spread their picnic rug, with the deep waters of the lake lapping gently at its base. The coastline was edged by a mixed woodland habitat with an assortment of dense evergreen vegetation and thick undergrowth, overshadowed by some tall trees whose canopies touched at mid-level to afford some welcome shade. A pair of shy, bespectacled weaver birds had flown noisily above the rock as if in protest for having been disturbed and the ubiquitous colourful butterflies fluttered to and fro, without a care in the world. An African fish eagle, with its white head which contrasted magnificently with its chestnut belly and shoulders and black wings, was perched nearby at the top of a sizeable dead tree with a commanding view over the lake. Seemingly aware of the occasion, it bid Mathew an African farewell by throwing its head back to utter its far-carrying gull-like call, which so well represented the characteristic and evocative 'Cry of Africa'.

Lucienne had gone out of her way to provide a picnic to beat all the previous picnics that she had provided Mathew with during her almost weekly visits to his hut at Kahuzi-Biega. Slices of water melon, portions of smoked fish, legs of chicken, a salad with boiled eggs, tomatoes and spring onions, along with the added benefit of Lucienne's special home-made garlic and olive oil dressing – her own carefully guarded recipe. This was followed by scoops of vanilla ice cream, skillfully wrapped to stop it from melting, each topped by a teaspoonful of Amarula cream liqueur. The drink is made from the small yellow fruit of the Marula tree, the berries of which are so much favoured by elephants that the trees are frequently referred to by locals as 'elephant trees'.

In addition to this, Mathew had managed to secure a couple of bottles of Chablis, which he had carefully brought along in a freezer bag to serve perfectly chilled. After they had both enjoyed the delights of the picnic, the agreeable relaxing and rather intoxicating effects of having consumed a bottle and a half of the Chablis Premier Cru and amply sampled the special blend of the Amarula liqueur, they had both gone to sleep under the shade of an acacia tree on the top of the rock, with Lucienne's head gently resting on Mathew's chest. Some time later, Mathew had suddenly been awoken by the shot of a gun which had appeared to have been quite close to them. His reaction had been to quickly jerk his body to a sitting position, which caused Lucienne's head to slip off his chest and her slumbering body to slide down the boulder into the lake. As soon as she had been momentarily submerged, the coolness of the water was quick to bring her to her senses – she threw up her arms and cried out for help, and it was immediately obvious to Mathew that Lucienne was unable to swim and was well out of her depth.

'Lucienne! Don't worry... I'm coming...' Mathew tore off his bush jacket and shoes as she thrashed helplessly around, gasping for breath and taking in mouthfuls of water. He slid down the rock and quickly swam to Lucienne's sinking body, immediately putting into practice the life-saving exercise that he had learned from a St John Ambulance team that had once visited Wellington College.

'Lucienne, stay calm, trust me...' he shouted while swimming up to her, turning her struggling body onto its back and placing both hands on either side of her face. He turned onto his back and holding the now almost lifeless form of Lucienne above him, he swam to the nearby beach and managed to pull her on to its soft, warm sands. Then, to Mathew's utter horror, he saw that her breathing had stopped.

'Lucienne... come on, don't do this to me... start breathing

... please...' He knelt by her and swallowing back the lump in his throat, quickly applied compressions to her chest, desperately trying to remember what those St John Ambulance men had shown him all those years ago. After approximately thirty compressions he lifted her chin to open the airway, pinched her nose then blew a couple of times into her mouth and, after having repeated this procedure on two to three occasions, to his immense relief she started to breathe lightly. Mathew resumed the chest compressions in a more composed manner; alternating thirty pumps with two more 'kisses of life' before he was satisfied that Lucienne had started to breathe regularly.

After wrapping Lucienne's body within the folds of the picnic rug, he took her cold hands in his and they soon responded to his touch as her body warmed up. As Lucienne regained consciousness, through spasms of delayed shock, she started to whimper slightly before her dark brown eyes began to focus more clearly on Mathew's worried countenance. She smiled and on releasing his hand, flung her arms around him to take him into her full embrace. They lay together for quite some time, while Mathew gently stroked the back of her head and the long, curly hair that hung loosely over her neck and shoulders. And as the sun warmed and dried their damp bodies and clothes, they felt each other's hearts almost beating in unison.

It was then, as if it was the most natural act of relief, compassion and friendship in the world, that they gently made love. Such a physical and romantic experience had been the first time either of them had experienced the ecstasy of intercourse, culminating as it had done with such a blissful integral union of their loving bodies.

3

Conflicting Sentiments

On Mathew's return to the UK from Kinshasa, prior to flying up to his home in Yorkshire, he had arranged to meet with some of his old Wellingtonian friends in London. While in the city he had stayed at the original Cavendish Hotel in Jermyn Street, where there had always been a room made available for a member of Sir Colin Duncan's family. His grandfather, Sir Reginald Duncan, had been at the Cavendish soon after the famous Rosa Lewis, the 'Duchess of Jermyn Street', had taken over the lease of the hotel in 1902; he was purported to have participated in many of the discreet and colourful dinner parties that had taken place there during the years prior to the First World War. It was Edith Jeffrey (Rosa's companion for over fifty years and a long-time friend of his parents) who was the first familiar face to welcome Mathew back to his homeland.

Rosa Lewis had initially worked at the end of the nineteenth century for Lord and Lady Randolph Churchill when she first met their young son, Winston – still a schoolboy at Harrow at that time. Rosa's cuisine met with the royal approval of the Prince of Wales, later King Edward VII, who was to summon her on numerous occasions to cook for him and his guests. Such was Rosa's fame that on 25 February 1909, soon after she had acquired the lease of the Cavendish, the London *Daily Mail* carried the headline 'England's Greatest Woman Chef'. The framed cutting of the article could be seen hanging on the wall just outside Miss Edith's small office. It read:

SOMEONE WISHES TO SPEAK TO YOU

Mrs Rosa Lewis is, as every gourmet knows, *the* woman chef of England. In November 1907, by special request, she cooked for the German Emperor (Kaiser Wilhelm) while he was staying at Highcliffe. She has cooked for the King, and among the long line of her patrons one finds the names of all the prominent members of the English aristocracy and the leading American magnates.

Miss Edith, even at this very much later date, was unlikely to accept people to stay at the Cavendish unless she knew their family or they were fortunate enough to have a personal letter of introduction.

It had been during Mathew's few days of partying with his friends in London that he had begun to recognise how difficult it would be for a person of Lucienne's ethnic and social background to fit easily into such an alien world. He was also conscious of the fact that growing up in the social milieu of the English upper class had left him vulnerable to a degree of snobbery – a subconscious attribute that he was now desperately attempting to shake off.

Mathew could not help being aware of some of the social ramifications if he were to bring Lucienne back to England. No doubt he could well be ostracised by the majority of his society friends, and perhaps even become alienated from a few of his very socially conscious family who in all probability had never met an indigenous African. The more Mathew dwelt upon the absurdity of such social dilemmas, the more illogical he considered the racial boundaries that were currently in place in England, although he had seen some integration of ethnic minorities in Bradford that was considerably more progressive than anything he had witnessed in America's Deep South.

He had already started to miss Lucienne greatly, but recognised that on his return to Atlanta it was very important that he shouldn't keep telling her how very much he had missed her. Unless, by the time of their reunion, he wanted his love for her to progress into something more long term, perhaps even marriage. In the meantime, he knew that he would always have the memory of their last afternoon together on the shores of Lake Kivu; the drama of her having almost drowned, and the subsequent blissful fulfillment of their deep friendship and love for one another.

While Mathew had been trying to resolve some of his fears on how socially alienated he might be should he decide to take Lucienne as his bride, he knew only too well, as had always been the case since his school days at Wellington, how important it would be for him to make up his own mind. He must not in any way be influenced by the suspected racial bias of his family and friends and consequently abandon the very person he considered that he had fallen so much in love with.

'Mathew! Oh! Let me look at you... I can't believe you're finally home!' said his mother, Lady Sally Duncan, wrapping him in her arms on his arrival at Leeds/Bradford International Airport. She had not seen her younger son for over a year. Lady Sally bombarded Mathew with questions as she led him out of the airport to where Sid Stockdale, the family's chauffeur-come-butler, was waiting to drive them home in Sir Colin's highly polished new black Daimler 250 V8. As they drove through Otley and Burley on their way to Hartington Hall, to the south-east of Skipton in southern Wharfedale, Sally Duncan held tightly onto her son's hand as if she never wanted to be parted from him again, at the same time continuing her interrogation. 'Mathew, I want you to tell me absolutely everything. Did you meet interesting people and make some good friends while you were there? Do tell me you managed to avoid catching one of those awful tropical diseases... Oh ... and how did the field studies go with those dangerous gorillas? I hope you weren't in any danger, one hears such terrible stories.'

'No Mother, no danger whatsoever – not from the gorillas anyway.'

'So how successful was your time in Bukavu overall? Was it worth going all that way?'

Mathew responded to the inquisition in his usual quiet and confident way, being careful not to make any reference to his love for Lucienne.

The two famous Cow and Calf rocks stood proudly on the skyline of the moors above Ilkley, known as the 'gateway to the Yorkshire Dales'. The winding road north through Bolton Abbey, past the Duke of Devonshire's hunting lodge and the gothic grandeur of the twelfth-century Bolton Priory was squeezed in parts by the sombre grey dry-stone walls so characteristic of this part of the north of England. During the majority of the journey the road had clung to the banks of the River Wharfe, prior to twisting its way over the heather-covered grouse moors of Lower Wharfedale, and down to the lush valley embracing picturesque Burnsall. Here, infant lambs skipped around their mothers in celebration of their new-found freedom in the verdant meadows of the surrounding countryside. Seeing once more the familiar landscapes of natural beauty and rich diversity, Mathew had found himself with a growing feeling of belongingness in this return to his birth place, an environment that could hardly be more of a contrast to the Central African montane forests of Kahuzi-Biega.

As the Daimler drew up in front of the impressive main entrance to Hartington Hall, Sir Colin had been quick to descend the expansive flight of limestone steps to greet his younger son. As Mathew stepped out of the car, his father for a moment dropped his usual formal approach by embracing him with insuppressible emotion, such was his delight in seeing his son again.

CONFLICTING SENTIMENTS

'Mathew! My boy! So good to see you... Let's have a look at you then... Glad to see you're all in one piece. Not quite as warm here as you're used to, I dare say.'

'It's so good to be back on home ground – I can't tell you how beautiful it looks!'

'Quite so, we're very lucky. Well, come in, come in... We've got a lot of catching up to do.'

Over dinner that evening, Mathew provided his parents with as much information about his time in Africa as he considered appropriate. It felt rather like the prodigal son returning to his home from afar, with the fatted calf having just been slaughtered. He told them about the great variety of people he had been privileged to have encountered; the diversity of the environments he had seen during his travels around Lake Kivu, including the dramatic beauty of the Virunga volcanoes; the tremendous respect and admiration he had gained for the gorilla family he had studied, in particular the quality of their social life; the great help his professor's introduction to Adrien Deschryver had been, on behalf of Emory University and the Yerkes Primate Research Center; and how grateful he was that his father's grouse-shooting friend, the Belgian CEO of Amiza, had sponsored his accommodation.

After Mathew had finished summarising as many of his experiences as the conversation at the dinner table had allowed, he moved on to his future plans. 'Over the next few months, while I'm here with you, my priority has to be to analyse and compare all the data I've gathered on gorillas in captivity and those living in the wild state. Once I've finished that analysis, I have to start writing up my doctorate thesis – I'm due to be interviewed by an Emory University examination board at the end of November, under the chairmanship of my mentor, Professor Osman Hill.'

'It sounds as though you have it all thoroughly planned out, darling,' said Lady Sally. 'So you'll be able to stay for quite a while, will you?'

SOMEONE WISHES TO SPEAK TO YOU

'It all depends on how much work I can get done without access to the library at the Yerkes Center, but I do expect to be here for the next five to six months, at least...'

Sir Colin Duncan had been born in 1910 and was only four when his father, Sir Reginald, acquired his baronetcy at the start of the First World War. In 1928 he was appointed Head Boy of Sedbergh School in north Yorkshire, and the following year he embarked upon a three year BSc (Hons) Countryside Management course at the Royal Agricultural College at Cirencester. After attaining his degree, he spent the next five years gaining valuable experience by carrying out management responsibilities on two sizeable country estates, one in Westmorland and one in the lowlands of Scotland, prior to taking over the running of the Hartington Hall estate, which had been in the Duncan family since the mid-seventeenth century.

In 1937, he had married Sally Parkinson, the daughter of a wealthy property and upmarket department store owner in Bradford. The wedding had taken place at Bolton Abbey, followed by a lavish reception at the nearby Devonshire Arms. The honeymoon had been spent in the Italian lakes at the luxury Grand Hotel Villa Serbelloni at Bellagio, on the shores of Lake Como.

Sally Parkinson had been born at the family's manor house, Howgill Hall, in Gilstead near Bingley, Yorkshire. After schooling at Harrogate Ladies' College she had spent a year at the famous Swiss ladies' finishing school of Château Mont-Choisi in Lausanne, undergoing classes in etiquette, training in cultural and social activities, as well as learning French and Italian. Since marrying Colin Duncan she had wholeheartedly thrown herself into charity work for the underprivileged and energetic fundraising for the cottage hospitals in Ilkley and Skipton. Although she had always been desperately anxious not to be considered by others as a snob, she had found it almost impossible not to socially pigeonhole the people she met. Did they have a handle to their name? Were they from the top social drawer, or perhaps from the second drawer? Or could they be categorised as rather undesirable – would it be rather counterproductive to be seen in their company?

One of his mother's ancestors, Robert Milligan, had settled in Bradford in 1810 when it was only a small village. He had taken an active interest in public affairs and had soon become an influential figure. He served as the Borough of Bradford's first mayor during 1847-1848 and in 1851 was elected as a Church Liberal MP. Following the Slavery Abolition Act in 1833, the Milligan/Parkinson family, the second generation of which had married first cousins in order to keep family wealth within their ranks, had always been immensely proud of their ancestor's support for the total abolition of black slavery in the British colonies, as well as his active interest in promoting the emancipation of West Indian slaves. Mathew's maternal grandfather, Albert Milligan Parkinson, had died in 1932 and had left his only daughter a sizeable fortune.

The Duncans' first child, Sebastian, had been born just prior to the outbreak of the Second World War, in May 1939. It had not been long after his birth that their father had volunteered to join the British Army and gained a commission in the 12th Royal Lancers. The regiment had been raised in 1715 against the threat of the Jacobite rebellion, and seventy-four years later had a young Duke of Wellington serving in it as a subaltern. The 12th Lancers were proud of the fact that their first battle honour had been won in Egypt in 1801, a country in which 2nd Lieutenant Duncan was soon to serve. During the war the regiment played a key role as an armoured car division in shielding the British Army's retreat from Dunkirk, and it was during this time that Colin Duncan was 'mentioned in dispatches'. Subsequent to Dunkirk he was with the regiment when it fought with distinction at the Battle of El Alamein and, later on in the war, the 12th Royal Lancers played a significant role as a corps-led reconnaissance asset with the Allied Forces in their advance through northern Italy.

After being promoted to captain, it was due to his bravery in single-handedly taking out a German machine gun post that Captain Duncan was awarded a Military Cross. In April 1945 the regiment entered Venice, and after D-Day he celebrated with his fellow officers at the famous Locanda Cipriani restaurant on the nearby island of Torcello. It had been during the Italian campaign that he had become great friends with a brother officer, Roger Willock, who prior to the war had joined the Diplomatic Corps. This friendship was to prove most advantageous to Mathew in years to come.

In 1962, while Mathew was at Wellington College (a school that his father had most probably chosen for both of his sons due to his regiment's association with the Duke of Wellington), that Mathew's eighty-five-year-old grandfather had died and his father had inherited the baronetcy. Sir Colin was a tall, handsome man with a charismatic, commanding presence and a full head of snow-white hair, which was suitably matched below his twinkling blue eyes by a whiter-than-white well-trained military moustache. There was something in his manner, an emanation of kindness, which put people at ease although he was a man of high principles who always expected others to have the same level of integrity. He would never suffer fools gladly. During the next ten years, Sir Colin was appointed High Sheriff of North Yorkshire; awarded the Life Presidency of the North Yorkshire Branch of St John Ambulance; and selected to by an Honorary Colonel of his old regiment.

Mathew's brother, Sebastian, had always wanted to be a professional soldier. After leaving Wellington College, which had been built as a national monument for the Duke of Wellington and opened as a school in 1859 with its motto

'Fortune Favours the Brave', he gained entrance to the Royal Military Academy (RMA) at Sandhurst. After two years of intensive training, he narrowly missed gaining the academy commandant's much-coveted Sword of Honour, but was awarded the Queen's Medal as the officer cadet achieving the highest scores in military practical and academic studies.

Prior to entering Sandhurst, Sir Colin had recommended that his eldest son and heir should aim at gaining a commission in the Household Brigade. So Sebastian took the opportunity to make friends with members of the brigade and, due to his family's many social connections and his evident military prowess, he was soon to be sponsored throughout his two years as a cadet as a potential future officer in the Life Guards (which together with the Blues and Royals, represented the oldest and most senior British cavalry regiments). Toward the end of his training, a place in the regiment was confirmed. At the time of Mathew's return to Hartington Hall, Sebastian was serving as a senior captain with his regiment as part of an armoured unit on his second tour of Northern Ireland.

Before Mathew was accepted by Scaife University in Tupelo, Mississippi, his mother had schemed as much as possible to pair him off with the oldest daughter of the Earl and Countess of Drysdale, the eighteen-year-old Lady Antonia Clinton-Kemp. Antonia was just the type of person she would like to see her youngest son betrothed to. She was five feet six inches tall, with light-blonde hair and an English rose complexion. These attributes were matched by her fine cheekbones, clear blue eyes, and a countenance that gave her a kind of delectable innocence as well as, to Lady Sally's reckoning, the fact that she was 'a perfectly nice young lady'. Adding to such agreeable qualities, she sat on a horse well and rode to hounds impeccably, she was intelligent and also a fine shot. So in Lady Sally's estimation, Antonia possessed the majority of the social attributes that she considered were essential for the next generation of the Duncan family to reproduce from.

SOMEONE WISHES TO SPEAK TO YOU

Prior to having embarked on his African field studies, Mathew had had a brief flirtation with Antonia at the annual January Bramham Moor Hunt Ball at Wetherby. The encounter had been rather champagne-fuelled and had been restricted to a few furtive kisses, cuddles, and a lasting embrace, within the confines of the front seat of his MGB GT. But in spite of Mathew having enjoyed this first physical contact with a member of the fairer gender, he could not help regarding Antonia as just a delightful, attractive, sporty friend who shared his social circle; not a person to attempt to deflower and thereby dishonour.

It was well known that girls within his set would be quick to warn each other of the boys who had 'tried to pounce', and word would soon get around that they were NSITs – 'Not Safe in Taxis'. On the odd occasion the behaviour of one of his social group had been considered by his peers to have gone too far, to have breached their moral code, they were quickly ostracised from the circle. However, due to his mother's continued scheming it was not long after Mathew's return to Hartington Hall that she announced Antonia was soon due to return to her nearby family estate, Bardon Towers, for her summer vacation from Girton College. Her mother, the Countess of Drysdale, had informed Lady Sally that Antonia had told her she would like to see Mathew again and was keen to hear all about his encounters with gorillas in 'Darkest Africa'.

The view out of the mullioned bay window of Hartington Hall's library, with its floor to ceiling shelves of leather-bound books, could not have been a more agreeable and peaceful environment for Mathew to work in. Wisteria cascaded over the balustraded upper terrace, which featured splendidly elaborate gazebos at either end of the lichen-speckled wall, through which an imposing double flight of steps led down to an ornate wrought-iron gate giving access into the undulating meadows of the 'Home Park'. At the bottom of the park could be seen the slow-flowing, shallow waters of the River Wharfe, with its backdrop of trees which gave way to the heather-covered moors and hills of the Dales.

Since returning to Hartington, Mathew had slipped into a carefully disciplined routine from Mondays to Fridays, leaving each weekend to socialise with his parents and friends. After rising at dawn, showering, and taking a mug of hot, strong, black Kivu coffee (numerous bags of which he had brought back from Bukavu with him), he would make his way to the stable yard. During Mathew's formative years, the stable yard had represented a place of sanctuary – a place he had shared with his father's Labrador gun dogs, Jock and Paddy, and his half-bred chestnut-coloured hunter out of an Irish Draught horse lineage; The Mouse.

In the middle of the flagstone yard was an attractive fountain whose waters tumbled gently over the figure of Artemis, the Greek goddess of hunting and of the woodlands, into a font-like trough where horses had refreshed themselves for generations. White fan-tailed pigeons fluttered from their loft above the main coach house to bathe in the clear water. Spacious wood-panelled loose boxes and stalls, topped by metal bars which enabled the horses to communicate with each other, and the two mahogany-panelled harness rooms with their glass-fronted sliding doors, had no doubt once boasted some of the best saddlery in the North of England; all of which presented a scene of former opulence. Before the advent of the car the stables probably accommodated well over twenty horses, but now there were only four. The Mouse had died several years previously.

Riding his father's highly spirited grey thoroughbred hunter Winston, who stood at 16.3 hands high, Mathew would take an exhilarating early morning gallop in the Home Park as far as the lodge at the end of the mile-long south drive. He would then rub Winston down in his spacious loose box and give him a reward of a good feed of oats. After returning to the hall for more cups of Kivu coffee and a light breakfast, he would isolate himself in the library. There he would remain mostly undisturbed with his note books for the majority of the day, only breaking briefly for a snack at lunchtime in the hall's flagstone-floored kitchen.

It had been on a Saturday morning when Mathew was having breakfast with his parents that Sid Stockdale had brought in the morning papers, *The Times* and the *Telegraph*, together with the day's post. And, as always had been Stockdale's custom, he placed the small pile of letters ceremoniously to the side of Sir Colin.

'I also had to sign for this package that came by registered post from Africa,' he announced in his usual regimental fashion. Seeing that this was for Mathew, Lady Sally was quick to take possession of the package before passing it onto him, seizing the opportunity to glance at the rather flowery backward-slanting writing and noting that the sender's name and address was L. Luzembo, from the National Park Office, Bukavu, Zaire.

'What a lovely lot of colourful stamps there are on that package! We must find a small boy to pass them on to... Who is "L. Luzembo", Mathew?'

Although Mathew had found it difficult to disguise his excitement in receiving the package from Lucienne, he made an attempt to be as casual and as uninterested as possible. 'Oh... Lucienne is Adrien Deschryver's assistant; I was working with her in Bukavu. She's can speak four languages – one of which is English – she helped me a huge amount while I was there.' Whereupon his mother, with the benefit of maternal instinct and feminine intuition, sensed that Mathew was being rather guarded in what he was saying; perhaps there was more to it than a working relationship, she thought.

Mathew had decided that it would be prudent not to open

the package until he had returned to the privacy of his bedroom; he was well aware that his mother would have been studying his expressions and reactions like a hawk. He was determined, at this stage of his relationship with Lucienne, not to give anything away about how he felt. Once he had returned to his room, it proved to be just as well that he was by himself.

Dear Mathew,
I just had to write my feelings down before they overwhelm me. Do forgive me if my letter doesn't make sense, this is the first time I've ever written to anyone like this.

Since our afternoon together on the shores of Lake Kivu my life has changed, I think about you all the time. I understand why you needed to return to England, I just wish that circumstances were different and you could have stayed here with me. Our time together was so special; I would have loved it to carry on like that forever.

But, my dearest Mathew, I am hoping that you are thinking about me too and although I would never wish you to be unhappy, I would like to think you too are at least a little sad at our separation.

At least there is light at the end of the tunnel – although it seems a long way off. I yearn for the day we meet again in Atlanta, when I can take you in my arms and hold you close once again.

With deepest love and affection, always,
Lucienne xxxxx

Within the folds of its scented pages was a gorgeous photograph of a smiling Lucienne, dressed in a colourful sky-blue kaftan, sitting with a glass of wine in her hand on the balcony of the Bistro Zanzibar overlooking Lake Kivu, with the mountains of Kahuzi-Biega as a dramatic backdrop. On the back of the photograph, Lucienne had written in red ink:

'How I so much wish that you were here with me now, so that I could once more be in your loving embrace. Here's to our reunion in Atlanta. With lots of hugs and kisses, Lucienne xxx'.

The package had also included a second, more formal, typed letter to bring Mathew up-to-date and to report that she had been accepted by Emory University's Department of Psychology to undertake a three-year degree course to study both Primate Social Psychology and Animal Behavior and Evolution. A copy of Osman Hill's letter to her was enclosed with regards to the funding he had arranged for her air ticket to Atlanta, and the stipend he had organised for her in connection with the research she was to undertake at the Yerkes Center for Volume 9 of his primate monograph.

Lucienne had also included in the package a selection of recent photographs of Mathew's study group of gorillas, and one of Deschryver communicating with Casimir, which had the effect of engulfing Mathew in a mist of nostalgia. After reading and rereading her loving sentiments, he kissed the photograph a couple of times, as well as her signature, prior to placing the pictures and the scented letter back into the package, and carefully secreting it among his belongings.

Taking care not to bump into either of his parents, he made his way to the stables, saddled Winston and galloped through the Home Park, scattering the herd of Friesian cattle as he passed through their midst. He just wanted some time on his own to attempt to reconcile the strength of his feelings for Lucienne and to arrive at some degree of normality as to the ever-increasing conflicting emotions that had started to haunt him. He was fully aware that as far as his parents were concerned, if he were to become engaged to be married they would expect him to chose a person from a similar social background, who would thereby be easily able to fit into the privileged world that he inhabited. Mathew could only conclude that if he were to become engaged to Lucienne and bring her back to England, it would be extremely unfair for her to have to be exposed to such a parochial environment and high degree of social bias, and for her fun-loving, intelligent personality to be inhibited by the unacceptable, entrenched, short-sightedness of his peers.

While riding at a more relaxed pace along the riverbank, Mathew reflected on his experiences during his time at Scaife University. He reminded himself that in spite of the US 1964 Civil Rights Act, sizeable forces in the Deep South still resisted change, resulting in various degrees of racial tension and divide still remaining apparent. He also wondered how long it would be before such current, almost tribal uncertainties between the races became a spectre of the past. But regrettably, the more he thought about such a social bias-based imbroglio, the more he came to the conclusion that the way he felt about Lucienne was almost insurmountable.

Mathew knew that once he gained his PhD, if he were to marry Lucienne, which would in all probability distance him from his family and friends in England, he would at least be able to gain employment as a university lecturer in either Africa or even in the USA, but he had to confess that a totally academic teaching career had never appealed very much to him. However, by the time he had returned Winston to his loose box, he had concluded that it was of the utmost importance not to allow such a conflict of emotional loyalties to distract him from his priority; the analysis of his field notes. Otherwise, his moral dilemma could well undermine his immediate objective, that being the attainment of his doctorate from Emory University.

After returning to the hall, Mathew joined his parents for lunch in the nineteenth-century orangery, taking with him the selection of gorilla photographs that Lucienne had sent. He showed them the photographs and described in great detail each member of Casimir's family, highlighting their individual temperaments, characteristics, and how they interacted with

SOMEONE WISHES TO SPEAK TO YOU

each other. Although both parents tried to show as much interest as possible, their only remarks were how brave he was to have been in such close contact with such 'large, black, human-like apes'. After he had told them about the threats that the eastern lowland gorilla species had been subjected to, prior to Adrien Deschryver's dedicated work for their conservation in Kahuzi-Biega, the only question his mother asked was what Luzembo's Christian name was. And in a similar somewhat distracted fashion, his father had rather tactlessly asked him whether there was any good big game shooting in the area.

The following week, the Duncan family received an invitation from the Earl and Countess of Drysdale to a dinner party at their nearby estate, Bardon Towers. It was an event to celebrate Antonia having just come down from Cambridge for the summer break. Sir Colin regretted that all such evenings were no longer 'white-tie' occasions as they always used to be in pre-war days for, as far as he was concerned, just having to don a dinner jacket and black tie represented a retrograde step. Prior to such a formal dinner, he always made this a point to lament about.

On the Saturday evening of the dinner, while they were waiting for Sid Stockdale to arrive at the hall's front entrance with the immaculately polished Daimler, Mathew had joined his father in the study to take a glass of chilled Harvey's amontillado sherry. 'Fancy a smiler, Mathew? We'll have a lot of talking to do tonight!' Having a 'smiler' was a family custom that was often observed before attending social gatherings.

'Yes please, I think I'll need it.' Mathew had been particularly pleased to accept the offer for he knew it would help to calm his nerves prior to being cross-examined by the somewhat imperious Countess of Drysdale, as well as in seeing Antonia again after such a long time. When it was time to leave,

CONFLICTING SENTIMENTS

Lady Sally joined the two of them in the hall, dressed in an elegant floral-patterned silk evening gown, and wearing around her neck a perfect double string of fine Cartier pearls.

'Mathew, you look positively smart – the smartest I've seen you since you came back. Even your hair is neat, and that is certainly a rarity.' She glanced at the little finger of his left hand to see whether he was wearing the gold signet ring with the family crest engraved upon it that she had requested him to put on for the evening. She smiled in satisfaction that he had complied with her wishes. As the family trio descended the wide front steps of the hall in their evening finery, Mathew reflected on how some of his student friends in Atlanta would have viewed such a regal spectacle.

A dinner at Bardon Towers had always followed a similar procedure, with the Earl's family butler, wearing white kid gloves, serving flûtes of champagne from a large silver tray in the drawing room, which rejoiced in a commanding view over the deer park.

'Ladies and gentlemen, if you would like to proceed into the dining room – dinner is served.' The gong had sounded and the party was led to the spacious dining room with its minstrels' gallery and tapestry-adorned walls which, at intervals, were punctuated by a series of rather stern-looking family portraits. The butler, holding a small table plan, ceremoniously gestured with his free hand to indicate to the guests the shortest distance to their designated place at the enormous Chippendale table.

When each guest arrived at their chair, in order for there to be no last minute confusion or exchanging of places, their name was neatly written on a small gilt-edged card, supported by a silver place-name holder positioned in front of each table setting. Once Mathew had located his place and stood behind his chair, he was delighted to be joined by Antonia, who was to be seated to the right of him. No doubt, he guessed, on her insistence.

SOMEONE WISHES TO SPEAK TO YOU

After the Earl and Countess had seated themselves at each end of the long table, Mathew pulled out Antonia's chair. 'Allow me,' he said as she slid into her seat, smiling.

'So lovely to see you again Mathew, it's been an absolute age. You must tell me all about Africa – rather more exciting than Cambridge, I'll bet... Jolly good, this is Daddy's favourite Premier Cru Chablis, you must try it,' said Antonia as the wine was poured into exquisitely cut crystal glasses. Mathew took a sip and decided the evening might be tolerably pleasant after all. The five courses were served on the family's fine gold-leaf edged porcelain, all of which had their coat of arms with the crest on each plate being positioned carefully at twelve o'clock in front of the diner. At either side of the placement had been a set of monogrammed Georgian silver cutlery. During the meal, each dish was accompanied by a generous amount of vintage wine, which included some fine claret from the Earl's renowned cellars. Three tall candelabras gave flickering light to a selection of rather over-ornate gold family heirlooms, which had been positioned at intervals along the length of the table. Two sizeable Venetian chandeliers hung on long, gilded chains from the vaulted ceiling, providing some welcome additional illumination to this formal setting.

The conversation between Mathew and Antonia flowed easily. 'Do you know,' said Antonia, 'I do so enjoy Girton. I love studying History of Art, and the college itself is just wonderful – we really have so much freedom, and there's just so much going on. One can never complain of being bored!' While she was talking about her new life in Cambridge, Antonia had left her knee touching his, which Mathew had found surprisingly agreeable, although after a while he had decided it was prudent to move away. He found it difficult to decide whether this contact had been intentional. As they had been getting on so well, Mathew had hoped that it was.

As the evening progressed, it was as they shared a joke together that she had momentarily gently squeezed the top of his right leg and Mathew recognised that Antonia was still attracted to him. But while they had been talking about mutual friends and the privileged lifestyle they had always both so much enjoyed in their youth, he had become conscious of how very much they had in common. Mathew could not help thinking how Antonia still possessed that rather delectable countenance of innocence that he had previously found to be so enchanting, and how he found her to be so much more mature than ever before.

'Gentlemen, the ladies will take their leave of us for a while before we join them for coffee.' Following the Earl's lead, Mathew and the other five male guests rose to their feet while the women followed the Countess to her boudoir. Here, without the presence of the menfolk, they could discuss various upcoming social events, as well as the ramifications of some society scandal that had recently come to their attention.

On the other hand, Mathew found that while the decanter of port was being circulated and the cigars were lit, the men's conversation was rather limited. 'Do you think the heather will be right for the grouse? We want them to be ready for us on the Glorious Twelfth!' 'Last winter it was so cold, the moat froze – I don't remember that happening since '47 and '63. Unlucky, what?'; and some more detailed discussion about the different types of feathers some of them had chosen to fish for brown trout in the nearby River Wharfe. Discussions had concluded by the fox-hunters among the guests having spoken about how well the new whippers-in of the Bramham Moor Hunt had controlled the hounds during the last season, and how many fox kills each of them had witnessed.

Half an hour later, the men rejoined the women in the drawing room to take coffee, and to have a choice of either one of the Earl's fine cognacs, or a liqueur. To Mathew, the evening had gone off surprisingly well and being seated next to Antonia had proved to be an unexpected pleasure. The back-slapping, red-faced, jovial Earl had been in cracking form and could not have been a more welcoming and generous host. The Countess had been as gracious as ever, but always managed to maintain the formal decorum of her considered social status. No doubt as far as she was concerned she had performed her duty ably by providing her husband with four children, particularly by producing a son and heir. Young Alistair was about to go to his father's old school, Winchester College; a second son, Philip, (whom she always referred to as a 'spare') had just entered the Pilgrims Preparatory School; and Antonia's younger sister, Penelope, had just entered Benenden School in Kent at the age of eleven.

When Mathew had been enthusiastically telling the Countess, Antonia and her siblings about his gorilla studies, he could not help feeling that the last thing this aristocratic lady would wish would be for a man whose only evident ambition in life was to study different types of monkeys in 'Darkest Africa' to become betrothed to her eldest daughter. Also, as Mathew was the younger son, it would be Sebastian who would inherit the Duncan baronetcy.

When the evening came to an end just after midnight, Antonia mentioned that the annual summer tennis tournament at Bardon Towers was soon due to take place. 'What would you say to partnering me in the doubles? I know you're rather handy with a racket... It's always such fun.' 'That sounds like an excellent suggestion, I would be delighted to accept,' replied Mathew, although he could not help wondering what Lucienne would have to say about it. He had always rather prided himself on his skills as a lawn tennis player, and he knew how well the grass court at Bardon Towers was maintained.

Fond farewells were bade, with additional superlatives from all to the Earl and Countess as to how wonderfully enjoyable the whole party had been. When Antonia said goodbye to Mathew, she gave him a gentle kiss on both cheeks. 'I'm looking forward to playing tennis with you, I'm sure we'll make a formidable partnership. You know, you could always come to visit me in Cambridge when you have time,' she whispered with a mischievous smile. 'Anyway, if you're back in England by the New Year, I would love an invitation to be your partner at the Bramham Moor Hunt Ball. I seem to remember we had lots of fun at the last one...'

During the drive back to Hartington Hall, with Mathew's mind well lubricated from imbibing an agreeable amount of vintage wine followed by the Earl's fine 1963 Dow's port, he reflected just how convivial, alluring, desirable and seductive members of the fairer sex can be. In comparison to his kingdom of gorillas, how was it that Western civilisation had adopted monogamy as its *status quo*? He reminded himself how jealous he was when Lucienne had appeared far more interested in Patrice Daman than him as they were leaving the research institute near Bukavu. Remembering those feelings of possessiveness helped Mathew come to the conclusion that perhaps in the long term, monogamy would be by far the most sustainable path for him.

The following morning, having been concerned about the conflicting emotions he had experienced in his dreams during a rather turbulent night, he wrote what he hoped would be a philosophical and tactful letter to Lucienne. He apologised for not having responded to her most welcome letter before, but emphasised how extremely tied up he had been in working on the analysis of his field notes. He mentioned how very much he had appreciated receiving her loving sentiments, and he had reciprocated to these by saying that he too had been missing her greatly and how much he was looking forward to seeing her again in Atlanta, in just over two months time.

However, Mathew was careful not to over-emphasise any of his deep-rooted intimate romantic thoughts about her, in spite of feeling that he loved Lucienne more than anybody else in the world. This reserve was due to his understanding that when they met again, the environment would be quite unlike that of Bukavu; things might turn out to be very different. Should their relationship fail to blossom, Mathew would hate to let her down. He had genuine concern for her ultimate future happiness, and wanted to avoid damaging her self-confidence and self-respect at all costs.

Just under a month before Mathew was due to return to the USA, he received a letter from a Professor Carl Benirschke of the Centre for Interdisciplinary Research at the recently established Bielefeld University, Germany. The Professor had been given Mathew's details by his old academic friend and colleague Osman Hill, who had highly recommended Mathew as an ideal person to step in to present the keynote address at a forthcoming symposium on 'Captive Propagation and Conservation of Primates'. A sudden illness had caused the previously nominated academic to have to withdraw. All travel and accommodation expenses were to be paid by the university and, if Mathew was able to accept, he had been asked if he could highlight in his address the significance of facial signals and vocalisations of the eastern lowland gorillas he had studied at Kahuzi-Biega, and their particular relevance to human communication. Mathew was quick to accept the invitation; he was honoured Osman Hill had put his name forward and the subject matter was ideal for him. It would also make an excellent addition to his CV.

Ten days later, Mathew flew to Hanover, then travelled by train for the 110 km onward journey to Bielefeld. 'Mathew Duncan?' asked an earnest-looking young man waiting on the station platform. 'That's right,' replied Mathew, putting his cases down to shake hands. 'My name's Michael Lamb, I'm a student of Professor Benirschke – he's asked me to, you know, look after you and help you with things while you're here. My car's right outside, let me take you to your hotel.'

While Michael drove, he told Mathew a little more about himself. 'I graduated from the University of Durham and went straight into the British Diplomatic Service. They sent me here to learn German – I'm doing a one-year crash course at Bielefeld.'

'Is it working? A year is such a short time – I've always found German rather a tricky language.'

'Oh, so do I, absolutely, but Professor Benirschke is an excellent teacher and actually living in Germany makes all the difference so I feel as though I've quite got the hang of it. In fact, they've asked me to translate the abstract of your paper so it can be circulated tomorrow morning, before the presentation.'

Michael dropped Mathew at his hotel, promising to pick him up in good time in the morning.

The next day, everything went according to plan and Mathew delivered what was a very engaging and well-received presentation. Michael had done an excellent job in translating the abstract and keywords of the paper, also carrying out some valuable interpretation during Mathew's speech as there was no simultaneous translation. When Mathew had projected various mugshots of his gorilla study group, Michael had been able to emphasise how much Mathew had to depend upon his sketches and photographs of each individual's noseprint for identification purposes. Just as George Schaller had recorded during his epic year studying the gorilla kingdom, whereas no two humans have exactly the same finger-prints, no two gorillas have the same 'nose-print' – the shape of their nostrils and the outstanding troughs on the bridges of their noses.

Over a much-needed cup of coffee after the presentation,

Michael said, 'I found it absolutely fascinating what you said about how gorillas interact with each other and how there's often a family likeness in both looks and aspects of behaviour. I never would have considered it before – nor what you said about how their interaction could be relevant to human communication.'

'I'm so glad to hear that, I hope you're not the only one!' Mathew laughed.

'Oh I shouldn't think so! I've also made a note of your point about not staring at gorillas directly when you're making observations, that it can constitute a threat – as it can with humans. That may come in very useful.' Michael reflected on how the study of such cognitive skills could well benefit his long-term ambition to work under cover for British Intelligence.

On Mathew's return from Germany, he was delighted to hear from his elder brother in Belfast that he had arranged to take some leave in order to spend a week at Hartington Hall with him prior to his return to the USA. Mathew's disciplined weekly work routine had resulted in having completed the analysis of his gorilla field notes and he was free to relax.

When it came to the weekend of the tennis party at Bardon Towers, Mathew was ready for the opportunity to unwind and meet up with a number of his old hunting and grouse-shooting friends, as well as to be introduced to a variety of the Drysdale's rather eccentric house guests. On such occasions it was mandatory for all participants to wear immaculate white tennis gear, more often than not enhanced by tennis or cricket club sweaters.

The provision of ice-cold jugs of Pimms, platefuls of smoked salmon and cucumber sandwiches, scones with clotted cream and strawberry jam was *de rigueur* for a weekend tennis gathering at a British stately home. Antonia and Mathew had won the doubles and, in the singles, Mathew was only just beaten in the semi-finals by the person who had gone on to win the contest. As Mathew relaxed on the veranda of the thatched summer house, under the shade of two century-old oak trees, he considered how much the setting contrasted to the small veranda in front of his rodent and insect-infested hut near to the entrance to Kahuzi-Biega. An environment that he very much doubted any of his fellow tournament players would have enjoyed or even survived in.

Comparing the two lifestyles, he had found it almost impossible to come out in favour of one against the other, and considered the possibility of merging them both. It had been whilst sitting in this agreeable environment that he attempted to understand the depth of his freshly kindled fondness for Antonia, and how such feelings had contributed to the emotional dilemma and moral contradictions that had now started to haunt him. He also deeply regretted that since he had been back in England, he hadn't mentioned anything to either his parents or his closest friends about his deep love and intimate relationship with Lucienne.

The arrival of Captain Sebastian Duncan back at Hartington Hall was greeted with great warmness by everybody, including the staff. Even Sid Stockdale, an ex-National Service trooper in the Household Brigade, was quick to act as if he was the Captain's batman by proudly unloading his brown leather monogrammed suitcase from the Daimler, and carrying it personally up to Sebastian's bedroom, This would have been conveyed by a lesser mortal under normal circumstances. Although Lady Sally wanted to arrange a number of social events while she had her two sons back at home again, Sebastian and Mathew had managed to persuade her to confine such visits to just close family members; neither of them wished to become involved with the intricacies of their mother's matrimonial match-making.

SOMEONE WISHES TO SPEAK TO YOU

Much of the family conversation during Mathew's final few days at Hartington Hall revolved around the future running of the 1,800-acre estate, and the financial constraints that would be required during the next decade on the two estate farms in order to make them more economically viable. However, Sir Colin had highlighted the financial viability of both the annual four-month grouse and five-month partridge shoots.

'The estate has recently become an integral part of the Yorkshire Dales National Park,' Sir Colin told his sons. 'Do you know, nearly the whole park is under private ownership? We're all extremely fortunate to have Hartington Hall as our ancestral home – we've all benefited from the magnificent scenery of the Fells, grouse moors, hill farms, dry-stone walls ... the streams that tumble down from the hills...' As if their father were working on behalf of the Yorkshire Dales Tourist Board, he highlighted how the rain, wind, fog, frost and snowfalls that regularly occurred throughout the winter months contrasted so magnificently with the beautiful, bright, clear days that they were currently experiencing and how such significant changes had always contributed so much to the Dales' rich biodiversity.

While their father was painting such an idyllic picture, Sebastian and Mathew knew only too well that was leading up to a matter of major importance to him. 'In seven years time I'll be celebrating my seventieth birthday... I'm no longer in the best of health and I sincerely doubt that after 1980 I'll be in a position to carry on running the estate successfully, with its best interests at heart. In order to safeguard the long-term financial viability of Hartington Hall and it environs, would either of you be interested in stepping into the breach, as it were?'

Sebastian was the first to speak up. 'You know how important Hartington is to me, Father, and I want to help, but I've been told by my commanding officer that by the end

CONFLICTING SENTIMENTS

of the year I'll be gazetted as a major in the Life Guards – my future responsibilities will be split equally between the regiment's ceremonial mounted duties, and the Household Cavalry's armoured reconnaissance operational activities. I've been given the chance to lead the Life Guards' half of the Sovereign's Escort at the next Trooping of the Colour.' Sebastian looked down. 'I don't want to give it up. It's my life, it suits me and to tell you the truth, I don't think I'm cut out to run this place, much as I love it.'

Although this was not the response that Sir Colin would have wished for, he was delighted with the success of Sebastian's military career. 'Quite right,' he acquiesced. 'It seems the Life Guards is the place for you for the time being – you stay put. What about you, Mathew?'

Sir Colin found his younger son's future career path more difficult to comprehend.

'Well, for my part,' began Mathew, 'I'm hopeful that I'll be awarded the PhD by late autumn, and after that I plan to come back to Hartington for Christmas and New Year. That's when I'll be looking at all my options – which, in years to come, could well include taking over the estate.'

However, Mathew had gone on to explain how his current ambition was to return to Africa for a few years to continue with his studies on primate behaviour. 'I really believe there is so much that could be learnt from the communicative skills of the monkey kingdom that could be very relevant to human knowledge. I want to expand my studies into other groups of primates.' Mathew's plan was to study within the African guenon group of primates, belonging to the *Cercopithecus* species.

'So you're planning to go back to Africa… What do you think of Rhodesia, would that be any good to you? I've just heard from a great friend of mine, Sir Roger Willock. He served as a brother officer of mine in the 12th Royal Lancers during the Italian Campaign. He's soon to take up the appointment as Britain's senior representative in Ian Smith's Republic of Rhodesia. At the end of the year, if you're still keen to return to Africa to carry on with your field studies, I'll write to him – I'm sure he'll be only too pleased to help you in any way possible.'

This was exciting news; Mathew was already aware from Osman Hill's primate monograph No. 6, which included all members of the superfamily *Cercopithecoidea*, that both the Vervet monkey, *Cercopithecus pygerythrus*, and a rarer subspecies of the Samango group of monkeys, *Cercopithecus albogularis*, inhabited the south-eastern district of Rhodesia.

So it was agreed that if Mathew had still got his mind set on pursuing post-doctorate primate studies in Africa, his father would write to Sir Roger when he returned to the UK for Christmas. Sir Colin felt immense gratitude towards his younger son for giving him a glimmer of hope that one day he might take on the management of Hartington Hall.

Sebastian and Mathew, in spite of their very different careers, had always been the greatest of friends and they both relished the week that they had together prior to Mathew's return to the USA. On their final ride out in the Home Park, the brothers discussed the idea of Mathew taking over the running of the estate. 'What do you think of the idea, Sebastian? You are the older brother, and I certainly don't want to tread on your toes, but I can see you don't want to give up the Life Guards.' 'I think it's a splendid idea! Father will be absolutely delighted that one of us is considering the idea of running the estate, and you're quite right, it really isn't for me. You go ahead with my blessing, Mathew – you know I'm always there for if you need my help.' Sebastian was well aware that his father would never have requested him to resign his commission, for ever since he had been awarded the prestigious RMA's Queen's Medal at Sandhurst, Sir Colin had recognised that he would always be a career soldier and would always nurture the ultimate accolade of becoming colonel of his regiment.

CONFLICTING SENTIMENTS

On their return to the stable yard, Mathew was tempted to tell his brother something about Lucienne, but failed to do so and felt quite deceitful as a result. He considered that his inability to speak about his feelings had something to do with the two contrasting worlds of Bukavu and the Hartington Hall estate. All Sebastian had become aware of with regards to any enthusiasm that his younger brother had for a member of the fairer sex, was when he had overheard some of Mathew's telephone conversation with Antonia Clinton-Kemp. He had been passing through the hallway when he heard his brother say, 'Antonia, I must say it's been delightful to see you again. We made a fine team at the Bardon Towers tournament, don't you think? Yes, quite... I'm just calling to say I'll be back by Christmas, I'll be in touch if you're down from Cambridge... Yes, that would be splendid...'

On the 1 August, 1973, Mathew landed on a British Airways Boeing 747 jumbo jet at Atlanta's Hartsfield-Jackson International Airport, and was met by an enthusiastic Lucienne Luzembo.

4

A Moral Dilemma

After having been away for almost eighteen months, Mathew took some time to readjust to his life at Emory University. Going from the tranquility of the Yorkshire Dales to Atlanta was almost as much of a contrast as that between his small, isolated cabin by the entrance to the Kahuzi-Biega National Park and the opulent environment of Hartington Hall. The constant noise of traffic in downtown Atlanta, the bustle of people and the piercing sirens were all starting to have a rather suffocating effect upon him, and he was beginning to yearn for the secluded lifestyle that he had so much enjoyed during the earlier part of the year.

On Lucienne's arrival in the USA four months previously, Professor Osman Hill had arranged suitable accommodation for her in easy reach of both Emory University and his office at the Yerkes Regional Primate Research Center. Lucienne had started to settle into her undergraduate life in Atlanta by the time Mathew arrived. The professor's wife, Yvonne, had been particularly welcoming by making sure that she had everything she required and taking her to see some of the city's major landmarks. Within a week of Mathew's return to America, he and Lucienne were invited to dinner at the Hills' home in the fashionable uptown district of Buckhead, as the professor was so eager to hear first-hand about his observations on the eastern lowland gorilla species in the wild.

A MORAL DILEMMA

During Mathew's first few days back, he kept reminding himself about the strength of his recent emotions for Antonia Clinton-Kemp and to be guarded in his affections towards Lucienne in case he gave the impression he wanted a committed long-term relationship. However, in spite of such a righteous intention, he was surprised how quickly his deep feelings for her were rekindled and how very much he enjoyed her ebullient company.

So it was on a hot and rather humid August evening, with thunder in the air, that Mathew had picked Lucienne up in a taxi from her small flat. As they drove through midtown Atlanta, they shared their excitement about the evening ahead.

'I must say I feel very honoured they've asked us for dinner at their home,' said Mathew. 'I've never been invited before so it'll be interesting to see Osman Hill in his own environment. He's supposed to be an excellent host.'

'I've spent quite a bit of time with Yvonne, she's been so kind to me, but it will be great to get to know the professor on a more personal level,' replied Lucienne. She took Mathew's hand and began to speak in a hushed tone. 'I was thinking that it might be best if we project our relationship as friendly but professional. If they think there's anything going on between us it might not look good, you know... They might think it will get in the way of our work.'

'That's a good point. Well, there's no reason for them to think anything other than that we developed a friendship while I was studying the gorillas of Kahuzi-Biega and that we share a professional interest.'

'And in many ways that's true, but I think we should emphasise that we have a mutual ambition to do as much as possible to promote the future conservation of the eastern lowland gorilla in the wild. In fact, we could jointly organise some fundraising activities in support of Adrien's anti-poaching patrols in Kahuzi-Biega... What do you think?'

In spite of Mathew's previously vowed intention to become

more reserved during his meetings with Lucienne, throughout their taxi ride they had held hands with the enthusiasm and intensity of two young lovers. It was almost as if their almost six months of separation had only been a matter of a few hours, with the intimacy of Mathew's rescue of Lucienne from Lake Kivu fresh in their memories.

Mathew had always found his professor to be extremely supportive to any student of natural history, no matter what their background or what level of education they had achieved, as long as they showed enthusiasm and dedication to the subject. Osman Hill was well respected for his eagerness to help young researchers in any way he could. The more Mathew got to know his mentor away from his academic teachings, the more he came to recognise his strong sense of humour and his quick and ready wit. Also, within his small, close-knit academic circle of friends, he was well acknowledged to be an excellent host, a connoisseur of good wines and the producer of a variety of exotic dishes. Mathew had been amused to hear a rumour that some of Osman Hill's colleagues and staff at the Yerkes Center viewed him as 'the archetypical English scholar-gentleman who was inclined to view those from the "colonies" as a step below the British!'

'Put me out of my misery, Mathew – I must hear all about those gorillas in Kahuzi-Biega – I want every detail, don't leave anything out,' smiled Osman Hill almost as soon as they sat down. Mathew was in his element as he described the make-up and social grouping of his study family; the way they interacted with one another and his interpretation of their vocalisations, facial signals and eye flashes. 'Apart from George Schaller's excellent observations on the mountain gorilla, and some more recent papers by Dian Fossey, there's really been little research and even less published about the eastern lowland gorilla,' explained Mathew. 'That's what made this particular species of such interest to me.' After almost an hour of quite intensive questions and answers, it had been obvious to Lucienne that Osman Hill had been totally absorbed in and had very much enjoyed what his doctorate student had been able to tell him.

'I would very much like to see your sketches of the facial patterns next time we see you... I did the anatomical figures for the first six volumes of the primate monograph,' said Yvonne, finally getting a word in edgeways in the question and answer session between her husband and Mathew.

'When I was first a visiting scholar at Emory,' continued Osman Hill, 'it must have been 1958, we had Jane Goodall studying here.' Jane Goodall had studied primate behaviour under him in preparation for her long-term and now famous field studies of wild chimpanzees at the Gombe Stream Research Centre in Tanzania. 'Have you seen her book *In the Shadow of Man*? It's just been published, and she's done a very professional job of presenting her field studies – fascinating, you must read it.'

As the friends enjoyed the generous supply of fine Californian wine, the conversation became more general. Yvonne suggested Mathew and Lucienne might enjoy a visit to the town of Macon, some 140 km to the southeast of Atlanta. 'It's known for having a Cherry Blossom Festival and as the home of the Georgia Music Hall, but the reason I'm suggesting that you visit is to see a major private collection of African-American art and historical and cultural artefacts. There are some fascinating pieces. The owner is one of our friends, Dr Murray Cohen – I'm sure he'd be delighted to show you around.'

'We may well think about that,' said Mathew, winking at Lucienne across the table. 'I could do with a break. Now, Professor, enough about me. Why don't you tell us about your career before you ended up at Emory?'

Osman Hill went on to give a fascinating account of his early days after qualifying as a doctor at the University of

Birmingham's medical school. In 1930, his career had taken him to Sri Lanka (then Ceylon) where he had been appointed as Professor of Anatomy at the University of Colombo Medical College. What Mathew had found of particular interest is that apart from the professor's university teaching and academic responsibilities, he had taken the opportunity to pursue anthropological studies of the indigenous people as well as researching the comparative anatomy of some of the local primates.

Although Osman Hill's international reputation was that of a distinguished anatomist and eminent primatologist, Mathew had found it most revealing to hear about his breadth of interests in so many other aspects of natural history. He had managed to maintain a private menagerie of exotic and native species in Colombo comprising lorises, purple-faced leaf monkeys, cockatoos, red-fan parrots, star and leopard tortoises, a giant Galapagos tortoise and some ruddy mongooses. In the past, Mathew had rather struggled with the fact that to date, his academic studies had been rather restrictive and had prevented him from looking into other aspects of the natural world.

'Coffee, anyone?' asked Yvonne, carrying a tray into the room. It was then that the professor picked up a small museum-type specimen jar full of formalin, which had been partly hidden by a bowl of flowers in the middle of the dining room table and overshadowed on either side by bottles of Napa Valley Sauvignon Blanc and Pinot Noir. Although Mathew had noticed the presence of the bottle containing what looked to him like a foetus of some type of diminutive primate, he had not drawn Lucienne's attention to it. Osman Hill's deep-blue eyes were twinkling as he had held the bottle of formalin up to the light, rather like a small boy with his favourite conker.

'I've got something special here, take a look at this!' he said as he started to point out the anatomical features of a

A MORAL DILEMMA

neonate of the threatened South American Goeldi's monkey, *Callimico goeldii*. He clearly regarded this rare specimen to be the jewel in the crown of his collection. 'I can't tell you how pleased I was to get it – this neonate arrived from a research laboratory in Miami, just in time for tonight.' It was his *pièce de résistance* for the evening. 'I'm currently writing a paper on obstetric mishaps in marmosets,' he informed them with the enthusiasm of a surgeon about to carry out his first operation. 'Now I can include comparative observations of Goeldi's monkey. So little is known about the species, it's going to be fascinating,' he said, turning the jar around to look at the specimen from every angle.

After having thanked the Hills for the most enjoyable of evenings, Mathew had suggested in the taxi back to Lucienne's flat that they should take Yvonne's advice and hire a car to visit Macon. Lucienne was very enthusiastic and so the following morning, Mathew phoned Macon's tourist office who recommended that he make reservations at the Lakeside Inn. He duly reserved two rooms for the coming weekend, with views of Lake Tobesofkee.

With approximately three months to go before it was time to submit his dissertation, Mathew returned to his Hartington Hall weekday routine in order to finalise the writing up of his thesis. He had to restrict socialising with his university friends as much as possible. Whenever he had time to reflect on Lucienne and Antonia, he found it almost impossible to reconcile his respective deep feelings for them. This had not been helped at all when he had received a rather romantic letter from Antonia, who had written to say how much she missed his company, especially when she had returned home to Yorkshire, and that she did so much hope he would be back in the UK by Christmas. What with Lucienne's regular expressions of love for him, Mathew found himself in an emotional tug of war. He felt that he had adopted somewhat of a 'Jekyll and Hyde' attitude in his relationship with them both. However, with no foreseeable solution to his emotional disarray, Mathew decided to concentrate as much as possible on his priority; preparing his doctorate dissertation.

On Friday afternoon, Mathew collected an excited Lucienne from the Yerkes Center's reference library, and although the heat of the day was still intense, the drive down to Macon through the rolling hills proved to be a very enjoyable journey. They followed a sign to the shores of Lake Tobesofkee and soon arrived at the small, quaint-looking Lakeside Inn. While Mathew removed their overnight bags from the boot, he noticed that the 'Vacancies' sign behind a glass panel on the front door was being turned around.

As they entered the reception area of the hotel, a middle-aged man with the appearance of a bull mastiff glared at Lucienne.

'Did you read the sign?' he snarled at Mathew. 'There's no vacancies here tonight.'

'I've booked and paid for two lake-view rooms on my Amex card. Here's the confirmation reference.' Although taken aback by such a rude reception, Mathew was quick to find the slip of paper in his wallet and hand it to the increasingly angry-looking man, who then disappeared into a back office where he could be overheard almost screaming at someone. He returned a few minutes later.

'Well, there's been a mistake with these reservations. There's only one room with a lake view available, which you can have, but the black girl will have to take a room at the far end of the building. If the lady doesn't like it,' he sneered sarcastically, 'she can try a hotel in another part of Macon which she may find more ... appropriate.'

Shocked by such aggression, Mathew had to do everything possible to control his anger. Glowering back at the hotelier, after a long pause, he replied as calmly as he was able, 'Could

A MORAL DILEMMA

we see the rooms?' The man returned to the office and after more angry words from within they were joined by an agitated and tearful-looking lady, who took them upstairs.

'These will just about do – as long as my friend has the lake view room,' Mathew insisted. 'I'm sure you'll agree the other room is far from acceptable for a lady to sleep in.'

'I'm afraid you have to take the lake view room. My husband, Jed Jarman, he's the owner and he sticks to his rules. There's a notice at the entrance which says "Rights of Admission Reserved". It states that only Europeans are allowed to stay in this part of his hotel, non-Europeans have to be accommodated elsewhere.' The woman looked at the floor. 'I'm really sorry I can't help you, but those are the rules.'

Mathew was tempted to contact the local sheriff's office immediately and cite the 1964 Civil Rights Act that had officially ended such public segregation in the USA almost ten years before, but decided against it. Prior to leaving Atlanta (he had not considered it necessary to mention it to Lucienne), one of his friends had warned him that Macon was in a district of the Deep South where there was still quite a sizeable percentage of the white population who resisted change. His friend had warned him that should he encounter any 'rednecks' in Macon while out with Lucienne, to be careful not to overreact in case the situation should escalate.

That evening, in spite of the hotel restaurant being only half full, as soon as they arrived at the dining room they were immediately guided to a table in the far corner, as if Jarman wished to completely hide the presence of Lucienne from the rest of his hotel guests. However Lucienne, being the level-headed, mature mortal that she had always been, acted as if everything was in order and during the course of the meal she was as cheerful and as charming as ever. After taking coffee in the hotel lounge, where they had also been directed to a table in a secluded corner and received a few disapproving looks as they walked through the room, Mathew had accompanied Lucienne to her room at the far end of the building, passing as they went a bathroom with a 'Whites Only' notice on its door. After giving Lucienne a quick hug and kissing her gently on her lips, he said 'I'm so sorry to have brought you here... I'll take this whole despicable racist attitude up with the appropriate Civil Rights authorities in Macon before we go back. I can't believe people still think like this, I never expected it.'

'It's not your fault, Mathew. But we're here now and we can't do anything about it, so we may as well make the best of the weekend, don't you think?'

He smiled and kissed her again, impressed at her strength and resilience under such trying circumstances.

The following morning, after an early breakfast, Mathew phoned Dr Murray Cohen. As suggested by Yvonne, Osman Hill had provided them with an introduction to this friend of his, an archaeologist by profession, who had for many years been gathering African-American art and now had a sizable collection of artefacts and documents, with the idea of establishing an African-American Museum in Macon. Dr Cohen invited them to his home that morning.

'How lovely to meet you both! Any friend of Osman Hill is a friend of mine – come right in.' As soon as they entered Dr Cohen's house Mathew was tempted to tell him about Jed Jarman's extreme racist attitude, but he decided to leave the matter until later in the day.

While they were sitting on the veranda with some ice-cold lemon drinks, Dr Cohen told them that he had been awarded his doctorate from the University of Georgia as a result of the data he had collected during the major excavations of the Ocmulgee Monument, which had taken place in the 1930s.

'Much of the research we carried out was with a ground-

A MORAL DILEMMA

scanning instrument, very primitive compared with anything in use today but it allowed us to locate shapes underground.'

'Really?' said Mathew. 'Archeology fascinates me, but I'm ashamed to say I know very little about it.'

'Well, for this dig, it was the ground scanner that led to all the other discoveries. As we found the forms underground, we could identify the unearthed dwellings of an ancient civilization of mound builders. These were near the Ocmulgee River, just to the north west of what's now downtown Macon.'

'So what kind of things did you find?' asked Lucienne.

'Pretty much what we were expecting to find – pieces of domestic ware, animal bones, axe heads, even some fine decorative pieces – but the quantity and the analysis we were able to carry out meant that the site is now considered to be one of the largest Mississippi-period settlements in the eastern USA with mounds dating back about 1000 years. It gave us an incredible amount of data on how they lived their lives.'

Although the doctor's sizeable collection of artefacts was not currently open to the general public, he had made a room in an outbuilding available to schools as an educational resource devoted to the African-American experience as far back as 1619. As he showed them round, Mathew and Lucienne found the doctor's commentary about African-American art, history and culture during the past 350 years to be enlightening and enthralling. He was generous enough to spend the majority of the morning explaining in detail the historically significant achievements of African-American inventors, military leaders, artisans, musicians, writers and artists, as well as a number of outstanding heroes.

'Now this,' Dr Cohen explained, 'is one of the jewels of the collection. It's called "From Africa to America", a work by a contemporary Macon artist, Wilfred Stroud.' They took in the intricate mural in front of them, depicting the journey of Africans from West Africa to America beginning in the early seventeenth century, portraying significant events up to the twentieth century. It was an incredibly moving piece in which the artist had managed to capture the suffering of slaves and degradation of African-American people and their struggle against oppression.'

'Your collection is quite remarkable, Dr Cohen,' said Lucienne. 'It has a great historical value – do you have a plan for the future?'

'My dearest wish is that it will form the main nucleus of an African-American museum in Macon for all to benefit by, so that it can help educate and promote understanding.'

Once they had seen the collection and were back on the shaded veranda, Mathew decided the time was right to bring up the problem of the Lakeside Inn.

'Dr Cohen... I wanted to ask your advice on something. We arrived at the Lakeside Inn yesterday having pre-booked two rooms, and were treated with the most hostile racism I have ever witnessed. The owner, a Mr Jed Jarman, tried to pretend there were no vacancies and eventually, Lucienne was put in a room at the back of the hotel instead of one the lake view rooms I'd asked for – we were practically hidden from view at dinner. How should I go about complaining to the relevant authorities? We can't let Jarman carry on treating people like that.'

'I honestly can't believe this attitude is still going on in Macon... I am genuinely shocked by what you've told me. Coincidentally, I've just been elected as chairman of the city's Anti-Racial Discrimination Board and I will certainly do something about this as soon as I can, on Monday morning. In the meantime, I would recommended that on your return to Atlanta, you write a letter to the Mayor of Macon at City Hall on university note paper, with an open copy of it to the Chief of Police, both at the same address, as well as mailing a copy to him. That way I can table the letter at the next meeting of the ARDB.'

Dr Cohen realised how upset Lucienne must be, although

she hid it well. He guided them through his garden to an outhouse in order to show them his collection of written material about the part that Macon had played as the main armory for the Confederate forces during the American Civil War, and how the Union forces had laid a successful siege to Fort Macon in 1882. But he was particularly keen to show them both his sizeable collection of writings about the Civil Rights Movement, and how it had been less than ten years since African Americans had to enter a cinema by a separate door; drink from different water fountains; use separate toilets; and were segregated on city buses, in schools and in the majority of public places. Even park benches had notices on them denoting 'Whites Only'.

'At the height of the demonstrations in Macon against the passing of the Civil Rights Act in 1964,' he explained, 'I wrote a lead article for the *Macon Telegraph* voicing my strong support for the Democrats' intention to have the act passed by Congress. As a result of the article, my house was targeted by members of the local Ku Klux Klan. They painted a swastika in red paint on the most prominent part of my garden wall and wrote "The Home of a Nigger Lover" in large letters. They're a nasty bunch of fellas.'

'Were they ever caught?' asked an outraged Mathew. It was vile to think of such a decent and deeply humanitarian man being sought out for this sort of abuse.

'No, they're probably people I see all over town – storekeepers, bank tellers, mechanics – but they hide behind those white robes and become invisible. Over sixty-five per cent of the population of Macon are African Americans, but members of the KKK are still promoting their extremist, reactionary, far-right policies – the owner of the Lakeside Inn is probably an active Klan member. In spite of it being almost ten years since the Civil Rights Act was passed, the Mormon Sect are still not admitting African Americans to their priesthood. I should think it will take at least three generations, through education, tolerance and enhanced integration between the races, to breed out this narrow-minded bigotry.'

Mathew expanded on his own views on segregation and how, during his early days at Scaife University in Tupelo, he had joined the city's Civil Rights Movement and participated in a protest march. 'It surprised me how much criticism I received from some of the more hard-line fellow students for being so directly involved with the movement. I thought they would think the same way as I did,' Mathew explained. 'I had an ancestor, Robert Milligan, who was elected as MP for Bradford in 1851 – he was a dedicated disciple of William Wilberforce. During his six-year tenure as a member of Parliament, his main mission was to do as much as possible to promote the emancipation of slaves in the West Indies; a *raison d'être* that my family have always been immensely proud about.'

During the course of the morning, the doctor had taken a liking to Mathew and Lucienne and had been pleased by the way they had showed such enthusiasm about his collection, as well as to the background that had led up to the passing of the Civil Rights Act. As he was very embarrassed about their reception at the hotel and wished to minimise any further discrimination directed at these friends of Professor Osman Hill, he invited them to return to his home at 6.30 that evening for pre-dinner drinks, prior to taking them as his guests to a popular, informal Brazilian restaurant in downtown Macon. He told them that the restaurant's owner was an Afro-Brazilian immigrant from Salvador in the state of Bahia, and was not only his friend but also served as a valuable member of the city's ARDB.

After leaving the doctor's home, they drove along Riverside Drive to the banks of Lake Tobesofkee, and after enjoying a snack at a lakeside drive-in kiosk they walked hand-in-hand along the lake's attractive tranquil shoreline. On their return to the Lakeside Inn Mrs Jarman gave them their room keys, regarding them with a surly expression.

A MORAL DILEMMA

'You know, we've just spent the most fascinating morning with Dr Murray Cohen.' Mathew couldn't resist taking the opportunity; he knew whatever he said to Mrs Jarman would be reported back to her husband and he relished the idea of increasing Jarman's uneasiness about having them in the hotel. He delivered his *coup de grâce*. 'I don't know whether you're familiar with him, he's chairman of Macon's Anti-Racial Discrimination Board. He's been telling us about the problems that Macon is still facing with the implementation of the Civil Rights Act. As we're both keen to learn as much as possible about these ongoing problems, we've accepted an invitation from Dr Cohen to dine with him at a restaurant owned by a recent immigrant from Brazil, of African descent, so we won't be requiring dinner at the hotel this evening. Good day to you.'

Mrs Jarman stared after them, open-mouthed, as they turned and left the reception area.

The relaxed atmosphere at the candlelit Brazilian restaurant in downtown Macon could not have been more of a contrast to the previous evening. The cocktails the doctor had mixed and served to them on the flower-bedecked veranda of his home had greatly helped Mathew and Lucienne to momentarily forget the constraints and uneasiness they had experienced. The convivial ambiance of Padua Santos's Bahia Bistro reminded them both of their first meal together in Bukavu at Bistro Zanzibar; such was the friendliness of the clientele and of the patron himself. When the three of them entered the restaurant, it was evident by the way Dr Cohen was received what a high profile and popular citizen of Macon he was. Also, as they had walked past the crowded tables, Mathew could not help but notice the amount of admiring glances that Lucienne was receiving; he quickly recalled the possessiveness he felt when Patrice Daman had paid her so much attention on their first meeting.

SOMEONE WISHES TO SPEAK TO YOU

Mathew and Lucienne had a delicious black bean soup, a specialty of Bahia, and a king-size steak washed down by copious glasses of some most agreeable Californian wine, while learning more from the encyclopedic knowledge of their host about the history of Macon, the county seat of Georgia's Bibb County. There was little that could have made the evening more fascinating, informative or enjoyable for them. Although during the course of the meal, as the wine started to flow, Dr Cohen could not help seeing from the way his two guests sometimes interacted that their relationship went much deeper than just the professional involvement that his friend Osman Hill had purported it to be. Although he was aware that throughout the meal Mathew and Lucienne had attempted to keep their sentiments to themselves, by the end of the evening it had become increasingly evident to him that they were romantically entangled. This had been backed up by the subjects they had touched on during dinner, such as asking what the views of the citizens of Macon were with regards to mixed marriages. He had no doubt that Cupid's bow had scored a direct hit.

'Dr Cohen, thank you so much for a wonderful evening – meeting you has made this weekend so enjoyable,' said Lucienne.

'Absolutely,' agreed Mathew. 'It couldn't have had a worse start but today has been unforgettable. Do get in touch if you ever visit Atlanta.'

'I will certainly do that, and do send my very best wishes to old Osman Hill. But don't forget – send me a copy of your letter to the mayor so I can take some action on that. Safe journey!'

So just after midnight, Mathew drove the hire car slowly back to their hotel as the relaxed mood of the evening started to dwindle with the very thought of having to face Jed Jarman.

'Honestly Mathew, I don't know how Jarman thinks he can put anyone in that room.' Lucienne's resilience was

A MORAL DILEMMA

beginning to crack. 'The basin and shower are filthy, the lavatory seat is broken, the sheets are soiled and the furniture is dusty, I don't believe it's been cleaned or even checked on for days. The worst thing was there was scratching from behind the skirting boards, mice or rats, I don't know, and at one point I heard a noise next to my bed, turned the light on and saw an enormous rat – I've always hated rats, they are vile creatures – then it ran across the room and hid under a wardrobe.'

'Why didn't you tell me sooner? I knew it was dreadful, but I didn't realise just how bad it was. I can't bear you having to suffer such an awful mess while I have a perfectly good room... There must be something we can do.' Just before arriving at the hotel, Mathew drove the car into a small lay-by by the side of the lake. They discussed the potential of sleeping in the car for the night but Mathew came up with an alternative plan and in spite of the possible dangers involved, they agreed that on their return to the hotel they would put it into operation. The more Mathew thought about his scheme, the more it appealed to him; whenever he had embarked on some type of challenging escapade throughout his life, he was always stimulated by the atmosphere of uncertainty and the spirit of adventure.

A dim ray of light shone from beneath the office door to the rear of the darkened reception desk. Mathew rang the bell on the counter for attention and it seemed to take several minutes before the sullen-looking Jarman emerged from his office and scowled at Lucienne, as he passed the two bedroom keys over to Mathew. 'I need both your rooms vacated by 9 a.m.' he told Mathew, in his rather gruff Southern drawl, totally ignoring Lucienne. 'I have members of my local fraternity clocking into the hotel early for one of their monthly meetings.' He then added in a sarcastic manner, 'And I'll have to have your room cleaned thoroughly before giving it to one of the fraternity.'

SOMEONE WISHES TO SPEAK TO YOU

Mathew could not help assuming that the fraternity referred to was in all probability the Ku Klux Klan, and although he had read the notice on the back of his bedroom door stating that guests were not required to vacate their rooms until 11 o'clock on the morning on their departure, he decided that it would not be prudent to pick an argument with Jarman at such a late hour. His breath reeked of whisky and he appeared to be spoiling for a fight. So as Mathew and Lucienne started to go up the staircase, no doubt to Jarman's frustration, Mathew maintained his gentlemanly good manners by courteously bidding him goodnight.

As Mathew had done on the previous evening, he accompanied Lucienne along the winding corridor, past the 'Whites Only' bathroom to her room at the far end of the building. On switching on the bedroom light, and while Lucienne quickly gathered up her nightdress and dressing gown, a family of mice fled to the security of a hole in the skirting board. Lucienne removed her shoes and slipped her feet into the canyon-like openings of Mathew's heavy leather brogues. Then, in quite a loud voice Mathew bade Lucienne good night, saying that he looked forward to seeing her at breakfast later on in the morning. Mathew entered Lucienne's bedroom and closed the door, while Lucienne walked back along the corridor treading as heavily as possible in Mathew's footwear, so that if Jarman had been listening at the foot of the stairs he would have considered that Mathew had returned to his room.

Just after 2 a.m. when no lights could be seen in other parts of the hotel, Mathew put his animal-tracking expertise into effect, creeping along the corridor almost as silently as a leopard avoiding a confrontation with a hunter. On reaching his bedroom, he gently turned the knob of the unlocked door and went inside. A three-quarter moon shone its lazy beams through the half-open curtains and cast a shadow on Lucienne's slumbering figure. Locks of her curly dark hair were spread

A MORAL DILEMMA

in a seemingly coquettish fashion over the pillows, which contrasted magnificently with the whiteness of the linen sheets that enveloped her shapely form. After quietly locking the bedroom door, Mathew went into the bathroom, changed into his pyjamas and donned the hotel's white towelling dressing gown from behind the bathroom door. He sat down in the high-backed armchair by the window and, after having been stimulated by the exercise of deception and the degree of excitement that he had just experienced, he contemplated the pros and cons of the situation he now found himself in.

Mathew had considered that his feelings for Lucienne and Antonia had been balanced quite evenly, but now he was almost overcome by his desire to join Lucienne's slumbering form. At the last moment, his stoic reserve had suddenly checked his intention. He reminded himself how dishonourable it would be if he were to take advantage of this desirable dream of a person who was now lying so comfortably within the folds of his sheets.

While still trying to make up his mind what the most gentlemanly thing was for him to do in such an enticing situation, he recognised that the majority of his university friends would take full advantage of such a heaven-sent opportunity; alone in a bedroom in the middle of the night with such an attractive woman. But, while still in the process of going over all of the events that had occurred during the last twenty-four hours (the excitement of the evening; the effect of Dr Cohen's cocktails and the amount of wine he had consumed at Bistro Bahia; Jarman's aggressive nature; the thought of Lucienne's body – which was very much at the forefront of his mind) his tiredness got the better of him, he slumped into the hard upholstery of the armchair and fell into a deep sleep.

The loud cracks of a thunderstorm overhead woke Lucienne from her slumbers, and when she propped her head up on a snow-white pillow she saw the seemingly lifeless form of

SOMEONE WISHES TO SPEAK TO YOU

Mathew doubled-up in the armchair by the window. She threw one of her pillows at him in order to return him to full consciousness and, as he unsteadily gathered himself up from the chair, she slightly folded back the sheet covering the top of her body and spread open her arms as if in invitation for Mathew to join her. He dropped his dressing gown to the floor and crawled onto the bed beside her, and after wrapping his arms around her was to experience the joy and sensation of holding her naked body against his. Whereupon he gently kissed her forehead, the tip of her nose, her cheeks, before their lips met for a lasting kiss. Lucienne's eyes started to moisten with tears, such was her happiness in being in the security of Mathew's firm embrace, and while the heavens raged with resplendent flashes of sheet lightning, quickly followed by loud explosions of thunder above them, it was not long before they made love and experienced such ecstasy for the second time in their lives. And, as the storm moved to the mountains on the north side of Lake Tobesofkee, they were soon to fall asleep in what Lucienne felt was the blissful sanctuary of Mathew's embrace.

Just after eight-thirty on the Sunday morning, the phone rang in Mathew's room and he heard Jarman's brusque voice asking the whereabouts of his 'black girlfriend'. Jarman went on to say how his wife had tried to phone her room on three occasions but, as there had been no reply, she had sent a maid with a pass key up to see whether she was all right, only to find the bedroom empty. As they had not been at the table he had allocated for them in the corner of the dining room to have breakfast, he had demanded to know the whereabouts of his companion. Mathew, who had only just got out of his bed, was immediately taken aback by Jarman's aggressive tone but was able to compose himself and calmly told him that due to the deplorable conditions of the rodent-infested, dirty room he had provided her with, he had decided it to have been more appropriate for her to have shared his bedroom with him. He told the now irate-sounding Jarman that as they had only just got up, they would not be down for breakfast for another half hour but that this would be well in time for the hotel's advertised deadline for breakfast of 10 a.m. Such a philosophical and calm response had resulted with an explosion of expletives from Jarman, which Mathew had responded to by replacing the receiver, winking at Lucienne and going to take a shower.

When they went down the stairs into the hotel lobby and started to walk along the passage, they found the red-faced and angry-looking Jarman was blocking the door to the breakfast room. 'The kitchen is closed,' he told them gruffly. 'I want you both to leave the hotel within the next half an hour, otherwise I will call the sheriff's office and have you thrown out.' In order to underline his spurious degree of authority, he pointed to the notice 'Rights of Admission Reserved'.

'Don't you worry, I'll be reporting the appalling conditions of Lucienne's room to the city's Tourism Advisory Council, as well as writing to the mayor with regards to your inexcusably racist attitude toward us, completely contrary to the Civil Rights Act of 1964... I'll also open-copy both letters to Dr Cohen and to the city's Chief of Police.' As they started to return to their rooms to pick up their belongings, they saw Jarman pick up the phone on the reception desk.

'Operator? This is Jed Jarman at the Lakeside Inn. Put me through to the sheriff's office immediately, we have an emergency here and I need assistance. Right away, d'you hear?'

Once they were back in his bedroom, Mathew gave Lucienne a hug, grabbed the phone and asked the operator to put him through to Dr Cohen's number. She had never seen him looking so furious. As soon as the dialling tone had started to purr, the line suddenly became dead. He had been cut off. Mathew immediately left Lucienne in the room and stormed downstairs to the reception desk, where the now very worried-looking Mrs Jarman was sitting.

'I want you to put me through to this number immediately,' he demanded. Before she could do anything, Jarman appeared, grabbed Mathew's arm and almost frog-marched him back to the foot of the stairs. 'I want you off these premises before the police arrive and help me throw you out!' Mathew had not experienced such an aggressive physical contact since being a 'fag' during his first year at Wellington College. His immediate response was to deliver a sharp slap to Jarman's left cheek.

While Mrs Jarman retreated to the safety of the office, a state of bedlam pursued in the hotel lobby with Jarman roaring with a similar ferocity of that of a silverback gorilla in its attempt to become the dominant male. He reached to grab a stage-coach whip from the nearby hall stand, but while in the process of unraveling its tassel of leather thongs, the sirens of the sheriff's car could be heard arriving outside.

The whip was quickly put back into its place in the hall stand, while Jarman managed to grab the arm of the retreating Mathew again and pull him roughly from the staircase, marching him to the hotel's front entrance. At the same time, two armed policemen from the sheriff's office burst into the lobby and, after calling Jarman by his Christian name, asked him whether the man he was firmly holding by the arm was the culprit he had called them about. Before Mathew realised what was happening, he found that his wrists were manacled behind his back and he was being almost dragged upstairs by one of the policemen. Jarman used his pass key to throw open the bedroom door, revealing a startled Lucienne standing by the window.

'Get out of this room now, get your things and leave this hotel within the next ten minutes,' he snarled at Lucienne. 'Then get your car off my property before I have it impounded.' Lucienne almost fled down the corridor in terror. 'If you ever want to see your nigger-loving boyfriend again, you can find him in police custody at the local sheriff's office on the north

A MORAL DILEMMA

side of Lake Tobesofkee. He's about to be charged with physical assault.'

Before the police took Mathew from the hotel, his handcuffs were removed for a short time so that he could pack his bag and leave it to be collected from the hotel lobby by Lucienne. However, after Mathew was jostled down the staircase, across the lobby and into the car park, he refused to get into the police car until he saw Lucienne leave the hotel safely and get into their hire car. At the same time, he saw a group of rather hostile-looking new arrivals talking to the now gleeful-looking Jarman by the hotel's front entrance. Mathew considered that these were doubtless all members of the 'fraternity' Jarman had been expecting that morning, who were in all probability fully paid-up members of the local KKK. The distasteful scene was concluded when the gathering of local rednecks all started to clap and whistle as the police car, with Mathew seated in the back with his right hand manacled to a policeman, drove out of the hotel's car park closely followed by a tearful Lucienne.

Mathew suffered three hours of confinement in a small, oven-hot, windowless cell at the police station before he was taken before the local sheriff. He clearly repeated his account of the events that had led up to him slapping Jarman's face and informed the sheriff that it was of the utmost importance for him to be able to make contact with his friend Dr Murray Cohen, the chairman of the city's Anti-Racial Discrimination Board, a request that visibly worried the sheriff. Mathew had to wait a further three-quarters of an hour before he was given permission to phone Dr Cohen.

'So perhaps you could tell me what it was that made you choose the Lakeside Inn as a little weekend retreat for you and your African girlfriend?' asked the sheriff, a hulking bully of a man, before Dr Cohen's arrival. 'Surely you must have been aware from past publicity that my friend, Mr Jed Jarman, led one of the main factions in opposition to the Democrats'

Civil Rights Campaign prior to the passing of the Civil Rights Act?'

'No, I've never been to Macon before and I've never heard of the Lakeside Inn. I called the local tourist office and was told that the inn was the best place to stay, so I went ahead and booked two rooms. They didn't ask the colour of our skin.'

'But surely you knew that during Jed Jarman's opposition to the act, how he always maintained a strictly "White's Only" policy for his hotel? He wrote several articles at the time which highlighted how ... um ... inappropriate it was for white Anglo-Saxon protestants to engage in immoral behaviour, which of course is fully in keeping with the teachings of the KKK. You had no idea, huh?'

'No,' replied Mathew wearily. He could guess what was coming next.

'Well, I would like to ask you whether, as a friend of Dr Cohen's, it was your intention to provoke Mr Jarman by arriving at his hotel with an African girlfriend, then inviting her into your bedroom with the intention of sleeping with her?'

'I refute this allegation entirely! I categorically deny that I knew anything about Jarman's abhorrent racist attitude prior to our arrival. What's more, I find it grossly deplorable that anyone can hold these outdated and discriminative opinions, especially in view of the Civil Rights Act...'

'Don't you say another word, or you may find that you are facing charges for character defamation as well as physical assault. Let's just say that everybody is entitled to their own personal views on such matters – the Lakeside Inn was a very bad choice for you.'

It was fortunate that Dr Cohen arrived at the sheriff's office when he did, as it was very much thanks to the doctor's quiet diplomacy and a number of his references to his chairmanship of Macon's ARDB, his friendship with the city's

A MORAL DILEMMA

mayor and many of Macon's other leading citizens that he had been able to redirect the majority of the sheriff's hostility toward Mathew and gain his release. This had only been accomplished after the doctor had agreed to pay a preliminary sum of $1000 bail, as well as to be held responsible for Mathew's return to Macon in the probable event of a court appearance.

After Mathew's wrists were released from the tightness of the handcuffs, a photographer was called into the sheriff's office to take a series of mugshots of him, for which he had to hold a small blackboard with a police reference number and his name recorded in white. Mathew was also instructed to fill in a copious amount of forms to provide the sheriff's office with as many details about himself as possible. These ranged from the reason for him and his 'African girlfriend' being in Macon for the weekend; recording his residential address and contact numbers in Atlanta; the name and department of the university that he was studying at and providing full green card and passport details. He was also asked to provide his place and date of birth, home address, and the names of both parents – information he was reluctant to give the sheriff – although he was careful not to include the fact that his father was an English baronet.

Finally, before he was allowed to leave the sheriff's office, he had to sign a police charge sheet to record that he admitted having slapped Jed Jarman's face and, as a consequence, was aware that the Jarman had charged him with physical assault.

'So, Mr Duncan,' said the sheriff in an imperious tone, 'at a date to be decided upon, you will be receiving a formal summons to appear before a Bibb County Magistrate Court (Civil Division) hearing – I recommend that you instruct an attorney to act as a lawyer for your defence.'

On leaving the sheriff's office, Mathew joined a tearful but relieved Lucienne, waiting by their car.

'Oh Mathew, thank goodness!' She threw her arms around

his neck and held him tight. 'I followed you here, I didn't know where else to go, and I was so worried what they might do to you. Thank you Dr Cohen, for helping us, I don't know what we'd have done without you!'

'That's my pleasure, Lucienne. It's terrible you've been caught up in this ridiculous situation. Why don't you both come over to my house, freshen up and have something to eat before your drive back to Atlanta?'

'I certainly won't turn that down,' replied Mathew. 'Being on the inside of a police cell is not an experience I'd care to repeat.'

'It'll give us a chance to discuss the best strategy to adopt to try and stop the assault case coming to trial.' They jumped into their cars and left the sheriff's office behind as swiftly as possible.

Once they were back at Dr Cohen's house, Mathew and Lucienne gratefully sat down to rest and discuss the morning's bizarre turn of events. 'I can't get over how hostile the sheriff was,' said Mathew. 'He was clearly a friend of Jarman's. I've never met such a blatant racist as Jed Jarman – what with that group of jeering rednecks, it wouldn't surprise me if he wasn't the staunchest member, if not the leader, of the local Ku Klux Klan.'

'There's certainly been a number of recent cases that have come to light where the KKK is known to have forged alliances with police departments in the Deep South. It's because of these very situations that the ARDB are trying to do everything possible to expose these irregularities – we aim to prosecute those found to be contravening the terms of the 1964 Civil Rights Act so that the message gets across loud and clear.'

'Macon is lucky to have you,' said Lucienne. 'Let's hope attitudes start to change to put an end to this awful hatred.'

Before they left Dr Cohen's house, he advised Mathew that it would be prudent to delay writing to Macon's mayor and the Tourism Advisory Council until the police matter was satisfactorily resolved.

A MORAL DILEMMA

Mathew and Lucienne were both stunned by the traumas of the weekend and only exchanged a few thoughts on their drive back to Atlanta. Mathew was particularly concerned about the possibility of being involved in a court case where he was accused of an assault and what would happen should any news get back to his family and friends in the UK. When he dropped Lucienne off at her flat, he turned down her invitation to go in and, after giving her an affectionate hug and kiss, he told her that he had to explain to Osman Hill what had happened as soon as possible, before Dr Cohen made contact with him. 'I'll call you on Monday evening,' he promised, holding her hands tightly. 'That should give me long enough to get in touch with Dr Cohen again, and hopefully to map out the best way forward.'

The following week started off well, with Osman Hill being very understanding about the horrific turn of events. He told Mathew that he would see whether he could be of any assistance in preventing the case from coming to trial. When Mathew phoned Dr Cohen, he was told that he had already made contact with a very bright African-American defence attorney who had done some voluntary legal work for the ARDB and who had offered to represent Mathew should the assault case go to court. Mathew felt incredibly grateful for this significant offer of legal assistance. The following day, he was able to send Dr Cohen a cheque for the US $1000 bail money that he had paid on his behalf.

On the Thursday morning, the unfortunate happenings of the previous weekend reared their ugly head. Dr Cohen called Mathew with news of some unfortunate developments.

'I don't want to worry you but it seems that a freelance investigatory journalist from Macon's local press agency has got to hear of last Sunday's debacle at the Lakeside Inn and the subsequent assault charge,' he explained. 'The sheriff obviously provided the journalist with all the information that you gave, including your home address and the names of your parents. The journalist interviewed Jarman about the implied assault, who took the opportunity to provide some overblown fictional details about the type of improper orgy that had taken place in your bedroom with an African girl that you had "lured" from another room. The journalist also found out that you're the son of a British nobleman who, within the next three months, is to submit his dissertation to his doctoral committee at Emory University. I've been told by a contact at the press agency that there's a draft of the forthcoming article with the heading: "*In flagrante delicto* – Son of British noble engaged in immoral behaviour with black girl ends up with an assault charge".'

The very thought of such a article arriving at Hartington Hall and being seen by his parents, and his university doctoral committee being informed about it, caused Mathew to enter a state of near panic. After quickly telling Lucienne what was going on and highlighting the many adverse ramifications should the article be published, he decided to return to Macon immediately. He needed to discuss with Dr Cohen and his attorney colleague what could possibly be done to prevent the publication of this almost libellous account of their stay at the Lakeside Inn. During his drive down to Macon, Mathew could not help reproaching himself and regretting the situation that he now found himself in. If only, in the early hours of Sunday morning while a thunderstorm had crashed in the heavens overhead, he had not succumbed to temptation and responded to Lucienne's open arms to join her in his bed, which had culminated in him having made love to her.

During Mathew's afternoon and evening meetings with Dr Cohen and the attorney, Otto Gwynne, they discussed all the potentials available to them in order to prevent the publication of the article, as well as how best to have the case of assault against him abandoned. Fortunately, a telephone call from

A MORAL DILEMMA

Otto Gwynne to the investigatory journalist had resulted in him agreeing to meet them on the Friday morning. As Dr Cohen was a senior member of Macon's Cherry Blossom Lions Club, thereby having many important contacts within the community, he had been able to set up meetings with a Deputy Commissioner of Police and the Chairman of Macon's Tourism Advisory Council for later on in the day.

The morning meeting with the freelance journalist had gone well after Otto had made it quite clear to him that should he go ahead and file his defamatory article, he would be sued for libel and the legal case against him would take him for every nickel he possessed. The chairman of the city's Tourism Advisory Council, who was also a senior member of the local Lions Club, expressed his sympathy about the incident at the Lakeside Inn the previous weekend. He did seem to show particular concern about the dreadful conditions in Lucienne's room and any adverse publicity if these became public. Dr Cohen told him that the state of affairs was soon to be recorded in Mathew's letter of complaint to the mayor and the Deputy Police Commissioner, as well as an open-copy to be sent to him personally at the Tourism Advisory Council. Although the chairman had not been aware that any of Macon's hotels still displayed such notices as 'Whites Only' on the doors of their bathrooms, he fully recognised that any publicity could well result in a major national news item and would be highly detrimental to his overall responsibilities in promoting Macon's tourist trade.

As a result of the meeting, the chairman told Dr Cohen that providing Mathew withheld his official letters about the appalling conditions at the Lakeside Inn and the racist discrimination that he and his girlfriend had experienced, he would do everything in his power to persuade Jarman to withdraw his assault charge against Mathew. The meeting with the deputy commissioner had also proved to be a positive one, for once he heard first-hand about the Jarman's attitude and that of the sheriff at the Tobesofkee district police station, he understood the amount of adverse publicity that would arise should this be highlighted at a future Magistrate's Court hearing.

The deputy commissioner concluded the meeting by saying that he would personally exert pressure on Jarman to drop his case against Mathew and, should he refuse to do so, he would threaten to prosecute him under the 1964 Civil Rights Act for still displaying 'Whites Only' signage at his hotel. He would also instruct the local police department to start to look more carefully at the Lakeside Inn's possible infringement of the licensing law when playing host to the monthly meetings of his KKK fraternity, which the local community had always been well aware of. Also, as he genuinely wished to cooperate with his good friend Dr Cohen to the maximum, he told them that he would be reprimanding the sheriff for unlawfully divulging confidential police information to an investigatory reporter.

On Mathew's return to Atlanta, he was quick to pass on to Lucienne and Osman Hill the encouraging discussions that had taken place during his thirty-six hours in Macon. He also took the opportunity to tell Osman Hill that he could not thank him enough for introducing him to Dr Cohen, who under the circumstances could not have been more helpful.

It was now only two months until Mathew was due to submit his dissertation to the doctoral committee and to defend it. As the American university system allowed a PhD student to choose a committee of his professors and other relevant university faculty members, who as a consequence had to receive and read the dissertation, he had chosen Osman Hill to chair the committee. With the defence of the dissertation being scheduled to take place a few weeks after its submission, Mathew considered that providing everything went according to plan, and that he was successful in achieving his doctorate degree, he should be in a position to return to England by mid-December. Then he would have the opportunity look at the potential merits of returning to Africa, perhaps to Rhodesia, in order to continue with his primate field studies.

In the latter part of October, Lucienne discovered that she was pregnant. She was devastated. Although she had been seeing quite a lot of Mathew since their weekend together in Macon, the intensity of their feelings for each other had started to wane due to the academic pressures on both of them. Lucienne had also become rather disillusioned when she found a letter in Mathew's flat written on Girton College notepaper from Antonia Clinton-Kemp. The sentiments expressed in it had made her, for the first time, aware that she was not the only girl in Mathew's life. She sensed that Mathew had become more distant and less affectionate. Partly due to this, and also as she was determined not to deflect Mathew's focus from his preparation for the defence of his dissertation, she decided for the time being not to let Mathew know about the unplanned pregnancy.

At the end of the month, Lucienne received an unexpected invitation from the Embassy of the Zaire Republic in Washington DC to attend a reception to celebrate President Mobutu Sésé Seko's private visit to the USA. He was to have a meeting with President Nixon at the White House. Lucienne was delighted, as it would take her away from Atlanta for a few days and give her time to reflect on her predicament and how to tell Mathew about it. The invitation was as a result of the embassy having decided to gather together a select number of Zairian university graduates who were studying in the USA. The Zairian Ambassador had also invited a cross-section of people from the US Foreign Service, in particular those working in the African Section of the State Department in Washington.

SOMEONE WISHES TO SPEAK TO YOU

It was at the Zairian Embassy reception that Lucienne first met Daniel Olingo, an African-American who had recently graduated from the University of Chicago and joined the ranks of the US Foreign Service, specialising in African Affairs. Daniel was immediately attracted to Lucienne. She looked stunning in a loose pink floral dress and seemed to be smiling every time he looked at her. Although, due to the presence of a closely guarded President Mobutu, it had taken some time for Daniel to arrange for an embassy official to introduce them, it did not take long after meeting her before they were thoroughly enjoying each other's company.

After the president had given a rather lengthy and laborious speech with regards to how the USA represented one of Zaire's closest allies and friends, Daniel grabbed the opportunity to make a suggestion to Lucienne.

'I hope you don't think me presumptuous,' he asked slightly nervously, 'but I was wondering if you would like to come to see the new African-American art exhibition which has just opened at the Smithsonian? Afterwards, I could show you around some of city's highlights and then perhaps we could have dinner. There's a little Afro-American restaurant in Georgetown which has great food – what do you say?'

Lucienne accepted, and the following day the two enjoyed a memorable day of sightseeing, conversation and laughter. She hadn't felt so happy and carefree for some time. On her flight back to Atlanta, she couldn't help reflecting on just how engaging she had found Daniel's company and how very much they had in common. 'I would really like to see you again, Lucienne,' Daniel had said when he drove her to the Zairian Embassy's guest residence to collect her suitcase. 'I could always come to see you in Atlanta...' Much to Lucienne's surprise, she responded by giving him her address and telephone number and adding, 'That would be lovely, Daniel – keep in touch.' She wasn't sure if her reaction was due to the combined uncertainties of her pregnancy and her unhappiness about the heart-felt deterioration of her relationship with Mathew (especially that he was soon to leave Atlanta and return to the UK), or if her feelings when she said goodbye to Daniel were genuine. If they were, it was yet another situation that she would soon have to resolve.

After Lucienne's return to Atlanta, she had only seen Mathew three times prior to the presentation of his dissertation although they had spoken on the phone on several occasions. This was not only due to the pressure of her personal academic commitments, but also to Mathew's preoccupation with the submission of his dissertation. However, in the last week of November Mathew received the news that the committee had awarded him the PhD. He called Lucienne immediately to tell her and to arrange a celebratory dinner at the earliest opportunity. He also sent a telegram to his parents and his brother, as well as a note to Antonia, to inform them that he had at long last been successful in attaining a Doctorate of Science at Emory University.

Mathew arrived at Lucienne's flat on the Friday evening feeling on top of the world, very much in a spirit of euphoria. Lucienne had her hair tied back with a colourful pink silk ribbon that matched the colour of her dress, and Mathew considered that he had seldom seen her looking so attractive. After a celebratory cocktail in her flat, they took a taxi to a new five-star Mexican restaurant, the Alma Cocina, in downtown Atlanta. During the course of the meal, and while enjoying some classic Californian wine, Mathew talked enthusiastically about his immediate future.

'I can't tell you what a relief it is, Lucienne. Now I can make the arrangements to go back to the UK before hopefully going on to Rhodesia. As my father has offered to provide an introduction to Roger Willock, the new British Senior Representative in Salisbury, I'm really hoping he'll be able to help with any problems I may have getting in to the country.'

'You're lucky to have a father with friends in high places! I'm sure it will make things much easier for you.'

'It should certainly help iron out some of the beaurocratic wrangles. I'm also hoping he'll be able to introduce me to people who'll be able to advise me on the best place to carry out the field studies.'

Mathew explained to Lucienne about the comparative methodology he planned to adopt. 'The Samango and vervet group of guenons are native to Rhodesia, and if I have time, I aim to make some observations on the social grouping of chacma baboons...' Lucienne listened, genuinely interested in discussing his plans, but changed the topic of conversation when the opportunity arose to tell him about her recent travels.

'I met some really interesting people at the reception and had the chance to have a look around Washington – it's a wonderful city. A diplomat I met at the Zaire Embassy took me to see a fascinating African-American art exhibition at the Smithsonian. Then he showed me round the city's major landmarks, there's a lot of beautiful architecture there.'

After the conversation had lapsed for a little while, Lucienne reached over the flickering candles on the table and took Mathew's hand.

'I've been putting this off but I can't leave it any longer. I'm two and a half months pregnant.'

Although Mathew looked as if a bomb had just exploded by his side, he squeezed her hand tightly, got up from his seat and bent over to caress her. Lucienne's eyes were soon moistened by tears as she tried to battle with her emotions in having at long last released herself from keeping her pregnancy a secret from him. Mathew returned to his seat, still holding tightly onto her hand, and silence prevailed for a while.

Eventually, Mathew said quietly, 'We must spend the day together tomorrow to talk about the future. We've got to do everything we can to make the right decision, for all our sakes.'

It had subsequently taken them the whole weekend of

A MORAL DILEMMA

mutual soul-seeking, weighing up all the pros and cons of a possible future of remaining together and even getting married, until they reluctantly concluded that the previous romantic magic of their intimate relationship was now a thing of the past. Although they both recognised that they were still extremely fond of each other and would always remain the greatest of friends, it was not just their contrasting cultural and ethnic backgrounds but the different career paths they had chosen that had started to separate them. They both acknowledged that even with the birth of their child, their future together would be unlikely to last the test of time.

It had taken a further two weeks before Lucienne had rather hesitantly agreed with Mathew that the best way forward was for her to undergo an abortion before the signs became too evident. Before Lucienne had told Mathew about her pregnancy, she read about America's Abortion Act, Roe v. Wade, which had only been passed by the US Supreme Court on January 22nd of that year. The law had nullified state restrictions on abortions and now allowed women in all fifty states to obtain an abortion within the first trimester, for any reason that a woman so required.

However, Lucienne was also aware of the strong feelings in the Southern States against the new law, with many people believing that an abortion should remain on the statute books as a criminal act. It was for this reason, and for not wishing in any way to experience the regrettable stigma attributed to women who had undergone abortions in some areas of Georgia, that she had decided to travel to a more liberal-minded and sympathetic part of America in order to go ahead with it. It was thanks to a very understanding college obstetrician that she was given the name of a well-respected private abortion clinic in San Diego. As Mathew wanted to be as supportive as possible during this emotional and stressful time, he had insisted that he should accompany her to San Diego and stay for the clinic's initial mandatory consultancy.

Although Mathew had told Lucienne that he would be responsible for all travel expenses to and from San Diego, and the subsequent private clinic costs involved in carrying out the operation, Lucienne had made it quite clear to him that she wanted to be by herself when the operation took place and to be totally on her own when she returned to Atlanta. She insisted that Mathew go ahead with his travel plans and return to the UK in early December as planned. She promised to keep in regular contact with him.

During the course of Mathew's last week in Atlanta, he kept himself as busy as possible by gathering all the things that he had amassed during his time at Emory University and clearing out his flat prior to his imminent departure. Whenever he started to relax and reflect on the events that had taken place during the past month, his thoughts were preoccupied by his concern about the harrowing time that Lucienne was going through. He very much regretted that he had been unable to make Lucienne change her mind about travelling to San Diego alone. He had tried so hard to impress on her that he considered it to be very much his responsibility to be with her, and to keep her company throughout the traumatic times ahead. He had also reiterated that he would be only too willing to delay his departure from Atlanta in order to be with her; Lucienne had refused to be swayed.

The only highlight of their last few days together was a dinner given for them both by Osman and Yvonne Hill. The circumstances were very different to the last time they had visited, when Mathew had just returned to Atlanta after staying in the UK, and they had held hands excitedly throughout most of the journey. This time, despite her sadness, Lucienne looked as attractive as ever and was as outwardly cheerful as any host could have wished a guest to be.

'It couldn't have turned out much better under the circumstances,' said Mathew as they discussed the outcome of the potentially disastrous situation in Macon. 'Dr Cohen

A MORAL DILEMMA

and Otto Gwyne negotiated brilliantly with the Police Department and the Tourist Advisory Council, successfully persuading them how badly it would reflect on the town if the incident were made public.'

'I wouldn't be surprised,' added Osman Hill in a rather jocular fashion, 'if the dropping of the court case didn't owe something to Murray Cohen having so many influential friends among the elite of Macon society and his involvement with the upper echelons of the Cherry Blossom Lions Club.'

'Whatever it was, it worked and I'm immensely grateful. I never want to see the inside of a police cell again!'

The conversation moved on to Mathew's return to Africa and his hoped-for field research, which he promised to keep his professor fully informed about. Osman Hill also took the opportunity to say how very impressed he had been with the high standard of the data collection that Lucienne had carried out on his behalf, and just how important this had been in the writing of volume 9 of his primate monograph.

It was a convivial evening, though for Mathew and Lucienne it was poignant that circumstances differed so greatly to their previous dinner at the Hills' home. There had been a great deal of happiness during their time in Atlanta, but now it was time to move on.

When the day of Mathew's departure arrived, Lucienne had decided that it would be less traumatic for her if they had a quiet farewell lunch together at her flat rather than if she accompanied him to the airport. There was an understanding that they would talk about anything but her forthcoming trip to San Diego, which was due to take place at the end of the following week. It was a sombre and tearful occasion when Mathew caressed Lucienne for the last time, as he found himself saying goodbye to someone who he respected and loved so much. They had shared so many diverse and wonderful times in Africa and in North America during the past eighteen months. As Mathew's taxi drove away from the flat to take him to the airport, Lucienne put on the bravest of faces and amidst a flourish of farewell waves, she blew him a final kiss.

Later on that evening when his British Airways flight had lifted off from Atlanta, it was an extremely depressed and dejected-looking Dr Mathew Duncan that was to be found seated in business class with a double whisky and soda clasped in his right hand. Mathew had found himself in a state of emotional disarray and emptiness of spirit, and he could not help feeling that he had not only greatly let down a person who he admired and loved so much, but that he had also failed to satisfactorily live up to the moral standards of his upbringing and the faith and confidence that he once had in himself.

By the time Mathew's flight had landed among the mists of Heathrow the following morning, Lucienne had been in contact with the clinic in San Diego to cancel her appointment for the termination. She had decided some time ago to continue with her pregnancy and keep the child that had been fathered by a man she had loved so deeply. Lucienne had also made up her mind that Mathew would not be told about the birth of their child, due in the spring of 1974, for many years to come.

Part Two

A Return to Africa; 1974–1979

5

Leopard's Rock

The route through the attractive township of Umtali on the south-eastern border of Southern Rhodesia with Portuguese East Africa (PEA), took Mathew along avenues lined with blazing flamboyant blossoms, intermingled with the pinks and yellows of the aloes. The tarmac road soon gave way to an impacted earthen surface that wound its way some 32 km up into the Vumba Mountains. As Mathew drove his newly acquired (second-hand) 4 x 4 Land Rover higher into the densely forested mountains, a thick mist or *guti* came rolling down, reducing visibility in places to less than 10 metres. Here, thick vegetation flanked the track, sometimes meeting overhead to form a tunnel then clearing suddenly to reveal precipitous ravines, leading eastward to the dramatic range of Chimanimani Mountains. At intervals, crystalline streams could be seen cascading down the mountainside, flanked by abundant forest ferns and lush tangles of vegetation. Mathew was delighted to see laughing doves and purple-crested turacos swooping to and fro through the spray.

This was the type of environment that Mathew felt very much at home in, and he was already finding that his recent return to Africa was acting as an effective tonic to all the traumas he had experienced during the past three months. In particular, the emotional disarray that he had felt during his last few days with Lucienne in Atlanta, and the stress of their final parting when his mind had been so preoccupied by her insistence on both going to the clinic and returning to Atlanta alone. He had dearly wished to be allowed to support her.

On his return to England for the Christmas of 1973, Mathew had phoned Lucienne on a number of occasions from the privacy of the Red Lion Inn in Burnsall. She had told him how her doctor was very pleased with her progress, but he couldn't help feeling responsible for her and being concerned about her future welfare. During his time at Hartington Hall, Mathew often felt depressed and deceitful for keeping such a major event secret from not only his parents, but also from Sebastian and his close friends.

But now, after having been away from Africa for over a year, Mathew had returned to the continent that he so delighted in and found he had the opportunity to make a completely fresh start, hopefully with the benefit of the important lessons learnt over the past twelve months. He soon realised that in Ian Smith's Republic of Rhodesia, it was important for him to keep his liberal views on race to himself initially in order to focus his attentions on his field studies. He would be studying the samango and vervet monkeys; both groups lived in the idyllic, lush habitat of the Vumba Mountains, along with other representatives of Rhodesia's rich wildlife.

Before Mathew's journey to Umtali to begin his field studies, he had stayed for ten days with Sir Roger and Lady Devra Willock at their sumptuous home in Salisbury. During his stay, Sir Roger had been extremely helpful by arranging for him to meet a cross-section of the people who could be of the most assistance to him. Some of the many useful contacts he made included Dr Simon Vaughan-Jones, Curator of the Victoria Museum in Salisbury, and his wife Anna, who were both carrying out behavioural studies on a captive colony of vervet monkeys; senior members of Rhodesia's Game and National Park Departments (from which Mathew had to obtain permits) and the Professor of Zoology at the University of Rhodesia.

'When I arrived here,' Sir Roger had explained, 'it was quite without any publicity. Britain withdrew its High Commissioner soon after Ian Smith's Unilateral Declaration of Independence in 1965, and my appointment was a result of the findings of the Pearce Commission of 1972, to try to find a settlement that would be satisfactory to both the African and European communities. Since the High Commissioner was withdrawn, there's been no direct contact between the Rhodesian and British governments, so that's where I come in.' The Commission had recommended that as there was a degree of optimism in finding a political solution, it would be useful to have a senior British diplomat to set up a UK representative's office in Salisbury, which could act as a reliable conduit of recommendations from all sides of the conflict – and so appointed Sir Roger Willock to the task.

During Mathew's stay with the Willocks, he was delighted to hear more about Sir Roger's time serving with his father in the Second World War. They were both in the 12th Royal Lancers during the Italian campaign, in the course of which they had both ended up as captains.

'We lost far too many of our friends during the war, but we both felt very fortunate in having concluded our military activities with the liberation of Venice in April 1945. I'm sure your father's told you that after VE Day on 8 May, we celebrated in some of the best bars and restaurants around St Mark's Square. Nothing can compare to that experience, the sheer exuberance everyone felt once the war was over. No more fighting. People were cheering, shaking hands, hugging, kissing... The farewell dinner was at the Locanda Cipriani restaurant on Torcello, just off the Venetian coast – we had the finest food any of us had tasted since the beginning of the war. I shall never forget it. War can be utter hell; there's nothing like the joy of being alive when it comes to end.'

Mathew had to have a meeting with a superintendent from Rhodesia's Central Intelligence Organisation (CIO). Such interviews had recently become mandatory for any non-Rhodesian resident or passport holder who wanted to visit or stay in a border region with either Portuguese East Africa to the south-east or with Zambia to the north. The authorities had started to consider that due to the potential of increased insurgency by factions of the Zimbabwe African National Liberation Army (ZANLA) involved with Rhodesia's fledgling Bush War, these border areas could become areas of conflict in the future.

During his meeting at the CIO headquarters, it had taken Mathew quite some time to impress on the intelligence officer why exactly he had come to Rhodesia.

'I am neither a journalist investigating the success of Rhodesia's United Nations sanction breaking,' repeated Mathew slowly and clearly, 'or a British spy reporting on counter-insurgency operations. The only reason I have come to Rhodesia is to carry out my post-doctorate comparative primate research. I need to set up a camp in the best possible area to carry out this research. I already have the full support of Dr Vaughan-Jones and his staff at the Victoria Museum and have agreed to share all my field observations with the museum authorities. I will be giving talks to both museum staff and members about my observations and have accepted an invitation to present a paper at a forthcoming symposium to be held at the University of Rhodesia's Department of Zoology, on the subject of my doctorate field observations on the eastern lowland gorillas of Kahuzi-Biega in Zaire. Is there anything else you would like to know?'

During his last few days with the Willocks, Mathew had the great coincidence of meeting up again with Michael Lamb, who had acted as translator for his key-note address at Bielefeld

University in 1972. Lamb had only recently arrived in Salisbury with his American wife, Denise (who had the most bewitching of smiles), to take up the post of Private Secretary to Sir Roger as a part of the Foreign Office's small cadre of Britain's Diplomatic Corps presence in the country. Sir Roger told Mathew that one of the main priorities of his office was to help the politicians find a satisfactory way to break the current impasse between Rhodesia's African and European political factions.

'So you've been given permission to establish your research camp in the Vumba Mountains? It's so close to the international borders with PEA, I'm surprised they've allowed it,' said Michael as they discussed their respective reasons for being in Rhodesia. 'The freedom fighters of the Mozambique Liberation Front have become more active in that area – it could be dangerous.'

'Obviously they don't believe the danger is that great, for the time being at least,' replied Mathew.

'Well, when you come back to Salisbury from the wilderness I really hope that we have the chance to see each other again. Of course I'm interested in your primate studies, but I'd also like to hear what you think about the attitudes of the African and European residents of the border region – PEA is leading up to independence from its colonial masters in Portugal and things are set to change.'

During their conversation, Mathew had been surprised at Lamb's particular interest in the relationships between the black and white communities in this border region. As he had only just arrived in the country, Mathew was unaware of the seriousness of the ZANLA terrorist attacks on civilians from across Rhodesia's border. Neither was he really aware of Rhodesia's escalating Bush War. Most importantly, he had no idea that Michael Lamb was working under cover for the British Secret Intelligence Service, MI6.

* * *

Lamb hosted a small farewell dinner party for Mathew at his smart bungalow, at which his wife Denise introduced Mathew to Adeline Kinloch.

'Call me Addie, all my friends do.'

'Well then, Addie it is,' smiled Mathew. 'So how do you come to know the Lambs?'

'I recently graduated from the University of Rhodesia and wasn't sure what to do, when I heard about an opening in Sir Roger's office carrying out his confidential secretarial duties and those of his private secretary, Michael – Denise's husband. Sounds rather dull but it really isn't ... suits me down to the ground,' she smiled. Addie was of medium height, with a head of unruly curly auburn hair. Her ochre-coloured eyes had a lively sparkle to them and her smiling countenance was blessed by two dimples that appeared as small rosettes on each of her freckled cheeks whenever she laughed.

'I first met Michael years ago when I was giving a keynote address in Germany and he was acting as a translator,' said Mathew. 'I just happened to bump into him over here – Sir Roger is a friend of my father's, I'm staying with him for a few days before I head off to the border country to do some field studies.'

'Sounds fascinating,' smiled Addie. 'Tell me more.'

During the evening, Mathew found himself to be very relaxed in the company of these two attractive women; a feeling he hadn't had for several months. Although Denise and Addie's backgrounds were different, it was obvious by the way they interacted and laughed together that they had already become good friends. Mathew found both of them to be independently spirited and to have an extraordinary gift for friendship, as well as being intelligent, fun-seeking and to have a very positive and optimistic outlook on life, although he was quick to remind himself that at this early stage of his time in Rhodesia, he would have to be careful not to become caught up within the imbroglios of any further romances. He knew that the order of the day for him had to be the development of mature friendships, rather than more intimate associations. On Addie's part, she was attracted to Mathew's very Englishness, his quiet sense of humour and self-effacing disposition, and through her female intuition was aware that he found both her and Denise to be enjoyable company. At the end of the evening, Mathew asked Addie if she would like to join him for dinner one evening while he was still in Salisbury. They made an arrangement to meet three days later at a local restaurant.

Subsequent to the Lamb's dinner party, Sir Roger told Mathew that Addie's father, Group Captain Miles Kinloch, had served with distinction in the RAF during the Second World War and had been awarded a DFC (Distinguished Flying Cross) for his part in the Battle of Britain. Soon after having received the award from King George VI, the RAF had posted him to Southern Rhodesia to instruct at the Elementary Flying Training School (EFTS) at Guinea Fowl Airfield in central Southern Rhodesia. Here, more than half of the course members had been Australians, some were Rhodesians and the rest arrived from the UK.

'Sir Roger mentioned that your father was a flying instructor near Gwelo,' said Mathew over dinner at his second meeting with Addie. 'He must have met some interesting people.'

'Oh, indeed he did. One story I always love to tell is that my father, being a senior RAF instructor at Guinea Fowl, had to train the young pilot officer recruit Ian Smith, who in those days always had to salute him! After the war, my father decided that he'd enjoyed his time here so much that he wanted to settle in Southern Rhodesia. He bought an apple orchard in Inyanga, in the south-east.' Addie looked down at the table, suddenly a little unsure of herself. 'As my father's estate is within easy reach of the study site you're establishing in the Vumba, my father has asked me to say that you would be always welcome to spend a weekend with us there. My mother was killed in a road accident five years ago and as Daddy lives alone, he's always pleased to meet new people, especially anyone recently out from England.'

Mathew and Addie enjoyed a very amicable evening, although Mathew was careful not to behave in any way that might imply he was looking for anything more than friendship. Addie was without doubt attractive and they had much in common, but the invitation to spend a weekend at her father's estate has taken him a little by surprise and he knew he must tread carefully.

Rhodesia's National Parks Department had informed the warden of their Vumba Botanical Park, David Montgomery, about Mathew's forthcoming research activities and had requested him to cooperate fully. The chief CIO operative in Manicaland, and his counterpart in the Special Branch of Rhodesia's British South Africa Police (BSAP) headquarters in Umtali, had been asked to keep an eye on him. There had been a degree of suspicion expressed by security officials in Salisbury about Mathew's real objectives; they were apprehensive as to why he considered it to be so important to carry out his research activities so close to Rhodesia's international border with PEA. The District Commissioner's office had also been informed about Mathew's presence in the area.

With a letter of introduction from Sir Roger to the resident director of the Leopard Rock Hotel, Charles Seymour-Smith, Mathew was given a fine room at a very good discount, which he decided to stay in until he found an appropriate place to establish his camp. The hotel had been built by Italian prisoners of war in the early 1940s, and was nestled under the base of a steep, mist-covered mountainside named Leopard's Rock. Its turreted roof looked more like a French chateau within the woodlands of the Loire Valley than a hotel in southern-central Africa.

In preparation for his field work, Mathew had read as much as possible about the primate species that inhabited this region. Following Osman Hill's primate taxonomy for the samango group of monkeys, sometimes referred to as white-throated guenons (*Cercopithecus albogularis*), the group had been divided into twelve sub-species of which the Stairs' or Mozambique monkey, *C. a.* erythrarchus, had as a part of its distribution the mountainous eastern districts of Rhodesia, including the Vumba Mountains.

Mathew had read that samango monkeys were usually confined to quite densely forested areas with their distribution being fragmented, and as visual communication between troops in their forest habitat is always difficult, their vocal communication becomes more important. This added a new and potentially groundbreaking dimension to his research.

Soon after Mathew's arrival, Seymour-Smith was most helpful by advising where he would be most likely to have the opportunity to see a troop of the Stairs' – just to the rear of the hotel where the monkeys visited on an almost daily basis to scavenge.

Shortly after sunrise on Mathew's second day at the hotel, when the sun had just begun to dilute the heavy mountain mist with the warmth of its rays and the animal kingdom had started to become active with the birds of the forest singing their early morning anthems, Mathew had his first encounter with two adult Stairs' monkeys. At first he heard their abrupt, single coughs as they jumped and crashed down from the forest canopy: 'jack', 'jack'. Then he caught glimpses of their long tails swinging to and fro like bell ropes, acting as important balancing agents.

As Mathew became familiar with the monkey's vocalisations, it was evident that these low-pitched booming calls were used by adult males during inter-troop encounters and would often be followed by loud 'pant' calls which appeared to be a response to potential dangers, such as Mathew's sudden appearance in their midst. These would sometimes be followed by 'chuckle' noises and high-pitched bird-like calls as a reaction to a disturbance. When females and infants found themselves in trouble they would often squeal, chatter and scream. When Mathew first encountered a troop of some twenty Stairs' as they foraged by the hotel and they were disturbed by his presence, the succession of their calls was to re-echo around the rocky outcrops behind them, sounding not dissimilar to a fusillade of rifle shots.

While Mathew was in the process of searching for a suitable location to establish his research camp, David Montgomery, the director of the Vumba Botanical Gardens and Reserve, took him up through the forest to Castle Beacon. There, a long track had been cleared for the erection of a series of telephone poles to connect the few residents of the Vumba with Umtali and the outside world. The forest clearing also acted as a fire-break, which meant that when a troop of monkeys descended the mountainside during their daily foraging, they had to come down from the safety of the trees and could be openly observed as they crossed the clearing.

Mathew had decided that this would be an ideal place to establish his camp. Thanks to the help of two of Montgomery's botanical garden staff, it was not long before he was able to transport all of his equipment from the Leopard Rock Hotel and set up his tented camp under a stand of wild fig trees on the downhill side of the clearing. Here, Stairs' and vervet monkeys had frequently been seen to forage.

Mathew was aware from his research that the samango group of monkeys were a diurnal (daytime) species and quite gregarious in comparison to some other primates. During the night they rested in trees, individually or in small groups, hiding themselves among the security of the deep foliage of their forest habitats. Their daily activity usually commenced just prior to sunrise before they moved off for their early morning feed. The activity of the group Mathew was studying occurred in bouts and, after a period of resting high up in the forest canopy for between ten and forty minutes, one or two individuals would start to forage and the remainder of the troop would then follow their lead, these periods of foraging ending as quickly as they began. The Stairs' seldom strayed from the security of their thickly forested habitat, except temporarily when coming down to the ground to transit the line of forest that had been cleared on either side of Castle Beacon.

As Mathew had done during his field studies of the eastern lowland gorilla, he collected faecal samples from both the Stairs' and vervet monkeys whenever he was able to identify which of the species the samples were from. When Mathew had met with the Veterinary Department in Salisbury, they had agreed that the Public Health Pathology Laboratories used by their department's veterinarian in Umtali would analyse the food items found in samples and provide both the museum and Mathew with their findings. The samples had to be taken down to the Umtali laboratory each Monday, but Montgomery and Seymour-Smith said that should he be unable to deliver them himself, they would be only too willing for one of their staff to do so on his behalf.

It took Mathew over three weeks before he managed to gain the confidence of this group of Stairs' monkeys and to partly habituate them to his daily presence. His eventual success was mainly down to him placing bananas, nuts and seeds along the tracks that they regularly used through the grass of the forest clearing near to his camp. It was important for the troop of some eighteen to twenty individuals to become accustomed to seeing him at his base, while they foraged and feasted on the ripe figs in the trees above. He could see that as the monkeys spent the majority of their time foraging in the forest canopy, it would be extremely useful if he could observe them from the same level.

SOMEONE WISHES TO SPEAK TO YOU

In order to achieve this, Mathew decided that he – with the help of Montgomery's two assistants – would construct a wooden platform as high up in the forest canopy as possible. With Montgomery's enthusiastic cooperation, and the willingness of his two assistant park rangers, Edgar Chidzikwee and Joshua Dombo, a wooden-planked platform measuring 2 x 1.5 metres was constructed and successfully hoisted up to almost 30 metres above ground level, safely secured to one of the sizeable upper branches of the largest of the fig trees above Mathew's camp. To gain access, Chidzikwee and Dombo had managed to acquire some rope and wooden slats from the botanical garden stores to construct quite a practical rope ladder, which they insisted on testing prior to allowing either Mathew or their boss to try it out for themselves.

As had been the case with Mathew's field studies with the eastern lowland gorillas, he soon settled down to a well-disciplined weekly routine, carrying out five continuous days of field observations from just before sunrise until dusk, spending the majority of the weekends, or two other days, sorting out and writing up his notes, supplementing his food supplies, organising paraffin for his hurricane lamps and any other stores or equipment that he was running short of. During this early period of Mathew's time at Castle Beacon, he started to learn some of the basics of the local Manyika language from Chidzikwee and Dombo.

Charles Montgomery told Mathew that the Manyika tribe belonged to the Shona people and that the majority were indigenous to this eastern district of Rhodesia. The Manyika language, being a broad dialect of Shona, was widely spoken in Manicaland and in certain areas of the Manyica Province in PEA. This was because in the nineteenth century, it had been common practice for the European colonial powers to pay little attention to tribal homelands but rather to establish their political boundaries by topographical features such as rivers, lakes, valleys and mountain ranges.

Due to the significant benefit that the wooden platform gave to his behavioural observations, Mathew commissioned Chidzikwee and Dombo to construct a second platform, which he was only too happy to pay them a reasonable sum to accomplish. He decided that this platform should be located in the forest canopy further down the mountain from Castle Beacon, where the road from a substantial abandoned house to the Leopard Rock Hotel interrupted the forest. Here, the Stairs' monkeys would frequently descend to the ground, cross the road and raid the property's overgrown kitchen garden and orchard of fruits, which included such delicacies as guanos, mangoes, bananas, mulberries, granadillas and apples.

During Mathew's many hours of observations, he noted for the first time the many social interactions that occurred between troops of the Stairs' monkeys, and the more active and smaller vervet monkeys, as well as being able to observe the way both species foraged for and selected their favourite foods. Whereas ripe wild fruits were the commonest and the most popular foods, these would be frequently followed by eating flowers together with a handful of leaves. Apart from the fruits, dry and green leaves, flowers, pods, shoots, seeds and strips of bark, he had been able to observe both species eating insects and caterpillars, and on one occasion he saw an adult male Stairs' monkey extracting the gum of an acacia tree by tearing off small strips of bark with its canine teeth. Although at times he experienced a great deal of loneliness, this was soon compensated for when in writing up his notes he recognised how so many of his observations had never previously been recorded, and were therefore completely new to science.

It was a few days after Mathew's fourth week at his Castle Beacon camp that he received a message via the Leopard Rock Hotel that Group Captain Miles Kinloch and his daughter had made a booking for the coming weekend and had invited him to join them for dinner on the Saturday. Mathew was at first hesitant to accept the invitation; he didn't trust himself not to become involved with Addie.

However, after two days of heavy rainfall when he was unable to carry out any worthwhile observations and was confined to his camp, he decided that a brief change of venue would do him good and accepted the Kinloch's invitation. He also arranged with Charles Seymour-Smith to take a room at the hotel for three or four days in order to carry out some comparative studies between the monkeys at Castle Beacon and those that came down through the thickly vegetated slopes of Leopard's Rock itself.

The decision to meet the Kinlochs at this early stage of his time in Rhodesia had not been made easy for him; since his arrival, he had already received letters from both Lucienne and Antonia which had done little to help him resolve his mixed feelings for them. Lucienne's letter touched on how her literary research work for Osman Hill was progressing and how she was getting on with her degree course, but the greater part of it highlighted how much she enjoyed being with Daniel Olingo. Lucienne had written that after Mathew had left, Daniel, who was currently working in the African Section of the US State Department in Washington, had visited her in Atlanta on several occasions.

Mathew had to reproach himself for the absurdity of still harbouring such strong emotions, but he couldn't help feeling a degree of selfish possessiveness, even jealousy, in the knowledge that another man was having the benefit of her company. Antonia had expressed her fond sentiments in her letter and he was very aware of how susceptible he was to the attractions of female company, especially to women who had taken a particular interest in him. He knew how careful he would have to be in the future if he was to avoid any further social and emotional complications for the time being.

When Mathew met the Group Captain and Addie, they

were sitting at a table by the window in the bar of the hotel, overlooking the small lake and the valley below with the distant dramatic backdrop of the Chimanimani Mountains. When Mathew approached their table, Addie leapt up and much to his surprise, greeted him like a long-lost friend by planting a kiss on both of his cheeks. 'Mathew!' she exclaimed. 'How lovely to see you again! Meet my father, Miles Kinloch.' Addie's father took Mathew's hand in a warm, firm handshake. He almost personified the image of an aging RAF wartime pilot officer: he had a thick-set stature; a handsome physique; a generous crop of snow white hair, which was neatly parted down the middle; a bushy, well-manicured white moustache, curled upwards at either end and a rather flushed complexion that hinted at his many years of good living and exposure to the elements. His *bonhomie* was emphasised by the enthusiastic interest he showed in Mathew's field work. 'Addie's told me a little of what you're doing out here, I'm certainly looking forward to hearing all about it, sounds fascinating.'

'Delighted to meet you, Group Captain. It was very decent of you to invite me along – I hope you won't regret saying that you're looking forward to hearing about my work!' As the three sipped a couple of 'sundowners' in the bar and the conversation flowed, Miles Kinloch showed his curiosity by asking many pertinent questions about the methodology that Mathew was using and the main objectives of his research.

As the evening went on, while enjoying some of the culinary delights produced by the hotel's *maître de cuisine*, the topic of conversation changed from the study of primates to the escalation of Rhodesia's Bush War. In particular, the increased activities of Samora Machel's Mozambique Liberation Front (FRELIMO) activists, who had recently welcomed ZANLA's change of tactics by moving their forces from the Zambezi Valley east into PEA in order to provide them with easier access to Rhodesia from across the border. 'Mathew, with all the terrorism going on in this part of Manicaland, don't you feel at all concerned for your own safety?' asked Addie. 'The fighting is on the increase, it's only going to get more intense.'

'To tell you the truth – I'm afraid this makes me sound terribly naïve – but as I've been so preoccupied with the planning of my field research and the establishment of the camp, I've really had my head in the sand. I've done little to keep abreast with how the Bush War has been developing or whether Rhodesia's security forces have been winning their battle against ZANLA's insurgents.' However, Mathew had been delighted to learn from Chidzikwee and Dombo that Ian Smith had recently agreed with the President of South Africa, Johannes Vorster, to an immediate ceasefire, which had as its main objective to bring to an end the armed incursions from across Rhodesia's borders with both PEA and Zambia. Smith had also agreed with Vorster to the release of political detainees which had included, after ten years of imprisonment, the release of both Robert Mugabe, leader of the Zimbabwe African National Union's Patriotic Front (ZANU/PF) party, and Joshua Nkomo, the leader of the Zimbabwe African People's Union (ZAPU).

On the strength of this latter development, he continued, 'I do see the ceasefire and the release of Mugabe and Nkomo to represent a promising way forward towards ending the great sadness of the country's racial upheavals. I can only be optimistic and pray that a satisfactory political solution can soon be found so that the country can overcome its present regrettable impasse between its European and African communities.' Mathew was referring to the racial disharmony that had resulted, in some quarters, from Ian Smith's Rhodesian Front (RF) political party's UDI, some nine years previously.

'Well, from now on it could be in your interests to keep your ear to the ground, my boy,' said the Group Captain. 'I haven't heard of anything happening on your doorstep as yet, but as Addie says the fighting is intensifying not far from here, so stay on your toes.'

'I certainly will. I have some good contacts in the area so I'm confident I'll hear if the situation changes.' The conversation moved on to more light-hearted topics, although the reference to impending danger left Mathew with a slight feeling of anxiety.

After dinner they retired to the hotel lounge, and were joined by two couples who it transpired had tobacco and maize farms in the Arcturus district to the north-east of Salisbury. Mainly due to Mathew having consumed more alcohol during the course of the evening than he had done for several months, he was expressing his views freely and at length. He spoke enthusiastically about having recently got to know two of David Montgomery's botanical park assistants, Edgar Chidzikwee and Joshua Dombo, who had started to teach him the rudiments of the Manyika language and how Chidzikwee was the son of one of the local tribal chieftains, who had expressed an interest in having a meeting with him.

Continuing to dominate the conversation, he moved on to his time in Zaire. 'While I was carrying out my field studies, I helped an African university graduate, Lucienne Luzembo, an assistant to the director of the Kahuzi-Biega National Park, to gain a place at Emory University in Atlanta. In my opinion, there should be education for all sections of society, no matter whether black or white – we should all be given the same educational opportunities to progress.'

After Mathew had accepted a second balloon-glass of VSOP brandy, he went on to tell the party how one of his ancestors, Robert Milligan, had been a member of the British Parliament soon after the abolition of slavery in the early part of the nineteenth century, and how he had taken an active interest in the emancipation of West Indian slaves. It had been only then that Mathew had sensed the cordiality of those around the table had started to wane, as well as noticing how the expressions on the faces of the Arcturus farmers had become a picture of despondency. In all probability, the very last thing that they had wanted to have learnt more about was the degree of liberalism of his views. It was fortunate Mathew noticed how his audience was reacting before he launched into the story of his support for the Civil Rights movement, and his participation in one of their marches while studying at Scaife University in Tupelo.

Addie managed to interrupt Mathew's flow of information and to come to his rescue. 'By complete coincidence,' she said to the now rather sullen-looking farmers, 'one of my bosses in Salisbury, Michael Lamb, met Mathew a while ago at Bielefeld University when he presented a key-note address about his studies of gorillas in Zaire. Lamb was studying German at the university at the time.' The Arcturus farmers began to thaw slightly and the conversation resumed. Mathew had detected from some of the things that Addie had mentioned during the course of the evening that she must have already carried out a good deal of research about his background. In particular, that she was aware that he was the younger son of a baronet who had served in the Second World War with Sir Roger Willock and, amongst other things, that he had been educated at Wellington College in Berkshire prior to going to a university in the USA.

At the end of the evening, when the three of them were drinking their final nightcaps with the Arcturus farmers in the lounge, Addie made a reference to Mathew having been educated at Wellington College. Her father immediately picked up the gauntlet in an attempt to further lighten the still rather strained atmosphere and asked Mathew whether he was a cricketer. When Mathew had replied in the negative, he said, 'Before I joined the RAF in 1939, I was in Marlborough College's first eleven when, in 1937, Marlborough thrashed Wellington, winning the match by a wicket and ninety-three runs. Ha! Jolly good day that was.'

'If the Wellington side played anything like I do, I'm sure it wasn't a hard-won victory.'

'Nonsense dear boy, I'm sure that's not true. But you know,' he added reflectively, 'there's nothing better in the world than a bit of healthy conversation and competition and, from my perspective at least, what a shame it is that all such unfortunate conflicts between races and nations can't be played out and resolved on a cricket pitch.' After the resulting ripple of laughter had died away, the Arcturus farmers were quick to take their leave – doubtless due to their fear that the young British academic, whom they had only just met, may suddenly unleash another detailed discourse on his political views.

Mathew had already mentioned to the Group Captain and Addie that he had decided to remain at the hotel for a few days in order to carry out some further comparative observations between the Castle Beacon family of Stairs' monkeys and those of the Leopard's Rock group. As he wanted to start his observations immediately, he told the Kinlochs that he planned to be up before dawn the following morning. He turned down the offer of a further nightcap just prior to midnight but before he returned to his room, Addie asked whether he would mind if she could accompany him; he had talked so enthusiastically about his monkeys, she would love to see them for herself. Mathew was happy to take her along and they agreed to rendezvous in the hotel hallway at 6 a.m.

So just after dawn on the Sunday morning, Mathew and Addie, with the aid of the night watchman who let them out of the hotel's back door, ventured out into the damp forest mist and set off on their climb through the thick, moist, vegetation of the mountainside. They were both suitably clad with groundsheet capes covering the majority of their bodies, wearing waterproof trousers, canvas climbing boots and wide-rimmed khaki jungle hats. Some pied crows squawked their astonishment at seeing two humans appear, like miniature tents, in their midst at such an early hour; one of the birds followed them from branch to branch, as if curious to see where they were heading for. As they had climbed further up the trail, a number of small red squirrels (which Mathew was to later identify as the Swynnerton's red squirrel), could be seen dashing nervously above them, flicking their long luxuriant tails as if in apprehension, having been disturbed from their early morning foraging of ripe fruits, berries and pods.

After some twenty minutes of climbing over a number of tree-roots along the moist, peat-like surface of the path, they reached a gap in the forest that was caused by the sizeable glistening face of Leopard's Rock, a section of which had a small mountain stream tumbling over the top of it to a mirror-like pool below. Mathew knew that from this vantage point, Addie would have a good opportunity to observe a family of Stairs' monkeys as they always foraged in this area after they returned from their speedy visit to the hotel's bounteous bins. As the first warm rays of the sun managed to filter through the forest canopy, drying the soaked leaves of the vegetation, and song birds started their dawn chorus, it was not long before they heard some of the characteristic abrupt single coughs and the low-pitched booming calls of two or three male Stairs' monkeys.

'I can't believe they're coming so close!' whispered Addie as she caught her first sight of one of the monkeys, crashing down through the foliage from one tree to another before leaping onto a branch just to the left of her. She watched the large male intently as it used its long, thick tail as a balancing agent, scampering along a swaying branch above the pool, before descending to the ground to satisfy its thirst. The group leader was soon joined by other members of his family, with some of the females carrying infants clasped tightly to their chests and taking seemingly suicidal leaps as they came down from the forest canopy. Once on the ground, the rays of the sun illuminated the colours of their fur. 'Do you see that, Addie? That colouring? That's the main characteristic of the Stairs' monkey, in comparison to the much lighter fur of the vervet monkey, which is far more common in Rhodesia. Here, have a look through these.' He passed Addie his powerful binoculars and through them she could see the yellow tinges of the thick grizzled blackish body hair of their heads and shoulders, the long hair of their cheeks that formed side-whiskers which were slightly paler than the face and the white hairs of their throats and upper lips that attractively contrasted with the slightly more yellow and ruddy-brown-tinged fur near the base of their tails.

'It's amazing,' she said, looking intently through the binoculars. 'I can see all the colours so clearly with these. Aren't they beautiful?' Addie was spellbound as she watched the interactions of the family group as some of the monkeys leapt from rock to rock by the edge of the pool. 'I wish we knew what they were saying to each other, all those little coughs and high-pitched calls, they must mean something.' After some of them had quenched their thirsts with the cool waters of the pool and regained the security of the overhanging branches, the troop had started to move away from them, to leap further up through the dense foliage of the mountainside, all keeping in close contact with each other through their variety of vocalisations.

While Mathew was absorbed in taking copious notes about what they had just witnessed, Addie found his enthusiasm to be highly contagious. 'Thank you so much for showing me this, today,' said Addie. 'I knew absolutely nothing about these animals – and to have the chance to come to see them with such an expert is ... well, it's very special.' While Mathew told her as much as possible about the significance of the monkey's facial images and the underlying geometry of these signals and accompanying eye flashes, Addie was tempted to take his hand and to give him a kiss of gratitude for allowing her to accompany him. At the last moment she decided not to, for she was uncertain how this outwardly reserved Englishman would react to such spontaneous familiarity.

By the time they had retraced their slippery way down the

track to the rear of the hotel, some Stairs' had returned to forage among some recently discarded items of fruit and vegetable matter from the hotel's kitchens. After watching them until they had eaten their fill, Mathew and Addie joined the Group Captain for breakfast. 'Daddy, you wouldn't believe how close they were to us,' Addie said, highly excited after her early morning foray. 'Mathew has taught me so much about these monkeys – they really are the most amazing creatures. It was well worth getting up early, you really should have come with us.' She gave her father a blow-by-blow account of what they had seen, obviously entranced by her encounter with the troop.

As Addie and her father were due to leave the hotel after a late lunch, the Group Captain back to his orchard farm in Inyanga, and Addie to her flat in Salisbury, Mathew had made an arrangement with David Montgomery for them all to visit the Vumba Botanical Gardens.

'Do you know,' said the Group Captain on their way down to the gardens, 'I first visited here in 1952 when they were known as Manchester Park, developed by the Taylor family during and after the Second World War. I remember it clearly; they were quite beautiful. After that, they were bequeathed to the nation by Fred Taylor.'

'I've heard very positive reports. They cover a huge area, around 160 hectares I believe – their upkeep must be quite a formidable task.' As they arrived at the entrance to the gardens, David Montgomery was waiting for them under the shade of a tree.

'Group Captain Kinloch, Miss Kinloch,' he said shaking their hands. 'I'm so glad you had time to pay us a visit while you're in the area. Now, as we walk, let me tell you something about the incredibly prolific birdlife you may see as we walk around and the troop of Stairs' monkeys that frequently visits – they come to forage for all the fruit and berries that grow here. Would you like to come this way?'

After Montgomery had given them some background

information on the park's wildlife, Mathew and Addie walked ahead, seating themselves on a shady rock next to a small lake. Addie took Mathew's hand and said, 'You know, Mathew, I can't tell you how much I've enjoyed this morning. Really, I haven't enjoyed anything nearly this much since before my mother died.'

Although Mathew failed to release his hand from Addie's clasp, he stopped himself from saying how much he too had enjoyed their time together. Instead he decided to reply rather reservedly, 'I always enjoy explaining to people the ways the monkeys interact with one another, especially to someone like you, who shows so much interest in them.' Addie took Mathew's reserve to be that of a typical well-brought-up Englishman, and in response to what he had just said she gently squeezed his fingers, leant over and kissed him on the cheek, before letting go of his hand, standing up and quickly suggesting that they should make the most of the morning's opportunity to see as much of the botanical reserve as possible.

They walked along a network of footpaths between the ancient indigenous fern trees leading to borders of hydrangeas, fuschias, proteas, azaleas, lilies, begonias, and to many other introduced and indigenous species. Mathew decided to tell Addie something about the emotional entanglements that he had experienced over the last year.

'You see Addie,' he said rather shyly in an attempt to avoid any misunderstandings and to be as pragmatic as possible, 'I do very much enjoy your company, and would indeed like to see you again, but in this state of mind I just don't think I can handle a relationship. I genuinely hope we can become the best of friends.'

Addie greatly appreciated Mathew's frankness and spontaneously, and gave him another generous kiss. With a smile that highlighted the two attractive dimples on her cheeks, she confirmed that she too would be very happy to develop a friendship without romantic complications.

By midday they returned to the park's headquarters, where they found the Group Captain and Montgomery sipping a cool glass of Castle lager. As Addie's father had so much enjoyed his conversation with the park's director, he had asked him to join them for lunch. 'I would be delighted to accept,' said Montgomery. 'The Leopard Rock is renowned for its five-course Sunday lunches, they do an English carvery – roast beef, roast potatoes and Yorkshire puddings – all the trimmings, as they say. It's got such a good reputation, people come from as far away as Hot Springs and Melsetter.'

During the course of the meal, the majority of the conversation between Montgomery and the Group Captain was about the ramifications of the UN trade sanctions against Rhodesia. In particular, how these had affected tourism; the significant loss of revenue from admission fees to the country's extensive network of national parks was starting to cause a shortfall in meeting the day-to-day running costs. Mathew, not wishing to become involved with the political pros and cons of the UN sanctions strategy, spent the majority of his time responding to a flow of enthusiastic questions from Addie, who wanted to know as much as possible about what he was hoping to establish in the long term from the monkey groups that he was working with.

When they moved into the lounge to have coffee, Montgomery started to talk about the slippage of the Portuguese security presence in Mozambique and the joint operations that were increasingly frequently taking place across the border between Rhodesia's security forces (which included the expertly trained counter-insurgency specialists, the Selous Scouts), and the Portuguese army, against both ZANLA and FRELIMO.

'Because of all these joint operations against the freedom fighters going on across the border,' said Montgomery, 'the Parks Department Head Office in Salisbury sent out a publication called *Anatomy of Terror* from the Ministry of Information. Basically, it's a short history of insurgency terror tactics from 1972 to 1974, with numerous illustrations of some of the atrocities, quite horrendous. Although obviously it's a propaganda tool to highlight what Rhodesians are now having to deal with, it's also designed to alert those living in rural areas to be constantly on their guard and to inform the BSAP or local security forces about anything suspicious in their vicinity.'

'Do you think Umtali or this area of the Vumba mountains may be in current danger from terrorist attacks?' asked Addie.

'I shouldn't think so,' replied Montgomery. 'Not at this stage, but who knows what will happen in the future?' The happy mood of the party had become more melancholy and in an attempt to deviate from the seriousness of Rhodesia's escalating Bush War, Montgomery tried to take a slightly different angle. 'It was only a couple of years ago, July 1972, that I had the opportunity to speak to Lieutenant General Peter Walls, the officer commanding the Rhodesian forces, about the security measures that he had organised for this border region of south-eastern Rhodesia. I was very pleased to be able to tell him first-hand as a resident of the Vumba how effective the security forces had been against terrorist attacks.'

'And long may it continue!' said Addie.

'Indeed. The occasion in question was when General Walls was invited as guest of honour at Plumtree School's speech day to celebrate its seventieth birthday. We are both alumni of Plumtree – otherwise known as Old Prunitians. During his speech, the general highlighted the problems that Rhodesia was now facing due to what he considered to be the totally unjustified and unwarranted sanctions that had been forced on the country by the United Nations.'

A waiter came in to refill their coffee cups, causing Montgomery to pause just as Mathew was beginning to worry that the conversation was returning to the UN sanctions. 'So you think General Walls is employing the right tactics to tackle this cross-border insurgency?' he asked.

'His measures seem to have been effective so far. Another interesting point General Walls made in his speech was that for the good and future welfare of all Rhodesian citizens, whether European or Africans, it is of huge importance for both communities to do everything possible to act together in order to combat future terrorist incursions and possible tribal conflict.'

With such food for thought, the time had come for Addie and the Group Captain to make their respective ways home in order to reach their destinations before nightfall. Mathew could at least be satisfied in the knowledge that he had been honest with Addie and hoped that though in its infancy, the seeds of a genuine friendship had been sown.

6

Chief Chidzikwee

On 25 April 1974, a left-wing military coup ousted the right-wing dictatorship of the Portuguese Prime Minister, Marcello Caetano, which immediately threw into doubt the future of Portuguese overseas provinces, in particular Angola and Mozambique. While Ian Smith's government was attempting to settle with the British and Rhodesia's African nationalist opponents (ZANU), FRELIMO Marxist armed troops fighting against the Portuguese took advantage of the crossing of the Zambezi River in the Tete Province of Mozambique.

The presence of FRELIMO along Rhodesia's eastern frontiers meant that ZANLA, the armed wing of ZANU, had a safe haven in Mozambique from which to penetrate the adjacent tribal areas and so access the white farming areas of the region. During the latter part of the year, insurgency activities started to escalate Rhodesia's Bush War on its eastern borders. When Mozambique obtained its independence from Portugal on 25 June 1975, further concerns were raised when President Samora Machel's Marxist regime proclaimed a republic, with houses and businesses declared to be state owned, which resulted in a constant flow of Portuguese refugees crossing the border into Rhodesia.

During Mathew's first year in the Vumba Mountains, he developed many friendships within both the European and

African communities. His friends included a number of staff from the small Umtali Museum, who helped him to identify various plant and invertebrate species, and the vets and laboratory staff who analysed the samples he sent on a weekly basis. Through Edgar Chidzikwee and Joshua Dombo, he gained a workable knowledge of the Manyika language and took the opportunity to meet a number of their friends.

Umtali had first come to the notice of both the Portuguese and British colonial powers in the latter part of the nineteenth century, when prospectors discovered gold in the Penhalonga Valley. Both nations were vying for the attention and favour of Chief Mutasa, the dominant ruler in the area. The name Umtali is derived from the local word *mutare*, meaning 'piece of metal'. Following the granting of concessions by Chief Mutasa, a group of pioneers and a contingent of British South Africa Company (BSAC) police built a fort close to the chief's *kraal* in November 1890. During the next decade a police camp was established, an administrative building erected in the township headed by a Civil Commissioner and, after an Anglo/Portuguese treaty, a rail link between the eastern coastal port of Beira in Mozambique and Salisbury was started in 1897.

George Pauling (a British engineer working for BSAC, which had acquired the construction rights) completed the rail link from Beira to a point on the boundary of British territory, but was then confronted by a major geographical hurdle. How could a train negotiate the steep gradient of Christmas Pass to reach Umtali? The township was 10 km north-west of the pass in the Penhalonga Valley. After having advised Cecil Rhodes (Prime Minister of the Cape at that time) of this dilemma, Rhodes visited Umtali and it was decided to relocate the small township 15 km south-east of Christmas Pass where the railway could service the settlement and continue its construction onwards to Salisbury. In 1902, the first part of Cecil Rhodes' dream was achieved when his planned 'Cape to Cairo' railway reached Salisbury from the

CHIEF CHIDZIKWEE

Cape via Bulawayo, a through link of over 2,000 miles connecting Cape Town with Beira.

The new town of Umtali was surrounded on three sides by mountains, with Christmas Pass to the north-west, the main route to Salisbury. The township attained its city status in October 1971 and had recently become the centre of extensive commercial forestry operations, as well as agriculture involving the production of coffee, tea, and the cultivation of a range of deciduous fruit. The new Cecil Hotel had only recently been completed to replace the original building next door. With the expected increase of ZANLA activities from across the border, Rhodesia's military presence in the region had been significantly supplemented by territorials and the old Cecil Hotel building had been taken over as the official headquarters of 3 Brigade (Manicaland).

Whenever Mathew visited Umtali to deliver his various samples or collect provisions, he either lunched at the Cecil Hotel or at the Umtali Sports Club, of which he had become a member. On these occasions, Mathew would take the opportunity to play tennis with staff attached to either the Provincial Commissioner's (Manicaland) headquarters, or the District Commissioner's office in Umtali. He became particularly good friends with a District Officer (DO), Jerome Prior, who was responsible for the area that included the Vumba Mountains. Jerome, known to his friends as Jim, had been educated at England's oldest public school, the King's School, Canterbury and Hertford College, Oxford before going to Rhodesia just prior to the country's UDI. He had immediately fallen in love with his adopted home and fully concurred with the frequently quoted comment that Rhodesia was 'God's Own Country'. They not only played tennis together on a monthly basis, but Jim had also shown considerable interest in Mathew's primate comparative field studies and, whenever he undertook one of his regular tours of duty in the Vumba area, he always visited the Castle Beacon camp.

Now that the threat of terrorist insurgency was deepening, Mathew was aware of the many changes that were taking place in Umtali. During the last twelve months, the relaxed attitude of its citizens had become more apprehensive and despondent. The majority of customers in the bars of the Cecil Hotel and the Umtali Sports Club were members of the military security forces from the Rhodesia Light Infantry (RLI) and BSAP personnel, which included officers of the CIO. At these venues, Mathew found that (in spite of a new emphasis on self-censorship) the conversation usually centred around recent terrorist incursions from across the border and how best to combat the insurgency resulting from the recent escalation of the Bush War.

Although Mathew had been frequently asked about his views on the Royal Navy's blockade of Beira in connection with the UN international trade embargo on Rhodesia, he did everything possible to remain totally apolitical on all such matters. At times, he could not help thinking that if the worst possible scenario were to occur, with the Western powers being pressurised by the African Commonwealth countries to invade the country in order to overthrow the Smith regime, how ironic it would be should his brother's Household Brigade of Life Guards become involved. In particular, with British forces having to fight against so many of their fellow countrymen, the majority of whom had either come out to the colony of Southern Rhodesia from the UK with their parents, or had more recently emigrated to the Federation of Rhodesia and Nyasaland (FR&N) to settle. The majority of these immigrants considered they were there to help with the development of the country into a significant trading partner for the UK and other Commonwealth countries.

Edgar Chidzikwee was the second son of a tribal chieftain, a distant descendant of Chief Mutasa. Mathew's first meeting

CHIEF CHIDZIKWEE

with Chief Chidzikwee took place at the beginning of 1975 at one of the Tribal Trust Lands (TTLs), known as Mutasa North. The tribal area of the Umtali district stretched from the north-west to the south-west of the city, a large tract of land prescribed by law to be used and occupied exclusively by the black population of the region.

Before the meeting, Edgar gave Mathew some background information about the traditional hostility that there had always been between the Ndebele tribal chiefs in Matabeleland and the Shona tribes of the eastern part of Rhodesia, and the various degrees of conflict within the Shona sub-ethnicities.

Chief Jeremiah Chidzikwee lived in a small, whitewashed bungalow with a red-painted corrugated-iron roof, within the midst of an assortment of thatch-plumed windowless *rondavels*. The *kraals* were surrounded by the ubiquitous poultry, enjoying dust baths or scratching the earth in an attempt to locate any previously overlooked morsels. As Mathew's Land Rover drew up in front of the chief's house, an assortment of skinny mongrel dogs got up from their midday slumbers in the shade to start a chorus of barking, while a number of scantily dressed children gathered around the vehicle to see who had arrived within their midst. Two spiky acacia trees stood like sentries on either side of the steps leading up to the small, mosquito-netted veranda, and a boulder-strewn tall *kopje* acted as a backdrop to the bungalow, flanked on either side by tall strands of yellow elephant grass.

Edgar introduced Mathew to his father at the foot of the steps. '*Mangwanani*,' said Mathew, making the traditional Shona greeting. The chief took his hand in a vice-like grip and led him into the bungalow. 'Meet Emmanuel, my eldest son,' said Chief Chidzikwee in a clear English accent (which came as a relief to Mathew as his limited Manyika would not have allowed a very fluent conversation). He went on to introduce a number of his extended family, although there were no women present. 'Can I offer you a glass of the

SOMEONE WISHES TO SPEAK TO YOU

village-brewed "seven days" beer?' asked the chief. 'We make it by simmering maize and rapoon millet with well water. Or you may prefer a bottle of the European Castle lager – it doesn't taste as good, but it's up to you.' Wishing to be as polite as possible, Mathew opted somewhat apprehensively for a glass of the home-brewed 'seven days' beer, in the hope that it would be sufficiently palatable for him to consume without any undue mishap.

The chief was a well-built man, over six feet tall with skin as dark as coal and eyes set back in deep sockets of loose skin. He was wearing a Western-style navy-blue pinstriped suit, a white shirt with a maroon silk tie with a matching handkerchief loosely hanging out of his top pocket. His highly polished black shoes demonstrated how well he wished to present himself when he was receiving a respected visitor. Edgar had said that he had told his father a great deal about why Mathew was in Manicaland, and why he had decided to undertake his studies in Castle Beacon, but despite this, the chief maintained a steady flow of questions.

At the start of their conversation, Mathew found it quite unnerving that the chief's rather bloodshot eyes never for one moment left his own, set as they were in deep sockets behind the thick lenses of his horn-rimmed glasses. Mathew found it impossible to decipher the chief's expressions in order to identify his mood or his thoughts. 'So tell me,' asked the chief, 'what is your main reason for having chosen the Vumba Mountains for your studies?' He could not help feeling that his host was trying to establish whether his reason for being in this border region with Mozambique was genuine, or whether he was carrying out his field investigation as a front to cover the fact that he was subversively involved with counter-insurgency activities with the BSAP, or acting as an agent reporting to the Umtali headquarters of the CIO and the RLI.

'The rest of you, go now. I wish to speak alone with Dr

Duncan,' said the chief to his sons and other family as he refilled Mathew's glass for the second time. Once the others had left, the chief came straight to the point. 'When you first arrived and set up camp, I received a brief report about you from one of my Shona/Manyika tribal informers. I read that on your arrival in Rhodesia, you stayed in Salisbury at the residence of the UK Senior Representative in Rhodesia; you have been seen with the Curator of the Victoria Museum; you had a meeting with a professor at the University of Rhodesia; and before you came here, you did some field work in Zaire. I have now received a subsequent report about you, which states that while you were studying at a university in the USA you were actively involved in the Civil Rights movement. You are known to be a liberal-minded European.'

Mathew was extremely surprised to hear such a résumé of his background, but considered at this stage of his relationship with the chief that it would be inappropriate to ask him where and from whom he had managed to glean so much correct information. As the chief revealed to his guest just how much he already knew about his background, he carefully watched Mathew's every reaction to what he said. Chief Chidzikwee suddenly moved his chair closer and, staring straight at Mathew, said, 'Does your presence in Manicaland have any other objectives but those connected with your academic studies?' Mathew quickly responded to this politically loaded question.

'Chief Chidzikwee, as with my time in Zaire – where I was also fortunate enough to be granted a visa and a permit to undertake field work – I had been preoccupied with my PhD studies and did not wish in any way to become involved with the politics of a foreign country... I always share the results of my research activities with the relevant authorities of the country in which I'm studying.' After a slight pause, the chief rose from his chair, grabbed Mathew's right hand firmly with both of his and enthusiastically pumped it up and down. 'Everything my son Edgar has told me about you is true! He calls you his young eccentric British gentleman of a friend, whose only apparent interest in life appears to be the monkeys that he spends so much of his time studying.'

Before Emmanuel and Edgar rejoined their father and Mathew on the veranda, the chief mentioned in the strictest of confidence his concern about the increased level of terrorist insurgency from across the border. 'Some of ZANLA's freedom fighters have started to come in to the villages of the region, putting pressure on some of the younger members of the tribal communities in Manicaland to become directly involved with their terrorist activities. Ten months ago Herbert Chitepo, the National Chairman of ZANU, was murdered – I was educated with him at St Augustine's Mission School at Penhalonga. As far as I am concerned, Chitepo's death was the consequence of the mutual suspicions among the tribal groups within ZANU. His murder represents the climax of the struggle for power between the Manyika and Karanga Shona tribes; his death has led to the Karanga becoming supreme in the party's command.'

'I'm sorry to hear that, Chief Chidzikwee. It's a worrying situation.'

'It is indeed... And because it's getting worse, I think it's important that we should keep in touch with each other through Edgar. Should ZANLA freedom fighters become active in the Vumba region, I will ask Edgar to keep a close eye on your safety at Castle Beacon.' Chief Chidzikwee's final gesture of farewell was to grasp Mathew's hand in his vice-like grip and to say, 'If there's anything I can do to help you in the future, you have only to ask.'

On leaving the village, Edgar's face was a picture of happiness. 'My father is very much impressed by meeting you. He thanked me for giving him the opportunity to meet you – a genuinely honest, courteous and nice Englishman.'

'And I'd like to thank you,' replied Mathew, 'for the

opportunity to meet your father. He's a very important man, and I know very few visitors would get the chance to talk to him face to face. It's a great honour.'

'He said that now he has had the chance to talk to you in private, he is confident that your presence here is totally connected with your academic studies, for one of his informers had warned him that you could be here to carry out subversive activities on behalf of Rhodesia's security forces. And...' added Edgar rather sheepishly, 'he's made me promise that during these troublesome times, I must keep a watchful eye on the future safety and welfare of his new and first-ever European friend.'

Just before leaving the TTL of Mutasa North, Edgar requested Mathew to stop at a small gathering of thatch-plumed dwellings in order to introduce him to a cousin of his, the village headman, Gabriel Nkulu. Gabriel welcomed them into his quite spacious, windowless *rondavel*, and almost immediately presented them with two steaming mugs of over-sweetened local black coffee and a bowl of home-made *sadza*, a mixture of mealie and pumpkin. Mathew found the *rondavel* similar to those of the Pygmy trackers that he had visited near to the Kahuzi-Biega National Park. It was built from the mud of anthills, the floor made by mixing cowpats with water, which sets as smooth and as solid as concrete. In the centre of the floor was a round hearth with a charcoal fire, its smoke managing to gradually find its way through the dried-elephant grass thatched roof. Edgar acted as translator so that the others could converse, discussing Mathew's studies and Gabriel's duties as headman of the village.

Later, as they drove away from Mutasa North, the shadows of the eucalyptus trees fell across the corrugated brown earthen roadway, which had started to turn crimson as the sun sank on the horizon. Just as they regained the tarmac road leading into Umtali, Mathew experienced his first road block, manned by a European BSAP Superintendent and two African police officers. Although the Superintendent was polite in asking Mathew for his identity papers, he noticed the brusque tone that one of the African officers used in dealing with Edgar. He was surprised by the extra interest the police showed when Mathew told the Superintendent that they had just been visiting Edgar's father, Chief Chidzikwee, but before long they were permitted to continue on their way.

During Mathew's first eighteen months in the country, as he was almost totally absorbed in his observations of the Stairs' and vervet monkey family groups, he had only visited Salisbury occasionally. His first return to the capital was to give his promised talk at the symposium called 'Our Endangered Environment', about his field studies of the eastern lowland gorillas.

As the symposium had been organised by the Zoology Department of the University of Rhodesia, Mathew was concerned about the nature of some of the questions that he might receive after having presented his paper. Instead of being directed at some of the academic aspects of his behavioural studies, the majority related to what he considered the relationship was between the indigenous African populations and the European; in particular those who had lived in the Belgian Congo prior to its independence, and who had experienced some of the massacres that had taken place in the early 1960s in the Kivu province.

However, Mathew found the majority of the three-day symposium to have been a great success, as some of the presentations provided him with a much better understanding of the pressures to which Rhodesia's wildlife was currently being subjected. In particular, the slaughter of endangered species, like the black rhinoceros suffering from the increased presence of terrorist insurgents in the Zambezi Valley and within the protected areas of the country's national parks. He had also been able to make a number of additional useful contacts as some of the meetings had not only had been attended by the Willocks (with whom he was staying), Michael Lamb, Addie, Simon and Anna Vaughan-Jones and some of Simon's Victoria Museum staff, but also by a cross-section of university students, national park staff, conservationists, veterinarians, academics, politicians (Europeans), environmentalists, and even by two of the Arcturus farmers, John and Juliet Stobart, whom he had previously met with the Kinlochs at the Leopard Rock Hotel.

During the majority of Mathew's subsequent visits to Salisbury he accepted the hospitality of the Vaughan-Jones, whose home was in the attractive upmarket estate in the Gunhill district of Salisbury. The three of them shared so many common interests in natural history, in particular their respective studies in primate social behaviour, that they became close friends. Anna was delighted to compare data between Mathew's field observations on his habituated vervet family of approximately twenty-five individuals at Castle Beacon, with the smaller family group that she was studying in a semi-naturalistic environment within the grounds of the museum.

As a result of their friendship, Simon and Anna visited his Castle Beacon site on several occasions and were enthralled by the way Stairs' and vervet monkeys interacted with each other while foraging in the same trees. They were fascinated to observe the way the vervets managed to extract the gum of acacia trees by tearing at the bark with their canines, and how they appeared to be rather inept at catching and handling insects. As Anna had been working on the way her captive vervet monkey colony communicated with each other, she had been particularly interested to see the way the troops of vervets in their wild state always appeared to have 'lookouts' stationed around them, in order to warn the rest of troop should any danger present itself.

During one of Simon and Anna's initial visits to the Vumba, the benefits of such a precautionary regime had been perfectly demonstrated. When one of the vervet sentinels saw a python slithering through the long grass of a clearing where they had been foraging, it had immediately stood up on its hind feet and screeched an alarm call before quickly following the rest of the troop to the safety of the nearby trees. On another occasion, when the monkeys were feeding on berries in the forest canopy, they saw a tawny eagle swoop down in an attempt to pluck a juvenile vervet from the end of a branch. One of the sentinels immediately used a different alarm call to the one that had been used for the python; as soon as the group heard this, they withdrew to the thicker foliage of the canopy, into which the tawny eagle would find it more difficult to swoop. If it had tried, it would have risked damaging its wings. Anna was particularly thrilled to witness both of these as she had been able to record both of the alarm calls.

During Mathew's second stay with the Vaughan-Jones, they organised a *braai* (barbecue) in the grounds of the museum. 'Mathew, you must meet Jan,' said Anna, enjoying her role as the attentive hostess, introducing her guests. 'She lives near us on the Gunhill estate and she's one of my closest friends.'

Mathew was immediately struck by the loveliness of the woman that Anna was steering him towards. She was tall and willowy, with long, slender legs and the elegant frame of an athlete. As Jan turned towards Mathew, he saw the beauty of her fine cheekbones, framed by a soft curtain of blonde hair. 'Jan, this is Mathew,' smiled Anna. 'I'm very pleased to meet you,' said Mathew rather formally, reaching out to shake her hand. He felt suddenly gauche, his usual self-confidence abandoning him momentarily as he was quite literally left speechless by the beauty of the woman standing in front of him. Anna had to rush off almost immediately to attend to some other guests, leaving Jan and Mathew to talk. Although the exchange was rather stilted to begin with, the ice soon broke and they were deep in conversation.

During the course of the evening, Mathew spent as much time in Jan's company as possible. He had plenty of time to observe her gentle eyes and beautiful soft hair, which blended so aptly with her rather shy disposition. Mathew recognised in her the kind of delectable innocence that he first saw in Antonia. The more he talked to Jan and studied her different expressions, the more he considered what a perfect model she would be to any artist who wished to portray such a classic example of femininity.

While they talked, Mathew was reminded of Victor Hugo's advocacy that 'When a woman is speaking to you, listen to what she says with her eyes'. Combining this advice with the findings of the communicative facial images of his primate studies, he paid particular attention to her eyes as she spoke. It was clear to Mathew from the close attention she gave to everything he said that a considerable degree of empathy had developed between them. He was very aware that Jan would be able to see the effect her female magnetism was having on him.

'So what about you?' asked Mathew, after having given Jan what he hoped was a fascinating account of his research studies. 'Have you always lived in Rhodesia?'

'No, I was born in South Africa. My parents came here in the mid-sixties from Potgietersrus, a farming community in the northern Transvaal. Rhodesia is a beautiful place to live, but I haven't had the opportunity to travel abroad and there's so much I would like to see.'

'So you've never been to Europe?'

'No – it's top of my list, but I've never been there or to the USA. I've only ever read about them. Perhaps if … if we could meet up again, you could tell me more about what life is like there?'

'That would be a pleasure.'

As Mathew was beginning to feel quite close to Jan during the time they spent talking in the smoky shadows at the *braai*, and as he had consumed more cold Castle lager than he had recently been accustomed to, he willingly accepted the invitation to have tea with her at her home on the following afternoon.

However, on the way back to the Vaughan-Jones', Anna dropped a bombshell. 'You seemed to get on very well with Jan tonight,' she remarked.

'Absolutely, I found her quite delightful – in fact, extremely delightful.'

'Did she mention that she's married to Major Paddy Bushney, second in command of the Selous Scouts?' The Selous Scouts were the crack counter-insurgency specialist arm of the Rhodesian security forces. From the silence in the car that followed, it was obvious to both Simon and Anna that this was news to Mathew. 'Major Bushney is substantially older than her. He's away at the moment on counter-terrorist operations in the Tete Province...' It took well over a minute before Mathew was able to tell them he had already arranged to see her again.

'I had no idea she was married. I said I would go to her house tomorrow as she said she would like to hear more about the USA and England... Oh God, what should I do now?'

The following morning, just after the first light of dawn had crept through the thin curtains of Mathew's room, he could not help feeling a degree of foolishness in having been so beguiled by Jan's femininity. Now that he knew she was married, how could he possibly go round to her house in the absence of her husband? After recalling that during the course of the night he had dreamt about her, he knew that it was important for him to see her at least once again in order to bid her a friendly farewell. He had already deduced that the sudden infatuation he was feeling for Jan was no doubt the result of living such a solitary and celibate existence since leaving Atlanta. It would be foolishly counter-productive for him to become involved with a married woman, no matter how attractive or appealing she was. Although on reflection, he could not help believing that the feelings were reciprocated.

Fortunately, when Mathew went down to have breakfast with Simon and Anna, there was some welcome news.

'I've just telephoned Jan and given her a little talking-to. You see, I am ten years older than her and I have to keep her in line, you know. I told her I don't think it's at all sensible for her to have you round while the Major's away.' Mathew looked rather despondent, although he knew Anna was right. 'But I have invited her round for a sundowner this evening, if it makes you feel any better.'

'Anna, you are an angel! I had no idea what to do for the best.'

'Well, Major Bushney has recently been away from his home for long spells on military operations and I've almost adopted Jan as a younger sister. She gets very lonely, so she often asks my advice on things. As we're close, or so I like to think, I jokingly pointed out to her just how awkward it would be if her husband's RAR batman started to spread rumours about the Major's young wife entertaining a handsome young Englishman at his house, on her own, whilst he was away on military duties. Of course she laughed, but admitted she hadn't thought about the ramifications of her invitation. Anyway, the arrangements are made and Jan says she's really looking forward it.'

After Mathew returned from lunch with one of the museum's council members at the Salisbury Club, Anna decided it would be prudent to put him in the picture with regards to Simon and her relationship with the Bushneys. Over several cups of tea, she told Mathew that Jan had come from a comparatively poor family of Afrikaner farm managers, the Labuschagnes. 'It's such a shame,' Anna explained, 'she's really very intelligent but she just didn't have the financial backing to go to university. After leaving school she took a secretarial course and managed to get a job as a secretary with Rhodesia's Tourism Board, after which she went to work for the director of a safari company, which gave her a chance to travel around to some of the popular tourist destinations. While she was spending a weekend on Spurwing Island on Lake Kariba, she met Major Bushney – "Paddy" to his friends.'

'Is he very much older than her?'

'Yes, indeed – twenty-two years in fact. His wife had died two years previously from cancer. When he met Jan, she was just the type of attractive young woman that he immediately set his sights on to be his new bride. Jan, on her part, had just been in the process of getting over the traumas of a failed romantic attachment to an old-Etonian "remittance-man" who suddenly returned to England without any explanation. So it was all rather on the rebound; she was flattered by the attention given to her by this well-respected and ruggedly handsome military officer, many years her senior. It was certainly to the delight of her parents that she accepted Major Paddy Bushney's hand in marriage.'

'I suppose I can see their point of view on some levels...'

'Financially at least, they thought Jan would be well cared for and have a secure future. Anyway, the Major and Jan were married at a small service held in the chapel at King George VI Barracks in the spring of 1974, followed by a reception in the RLI's Officers Mess and a short honeymoon at the Victoria Falls Hotel. But since then, with all these terrorist attacks on white farmers and their staff, the Major's responsibilities have grown and he's constantly away from home on counter-insurgency operations. Usually he can't even tell Jan his whereabouts, or when he'll be home. This is strictly between us, Mathew, but neither Simon nor I are particularly close or friendly with Major Bushney. Of course, we respect him for his military acumen, but he's terribly arrogant and inconsiderate in his dealings with civilians. Worst of all, he can be inexcusably rude to Jan in front of other people.'

'No wonder she didn't mention her marriage last night,' said Mathew, growing more despondent on Jan's behalf. 'It sounds like a rather complex situation. You would think as a much older man, he would count himself rather lucky to have such a young, beautiful and intelligent wife.'

'That's not all of it. As the Major's away so much of the time, Jan has started to feel extremely lonely and often relies on me for support and advice. She's become increasingly unhappy, so much so that the doctor's put her on anti-depressants. Once, when she was particularly low, she confided in me that she regrets agreeing to marry him and blamed the constant pressure from her parents for such a rash decision.'

'I find it hard to reconcile that this is the same woman I was talking to yesterday evening, She seemed happy.'

'Well, Major Bushney wasn't there last night which is bound to have made a huge difference – and she obviously enjoyed talking to you,' said Anna, arching her eyebrows at Mathew. 'Although he's well respected by the majority of his peers because of his various military accomplishments, Major Bushney is very much an alpha-male with a short fuse. He has the reputation of being quite ruthless with people he has taken a dislike to. He is certainly not a person to trifle with. Now, changing the subject, how about you come with me to visit the vervet monkeys in the museum grounds? We could collect Simon from his office at the same time.'

'I would love to, Anna, that sounds like an excellent plan,' replied Mathew, feeling he would very much like to clear his head after all that he had heard.

As they walked, Anna came straight to the point. 'Mathew, I hope I'm not jumping the gun but would you mind if I give you some advice about any future relationship that you may be wishing to have with Jan?'

'You already know I'm utterly smitten by her. Please go ahead, I feel I could do with all the advice I can get.'

'This is probably more for Jan's benefit than your own – you're quite capable of looking after yourself. She is not only extremely unhappy in her marriage, but currently in a very vulnerable state of mind. She's very fragile, Mathew, and if any relationship develops, you must deal with her as carefully and as sensitively as possible.'

'I wouldn't dream of doing anything else, Anna. I only want what's best for Jan.' Having said this, Mathew felt a sudden pang of guilt when he thought of how things had ended up with Lucienne, despite the depth of the feelings he once had.

'You must be aware that in Jan's present state of mind, what she wants more than anything else in the world is the constant companionship of a man whom she can really love, which sadly has not been the case with her husband since soon after the wedding. It really is such a shame she's stuck in this marriage to Major Bushney, but I think it's going to be extremely difficult, if not almost impossible, for her to get out of it.'

That evening, when Jan arrived at the Vaughan-Jones' for sundowners, she appeared to Mathew to be a breath of fresh air – he wanted to be with her more than he had wanted to be with anyone since his relationship with Lucienne. Her sky-blue eyes seemed to sparkle whenever she was in conversation with him, and such was the effect she had on him that he saw her body language as a portrayal of enticement. The evening flew by. Just before it was time for Jan to return to her empty house, Mathew wished more than anything that he could take her in his arms, hold her in a tight embrace and kiss her delicate cheeks and lips. But he was quick to remind himself of Anna's warnings, and merely took her hand and responded to the brief kiss that she planted on both of his cheeks. Then, reluctantly releasing the tight grip of her hand, he rather embarrassingly stuttered, 'Jan, I'm so pleased to have had the chance to meet you. I really enjoyed your company at the *braai* last night – perhaps when I next visit Salisbury, our paths may cross again?'

'I would like that very much, Mathew. You must come back to Salisbury before too long.' Jan looked directly at him as she spoke, her eyes almost misting over with tears of yearning.

The year 1975 turned out to be an exceptionally busy one for Mathew. He spent innumerable hours carrying out his field observations, each evening meticulously analysing and writing-up his findings. He also found time to compile a number of scientific manuscripts which dealt with various aspects of his field observations on the eastern lowland gorillas, and was delighted that three of the papers he submitted were accepted for publication by three internationally well-respected peer-reviewed scientific journals: *Conservation Biology*; *The American Journal of Primatology*; and *Oryx*, the journal of the Fauna Preservation Society.

During the course of the year, apart from the rigours connected with the field work, Mathew had taken on a number of extra commitments. These included his symposium presentation at the university (the proceedings of which had just been published by its Department of Zoology) and a number of talks that he had given about his comparative studies of the Stairs' and vervet monkeys in the Vumba Mountains. During the illustrated presentations that he gave to the council, members and staff of the Victoria Museum, Umtali's Rotary Club, Sports Club and the local Women's

Institute, he had taken the opportunity to emphasise how some aspects of the monkeys' communicative skills could well be attributed to the way humans interact with one another.

On leaving the Women's Institute, Mathew was amused to spot two quite large jovial-looking ladies standing in front of a sizeable gilt-framed mirror in the hallway, making a series of rather furtive side-glances and winking at one another. Either they were trying out the friendly primate interactions he had just been talking about, or they were practising to see how attractive their respective eye flashes and grimaces could be in the future to impress some unsuspecting male conquest. Whichever it was, Mathew was pleased that some of his presentation had impressed at least two of the audience members.

On 11 November 1975, four and a half months after Mozambique had gained its independence from Portugal, the Popular Movement for the Liberation of Angola (MPLA) elected Agostinho Neto as the country's first Marxist president. Just prior to this, an estimated 300,000 people left Angola after experiencing the devastation of fourteen years of civil war, which raged from 1961-1975 between the National Union for the Total Independence of Angola (UNITA) and the MPLA. Mathew found that both of these pre- and post-independence events, coupled with the increased insurgency from across the Mozambique border, had started to cause Umtali's European inhabitants to become increasingly apprehensive about what the future may have in store for them. Particularly, what would happen should Ian Smith's government give way to one dominated by Africans who wanted to follow the example of the majority of neighbouring states that had gained independence from their colonial masters.

Since Mathew's first meeting with Group Captain Miles Kinloch, when he and Addie had stayed at the Leopard Rock

CHIEF CHIDZIKWEE

Hotel, he had visited the Group Captain's orchard estate in the picturesque eastern highland district of Inyanga on several occasions. Their house had become almost like a second home. When Addie first invited him to stay for a weekend as she was planning to make the 240 km journey from her flat in Salisbury, he could not help feeling slightly apprehensive as he was well aware that she would like their relationship to become more intimate. He just hoped that she remembered what he had said to her at the Vumba Botanical Gardens, that he wasn't ready to cope with any further emotional ties. Fortunately, apart from Addie taking his hand on a number of occasions when pointing out some of the dramatic landscapes of the Rhodes Inyanga National Park, and brief kisses on the cheeks during their meetings and farewells, their relationship had remained pleasurably platonic.

After Mathew had managed to achieve the deadline he had been given by *National Geographic* magazine to produce a 4000-word article, co-authored with Adrien Deschryver, about the status of the endangered eastern lowland gorillas of Kahuzi-Biega, he was pleased to receive an invitation from the Kinlochs to spend Christmas and New Year with them. Mathew was in much need of a break from the recent intensity of his work, and he looked forward to a period of relaxation with two people he now considered to be close friends. He also looked forward to seeing more of Inyanga's spectacular scenery, as well as hoping for the opportunity to record some observations on the sizeable troop of chacma baboons, *Papio ursinus*, that inhabited some of the nearby *kopjes* on the Group Captain's homestead, and were frequently seen around his estate.

On the road from Rusape into the Inyanga district, Mathew was fascinated to see how the landscape varied. Initially it was dominated by a scattering of boulders of every shape and size, which all appeared to have tumbled onto each other with some of the larger ones balanced precariously on top of smaller ones, as if wishing to do everything possible to defy the basic laws of gravity. As the boulder-strewn *kopjes* of the landscape disappeared, the habitat on either side of the road gave way to a mosaic of montane forest grasslands as it progressed into the Rhodes Inyanga National Park.

When arriving at the Kinloch's homestead, an attractive house of Cape Dutch design with whitewashed walls, a pitched-roof, and the typical triangular gable above its front entrance, Mathew would always be greeted by the Group Captain's two boisterous Rhodesian Ridgebacks. The dogs had been named Huggins and Welensky after the Federation of Rhodesia and Nyasaland's (FR&N) first two prime ministers, Godfrey Huggins and Roy Welensky.

'They were previously known as Van Royen's Lion Dog or an African Lion Dog, you know,' the Group Captain was always keen to inform his guests. 'You can tell Ridgebacks by that ridge of hair along their back running in the opposite direction to the rest of their coats. But don't worry, they're nothing like lions at all – they're very friendly with people they know, intelligent and extremely loyal but, above all, they are excellent guard dogs.'

During Mathew's ten-day holiday with the Kinlochs, Addie went out of her way to show him some of Inyanga's spectacular scenic sights. From beyond the rather luxurious Troutbeck Hotel and its golf course at 'World's View', he had been able to see across the vast escarpment to the distant hills of Mozambique. Due to the altitude, the Rhodesian Corps of Signals had set up an important and well-guarded command post there for signal communications within the army's counter-insurgency operations. Mathew was later told that the command post was not only able to assist telegraphic communications between every European dwelling in the area, but enabled specialist code breakers in the Corps to interrupt and decipher some of ZANLA's signals from across the border. Mathew's favourite sight was the Pungwe Falls, a totally unspoilt natural environment overlooking the Honde Valley, where the Pungwe

River dropped some 240 metres into a thickly wooded gorge beneath the waterfalls.

As late December was in the rainy season, the Falls comprised of several rapids as the fast-flowing river made its tumultuous way over assemblages of smooth-faced boulders, before disappearing under the curtain of the soaked foliage of trees and the ubiquitous ferns of the region, into the long, deep gorge beneath. After which the Pungwe River wound its way through the open plains of the escarpment into Mozambique, before entering the Indian Ocean at Beira.

Mathew and Addie rested on a large, flat boulder close to the top of one of the rapids.

'What I love about this spot is being covered in that thin mist of spray from the Falls, it's so refreshing,' said Addie, stretching out on the boulder. 'Not to mention the terrible din the water makes!'

'It's quite incredible,' agreed Mathew. 'Almost like thunder. I've never heard anything like it.' The river was moving with a swift current, passing by the side of them before plunging over the nearby rocks into the depths of the ravine beneath. 'Look, Addie, can you see those birds?' Mathew pointed to the top branches of a nearby tree.

'Oh... Yes, I can see some orange and brown plumage up there,' replied Addie, straining to see where Mathew was pointing.

'It's a pair of paradise flycatchers. As well as the orange and brown plumage you can see, they have – look, they're on the move now, you'll be able to see them.'

'Oh, aren't they beautiful?' gasped Addie. 'I could look at them all day.' As they watched the flycatchers flit to and fro, feasting upon the multitude of insect life that was present in small clouds over the nearby rock pools, they could see how the orange and brown plumage contrasted beautifully with their dark heads, blue eyes and blue-grey underparts. They heard the far-carrying ringing calls of an African fish eagle, which Mathew had first heard with Lucienne on the shores of Lake Kivu. After the eagle's call, they were fortunate enough to see it suddenly swoop down past them to gather up in its talons a sizeable fish, which had been left marooned in one of the pools, and take it to a nearby rock.

Here the eagle, with its snowy-white head and shoulders, chesnut-coloured underparts and much darker wings, seemingly oblivious to their presence, proceeded to tear the fish apart with its curved black beak. After devouring as much of the flesh as it required, the eagle then characteristically threw its head back to make another of its long-ringing calls, as if to proclaim its gratitude for having been so conveniently provided with such a welcome and wholesome meal, prior to flying off with what remained of its prey to its lookout branch further up stream. To Mathew, the overhanging moist branches on each side of the rapids seemed to resemble a delicate picture-frame that captured the magnificence of the river and its rapids. 'Thank you so much for bringing me here, Addie, it really is one of the most spectacular things I have ever seen. I hope that everyone who is fortunate enough to come here recognises what a significant masterpiece of the natural world this really is. Quite magnificent.' Addie smiled, and the two friends sat in comfortable and companiable silence, taking in the beauty and the sheer drama of their surroundings.

The Kinlochs and Mathew spent New Year's Eve at an informal festive dinner at the Rhodes Inyanga Hotel. 'This is where Cecil Rhodes built his original cottage in 1896,' the Group Captain told Mathew as they took sundowners on the hotel veranda. 'Then they built the hotel in 1933. Look at that view, right over the Rhodes Dam – quite impressive, don't you think?' They were joined by a small group of men who, after they had consumed a few cold Castle lagers, told them that they were part of a detachment from Rhodesia's Corps of Signals, currently operating from its regional headquarters at World's View.

CHIEF CHIDZIKWEE

Mathew and the Kinlochs particularly liked the officer in charge of the group, a middle-aged Scot by the name of Angus Whitton, so they had invited him to join their table.

'I've been in Rhodesia's regular army for almost twenty years,' explained Angus over dinner. 'I joined the Rhodesia and Nyasaland Staff Corps as a junior NCO in February 1956, now I'm serving as an acting major in Rhodesia's Corps of Signals. How time flies! So, Mathew, which part of England do you hail from?'

'I'm from Yorkshire, the Dales to be precise, in the North Riding. Do you know it?'

'I certainly do – I did National Service in the British Army in the early fifties and did my basic training at Catterick, which was then the headquarters of the Royal Corps of Signals. I got to know the area quite well.'

'Is there anywhere you particularly remember?' asked Mathew, eager to discuss his home territory.

'It's a good few years ago now but I remember visiting Ilkley, and there was a pub I recall visiting in Burnsall, the Red Lion I think it was.'

'I know it well! They serve a fine pint of Webster's Green Label. Ah, wherever you go in the world, it's hard to beat a good British pub.' Mathew was delighted to hear that this soldier, so many miles away from Yorkshire, had once enjoyed a pint or two so close to his ancestral home.

'Aye, that's the one! Lovely little place that was, and fine beer. That brings back some happy memories.'

'So what brought you all this way?' asked the Group Captain.

'Well, I spent the majority of my National Service as a Signalman on active service during the Malayan Emergency. Then in 1955 I answered an advertisement in the *Guardian* newspaper – after an interview with a Lieutenant Colonel R.A.G. Prentice, at 429 The Strand, the Federation of Rhodesia and Nyasaland's headquarters in London, I was accepted as a recruit of the Federal Army's Staff Corps. During the 1950s, there was a considerable increase of people immigrating here for a fresh start and a completely new life – it was considered to be one of Great Britain's most attractive colonies. I must say I've never looked back.'

When Angus finished providing them with this interesting insight into his background, he stressed how very fortunate he had always considered himself to have emigrated to a country that he had come to love so much. 'For a long time now Rhodesia has been the country that I refer to as home. It provides me with a lifestyle and standard of living that would be difficult, if not impossible, for me to have had I stayed put.'

'There are certainly many advantages to life here as opposed to Britain,' agreed the Group Captain. 'While I miss it in many ways, I never regret the decision to stay here. But now, things are far from stable, there are huge changes going on around us. What's your opinion on Rhodesia's future?'

'What really concerns me,' replied Angus, speaking with the passion of a man who had genuine strong feelings, 'is that if and when Southern Rhodesia gains its independence from Britain, whether an African-dominated government would be able to take over the responsibilities of running a democracy devoid of the degrees of corruption, bloodshed and autocracy that has proved to be only too evident within the majority of Africa's recently declared republics. The very last thing that I or any of my fellow Signalmen would wish to see happen in Rhodesia is the type of chaos and bloodshed that happened during the aftermath of the Congo gaining independence from Belgium in the 1960s, or to experience the massacres and horrors that took place in Idi Amin's Uganda after its independence from Britain.'

'I agree, there are so many horrific examples of what can go wrong, right on Rhodesia's doorstep,' said Addie. 'Do you think there's any measures that ought to be taken to prevent it?'

CHIEF CHIDZIKWEE

'In my view,' Angus concluded, 'if a satisfactory political settlement can be found for this, my adopted country, its future will rely on international observers ensuring that free and fair elections are able to take place. Also, that once a democratically elected government has been established, it will not be allowed to follow the abysmal example of the majority of other countries who have, since Africa's "Wind of Change", gained independence from their European colonial masters. And now, if you'll excuse me, I'd better rejoin my men in order to see in the New Year with them.'

As Angus walked away, after the three of them had listened carefully to his pessimistic appraisal of Rhodesia's chances of achieving a satisfactory future for all of its inhabitants, they heard the first chimes of the grandfather clock in the hall striking the midnight hour. Any further despondent thoughts about the country's future were cast aside as all the guests assembled on the veranda to hold hands and form one large circle, for the merriment of the evening to achieve its climax. The circle closed in and went back out, the dancers swayed to and fro, and some of the party-goers tried to outwit one another by attempting to recall the correct words of Robert Burns' poem. It was the traditional welcoming-in of the New Year. As soon as they heard the final strike of the midnight hour, they all managed to rather inebriatedly sing the familiar chorus: 'For auld lang syne, my dear, For auld lang syne. We'll take a cup o' kindness yet, For auld lang syne.'

It had been immediately after the party's repeated and enthusiastic rendering of the chorus that the majority of the men had gone around their fellow merry-makers to kiss as many of the women as they were able to reach. When Addie found herself surrounded by most of Angus's Signallers, Mathew protected her from having to be subjected to too many hugs and kisses, very much as a brother would have done for a sister. After having told Angus how much they had enjoyed his company, and bidding him and his men a final 'Happy New Year', the Group Captain drove his Bedford pick-up truck slowly back to his orchard estate, with Mathew and Addie seated on the vehicle's bench seat beside him. Mathew gently took Addie's hand in his; this was his way of demonstrating how much he respected her understanding of how he wanted their relationship to remain. During the ten days that they had spent together, they had developed the type of deep friendship, maturity, and understanding that could well have been the envy of a number of their married acquaintances.

It had been as a result of the depth of such a degree of empathy that had developed between them that they had become so relaxed and uninhibited in each other's company and were thereby able to speak freely about their respective values in life, and their varied aspirations. But in spite of Mathew having developed such a deep level of understanding and respect for Addie, he was unable to tell her anything about his current infatuation with Jan Bushney. Although during his stay in Inyanga he had experienced so much to distract him from his thoughts, he was unable to escape from the fact that he yearned for her. As a consequence, he decided that the only way he would be able to put an end to his mind becoming increasingly preoccupied would be to arrange another meeting with her at the earliest opportunity. He wanted to tell her exactly how strong his feelings were and to find out, no matter how counter-productive it might turn out to be, whether it was reciprocated.

When, two days later, it was time for Mathew to leave the Kinloch's home, he knew that he would miss them hugely on his return to a more solitary existence at his Castle Beacon camp. He had thoroughly enjoyed their company.

On Mathew's final night, they had a most enjoyable *braai* under a large oak tree on the front lawn of the homestead. The smell of roasted pork, the smoke of the fire and the celebratory atmosphere reminded Mathew vividly of the gathering in the grounds of the Victoria Museum on the evening he had met Jan. He remembered how he had been so instinctively attracted to her. During the night he dreamt about being alone with Jan, on safari in the wilderness of Rhodesia's pristine bushveld. While they relaxed in each other's arms by the side of a smoldering camp fire, having just consummated their love for one another under a sky studded with the brightest of celestial stars, the dream had abruptly come to a horrific end. A rifle shot had rung out and Jan's body, splattered with blood, had become limp in his embrace. At the same time, he caught a glimpse of a man in military fatigues disappearing into the night.

7

Spirit of Rhodesia

By January 1976, Umtali had become almost like a garrisoned township, with the presence of uniformed troops and military vehicles being a common occurrence. Mathew noticed how the previously carefree atmosphere of the city had become quite tense. The majority of civilians had become tight-lipped, reluctant to talk about the ramifications of the increased insurgency, although most knew only too well what the situation was.

Although he had observed the changes in Umtali life, Mathew was so taken up with his field studies that it had made little impact on him. He hadn't considered the relevance of the small groups of Africans that he had started to encounter on the mountain forest paths near his Castle Beacon camp. He had failed to note the significance of the number of unfamiliar African faces he had seen when visiting Edgar and Josiah's village to learn more about their Manyika language, folklore, and tribal traditions.

In early February, much to Mathew's surprise, he received a long letter from Lucienne posted from Washington DC to tell him that she had recently married Daniel Olingo, and that she was now expecting their first child. She went on to provide Mathew with a brief biography of her new husband which she had marked, 'Strictly confidential and for your eyes only'. Daniel had initially graduated from the University of Chicago's Department of Mathematics with a Master of

Science degree in Financial Mathematics. Soon after his graduation, he joined the US Foreign Service and was posted to the African Section of the State Department in Washington, known fondly by its officers as 'Foggy Bottom'.

In December 1973, Daniel was approached by a talent spotter for the Central Intelligence Agency (CIA) to see whether he would be interested in carrying out intelligence work. This approach had resulted from a First Secretary at the State Department informing a colleague how Daniel ticked two boxes on the list of the agency's requirements; as a mathematician that could be involved in code breaking, as well as a competent linguist. After a successful interview, Daniel embarked on a course at Langley, which resulted in him becoming a fully fledged CIA operative. She continued:

> This information about Daniel is in the strictest confidence, but as you are the first man I ever loved, I thought it was important that you should know all about the man I have married.
>
> In order to move to Washington, I had to give up the degree course at Emory – although I stayed in Atlanta until I'd finished the literary research contract with Osman Hill. You will be relieved to hear that one of my friends from Yerkes said that the professor was very pleased with the quality of my work – he and Yvonne invited me to their house for a farewell dinner to wish me well for the future. They have both been very good to me.
>
> So, within six months of my move to Washington, I got married to Daniel at St Mary's Roman Catholic Church in Chevy Chase, Maryland. After we returned from honeymoon on the Pacific Coast of Costa Rica, Daniel went back to his job in the African Section.
>
> I just wanted you to know that I am very happy with Daniel and with my new life in Washington. I hope everything is going the way you planned in Rhodesia –

I haven't received a letter from you since I left Atlanta, so do please write, even if just to let me know how your primate research work is going. It's a subject I will never tire of hearing about!
  Keep in touch.
  Love as always,
  Lucienne

P.S. If you find time to reply, which I very much hope you will, it would be best if you mailed it to my previous Atlanta address. For the time being, I'm using that for all my personal correspondence, especially from family and friends in Zaire. My former landlady has very kindly agreed to forward packages of registered mail to me in Washington. Write soon!

Although Mathew was pleased to hear that Lucienne was now settled into an obviously happy matrimonial life, he became slightly emotionally disturbed in being reminded about their many months of happiness together, in Africa and America. Her letter had brought to the fore his longstanding concern that he let her down badly by not marrying her when she became pregnant, and then persuaded her to undergo the awful experience of going to San Diego to have an abortion. It was a scar that he was certain he would always have to bear on his conscience.

During one of Jim Prior's visits to Castle Beacon, Mathew was interested to hear about the activities of the European and African civilians who belonged to the Psychological Operations Unit (PSYOP), which worked in conjunction with the military's Psychological Action Group (PSYAC).

'You know, the main objective of the Rhodesian Ministry of Information booklet *Red for Danger*, which was dispatched in its thousands to many different countries, was to highlight that the ZANU and ZAPU political parties were just cover organisations for Communist expansion in Africa,' explained Jim. 'It recorded that Robert Mugabe received support for terrorist activities against white-owned farms in Rhodesia from China and North Korea, whereas Joshua Nkomo received most of his support from Russia. The booklet stressed that as the Western countries were actively pursuing a policy of attainment, it was important that neither ZANU nor ZAPU should elicit support from the West.'

'I haven't come across it,' said Mathew, 'but David Montgomery, the director of the botanical gardens, showed me the Ministry's *Anatomy of Terror* booklet – quite horrific.'

'The chief aim of *Anatomy of Terror* was to summarise the crimes perpetuated by "Communist-trained thugs" and to record a chronology of the brutal attacks already committed against black Rhodesians from December 1972 to May 1974. As the Bush War has progressed and the government's control of insurgency operations has diminished, the 1st PSYOP of the Rhodesian forces has recently implemented Operation Split-Shot – basically the distribution of leaflets to promote fear among the black population. They have graphic images of ZANLA/ZIPRA recruiters forcing Africans into training camps, raping women in front of their children, spreading sexually transmitted diseases and killing defenceless civilians who fail to cooperate with them. The leaflets are telling them that all their worst fears will come to pass if the insurgents get a foothold.'

For these reasons, both the Provincial and District Commissioner's headquarters in Umtali were busy setting up protected villages in the TTLs and distributing brightly coloured stickers to be posted in shops, restaurants, bars and bus terminals, which contained a series of self-censorship slogans including: 'Think About National Security, Don't Talk About it'; 'What You've Said May Blow Up a Truck'; and 'Your Tongue Could Pull a Trigger'.

Jim showed Mathew one of the Ministry's most recently

SOMEONE WISHES TO SPEAK TO YOU

released pamphlets designed to highlight the strength of the Rhodesian security forces and the significant benefits for people living in the protected villages. As its main thrust, it underlined how many thousands of grateful Africans had taken refuge in the newly created defended villages, or lived in communities protected by security forces and the paramilitary wing of the Ministry of Internal Affairs. The leaflet also stated that although the terrorists were well-armed with modern automatic rifles, machine guns of communist manufacture, explosives, grenades and powerful bazookas, they were scared to come into direct contact with the security forces. Instead, they were pursuing 'soft targets' on which to inflict their mayhem.

'One of my civilian friends, a successful businessman whom I met in Salisbury,' said Jim, 'is currently serving as a territorial PSYOP operative in the Fort Victoria Shangaan area of Southern Rhodesia. While he's undertaking military duties, which take up almost six months of the year, he dresses as a civilian and works directly with Africans of the Shinga tribe. During his operations in the *bundu* (bush), usually working with a mixture of African army regulars and civilians, they visit tribal chiefs in order to paint as damaging a political picture of Robert Mugabe as possible. The PYSOP operatives try to convince the quite independent Shinga tribespeople that ZANU is no friend of theirs and stress just how counter-productive it would be if they were to support Mugabe and his political party in the future. During these propaganda missions, they always highlight that the main aim of the Rhodesia Front's government is to seek the most satisfactory solution possible for the future of all citizens of the country, both black and white.'

'Does your friend seem to think the missions are working?' asked Mathew. 'You said yourself the Shinga tribespeople are independent.'

'He's optimistic, but that's not their only objective. These field missions are also an attempt to assess the mood, hearts and minds of the tribal communities, as well as to glean as much information as possible about the sentiments and political views of the chiefs they talk to. Once they return to Salisbury, my friend says they report back to the military command operations in order to amongst other matters guide the security forces on any counter-insurgency measures that they consider may be required.'

Mathew had been so preoccupied with his studies that he had been unaware of much that Jim was explaining to him. He was at the beginning of a very steep learning curve.

Whenever Mathew had driven to the Kinlochs' property or to Salisbury, he always took time to stop at the top of Christmas Pass and pay his respects to the Kingsley Fairbridge Memorial, with its magnificent view over the vale of Umtali. The statue of Fairbridge had been unveiled by Queen Elizabeth, the Queen Mother, in July 1953 in honour of the man who had done so much at the beginning of the century to establish the Child Immigration Society (which was later to bear his name), to help orphaned and underprivileged children from the overcrowded slums of Britain. Over the years, the society had provided training at farm schools for several thousand children who had emigrated to under-populated regions of what was then the British Empire, which included Southern Rhodesia and, to a greater degree, Australia.

With Mathew's very liberal views on life, he could not help admiring how much this South African-born Rhodesian boy, and Oxford Rhodes Scholar, had helped to give a meaningful life to so many children who had, over the past half century, contributed so much to the quality, diversity and development of parts of the British Commonwealth.

In the spring of 1976, Mathew spent a weekend staying with Sir Roger Willock and his delightful, vivacious wife, Devra, whose company he always relished. On the Saturday afternoon, Devra had left the men to their own devices while she visited a friend. The civilized beauty of Sir Roger's flower-filled garden contrasted with the subject that dominated their conversation.

'It seems to me,' said Mathew, 'that since Mozambique's recent independence, the relationship between the European and African populations has deteriorated greatly. The effect the Zimbabwe African National Liberation Army insurgency is having on the morale of the European inhabitants of Umtali and the Manyika tribespeople is incredibly damaging, and getting worse all the time. Chief Chidzikwee seems utterly despondent.'

'As you're relatively new to Rhodesia, let me give you some background information about the events that led up to the UDI,' said Sir Roger. 'You may be surprised; it's not so clear cut as you may imagine. It began when Sir Roy Welensky dissolved the Federal Parliament in the summer of 1962, which led to the break-up of the Federation of Rhodesia and Nyasaland. The liberally minded Prime Minister of Southern Rhodesia, Sir Edgar Whitehead, lost the general election to the newly formed Rhodesian Front party led by Winston Field, with Ian Smith as his deputy. Indeed, when Whitehead lost, Harold Macmillan made a point of saying how "deeply grieved" he felt about the defeat, as Whitehead "had represented, to the best of his power, the more moderate leader of the European politicians, with a tradition of mediation and even of liberalism". When Harold Wilson led the Labour Party to victory in 1964, he was eager that an amicable settlement should be reached in Southern Rhodesia that would represent a satisfactory solution for both the European and African communities. When Ian Smith took over the leadership of the RF party and became Prime Minister of Southern Rhodesia, he was charged by the party to secure the country's independence and to restore order in the African townships. But, at the same time, Harold Wilson made it quite clear to Smith that independence without majority rule was non-negotiable.

'After Nyasaland gained its independence from Britain and became Malawi, Dr Hastings Banda became the country's first president; and when Northern Rhodesia gained its independence from Britain in October of the same year and became Zambia, Kenneth Kaunda became the first president. Whereas the Southern Rhodesians were warned that should its RF Government declare UDI, to expect international sanctions, abandonment, citizenship-stripping, non-recognition and expulsion from the Commonwealth. During the months leading up to the UDI, Harold Wilson was reported to have bent quite far in his attempt to reach a compromise with the man he called "the slippery Ian Smith" and, by doing so, had even risked the resignation of Shirley Williams, Edmond Dell and others from his Cabinet.

'But when UDI was declared on 11 November 1965 and Governor Humphrey Gibbs went through the motions of dismissing Smith and his Cabinet, which were predictably ignored, Wilson immediately recalled Britain's High Commissioner to Southern Rhodesia, John Baines Johnston; and Rhodesia's High Commissioner, Brigadier Andrew Skeen, was declared *persona non grata* and asked to leave Britain. It was also said that six Rhodesians who had been undergoing training at the RMA at the time were given the choice of remaining at Sandhurst and joining the British Army, or to return immediately to Rhodesia, which apparently they all did.

'The day after UDI, the UN Security Council adopted Resolution 216 condemning it as a declaration of independence "made by a racist minority". Although, as far as Ian Smith's RF Government was concerned, as more than ninety per cent of the Rhodesian white electorate had supported UDI, and at the same time were prepared to take up arms in order to secure the country's independence and to combat any interference from the outside, it would lead to the best future for both the European and African communities. The government also hoped that UDI would provide them with sufficient time to work towards a peaceful solution to the current stalemate between the two communities. In fact, the government declared that it would always be its ultimate goal to establish a multi-racial state, which would be of benefit to the African majority as well as to the European minority. But Ian Smith also made it quite clear to the outside world that he would not be rushed headlong into agreeing to majority rule, before his government had decided that the country was politically ready for such a democratically realised settlement.'

Sir Roger paused. 'You may not think this is all relevant to today's situation, but I want you to understand the background to this potential political volcano we're sitting on today. I know your reasons for coming to Rhodesia are apolitical, but I want to give you the facts so you can develop your own informed opinion.'

'I'm surprised to hear that the government declared it their goal to make Rhodesia a multi-racial state,' said Mathew, 'that must at least give us some hope that they are considering the whole population in their decision-making. But let me be the first to admit that my knowledge of the detail is limited, so please go on.'

'Indeed, you may be surprised by other things I have to say – but we'll come to those. The Organisation of African Unity, which included a number of the newly independent African Commonwealth leaders, was led by President Nyerere of Tanzania and President Kaunda in trying to pressurise Harold Wilson to use military force to bring down Ian Smith's illegal Rhodesian régime. Wilson publicly stated that the OAU had no hope of persuading his government to use force. The declaration was reported to have come as no surprise to Ian Smith and his Cabinet – they had already heard through their security channels that as far as Britain's Chiefs of Staff were concerned, any thought of military action would be a nonstarter. You see, that would be quite logical to anyone who understood the intimate and integrated relationship that existed between the British Army and Air Force and the Rhodesian forces, and the great loyalty and dedication which Rhodesia had always shown throughout the Second World War, and more recently during the Malayan Emergency.

'So, it's to Wilson's credit that in spite of the OAU and the African Commonwealth leaders persistently pressing him to supply arms and money, he publicly flatly refused the requests, and was reported to have stated that "All their arguments and blandishments failed to change our minds". So it seemed at the time that Wilson had learned from history not to fall into Sir Anthony Eden's 1956 Suez-style fantasy in thinking that Britain had the military capacity, or the willingness of its forces, to overthrow the Smith régime by military intervention.'

'I heard there were calls for Britain to use military force to bring Rhodesia into line,' said Mathew, 'and that Wilson was being put under pressure to do so, but I didn't think it would happen.'

'I'm telling you this in the strictest of confidence, you understand,' continued Sir Roger, 'but just after UDI had been declared, the British very nearly invaded Rhodesia. For during the months leading up to Ian Smith's declaration of independence from the UK, and in spite of Harold Wilson's aversion to making war on our "kith and kin" in the colony which he referred to as "rebel Rhodesia", the situation did not prevent the defence planners of the Chief of Staff Committee from drawing up contingency plans for invading the Country.'

Sir Roger continued, 'The first file that I was given to read had been marked "U.K. Eyes Only, Top Secret" which recorded that the plan must avoid risks which in other circumstances would be acceptable, and strongly advised the fledgling Wilson government against military intervention, for it said the consequence of failure would be appalling. It also mentioned that the current intelligence assessments did not give any ground for supposing that there would at present be anything but whole-hearted European opposition to any UK force introduced into Rhodesia. It also highlighted that striking the first blow at Rhodesia forces would have the most severe implications, and could well put strain on the loyalty of some of our own units. The report also warned against underestimating the strength of Rhodesia's RRAF, and the capabilities and resilience of Rhodesia's military units.

'In a subsequent Air Ministry report I was given to read prior to my appointment here, it stated that at the end of November 1965 Aden's RAF station Khormaksar had been put on stand-by, all leave stopped, and the 105 Squadron and other flying units put to "immediate readiness". It wasn't until a senior air staff officer addressed the officers to tell them they were going to invade Rhodesia that anyone knew what it was all about.'

Mathew listened intently as Sir Roger went on to tell him the details of the strategy that had been devised for the invasion. The aircraft were not only going to come from Aden, but also from Cyprus and the UK. It was emphasised that this was a top-secret mission and that the plan was for the Argosy Force, comprising of ten aircraft, to depart at fifteen-minute intervals, starting at 0400 hrs, and fly to Nairobi's Eastleigh Airport in Kenya to refuel and then onto Southern Rhodesia to airdrop 1 Para Brigade on the military side of Salisbury's civil airport at New Sarum, as well as on the commercial airport itself. Once the airports had been made secure, for little resistance was expected, the planes were to land, refuel, and return to Nairobi to collect more troops and equipment. The plan had been that once the Argosy Force had completed their mission, returned to Kenya and got their aircraft turned around and refuelled, there was to be a steady stream of more Argosies and Hastings aircraft arriving at Eastleigh until the airport was full to capacity.

According to the confidential report about the raid, the pilots were briefed that if the invasion were to go ahead, they would be departing Nairobi early the following morning, so as to arrive at Salisbury at first light. The idea was then for the Argosies and Hastings to air-drop the Paras onto New Sarum airfield, for the Beverleys to land and unload support hardware, and this to be followed by a stream of Britannias bringing in further reinforcements. The Labour Government's strategy was to carry out a peaceful takeover of the Smith régime.

On 2 December 1965, the senior air staff officer (SASO) told pilots that the invasion was 'on'. The RAF planes all had civil aircraft call signals, which was intended to lull the Rhodesians into thinking that there was just one civil aircraft. It was considered that Rhodesia's Air Traffic Control was not in possession of radar able to detect the huge throng of aircraft flying behind the leader. The report stated that on the flight southwards, the Argosies had been joined by No 41 Squadron's Gloster Javelins, and some of Aden's Flying Wing Hunters, to combat any opposition, for the RAF were aware that the Rhodesian Airforce also had Hawker Hunters.

However, as the 105 Squadron flew southwards at the head of what was probably the largest collection of transport aeroplanes over Kenyan skies since the Second World War, when they reached the boundary of Rhodesian airport control's authority over M'Beya, in Tanzania, they received what subsequently proved to be Rhodesia's *coup d'état*. The Salisbury airport controller asked the leading plane's navigator whether he would like the latest Salisbury weather, and when the reply was to the affirmative, the RAF navigator was given a forecast that could not have been more counter-productive to the invasion plans.

'Whether the airport controller was pulling the wool over their eyes or not in saying that visibility was down to 400 yards,' continued Sir Roger, 'they couldn't risk it as there was no way of checking. If it was correct the RAF couldn't drop paratroopers, as they couldn't see the ground. The invasion was called off at the eleventh hour and the Task

SOMEONE WISHES TO SPEAK TO YOU

Force diverted to Lusaka, over 500 km to the north-west.
'The next morning, the aircrews were very relieved to hear that the mission was to be abandoned. Apparently, although some furious OAU members threatened to sever diplomatic relations with London, it was Wilson's Chiefs of Staff that eventually made him drop any future invasion plans, by telling him how reluctant they would be to go to war against a nation that had fought so bravely at their side throughout the Second World War and during the Malayan Emergency. I saw a subsequent report recording how the majority of those in the Middle East *Argosy* and *Beverley* Squadrons had nothing but the highest regard for Rhodesia's security forces, both black and white, who had always treated them with great courtesy and affection during their many training flights to Rhodesia before the UDI. Many Rhodesians had close relatives in Britain, as well as comrades in the respective armed forces. And it wasn't just an Air Force operation – the Royal Navy were to provide a task force in the Beira Straits to carry additional manpower and military hardware.

'In my view, if the invasion had taken place it would have been absolutely catastrophic, not just for the military but for Rhodesia's civilian population, both black and white. It was very fortunate from the British Government's point of view that the whole operation received no publicity. This unsubstantiated theory that it would be unlikely for it to have experienced any serious opposition could not have been further from reality. The whole operation had not been given adequate thought or preparation, and if it had gone ahead, it would have reflected extremely badly on the British Government, and its armed forces in general.'

'We can only be grateful that sanity prevailed in the end – just think how many lives would have been needlessly lost if it had gone ahead. Well, Sir Roger, you've certainly enlightened me this morning, I can now see the situation in a very different light.'

Taking into consideration what Sir Roger had told him, Mathew could see a justification for the efforts of the RF Government to slow down ZANU/PF's and ZAPU's wish for immediate independence, with one man, one vote elections, in order for them to take over the country's government. Having had the opportunity to talk to so many people, both black and white, over the last year or so, he had become increasingly aware of how some of the country's minority and sub-tribal groups, like his Manyika tribal friends, as well as Rhodesia's European citizens, had become increasingly concerned about their possible alienation by the dominant Shona (and to a lesser extent Matabele) tribal overlords in the future.

That evening, Mathew accompanied the Willocks to a reception at the South African Embassy, at which Sir Roger introduced him to Lieutenant General Keith Coster OBE. Coster, like Sir Roger and his father, had served in North Africa in the Second World War.

After the afternoon's conversation with Sir Roger, Mathew was keen to get an opinion from this wise and highly experienced soldier. 'I've already lost far too many friends, both European and African, through insurgency attacks from across the borders,' he told Mathew gravely. 'I don't know where it's going to end up, but make sure you take the utmost care in the Vumba, don't take your safety for granted.' Mathew was glad to have made the acquaintance of the General; he found him to be a gentleman of considerable integrity and hoped their paths would cross again in the future.

Before Mathew returned to his camp at Castle Beacon, he spent a few days with Simon and Anna Vaughan-Jones, mostly to compare respective vervet monkey observations with Anna. Mathew showed Anna a series of facial mask drawings he had done on his vervet group, which vividly illustrated the elaborate facial signals that individuals use to communicate and when compared with those of his Stairs' monkey family, showed how diverse the signals were. He had rather hoped that he would have the opportunity to meet Jan again, but when Anna told him that she was away staying at the citrus estate that her father managed at Mazoe, he could not help feeling slightly relieved at not being plunged into more emotional turmoil. However, he was still determined to meet her again, in order to find out definitively whether his feelings were reciprocated.

On his return to Castle Beacon, Mathew soon settled back into his field studies. He had also agreed to take tape recordings of the monkey's vocalisations on Anna's behalf. The columns of the *Umtali Post* had begun to record some of the devastating events that were occurring in the newly independent Mozambique. It was reported that the Roman Catholic Church had been driven underground and baptism banned; the country's legal code had been abolished and replaced by military tribunals; an estimated 50,000 people, including 150 Catholic priests, had been incarcerated in concentration camps; and Mozambique's President, Samora Machel, had declared his country to be on a war footing with Rhodesia. After Mathew had read this, he was surprised to learn that Harold Wilson's Labour Government had only recently given £15 million of humanitarian assistance to Mozambique.

A radio broadcast brought some welcome news at the end of April, announcing that Ian Smith was about to bring a number of black ministers into the government, and that this was to include Bishop Muzorewa. Mathew saw this as an encouraging first step toward realising a peaceful political settlement for Rhodesia. This small beacon of hope was completely overshadowed when, on the 16 June, the South African police were reported to have shot at and killed children in the Johannesburg township of Soweto. When an estimated 20,000 high school students in Soweto started a march in support of better education, the police responded to the protest with tear gas and live bullets, which resulted in the killing of 176 of the rioters.

The slaughter immediately gave rise to an international outcry against the killing of children; the UN Security Council passed Resolution 392 which strongly condemned the incident and South Africa's apartheid régime. In South Africa, many white citizens became outraged by their government's actions. Over 300 white students from the University of the Witwatersrand marched through Johannesburg in protest against the killings; black workers went on strike and riots broke out in the black townships of other cities in South Africa. The African National Congress (ANC) exiles called for international action and more sanctions against South Africa, and issued posters calling for the release of Nelson Mandela from imprisonment on Robben Island.

In early July, Mathew received a message via Edgar that his father, Chief Chidzikwee, wished to have another meeting with him and that he would be grateful if he could go with Edgar to his Manyika Tribal Trust Lands at the earliest opportunity. As Edgar emphasised the urgency that his father put on having this one-to-one talk, Mathew agreed to visit the chief on the following Sunday.

Before the meeting, Mathew was aware that due to the increased security measures which had recently been put into operation in the region, he would have to inform both his friend the District Officer, Jim Prior, and the BSAP Superintendent that he had been directly involved with in Umtali since the establishment of his camp in the Vumba. Due to his well-known friendship with the chief and Edgar, Mathew was confident that he would get their written clearance to pass through the various security road blocks and permission to cross into the chief's particular TTL, to which entry had now become restricted to serving members of Rhodesia's security forces.

SOMEONE WISHES TO SPEAK TO YOU

When Mathew and Edgar drove down from the Vumba early on Sunday morning, they passed through three separate road blocks manned by BSAP personnel, who looked at their pass documentation with considerable suspicion. On arriving at a fenced-in guard post by the entrance to the TTL, a young second-lieutenant from the Rhodesia Light Infantry (RLI), backed-up by three African askari's brandishing FN MAG general-purpose machine guns, kept them waiting while he carefully examined their documentation. The young officer asked Mathew the reason for his visit to the chief, then went to his wireless operator to check with his regional commander in Umtali whether or not to allow Mathew's Land Rover access to this military-protected safe zone. The response from the RLI HQ was that they could only spend two hours in the TTL, and therefore would have to return to the same gate of entry by 1300 hrs.

After having driven away from the guard post, Edgar said, 'We're meeting my father at the village of my cousin, Gabriel Nkulu. My father says he wishes to draw as little attention as possible to the fact that he is having a private meeting with a European.'

Mathew guessed that whatever he was about to be told by the chief, it would be important for him to deal with in the most diplomatic fashion, for he recognised only too well how apprehensive and sensitive matters had become between the African and European communities.

Chief Chidzikwee was already waiting in Gabriel's spacious *rondavel*, and greeted Mathew warmly by grasping his hand in his vice-like grip before leading him to the far side of the dwelling, where their conversation would not be overheard. Soon after Mathew was handed a cup of black coffee, both Gabriel and Edgar left so that the chief could talk in complete confidence, which he knew Mathew would respect.

During the next hour and a half, the chief brought Mathew up-to-date with regards to his considerable concern about recent events that had taken place within his TTL.

'Recently ZANU/PF political activists and ZANLA insurgents from across the border have started to exert an increasing amount of pressure, sometimes even intimidatory threats, against any of my tribesmen seen to be cooperating with the country's security forces and Ian Smith's government. I regret to say that some of the younger members of the tribe are so influenced by ZANU/PF's propaganda that without any consultation with the elders, they have decided to cross the border into Mozambique and join the ranks of ZANLA.'

Chief Chidzikwee went on to say that due to the Selous Scouts recently implemented counter-insurgency policy of taking the war to the enemy, a strategy that had been promoted and very much supported by the government's Minister of Defence, P.K. van der Byl, some of the young Manyika tribesmen who had been involved in the fighting had been killed. Also, due to the subsequent success of the Selous Scouts' hot pursuit raids on terrorist forces across the border, the number of these deaths had increased, which had given rise to anti-white feelings among his Manyika tribe.

'You see, Mathew, all the turmoil being caused by this Bush War has made it very difficult for me to be seen to be cooperating with the security forces, or even now to be seen having a private talk with a European. It puts my authority in question. That is why I wanted our meeting to be secret. What I have to say is of the utmost importance. These frequent insurgency attacks from across the border and the growing degree of anti-white sentiments among some of my tribespeople mean that with the utmost regret, I can no longer direct Edgar to keep a watchful eye on the security of your camp, or act as a guarantor of your personal safety in the Vumba. Please listen to me Mathew and take heed – you must close down your research camp and leave the Vumba at the earliest opportunity. Only return if, and when, a peaceful settlement is reached.'

'Thank you for speaking so openly with me, Chief

Chidzikwee. Rest assured I will think carefully about what you've said.'

The two men said their farewells and shook hands for what they both knew could be the last time in the foreseeable future.

Although Mathew was grateful to the chief for expressing such a degree of concern about his safety, he was reluctant at this stage of the terrorist insurgency to heed his advice, for the Vaughan-Joneses were scheduled to visit his camp in early August. During his last stay with them, Anna told him how very keen she was to make some further recordings of the communicative vocalisations of his habituated family group of vervet monkeys, particularly when the monkeys were confronted by a potential predator. She said that should a live predator fail to put in an appearance, Simon had volunteered to bring with them two museum specimens, one of a caracal and the other of a python, in order to stimulate the monkeys' warning responses to the respective marauders. He didn't want to disappoint them unless it was absolutely necessary.

Before Simon and Anna's visit, the press reported what they described as the most audacious and successful raid of the Bush War to date. This had been a raid carried out by the Selous Scouts against Nyadzonya, one of the insurgents' main camps about 80 km east of Umtali.

After news of the raid was broadcast, Jim Prior visited Mathew to bring him the newspaper reports and tell him all he knew. 'Apparently it was thanks to the Selous Scouts having captured and carried out a detailed interrogation of a ZANLA fighter, a "turned" terrorist, that they gained a great deal of invaluable information about the Nyadzonya camp. It was estimated to contain up to around five thousand people, who were all connected with the insurgents and potential terrorists. The ZANLA captive had only recently passed through the camp and was able to provide the Scouts with a detailed description of its layout, command protocols, and the fact that the camp contained military recruits who had been indifferently trained and were largely unarmed. The Selous Scouts Commanding Officer, Lieutenant Colonel Ron Reid-Daly, found that the information the ZANLA captive gave fully endorsed that which he had previously received from his men, who had been monitoring the camp for some time. As Reid-Daly was now sure that the Nyadzonya camp was a major terrorist training and operational centre, he decided that it would have to be put out of action at the earliest opportunity.

'Because of the political process that is currently underway between Ian Smith's RF Government, the British Government and a number of African leaders toward all-party talks in October, the country's Special Operations Committee were reluctant to give their permission for the raid to go ahead. It was only after Reid-Daly made use of his direct confidential line of communication with Lieutenant General Peter Walls, who had personally appointed him to head-up the Selous Scouts, that permission was granted.'

Jim Prior went on to explain that the independent nature of the Selous Scouts' clandestine operations caused a number of major misunderstandings between them and the RLI, as well as between the Special Branch of the Scouts and that of the BSAP. Reid-Daly's direct communication with General Walls was tempered by a degree of professional jealousy and also frequently aggravated by the top-secret nature of the Scouts' operations, and their practice of not wishing to confide in others. Although reconnaissance work represented a prime ingredient of the Selous Scouts' record of success, such achievements were also due to the men's qualifications of physical discipline and single-mindedness of purpose. All these qualities, said Jim, had contributed to the *esprit de corps* of the regiment, and to the total dedication of their chief objective; to destroy the insurgency operations of ZANLA and ZIPRA.

As the raid had to be kept top secret for as long as possible, in order for the operation to come as a total surprise to the ZANLA combatants, their cross-border operation had been put into effect almost immediately. The Scouts were concerned that from their previous reconnaissance recces into Mozambique, there was clear evidence of cooperation between FRELIMO and ZANLA. If ZANLA had full access to the local FRELIMO transport and logistic infrastructure, the secrecy of the raid was imperative.

The Rhodesian vehicles of the Scouts' task force were given FRELIMO number plates and insignia and the manpower disguised in their uniforms, in order for them to be easily accepted as a detachment of the Mozambique security forces. The task force crossed the border along a little-known smuggler's route under the cover of darkness, soon after midnight. At one point they had to pass by a FRELIMO sentry box; the sentry received an authoritative command and greeting from one of the African Manyika Portuguese-speaking Selous Scouts and merely waved a desultory greeting in response.

On approaching the gates of the camp, the convoy had gained access to it after a sharp command delivered in Portuguese by one of the Scouts' Special Branch members, to two startled ZANLA guards, who were quick to lift the boom and salute the vehicles as they roared their way past them.

Once the camouflaged trucks had rolled into camp and come to a halt, the Portuguese-speaking operative, wearing the fatigues of a FRELIMO major, stood up and with the help of a megaphone, delivered a short speech, proclaiming the imminent fall of the illegal régime of the radical leader of the white settlers in Rhodesia. He invited his assembled comrades to gather around for more detailed news about some of ZANLA's glorious successes.

After the major had announced a further day's holiday to the one they had only just had, and the jubilant cheering and ululating crowd had started to move forward and assemble in front of the vehicles, one of the ZANLA operatives noticed a white soldier on one of the vehicles, manning a machine gun. He took a wild shot at him. The task force burst into life, maintaining a steady and disciplined controlled fire which resulted in an estimated death of over 1,000 camp followers, including both women and children.

The official government report on the raid subsequently recorded that the Selous Scouts' column had succeeded in reaching ZANLA's Nyadzonya terrorist camp undetected, and the whole operation had gone like clockwork. The great success of it had done great credit to both the skill of its architects and the brave soldiers, both European and African, who managed to inflict such a significant wound on ZANLA's terrorist forces. Also, the report stated that a small party of the Scouts had successfully destroyed the bridge over the Pungwe River, and had blown up a number of road bridges on their way back. The conclusion was that the whole operation had been a triumph, 'Without a scratch to man or vehicle'.

After Jim had finished giving Mathew as much information he had on the raid, the two men sat in silence for several minutes, each deep in their own thoughts. Finally, Jim got up and bade Mathew goodbye, adding, 'Remember, keep your eyes and ears open. You can always come and stay with me if it starts to feel uncomfortable out here. Take care.'

Although horrified by the raid, Mathew wanted to read as much as possible about it to try to exorcise the anguish that he felt. After Mathew had read all the newspaper reports Jim had brought, he reflected on how the mass killing of so many human beings had taken place just downstream from the tranquil surroundings of Inyanga's Pungwe Falls. He and Addie had spent such a memorable time together relaxing by the Pungwe River close to where its waters plunged over the rapids and into the gorge below, watching the feeding antics of some of the remarkable bird life.

The very thought of such crystal-clear waters having been discoloured and swamped by the blood of the dead and wounded, and the river claiming the lives of so many of those

SOMEONE WISHES TO SPEAK TO YOU

camp followers who had attempted to swim its fast-flowing waters only to drown, could not have been more repugnant to Mathew. It brought home to him that he was living in an environment that had become a focus of terrorist insurgency. The occasional cross-border sorties of the Bush War had turned into an outright conflict between the Rhodesian security forces and the liberation fighters of ZANLA.

Ian Smith was later to record that only about 500 terrorists, and not over 1,000, had been eliminated. He also reported how the success of the Selous Scouts operation against insurgents had reverberated around the world, and how congratulatory messages had been received from far and wide.

Perhaps as a direct result of the Nyadzonya operation – it was certainly almost immediately after the raid – a new phase of terrorist activities by ZANLA and FRELIMO began. From the ridge of mountains that straddled Rhodesia's border with Mozambique, a thirty-minute mortar attack was launched on the southern suburbs of Umtali. The attack concentrated mainly on the suburbs of Greenside, Palmerston and Darlington and, although there were no casualties, it showed that the citizens of Umtali were totally unprepared for this new development. An article in the *Umtali Post* subsequently highlighted accounts of how some residents had stood in their gardens watching what they thought to be a 'display of fireworks', prior to becoming panic-stricken when they realised they were under attack.

The residents of Umtali had to face a steep learning curve with regards to their personal safety and the security of their properties. Mathew attended a meeting organised by Umtali's Civil Defence in order to raise levels of preparedness. Soon after a senior BSAP superintendent called for silence, Mathew experienced for the first time the depth of patriotism that existed among the European community, the 'Spirit of Rhodesia'. The gathering had launched into a spontaneous rendering of 'We Are All Rhodesian', with its chorus:

We're Rhodesians and we'll fight through thick and thin;
We'll keep our land a free land from the enemy coming in.
We will keep them north of the Zambezi till the river's running dry – (Here, the local community had added: And we shall throw the terrorists back into Mozambique and listen to them cry)
This mighty land will prosper, for RHODESIANS NEVER DIE.

Mathew was later to learn that man who wrote the song, Clem Tholet, was Ian Smith's son-in-law and that his composition was being increasingly sung at such meetings. It was almost Rhodesia's unofficial national anthem.

8

Change of Direction

During the latter part of 1976, Rhodesia became the target of Washington's 'shuttle diplomacy', with President Gerald Ford considering that an American-driven solution in Rhodesia would aid his presidential re-election campaign by gaining him additional support from the ethnic minorities. It was his diplomatic troubleshooter, Henry Kissinger, who managed to persuade South Africa's President, John Vorster, to cut supplies of fuel and munitions in the hope of bringing Ian Smith nearer to a negotiated settlement with his African opponents.

In order to encourage the insurgents to arrive at a peaceful solution, Kissinger visited Tanzania and Zambia to assure Julius Nyerere and Kenneth Kaunda that Ian Smith would concede his authority and power after a short but phased transfer period. After Nyerere and Kaunda had sanctioned the plan, Smith was summoned to Pretoria to discuss the agreement with Kissinger and John Vorster. Although Kissinger told Ian Smith that he fully recognised how desperately he wanted the best for his people, and understood why he was fearful of black majority rule, he was emphatic in his belief that the deal on the table would be the best he could expect to receive.

Soon after Ian Smith broadcast details of the Kissinger Agreement to the nation, any hopes that had been mustered from the deal were dashed. Some members of his RF party thought it represented the 'death rites' of the country. Such

CHANGE OF DIRECTION

future negotiations had to be abandoned, for five of the Frontline African leaders had rejected the proposals outright. Due to the collapse of the Kissinger Agreement, Vorster decided to continue with the deliveries of war materials from South Africa, as he was well aware that its failure had been no fault of Ian Smith's government. It was also confirmed that the South African loan of $20 million to Rhodesia's Ministry of Defence, which was previously held back, had now been made available.

Due to the ramifications of this international political debacle, Ian Smith came to recognise that whatever future internal agreements could be arrived at between his government and ZANU/PF and ZAPU, there could be no finality without the approval of the OAU. A final settlement might even have to be sanctioned by their communist supporters in China and Russia.

So, after Mathew had read as much as possible about the political stalemate which had resulted in the majority of Rhodesians, black and white, having to suffer its implications, he was thankful that he was at least able to redirect his mind from the political tragedies that surrounded him to the continuation of his observations on the complex social interactions of monkeys.

When Simon and Anna Vaughan-Jones arrived at the Leopard Rock Hotel with the equipment that Simon had arranged for the museum to supply, Mathew could see that the taxidermist had done an excellent job in making the caracal lynx as lifelike as possible. The lynx looked very much as if it was in the process of stalking its prey. It had been mounted and fixed onto a small trolley, so that it could be pulled out in front of the monkeys as they scampered through the long grass. The 2-metre African python was mounted and prepared in a similar lifelike fashion so that when it was put before the monkeys, it would be sure to cause the maximum amount of alarm, the expression of which Anna had come to record. During their five-day stay at the hotel, the Vaughan-Joneses visited Castle Beacon each day, arriving at the camp soon after the strong rays of the rising sun started to evaporate the early morning dampness of the foliage. After Simon had helped Anna to position the caracal and the python and set up her three high-frequency tape-recorders, they waited for the monkeys to descend from the trees before pulling one of the 'predators' into their midst. The caracal was the first to come out, which succeeded in creating instant pandemonium among the group. There was a crescendo of alarm calls, ideal for Anna's recording. Similarly, when the python was introduced to a group of vervet monkeys, she managed to capture the sound as they screamed their specific alarm calls to warn the remainder of their troop of the presence of a predator.

The vervets appeared to be far more vociferous with their alarm calls than the more reserved and sedate Stairs' monkeys. As soon as one of them spotted either the caracal or the python, it would stand up on its hind legs, bob to and fro and screech its alarm calls, which would be immediately taken up by the rest of the group as they made a rapid escape from the long grass of the clearing and returned to the security of the trees. However, by the final day of Anna and Mathew's observations, although the monkeys still showed various degrees of suspicion at the mounted specimens they continued to run through the tall grass of the clearing to the forest below instead of returning to the safety of the trees. They just hoped that should a live predator put in an appearance, the monkeys would stop this complacency and head for the forest.

(The experiment was a success. Listening to the tapes in her office in Salisbury, Anna could detect the difference between the vervet's alarm calls when confronted by the caracal and the python. At this time, very little observational material on the reaction of primates to predators had been recorded or published.)

CHANGE OF DIRECTION

Simon and Anna invited Mathew to have a farewell dinner at the Leopard Rock Hotel, to thank him for all the help he had given them during their time at his Castle Beacon camp. As he usually led a relatively solitary life, Mathew was thoroughly enjoying the company of friends who shared the same interests as him.

'I remember a paper that was presented at a symposium called "Captive Propagation and Conservation of Primates",' said Mathew. 'Quite fascinating. A Dutch field worker studying chimpanzees in West Africa had filmed a scene in which he pulled a mounted stuffed leopard into their midst. While they all jumped up and down and screamed hysterically at their number one enemy, an alpha male broke off a sturdy branch from a nearby tree, then appeared to use it as a weapon, beating it repeatedly on the ground in front of the predator. As far as I know, chimpanzees have been recorded using tools, such as twigs to poke into the holes of trees to extract termites, but they've never been seen selecting something to protect themselves with. I think that's the first time an anthropoid ape has been seen using an implement for either defence or attack.'

'I've heard about that piece of footage... Oh, Mathew – I've just remembered something. I'm so sorry not to have given it to you before,' Anna said rather sheepishly. 'It sounds awful but to tell you the truth, I'd quite forgotten about it. I just came across it while repacking my equipment! Here, Jan asked me to pass this on.' Anna handed him an envelope.

Mathew was relieved that he was in a dimly lit environment as he felt himself blushing slightly. He just hoped that neither Simon nor Anna noticed his reaction as he tucked the letter into his pocket to read when he was back at his camp.

After the friends had said their farewells and Mathew was driving the short distance back to Castle Beacon, he reflected that in all probability Simon had reminded Anna about the note and insisted that Anna should pass it on to him. On one occasion, while Simon and he had been walking by themselves on one of the mountain paths above the hotel, he had said, 'To tell you the truth Mathew, I can't stand the way Paddy Bushney treats Jan much of the time. It's almost as if he merely regards her as some type of trophy, the consequence of a successful military campaign; one which provided him with the possession of such an obedient, faithful and beautiful young wife. I probably shouldn't be telling you this, but on one of Jan's visits to the museum she told me how very much she hopes that when you next visit Salisbury, she will have the opportunity to meet you again. She told me that she not only very much enjoys your company but would love to have you as a close friend, a confidante. In fact, she almost made me promise to arrange a reunion with you.'

When Mathew opened the envelope, under the light of his hissing paraffin lamp, he found attached to the two-page neatly written letter a colour photograph of Jan with her arms around the neck of a sub-adult cheetah. She was wearing a powder-blue cotton dress that hung loosely over her shapely body and, impulsively, Mathew could not prevent himself from kissing the photograph. The beaming smile on her face seemed to mirror her very happiness in being in the company of such an endearing creature, and she had written on the back of the photograph that while she had her arms around the cheetah and gently stroked and caressed him, he had maintained a continuous purr as if in appreciation of her attention.

Dearest Mathew,
This photograph was taken at the Imire Wildlife Reserve, which I recently visited with my sister, Mariette. It's around 150 km to the east of Salisbury, at Marandellas. Mariette lives nearby with her husband, Willie Smoelke, on a farm that he manages at Macheke. It was thanks

CHANGE OF DIRECTION

to an introduction that Simon and Anna had given me to Norman Travers, the founder of Imire, that I was given the privilege of being introduced to one of his many pets, this young male cheetah that he calls Peter. I mentioned that I am a friend of the British primatologist carrying out post-doctorate studies on the Stairs' monkeys in the Vumba, and Travers told me how very much he would like to be introduced to you. He said that although he had listened to your lecture at the university last year, he was yet to meet you in person.

As Marandellas is on your way up to Salisbury, and my sister's home is in Macheke, I could quite easily revisit Imire to meet up with you again. I would love to have the opportunity to introduce you to Norman Travers.

Mathew, I must admit I'm becoming very concerned about the isolated location that you have chosen to carry out your field studies. I recently overheard my husband speaking to some of his fellow officers about how Manicaland is becoming a terrorist hub, and that as a response to their successful Nyadzonya/ Pungwe raid, the security forces are expecting an increased level of ZANLA insurgency and terrorist attacks from across the Mozambique border.

[She had written the next paragraph in red ink:] For all of your friends' sakes, including mine, I implore you to move to a safer location to carry out your work with primates. I would simply hate any harm to come to you. How I so wish to have the opportunity to meet up with you again.

Please, please take heed of what I say, I implore you.
With greatest affection,
Jan xxx

Mathew found that the photograph of such a happy-looking Jan, and the sentiments expressed in her letter, had an unsettling effect on him rather than a feeling of contentment that she should be so concerned about his welfare. At the same time, he realised from what Anna and Simon had told him about the unhappiness of Jan's marriage, how potentially emotionally explosive it would be if he were to become intimately involved with her in the future. However, in spite of such forebodings, there was no denying that he had experienced 'love at first sight' when he met her. To get to know her was one of his main ambitions; to see if the feelings were mutual and to what degree she would respond to his courtship. In the isolation of the hut that Edgar and Joshua had recently constructed for him, looking once more at Jan's photograph, he could not imagine anything more desirable in the world than to gain her lifetime love and affection.

Less than two weeks after Simon and Anna returned to Salisbury, there was a spate of insurgency attacks on rural communities. Jim Prior told Mathew that the BSAP had found an increased incidence of young collaborators (known locally as *mujibas*) passing information on to ZANLA about troop movements – in some cases also conveying weapons for the insurgents or carrying out small instances of sabotage. Jim had added that at the beginning of the Bush War, local people were only too willing to report insurgents coming across the border. But now these reports had stopped altogether. This could either be down to ZANU/PF's 'reign of terror' on the local tribal communities, or the increased numbers of their fellow Africans being killed by Rhodesia's security forces during their counter-insurgency raids into Mozambique.

Just a few days before Christmas, the press reported that a large group of workers at the Honde Tea Estates in the Eastern Highlands had been brutally bayoneted in front of their families. The terrorists were purported to have told the onlookers that the killings had taken place as a punishment to all people working for the white man, and had given the reason that as their wages were so low, they were better off dead. After the slaughter, the insurgents quickly disappeared and returned across the border to their terrorist camps in Mozambique. Rhodesia's European community, as well as some of the peace-loving Africans, had been greatly shocked, with the Minister of Defence, P.K. van der Byl, stating that it was 'an act of unspeakable brutality'. The UN voted overwhelmingly to tighten sanctions on Rhodesia, and Britain decided to increase its humanitarian aid to Mozambique.

Soon after his return from another enjoyable Christmas and New Year spent with the Kinlochs, Mathew had what turned out to be his last meeting with Edgar and Joshua at his Castle Beacon camp. He found them both very different from the jovial young men he was accustomed to; their broad smiles had been replaced by expressions of solemnity and dejection.

Due to the increased level of intimidation in the villages dotted around the Vumba by the ZANU/PF political activists, and the growing level of insurgency within the Vumba region, the National Parks Department had directed David Montgomery to close down the botanical gardens, board up its buildings, pay off his staff and return to Salisbury at the earliest opportunity. As so many Europeans had already decided to leave the region for their own safety, bringing unemployment upon a large number of Africans, ZANU/PF intimidation within the community had become quite a common occurrence.

'Edgar, what on earth happened to you?' asked Mathew, shocked by the prominent scar over his right eye. Edgar was initially reluctant to tell him, but after a couple of Mathew's lagers he spoke more freely. 'I will agree to tell you, as long as it goes no further. I know I can trust you. It was an activist from ZANU/PF – he attacked me on the way to work and took me to their camp in the forest. First of all, a few of them interrogated me about my friendship with you, the "white-man" living at Castle Beacon. They tried to force me to sign a document stating that "Dr Mathew Duncan is using his time studying the monkeys in the forest just as a front, and is stationed in the Vumba to act as an informer to the security forces". I said I wouldn't sign it – nor would I move the weapons that they asked me to. So they beat me with a truncheon, kicked me and left me in the forest.'

'It distresses me greatly to think that they targeted you because of me. I'm so sorry, Edgar, that our friendship led to you being hurt like this.'

'The leader told me that when I returned to the village, I was to carry a warning to my father. He said that Robert Mugabe expected all members of the Manyika tribe to support the ZANLA freedom fighters in their efforts to overthrow the racist government of Ian Smith. He wanted the Manyika tribesmen to help the insurgents cause as many problems as possible for the Rhodesian security forces while they carry out cross-border raids on their camps in Mozambique. He said we should help because these raids have already accounted for the deaths of so many of our fellow tribesmen.'

Mathew could not have been more thankful to Edgar and Joshua for their help and friendship over the last eighteen months. When it was time for them to leave, speaking in the Manyika dialect that they had taught him in happier times, he promised to make contact with them through Chief Chidzikwee as soon as the political and racial problems in the country could be successfully resolved. As he grasped their hands and patted them both affectionately on their backs, gestures of a sad farewell, he gave each of them an envelope containing some Bank of Rhodesia currency to add to the small retention wage that they would receive from the National Parks Department, to help them to maintain themselves during this uncertain period of unemployment, distrust between races and conflict.

CHANGE OF DIRECTION

Prior to them leaving Castle Beacon, Edgar took the opportunity to speak to Mathew out of earshot of Joshua. 'When they attacked me, I heard the names of three of them. Here – I've written them down.' He passed a scrap of paper to Mathew. 'Two of them work locally, so you must keep out of their way at all costs. Be careful.' Mathew noticed that while his friends were trying to smile as they said goodbye, their eyes were welling with tears. They left his camp to retrace their tracks down the mountain to the botanical gardens, to help David Montgomery close it down for an indefinite period, then to return to their respective 'protected' villages in the TTLs.

Mathew wished that he was in a position to employ Edgar on a regular basis and perhaps take him along to Inyanga. Although, bearing in mind the misery and uncertainty among the African communities that had resulted from the massacre on the Honde Tea Estate, this might have been a very dangerous course of action.

Although Mathew had yet to decide whether he should remain in the Vumba, he had almost completed his field observations on the Stairs' monkeys and the comparative work he had more recently carried out with the vervets. Therefore, if terrorist attacks were to occur in the area (members of the security forces had already warned him that it was very likely to happen), this could well be an appropriate time to close down his camp and leave what could easily become the next hub of insurgency.

During his recent stay with the Kinlochs, the Group Captain had tried to persuade him to transfer his camp to the much safer environment of his orchard estate. He had already offered his home as a future base for Mathew's field studies when Mathew mentioned his interest in carrying out some comparative observations on the social life of the ubiquitous chacma baboons, *Papio ursinus*, which occurred in quite sizeable numbers in the Inyanga National Park. Apart from Addie's regular weekend visits, he lived on his own for the majority of the time and he had said how very much he would enjoy having Mathew as company. 'But if you decide to come to stay with me,' he had told Mathew emphatically, 'I want no more of this Group Captain nonsense – I insist you call me Miles.'

Just over a fortnight after David Montgomery closed the Vumba Botanical Gardens to the public and returned to Salisbury to take up the appointment as senior botanist at the National Parks headquarters, the Leopard Rock Hotel received a direct hit from a terrorist mortar attack. This was successful in setting fire to and destroying the hotel's southernmost wing. The attack had taken place in the early hours of a Sunday morning, and luckily, as it was in the middle of the winter months, few visitors had ventured up into the cold mountain mists of the Vumba. The Osborne-Smiths were away and there were no guests at the hotel at the time of the fire. The assistant manager and his staff were reported to have done an excellent job in managing to contain the fire to the rubble of the southern wing, preventing it from spreading to the heart of the magnificent baronial building. Security personnel had flooded the Vumba by early the following morning. By midday, Mathew received a visit from Jim Prior, accompanied by an RLI major and a BSAP superintendent.

'As D.O. for the Vumba region, I have to request that you vacate the camp and the Vumba Mountains at the earliest opportunity. Due to the increased number of reports of terrorists at large in the area, this should be within the next twenty-four hours. I'm sorry that I have to do this Mathew, but all the other residents of the Vumba have been told to board up, leave their properties and to go to Umtali by tomorrow afternoon.'

'Don't worry, Jim, I know you're only doing your job. I was already thinking that it was time to move on.'

CHANGE OF DIRECTION

'For the time being, Dr Duncan,' said the major, 'the security of the Vumba Mountain region of Manicaland is to come under my jurisdiction. It is therefore to be considered a military zone. The Leopard Rock Hotel has been closed down, to be protected by a contingent of the RLI and, in future, only civilians who are granted prior permission directly from myself will be allowed to return to the Vumba, should they wish to check on their properties.'

The mortar attack on the Leopard Rock Hotel effectively made Mathew's decision for him. He was able to make contact with Miles (as he must now get used to calling him) through a radio connection in the major's jeep, and gladly accepted his offer of accommodation. 'As long as everything goes according to plan,' he told his new host, 'I should arrive at the estate some time tomorrow afternoon. Would you be kind enough to make contact with Sir Roger Willock and the Vaughan-Joneses on my behalf? I should let them know that I'm moving on.'

Mathew was saddened to have to leave the Vumba Mountains at such short notice. It had proved to be an ideal environment for him to have lived in and been a part of for so many months, as well as having been such a productive place to carry out his primate research. Although, as far as his study groups of monkeys were concerned, he was at least relieved to know that unlike those in West Africa where some tribes hunted monkeys for bushmeat, his precious families of Stairs' and vervets were safe from human predation. Primates in this region of Africa had never become a delicacy or found their way into the villagers' 'stew pot', so had not suffered the detrimental effects of the unsustainable West African trade in bushmeat.

Later on in the day, while Mathew was in the process of packing up his few belongings in readiness for his departure the following morning, he received a further visit from the BSAP superintendent. After Mathew organised a mug of tea for them both and they were seated on the two remaining canvas camp chairs, the policeman's attitude suddenly shifted a gear. He had begun in quite a relaxed manner, going over some of the security measures that had just come into force in the Vumba. Then he became quite aggressive and practically interrogated Mathew about his long-standing friendships with Edgar Chidzikwee and Joshua Dombo, as well about his reputed connection with Chief Chidzikwee. He demanded that Mathew told him as much about his relationships with them as possible.

'Now, I've been told that you recently had quite a lengthy meeting with Edgar Chidzikwee and Joshua Dombo at your camp, and that Edgar had a visible wound on his forehead. As the security forces have received a number of reports about small groups of Africans being seen travelling in this region of the Vumba, especially after dark, I want to know exactly what you were told by your two African friends. I want to know whether you consider either of them was either directly or indirectly connected with the terrorist activities of ZANU/PF, or with ZANLA's insurgency, or with the conveyance of military equipment from across the border. We know that you recently had talks with Chief Chidzikwee – did he give any clue as to whether he's sympathetic to the objectives of ZANLA's freedom fighters?'

Although Mathew was anxious to help the policeman, he objected to the way he was being questioned and was determined to keep the long-standing relationship that he had nurtured with his African friends as confidential as possible. 'I can assure you that in no way is either Edgar or Joshua involved with those African insurgents currently carrying out terrorist attacks.' He refrained from telling the superintendent about Edgar's experience at the hands of the ZANU/PF gang. 'As far as I'm concerned, I'm as anxious as my two friends are that having just lost their employment, the present political imbroglio between the races is resolved as quickly and as peacefully as possible.'

CHANGE OF DIRECTION

'Thank you, Dr Duncan, for giving me your assurance that your friends are not in any way involved with the insurgency. Your cooperation is appreciated.' Mathew could not help feeling that the policeman was well aware that he had only been provided with a fraction of the information he was seeking, which no doubt his report on this interview would reflect.

Prior to turning in for his last night at Castle Beacon, Mathew took his time to drink the remains of a bottle of Scotch and to dwell on his time in the Vumba. Eventually, he climbed into the folds of his old faithful double-sized hammock under the canopy of a faded and much repaired mosquito-net, both of which he had purchased with Lucienne in Bukavu.

After turning off the paraffin Primus lamp, Mathew spoke aloud against the background of a nocturnal chorus of amphibians and the continuous sonorous singing of a multiplicity of invertebrates, and prayed that a peaceful and satisfactory settlement for both the European and African citizens of Rhodesia could be arrived at as soon as possible. Since he had arrived in the country in 1974, he had witnessed the escalation of the Bush War and was very much aware of the great suffering that had been experienced on both sides of the political divide between Rhodesia's black and white citizens. He could only hope for a successful future for this priceless gem of what used to be Central Southern Africa's 'bread basket'. Rhodesia was a country that he had come to love.

The following morning, Mathew drove his fully loaded Land Rover down from the Vumba. His journey was interrupted on several occasions by security road blocks. On his arrival in Umtali, he stopped briefly at the veterinary pathology laboratory to collect the last results from the faecal samples he had recently sent, and to thank the assistants for having provided him with so much invaluable information. He then drove to the Umtali Sports Club to have a farewell lunch with Jim Prior. Once he had passed through a police checkpoint at the front gate and entered the club house, he found that the majority of those present were in uniform. It resembled a well-guarded military base rather than a centre for recreation.

During their lunch, Jim updated him on the increased number of terrorist attacks, now coming from different locations across the border. 'The local Africans have had a complete change of attitude. They're not willing to pass on information about the movement of unfamiliar people travelling through their villages, which they used to do readily. As some of my European staff are at present serving their obligatory time with the army's Territorials, all of this has placed untold pressure on the D.O.'s headquarters. I just hope it's resolved soon.'

On their parting, Jim mentioned to Mathew that the BSAP superintendent who had visited his camp on the previous evening had enjoyed talking to him, although he had felt that Mathew did not confide in him as well as he had hoped he might. 'He did say that his talk with you had been at least of some use, as after you gave your opinion that your two African friends were not involved in any way with the ZANLA operatives, you exonerated them from suspicion. In other words, you prevented either of them from been taken into police custody or subsequently facing detention.'

'I can't tell you how relieved I am to hear that,' said Mathew. 'It would have been awful if they'd been arrested as a result of the mere suspicion of a policeman, subjected to a terrible miscarriage of justice.'

'Yes, it's extremely lucky that you were able to vouch for them and that the superintendent took you on your word, or who knows what would have happened. Well, I'm sorry to see you go, old chap – as soon as things are more settled, which I pray will be soon, how about I come to visit you at your new base in Inyanga? Keep in touch, won't you.'

The two men bade their farewells, saddened by this enforced severing of their friendship.

On the outskirts of the city, Mathew called in at Umtali's recently reconstructed museum in order to thank the staff, in particular the botanists, for all the plant and invertebrate identifications they had done on his behalf. He promised to send them reprints of any of his published scientific papers that referred to their findings. After leaving the now-garrisoned city and passing through two further police checkpoints, Mathew stopped at the top of Christmas Pass to have what could possibly be his last sight for quite some time of the wide exposure of Umtali and the breathtaking view of the mountains surrounding it. The view included his much-loved Vumba, and the monkeys that the mountains held so securely within their embrace.

Mathew stood once more by the memorial of the benefactor Kingsley Fairbridge, at the age of twelve, with his African friend Jack and his little dog, Vixen. Here, he reflected on Rhodesia's sad evolution since the statue was unveiled by Queen Elizabeth, the Queen Mother in 1953: how such a progressive country, which had so greatly helped the advancement of both the African and European communities, had now descended (seemingly so irretrievably) into the abyss of political unrest and killings.

After turning off the Salisbury road at Rusape, he was stopped by yet another police checkpoint manned by four African BSAP constables. Mathew's visitor's permit and passport were studied with an exaggerated degree of attention. When they asked him where he was heading for in Inyanga and he told them that he was to be the guest of Group Captain Miles Kinloch, their rather hostile expressions blossomed into smiles. Before a constable raised the boom across the road, they all insisted on shaking him warmly by the hand and wishing him the most enjoyable of visits. (Miles later told Mathew that whenever he was stopped at that particular police checkpoint, he always gave them some money for their families and a sizeable bag of apples to share.)

As Mathew drove up the winding earthen drive to the Kinlochs' homestead, he was met by Huggins and Welensky as they ran around his Land Rover, which they recognised immediately and loudly barked their greetings to him. On hearing the commotion, Miles descended the steps from his front door and before Mathew was allowed to start unloading any of his kit, he was led into the house to share an earlier than usual sundowner with his host. Miles particularly wanted to be told as much as possible about Mathew's recent experiences in the Vumba, in the aftermath of the terrorist mortar attack on the Leopard Rock Hotel.

During dinner later that evening, Mathew's host had to remind him of one important point. 'As this is to become your future base, I want your stay with me to be as pleasant and as informal as possible – so I insist you call me by my Christian name.' Initially, due to Mathew's very conservative upbringing in the UK and the fact that he always had an inherent respect for a gentleman from a previous generation, he had found it difficult to call Addie's father 'Miles', but as his host clearly wasn't going to have it any other way, he soon relaxed into the informality of the situation.

Mathew spent the following day unpacking his kit and arranging some of it in a small outhouse that Miles had given him to use as an office. Here, he was able to place his small library of reference books and diaries, his tape-recorder, camera, binoculars, and other items of equipment that could well be useful if his intended observations on the local troops of chacma baboons proved to be a viable research programme.

'I'm sure you've made the right decision,' said Miles while Mathew took a brief pause from his labours. 'I must say Addie was hugely relieved, it should be so much safer for you here than in the Vumba. Both Sir Roger and Simon Vaughan-Jones called after they heard about the mortar attack

CHANGE OF DIRECTION

on the Leopard Rock Hotel to say how glad they were that you're relocating to Inyanga. The mortar attack got a great deal of coverage in the media, you know. They both said that they will be sending letters to you via Addie – she's due to visit next weekend.'

Mathew spent much of the week before Addie's visit reading as much as possible about the chacma baboons that inhabited the Inyanga area. It was interesting for him to note in the eighth volume of Osman Hill's primate monograph that the chacma was one of the earlier elements of the South African fauna to attract the attention of travellers. In the mid-seventeenth century, van Riedbeck had frequently recorded the presence of chacma baboons in his diaries; they were also mentioned by subsequent travellers in the region during the eighteenth century. Hill described eight sub-species of chacma baboons, of which the Rhodesian sub-species of chacma, *Papio ursinus griseipes*, was first described by R.I. Pocock in 1911 as being distributed to the north of the Limpopo, extending northwards through Rhodesia into southern Zambia.

As troops of chacma baboons were quite a common sight among the rocky *kopjes* of Inyanga, Mathew knew that he would have few problems in locating their favourite daily foraging sights, or the places that they chose to sleep at night. However, what concerned him more than anything else was whether he would be able to habituate a family group to his presence as easily as he had done with his Stairs' and vervet monkeys. The chacmas in this region were frequently shot on sight whenever they entered people's properties or were seen feeding in fruit orchards, so were, on the whole, apprehensive of humans and frequently beat a hasty retreat whenever they came into contact with them. Mathew saw a series of dramatic magazine photographs showing a large, powerful, male baboon defending itself from an attack by two Norfolk terriers, both of which were bleeding quite profusely from the encounter. The pictures well illustrated the length of the baboons' long canines and the ferocity of their characters. This was a species that Mathew could see would require a great deal of time and patience to acclimatise to his presence.

Since the Kinlochs and Mathew had first met Angus Whitton on New Year's Eve, just over a year ago, Angus (who had by now received his majority and was gazetted as a major), had become a good friend of Miles and was quite a regular visitor to the Kinlochs' homestead. Angus was able to keep him up-to-date with security matters, in particular news about any insurgency attacks from across the border. One evening when he joined Mathew and Miles for dinner, he described an incident that at first had appeared to be the consequence of a terrorist attack on the Chavhanga Missionary School. By coincidence, Angus was with a unit of his Rhodesian Signals accompanying a large scale counter-insurgency operation in the area in the early hours of the morning, when they saw flames and clouds of smoke coming from the direction of the school. As the military feared that it had been subjected to another terrorist attack and massacre similar to that which had taken place at the Elim Mission in June 1978, a detachment of RLI and Angus's unit had immediately gone to investigate.

Angus told Mathew and Miles that as they approached the burning school with the utmost caution, with their weapons at the ready, they were all stunned by what they saw. 'Honestly, it was like something out of *The Sound of Music*. Instead of coming across a bunch of terrified, sobbing youngsters, and perhaps some dead bodies, there was a line of girls clad in their dressing gowns and slippers walking in an orderly crocodile fashion around the school's blazing kitchen outhouse, under the supervision of a few determined-looking nuns. They were all enthusiastically singing "Onward Christian Soldiers marching into war; With the cross of Jesus going on before..." It was like something straight out of the pages of the Old Testament – it did great credit to the missionaries who founded the school in the first place!'

CHANGE OF DIRECTION

'So if it wasn't a terrorist attack,' Miles asked, 'what caused the fire?'

'Well, they later established that a cauldron of cooking fat had caught alight after having been left on the kitchen's log-burning stove. Unfortunately, it wasn't seen until it was too late for the cauldron to be removed and the fire to be extinguished. When some burning fat overflowed on the stove, it set the entire kitchen block ablaze, but fortunately none of the girls or the missionary staff was harmed. It makes a pleasant change when things turn out to be nowhere near as bad as you're expecting ... they're usually far worse.'

Another evening when Miles and Mathew were dining alone, Miles was explaining to Mathew how much the annual income of most Rhodesians had plummeted since the tightening-up of the UN trade sanctions and how the Rhodesian pound continued to be devalued by international currency markets. 'Before the sanctions, over two thirds of the apples grown on this estate were exported to Europe, with the majority ending up on the English market. Not any more. Although I still get a small pension from my days in the RAF service and I have shares in a property in Salisbury, I no longer benefit from some of the luxuries that I used to enjoy – the annual holiday in the Cape, a trip back to see the few relations left in the UK – although I still have a very comfortable life.'

'I must admit I was very fortunate in that my grandfather, Sir Reginald Duncan, set up a trust fund for my brother and I so that once we reached our twenty-second birthdays, we would get an annual grant.' Mathew was reluctant to say too much about his own financial situation, but wanted to be open with his host. 'Having the guaranteed income has given me the financial security and the freedom to carry out my post-doctorate primate field studies wherever I wished to do so. As for my brother Sebastian, it's enabled him to be an officer in the Household Brigade and to serve in the Life Guards.'

'You're a fortunate man, Mathew,' said Miles. 'Being free

SOMEONE WISHES TO SPEAK TO YOU

from financial pressures has allowed you to follow your own path. Not many of us can hope for that, although I can't complain, I loved every minute of my time in the RAF, and have never regretted the decision to set up home here in Rhodesia. I wouldn't have had it any other way.'

Mathew's first encounter with a family group of chacma baboons took place only three days after his arrival in Inyanga. He first spotted a troop of about thirty individuals made up of adults, juveniles and infants, the latter either riding like jockeys on their mothers' backs, or hanging like hammocks under their bellies, as the troop ambled across one of the national park's minor earthen tracks. This was in an area particularly renowned for the clusters of impressive dome-like *kopjes* in which large boulders balanced precariously on top of one another, and small trees, shrubs and long grasses gave shade and security to passing animal life. When two of the large, powerful-looking alpha male baboons saw Mathew's Land Rover slowly making its way towards them, they remained behind the rest of the troop as if to act as security guards for their family.

Once Mathew had stopped his vehicle and wound down the window to study the two sentinels through his powerful binoculars, they both uttered a series of short warning barks, which caused the rest of their troop to scatter quickly to the security of the *kopjes*. Mathew had read that baboons have quite a varied vocabulary spanning from short warning coughs, grunting sounds, frenzied screams and squeals when alarmed, to soft, chattering noises of pleasure. They were recognised to be extremely powerful members of the monkey kingdom, and with their long, somewhat square-jawed, dog-like muzzle, were known to be frequently quick-tempered, chastising very freely any younger member of their troop that had the misfortune of getting in their way.

CHANGE OF DIRECTION

While Mathew continued to make notes on the grizzly, olive-yellowish colour of the body of the male he was viewing through his binoculars, without a hint of any warning it rushed at his drivers' side door, screaming as it did so. Mathew was fortunate to have reacted as quickly as he did, managing to wind up his window in time to avoid being bitten. When the irate baboon failed in its surprise attack, it jumped onto the Land Rover's bonnet bark-coughing loudly, and after being joined by an accomplice, managed to tear off one of the vehicle's windscreen wipers.

Mathew's reaction to this hostile reception was to immediately 'rev up' the Land Rover's engine and, with his hand on the horn, to accelerate as quickly as possible away from the scene. This resulted in the baboons sliding off the bonnet onto the ground, although when Mathew looked into his rear-view mirror to see what had happened to them, he couldn't help being amused to see the two large males squabbling over the windscreen wiper trophy that had been so unceremoniously wrenched from his vehicle. His plan to habituate the group and make a study of them wasn't going to happen overnight.

Mathew was very much looking forward to the following afternoon, when Addie was due to arrive for the weekend. Not only would it be good to see his close friend and confidante again, for they hadn't had the chance to meet for some time, but she had said on the phone that she would be bringing with her a number of letters, including those from the Willocks and the Vaughan-Joneses. She also mentioned that Anna had given her a sizeable package of correspondence that she had just collected from his personal Causeway post office box number in Salisbury. Early on in his friendship with the Vaughan-Joneses, Mathew had given Anna the authority to collect this post office box mail on his behalf. During the last two years, whenever Mathew was unable to get up to Salisbury at regular intervals, Anna kindly collected any correspondence that she found in his post office box and

SOMEONE WISHES TO SPEAK TO YOU

sent it to him in a registered package, care of the Osborne-Smiths at the Leopard Rock Hotel.

As soon as Huggins and Welensky saw Addie's car pulling up in front of the homestead, there was the usual frenzy of excitable barks. After she had patted and hugged them both, she greeted her father with a similar degree of affection. Seeing Mathew walking towards her from the shade of a large mop-head acacia, she warmly kissed him on both cheeks. After the houseboy, Moses, had carried her suitcase to her room and she had taken a shower to freshen up, Addie returned to the fly-screened veranda in time for a sundowner. She gave Mathew the letters and the package.

Mathew was reluctant to open any of his mail while enjoying his whisky and soda, being brought up-to-date about how everything was going in Salisbury and whether the escalation of the Bush War was causing any additional problems in the capital. His reluctance had to be put aside after Addie mentioned that when Simon had come round to her office to give her his letter, he told her that it contained, as far as he was concerned, a most important and exciting offer which required a response at the earliest opportunity. Mathew had no alternative but to open the envelope in front of his hosts; after scanning through its three pages quickly, and then returning to read one part of it more carefully, he stood up to make an announcement. 'Well, it seems that the University of Rhodesia have offered me a position as a Visiting Senior Lecturer at the university's Department of Zoology. I think I may have to accept!' The sundowner glasses were quickly refilled and clinked together, and father and daughter proposed their individual toasts of congratulations to their guest.

After the most convivial of evenings, Mathew recognised that through the excitement of the university offer, he had drunk too much. But when he returned to his room carrying the rest of his as yet unopened mail, he was determined to have a cursory look through before turning in for the night.

CHANGE OF DIRECTION

The letter from Sir Roger and Devra Willock said how very pleased they were to have learnt from Addie that he had now transferred his base from the Vumba to her father's orchard estate in Inyanga. Also, as Sir Roger had heard that the terrorist attack on the Leopard Rock Hotel had been covered in the UK press, he had already cabled Mathew's parents to let them know that their son was safe and sound and had now moved to another much safer location. The Willocks had ended their joint letter by saying how very much they looked forward to Mathew's next visit to Salisbury, when they hoped that he would take the opportunity to stay with them once again. They were both very keen to hear about his recent experiences in the Vumba Mountains.

The package of letters that Anna had collected from his post office box, some of which had been there for some time, comprised of a good cross-section of correspondence from his parents and brother, from Antonia Clinton-Kemp, from some of his old school friends in England, a few from his university friends in Atlanta, and a long letter from Osman and Yvonne Hill. But it was an envelope with a postal cancellation stamp from Washington DC, written in Lucienne's elaborate hand, which gave him the greatest surprise. Although he knew that her letter was in response to the one he had posted to her just over a year ago, mailed as she had requested to her old Atlanta address, he had not expected to receive any response from her.

Dearest Mathew,
I hope this letter finds you well. I'm writing to give you the exciting news that Daniel has just been promoted, and later on in the year is to take up the appointment as Cultural Secretary to the US Embassy in Lusaka. I'm hoping to join him as soon as the US State Department's administrative authorities consider Zambia to be safe enough for me, our baby daughter Polly and adopted son, Marcus.

I very much hope that once we are settled there, we can arrange to meet. That is, of course, if Ian Smith's illegal regime will allow you to travel to Lusaka across Rhodesia's war-torn border with Zambia. Daniel recently told me that what he calls the freedom fighters' Bush War has effectively come to the border of Zambia and Rhodesia, so the conflict now extends some 600 miles from the Zambezi River in the north to the Limpopo River in the south. I hope you're being careful to keep out of danger.

I'll contact you once we arrive in Zambia so that we can make arrangements. It goes without saying that I can't wait to see you again, and I so look forward to introducing you to Daniel and the children.

Until then, dear Mathew, take care.

Lucienne xxx

Lucienne and Daniel had often thought about what the most appropriate age would be to inform Marcus that she was indeed his real mother, but Daniel was not his father, although he had adopted him as his son prior to Polly's birth.

Lucienne also often weighed up the pros and cons of letting Mathew know that back in 1973, the abortion had not after all been carried out and that Marcus, whom she considered would undoubtedly develop into a fine, handsome young man, was the product of their own very first intense love affair. As such, he was a love-child whose life would always have to be both celebrated and cherished.

9

An Imire Rendezvous

Professor Tom Martin was a charismatic, highly motivated academic and a native of South Africa. He had studied at the Department of Zoology and Entomology at the University of Pretoria, where he had gained his BSc (Zoology) and MSc (Ecology), before embarking upon his detailed study of acarology for his doctorate thesis. During two years of research for his PhD, he had undertaken exhaustive field work studying ticks in the Transvaal and north-western Rhodesia.

The professor had seen Mathew's presentation at the university the previous year and had been very impressed with his enthusiasm, depth of knowledge and communicate skills. He began the meeting by giving Mathew an overview of his responsibilities as Senior Visiting Lecturer.

'It's a great opportunity, Professor Martin. I'm really looking forward to working in the academic world again.'

'For a start, you must call me Tom. Now, let me fill you in on the details of the position. Your first tutorial on the subject of animal communication will be during the first week of the forthcoming autumn term. In addition to your wages, the university will provide you with the use of a small flat on the campus if required, and an office within the department. I don't know whether you've made any arrangements but when I first discussed the potential of you taking a post here with Dr Vaughan-Jones – Simon – he did say that he and Anna very much hoped that you would accept their invitation to lodge with them.'

After asking Tom Martin a comprehensive list of questions about his position, the department and the university, the productive meeting came to an end and a very up-beat Mathew left for Salisbury to have lunch with Addie at the Meikles Hotel.

'The initial contract is for a year, and I start in four months' time,' he told her. 'I'm happy to be returning to academic life – but if it's still convenient for you and your father, I'm still keen to keep my base at your home in Inyanga in the meantime. I want to take the opportunity to carry out a preliminary study of the chacma baboons. Though, of course, that's completely dependent on whether I can sufficiently habituate a baboon family to tolerate my presence. They don't seem particularly keen on having me around at the moment.'

'In that case Mathew, they don't know what they're missing. Of course we would love to have you – I'll call Daddy later and tell him the good news. Now, I must get back to work or they'll be sending out a search party. I'll see you back in Inyanga.' Addie gave Mathew the customary light farewell kiss on the cheek before rushing out of the door.

Soon after Mathew had accepted Tom Martin's offer of a post, he was contacted by the President of the Zoological Society of Rhodesia to ask him if he would be willing to present a talk to its members on his views about the society's ambition to establish a zoo in Salisbury. After accepting the invitation, he was taken to the large, picturesque Graniteside site. There were a series of flooded quarries where the Zoological Society considered some natural environments could be developed and Rhodesia's first national zoo could be established. As Mathew knew little about zoos, other than remembering how saddened he had been to see the chimpanzees in cramped cages at the Lubumbashi Zoo, he asked Simon what his views were, and those of his Museum Board of

Governors. Their collective viewpoint was that they would support the zoo's establishment, providing it could be used as an educational resource.

Before Mathew prepared his talk, he tried to reconcile his thoughts about animals being taken from their natural habitats into a captive and controlled environment. However, after reading a recently published book, *The Stationary Ark* by Gerald Durrell, which recorded the work of his Jersey Wildlife Preservation Trust, he had become more aware of how in recent years many of the world's more conservation-minded zoos had changed significantly from museum collections of exotic species to important centres of education, research and conservation.

Mathew composed a presentation emphasising that although the country had an abundance of wild animals, the bulk of the urban population, especially Africans, had little or no opportunity to see them in the wild. He came to the conclusion that the development of a zoo at Graniteside, to exhibit only indigenous species in as naturalistic surroundings as possible, could be an effective way of helping people to realise the importance and urgency of conservation.

After he had given the lecture at the university, the President of the Zoological Society approached Mathew to congratulate him. 'Well done – your address was very well received. You raised some very valuable points. There seems to be a default rejection of zoos in so many people's eyes. Your words have really helped some members of the public to become more aware of the role of a modern zoo, so that they're no longer in opposition to the planning permission being granted for a zoo here in Salisbury. Apart from my work here, I'm also the editor-in-chief of the *Rhodesia Science News* – I don't suppose you would write us an article setting out the arguments that you made today?'

* * *

SOMEONE WISHES TO SPEAK TO YOU

As Mathew had promised the Willocks that the next time he visited Salisbury he would spend at least one night with them, he accepted the invitation to be their guest on the Friday night. He arranged to stay with the Vaughan-Joneses for the rest of the weekend, before returning to Inyanga on Monday. The Willocks had arranged a small dinner party but before he joined the other guests, Mathew telephoned his parents in Yorkshire and his brother in Northern Ireland. They had all read about the mortar attack on the Leopard Rock Hotel in the British press, and were very relieved to hear that he had moved to a much safer environment. Since Mathew's arrival in Rhodesia four years previously, he had only returned to Hartington Hall for a brief visit in 1976. He promised his parents that he would arrange another visit in mid-September before starting at the university.

Michael Lamb and his charming wife, Denise, were among the guests at the dinner party. Before going into dinner, Mathew was introduced to a Major Piet Erasmus who had recently taken up the post of military attaché to the South African Embassy in Salisbury. As had become commonplace at such social occasions, the majority of the conversation centred around the current political situation within Rhodesia, the Bush War and the damaging effect that the UN sanctions were having on the country. During one of these conversations, Mathew heard the unwelcome news from Sir Roger that in March, Cuban troops had marched into Zaire's Katanga Province after fighting with UNITA forces in southern Angola. Mathew could not help worrying whether Zaire's internal problems would escalate to Kivu Province, and thereby affect the security and welfare of his beloved eastern lowland gorilla population in the Kahuzi-Biega National Park.

'Because of the presence of Cuban troops just across Zambia's northern border,' explained Sir Roger, 'P.K. van der Byl has found an unlikely ally in Kenneth Kaunda, who referred to the Soviet-surrogate presence on his border as "a tiger with its marauding cubs". The British Government is troubled about Fidel Castro and Soviet President Podgorny's tour of Southern Africa, and about Russia's increased support of Robert Mugabe and his ZANU/PF party, as well as their increased supply of arms to the ZANLA freedom fighters in Mozambique. On top of all that, Britain's Foreign Office is having to deal with the aftermath of Idi Amin's ousting of Milton Obote, in Uganda. The latest figures estimate that more than 90,000 Africans have been killed in the ongoing genocide – worse still, if that's possible, is that reports suggest Idi Amin participated personally in some of the slaughter.'

The conversation switched to the subject of Ian Smith seeking an internal settlement after the abandonment of the Geneva Conference proposals, a strategy that Piet Erasmus said his Pretoria Government had just given its full backing. Also, Mathew was pleased to learn that Smith's government had recently announced the excellent news that the Land Tenure Act, which segregated certain areas of the country on racial lines, was soon to be scrapped.

'I wholeheartedly welcome Ian Smith's statement that his government is irrevocably committed to majority rule,' said Sir Roger. 'The British Government has been striving for this since the break-up of the Federation in the early 1960s. The problem is that Smith's timetable for Rhodesia's African majority to achieve political franchise is very much slower than the British Commonwealth is demanding, or will accept. I'm sorry to say that in my view, the current political impasse is still irrevocable.'

At the end of the dinner, when the female guests left the table to leave the men to enjoy their cigars and some Cockburn's vintage port which Sir Roger had brought out from England, Mathew could not help feeling that both Michael Lamb and Piet Erasmus had started to quiz him too deeply about his Manyika tribal friends and, in particular, about his friendship with Chief Chidzikwee. Although he would have been happy to talk about his relationship with his African friends, it appeared that they required the type of information that could have been of interest to international intelligence agencies or the security forces.

It was obvious from the type of direct questions that Major Erasmus was asking Mathew that his main interest was whether he had any information about the movement of African National Congress (ANC) activists from across the border, and whether he had any evidence that ANC activists had joined forces with the ZANLA insurgents. 'The South African Embassy has known for a number of years that the ANC have been directly involved with the forces of FRELIMO,' Erasmus explained, 'but has only recently become aware that some of its more terrorist elements have joined forces with ZANLA. What's more, from some of the reports that South Africa's Bureau of State Security (BOSS) have received, it's evident that ZANLA operatives have been assisting the infiltration of ANC activists from across Rhodesia's border into the Northern Transvaal.' Mathew resented the feeling that he was yet again being interrogated, and chose his words extremely carefully.

Sir Roger said how much he was saddened by the unsubstantiated reports by the BBC and the *Observer* newspaper that the Rhodesian Army had been responsible for the murder of seven Catholic missionaries at Musami Mission, which had subsequently proved to have had no credibility whatsoever. 'In all probability, the report was the product of ZANU/PF's propaganda machine in order to keep the name of the supposedly still-practising Roman Catholic, Robert Mugabe, as snow-white as possible. But mud sticks, it's a bad mistake to make.'

Once the guests had been reunited in the spacious drawing room, the conversation became less politically dominated. The ebullient Devra Willock was always keen to talk about something less controversial and, for that evening, she had chosen to discuss one of her favourite subjects; gardening. 'What do you consider is the best variety of annuals to plant in the garden during the dry season?' she asked her guests. 'I'm very much looking forward to October, when the purple mist of the jacaranda trees appears to envelop almost every main street in the city. It's so beautiful, I would think it's almost worth a special visit to Salisbury for people who have never seen it.' Although it seemed a strange contrast to the talk of killing and hatred, Mathew was relieved to be out of the spotlight.

Later on in the evening, when all the guests had departed, Sir Roger apologised to Mathew about what he considered to have been the tactless and undiplomatic questions that Major Erasmus had directed at him. 'I wouldn't be at all surprised if once the South African Embassy knew that you were going to be one of the guests, Erasmus was told to glean as much information as possible, particularly about the cross-border movements of Africans from Mozambique and South Africa.'

'Don't apologise, Sir Roger. It's not your fault. It's bound to happen, in fact I'm getting quite used to it, although being interrogated is not my idea of enjoyable after-dinner conversation.' As was always the case when Mathew was queried about his various relationships with the indigenous African population, he had been careful to confine his responses (probably to the frustration of those querying him), to speaking about the friendliness of the tribal people that he had been fortunate enough to meet. He also mentioned how much he enjoyed learning the Manyika dialect, which had enabled him to talk to Africans who couldn't speak English.

On the Saturday morning, Mathew joined Simon and Anna at the Victoria Museum, where Anna was observing her family group of vervet monkeys. One of them had just given birth to its fourth infant.

'I've just received a very welcome letter from the editor of the *International Journal of Primatology*,' Anna told Mathew. 'He expressed an interest that I should submit a paper on my behavioural research work. He particularly wants me to highlight the comparisons in the social behaviour of my captive colony with that of a habituated family group in their natural environment, which – very much thanks to you – I've been able to study at Castle Beacon. As you've helped me so much, would you be willing to co-author the paper?'

Mathew was only too happy to agree to Anna's request, as he knew that to be the senior author of a published paper in a well known peer-reviewed journal would represent a significant addition to her list of publications. By the end of the academic year, Anna, as an external graduate of the University of Pretoria, was due to complete the MSc degree examinations that she had been working so hard towards.

'I've just received an invitation from Paddy Bushney to a *braai* at their house this evening,' Simon told Mathew over a quick lunch at the museum. 'After I told him that we had our friend, Dr Mathew Duncan, staying for the weekend, he said that we were to bring you along – he said he's already heard something about the "doctor scientist" from his wife, and would be pleased to meet you, so I've accepted the invitation on all of our behalf. I hope that's all right with you. He said most of the guests will be commissioned and non-commissioned officers from the Selous Scouts and the RLI. They're just back from a successful raid on a terrorist camp. He's hosting it for the NCOs, as they wouldn't be allowed to celebrate in the Officers' Mess – which does seem rather unfair, after the part they played in the operation.'

Although the raid on a terrorist camp close to the Mozambiquan town of Mapai had greatly raised the morale of all those involved in fighting Rhodesia's terrorist insurgency, it had drawn widespread international condemnation. The US State Department referred to it as a ploy to draw Cuban troops across the border into Zambia from Zaire, in order to create the suggestion that they might become directly involved in Rhodesia's Bush War. The raid also led Jimmy Carter to warn white Rhodesians not to expect to be rescued by American troops, and for the British Foreign Secretary, David Owen, to ask Parliament to send British troops to Rhodesia to overthrow the Smith regime. This was, of course, a strategy that the government was reluctant to adopt. The Rhodesian Government's response to such international criticism was to issue a statement that the country's security forces' only intention had been to protect its citizens, both black and white, from the ongoing terrorist activities of ZANLA.

When the time came for them to walk to the Bushneys' home, Mathew felt very apprehensive about meeting the husband of the woman he had fallen so much in love with. He was nervous about seeing Jan in such a military environment, for whenever he reflected on their first meeting, and how instantly besotted he had become, he had in his mind an almost unimpeachable image of her. Whereas Winston Churchill was purported to have once suggested love to be the most important force in the world, Mathew found that such strong feelings had an unsettling effect on him, rather than anything pleasurable.

When they arrived, there were over forty people gathered on the lawn in front of the spacious veranda. The carcass of a bush pig slowly turned on a spit, above the intense heat of the embers on a sizeable barbecue. The majority of the guests were men and in typical Rhodesian fashion, they were congregated in close proximity to a long table from which the drinks were being served, swigging their beer from bottles. The women were dotted about in small groups across the lawn, some distance away from their respective partners.

Simon introduced Mathew to Major Paddy Bushney, who

took his hand in a grip so firm it was as if he wanted to crush every finger within its grasp. 'Welcome to our home, Mathew. I'm very pleased to meet you. My wife has already told me what an interesting person you are.'

'Thank you, Major Bushney,' said Mathew, doing his best not to flinch. 'It's very kind of you to ask me along.'

Bushney said that he had laughed when Jan had told him, in her rather Afrikaans accent, that prior to coming to Rhodesia he had studied guerillas, and not gorillas, in Zaire.

'I sincerely hope you've been able to avoid becoming mixed up in the Rhodesia's internal politics,' said Bushney, 'or anything to do with the Bush War. These are troubled times.' (He had been informed by the Special Security Branch of the Selous Scouts that Mathew was a liberal-thinking friend of the UK's Senior Representative in Salisbury.)

'It's always been my policy to keep well away from internal differences of opinion and conflict in a country that's been agreeable enough to grant me permission to continue with my academic studies. I try to keep up with what's going on, but I never get involved.'

With a smile, Bushney summoned an African civilian batman to bring some drinks over to them.

'Well, I hope you all enjoy the party.' He added, as somewhat of a passing shot, 'I find it most regrettable that after having served with many delightful British servicemen in the Malayan Emergency – at the time I always referred to Great Britain as Rhodesia's "mother country" – these loyal subjects have now been tragically deserted.'

The first sight that Mathew had of Jan was as she was speaking to a small group of women close to the veranda. It was some twenty minutes before she approached Mathew and the Vaughan-Joneses. After embracing Simon and Anna, she rather shyly touched his cheeks gently with her lips, and said how pleased she was that he had been able to come to her husband's celebratory party. Mathew was alarmed to see

AN IMIRE RENDEZVOUS

how dejected Jan seemed, and distressed that she left their company almost as quickly as she had arrived, which he only hoped she was reluctant to do. Playing the role of hostess, she moved on to speak to a small group of women who had been abandoned by their macho partners. The men remained gathered around the drinks table, no doubt boasting about their recent accomplishments.

During the course of the evening, Mathew found himself feeling increasingly uncomfortable in conversation with some of Bushney's military colleagues. For, as more Castle lager was consumed, the group of officers and NCOs he was talking to started to boast about how many terrorists they had personally managed to account for during the Nyadzonya/Pungwe and Mapai anti-terrorist raids. The conversations reminded Mathew of those that would follow a successful grouse shoot after the Glorious Twelfth, with the guns boasting amongst themselves about how many birds they had managed to bag.

However, it was obvious to Mathew how much Paddy Bushney was respected by both European and African members of the military. He had an unorthodox and fearless leadership style; he always led by example by frequently placing himself in the most dangerous of situations when leading a counter-insurgency raid on ZANLA's terrorist operatives. Mathew had assumed that Bushney would be racist in his attitude toward Africans, but was interested to learn from his colleagues how he fully supported Colonel Reid-Daly's concept of introducing and promoting black special force personnel to the rank of a commissioned officer. As a result of this policy, the Selous Scouts could claim that nowhere in the armed forces was integration quite so comprehensive as it was within its ranks.

It was a conversation between a 2nd Lieutenant and a couple of NCOs that particularly concerned Mathew, for it highlighted the degree of hatred that so many of the military had toward ZANLA and its associate activists in ZANU/PF and ZIPRA. 'I'd be only too happy to assassinate Robert Mugabe,' said the lieutenant. 'As far as I'm concerned, Mugabe and his terrorist thugs have already demonstrated the various degrees of ruthlessness and savagery that they're prepared to sink to in their attempt to overthrow the Smith regime and become the country's next elected government. As far as I'm concerned, this attempt has to be stopped by any means currently available to the country's security forces.'

Simon, Anna and Mathew enjoyed generous portions of roasted bush pig, along with all the trimmings, washed down by some agreeable South African red burgundy from the Alphen vineyards in Constantia. Just after 11 p.m. they decided that the time had come for them to leave the party. While crossing the lawn to say goodbye to their hosts, they saw some of the fun-loving guests starting to play one of their favourite party games, known as 'Pass the Bottle'.

This involved men and women forming a tight circle and passing a beer bottle to one another by wedging it between their knees, until one of them allowed the bottle to fall, after which they had to leave the circle. It was customary for the winner of the contest to be presented with the beer bottle as a trophy and for its label to be dutifully signed by all of the contestants, which would frequently include some very ribald and thought-provokingly intimate comments.

Soon after a number of the more riotous guests had started to sing loudly, in true rugby club fashion, some of their favourite songs such as 'Comrade in Arms', 'Hold Him Down, You Zulu Warrior' and Clem Tholet's 'We Are All Rhodesians', some of the Rhodesian-born soldiers changed the words in the chorus of the traditional Afrikaans folk song, 'Sarie Marais' from: 'Oh take me back to the old Transvaal to my sweetheart Sarie Marais' to 'There's twenty thousand bastards in the old Transvaal thanks to the efforts of Sarie Marais'. As soon as they started to repeat their version of the chorus, a small fight broke out in the corner of the garden between a few

AN IMIRE RENDEZVOUS

inebriated South African-born NCOs with their Rhodesian-born counterparts. A thunderous command in Afrikaans, issued from the steps of the veranda by Paddy Bushney, restored immediate order to the party, but had such a stifling effect on the possibility of any further merriment that it signalled an end to the evening's festivities.

Bushney was quick to retire into his house with some of his closest Selous Scouts regimental friends and to leave his henchmen to bid farewell to those that had started to dwindle away from the floodlit lawn. Just as the Vaughan-Joneses and Mathew reached the drive, Jan suddenly joined them from out of the shadows, this time looking far more relaxed than she had done earlier in the evening.

'I'm so sorry for the way they behaved towards the end,' she said. 'That's what usually happens I'm afraid, when you get a large group of the military at a party together.'

Although Jan's deep-blue eyes no longer had the star-like sparkle to them that Mathew clearly recalled from their first meeting in the grounds of the museum, and her face did not portray that most attractive and beseeching of smiles, he still considered her to be the most desirable person he could ever meet.

While Jan was wishing them goodnight, she stood with her back to a tall eucalyptus tree and kept looking rather nervously in the direction of her house, as if she was worried that she was being observed by her husband, who was well known by his peers to have a highly possessive disposition. As Mathew sensed the uneasiness of the situation and recognised that her formality towards him was in all probability due to the nearby presence of her jealous husband, he decided not to attempt to kiss her goodbye but rather to just gently squeeze her hand. She immediately responded with a similar gesture of affection. However, as she did so, she managed to slip a small envelope into his grasp, which he quickly slipped into his trouser pocket without anyone noticing.

SOMEONE WISHES TO SPEAK TO YOU

Before turning in for the night, Simon offered Mathew a nightcap. After Anna went to bed, they stayed up until the early hours talking about the various goings-on at Paddy Bushney's party, whereby Simon provided Mathew with some more information about Bushney's military background. During the time of the Federation of Rhodesia and Nyasaland (FR&N) he had served as a 2nd Lieutenant in the Rhodesian African Rifles (RAR), which comprised black soldiers and non-commissioned officers, and was commanded by white officers. During 1956 and 1957, he had served with the RAR as a contingent of the British Commonwealth armed forces in the Malayan Emergency campaign, a long-standing conflict between the government and the Malayan National Liberation Army (MNLA), the military arm of the country's Communist Party.

Although both Bushney and his now commanding officer, Lieutenant-Colonel Ron Reid-Daly, had served in Malaya at the same time, the then Sergeant Reid-Daly had been seconded into C Squadron of Britain's SAS regiment so their military paths had not crossed. On Bushney's return from Malaya, he was posted to the Rhodesia and Nyasaland Staff Corps (R&NSC) and after UDI he had served in the Rhodesia Light Infantry (RLI) until the outbreak of the Bush War. Due to the reputation he had gained during his counter-insurgency operations in Malaya and his much-respected leadership skills, the newly appointed commanding officer of the recently formed Selous Scouts appointed him to be his second in command, with the operational rank of major.

'I'm telling you this in confidence,' said Simon, 'but Jan has told Anna that as the Selous Scouts' counter-insurgency activities have become more intensive, she seldom sees her husband in a relaxed state. She said that when he comes home from an operation, he's often been very insensitive and rough and, on some occasions after he's been drinking, she's become quite scared of him.' Mathew only wished that he were in a position to act as a 'knight in shining armour'; to rush to her house, gather her up in his arms and whisk her away from such unhappiness.

When he returned to his bedroom, he opened the small envelope that Jan had furtively slipped into his hand. He could not have been happier to read the words written in her small, neat handwriting.

Dearest Mathew,
Ever since I first met you, almost two years ago, I've been praying for the chance for us to meet in private. I've dreamt about being alone with you, I know we have so much in common and I realised some time ago that you feel the same way.

It's getting worse every time my husband returns from a counter-insurgency operation. I hate hearing about how many people he's killed – he often goes into horrific detail.

I only wish that I could find a way to escape from this unhappy existence, living with a husband that I no longer love, who frankly scares me at times. If it wasn't for Anna's friendship and support, I would by now have left to seek refuge with my uncle and aunt who live across the border at Louis Trichardt, in the Northern Transvaal. Should things get any worse between Paddy and myself, I may well go anyway.

Every two to three weeks, Paddy allows me to spend the weekend with my sister Mariette, at the farm my brother-in-law manages at Macheke. As you know, Macheke is on the Umtali side of Marandellas, near to where Norman Travers has his Imire game farm, where the photograph of the cheetah was taken. I'm sure that we could arrange a meeting with each other at Imire, without causing any suspicion.

Jan had signed off her letter with the signs for a hug and

two kisses, with a P.S. that said should her marital problems deteriorate any further, she would hate to have to leave Rhodesia without having the chance to talk alone with him again. At the bottom of the page, Jan had written her sister's address and telephone number, and mentioned that in three weekends' time she would be spending all day on the Saturday at Imire and beseeched him to meet her there. She asked him to contact Mariette to confirm whether he would be able to come.

Prior to getting into bed that night, Mathew found the picture of Jan with the cheetah and kissed it. He had already made up his mind that in spite of the potential complications involved in agreeing to meet a young married woman in such a clandestine fashion, he had such a desire to be in her company that whatever he was confronted with during the next few weeks, he would guarantee to make the proposed rendezvous with her at Imire. As Mathew fell asleep with Jan's letter under his pillow, he could not have been more gratified to know the depth of her feelings for him, or that she had known for quite some time that he felt the same.

The following day, Mathew decided not to mention anything about Jan's note to Simon or Anna, or to refer to the planned meeting with her at Imire. After attending the Sunday morning Communion service at Salisbury's Anglican Cathedral, they had lunch at The Ridgeway Hotel, where Mathew helped Anna with some preparation for their forthcoming joint publication. At sundowner time, Anna received a phone call from Jan who said that her husband had just left to go on military operations, and asked to have a quick word with Mathew to apologise for having been so unsociable the previous evening.

Mathew took the receiver.

'Mathew... I must know, have you read my letter? Will you come to Imire?'

'Yes.' Mathew was desperately trying to disguise his

enthusiastic reply. 'Yes Jan, it was a very nice evening. Perhaps if we do see each other again, you'll be able to spend a little longer talking to us,' he said laughingly. After replacing the receiver, Mathew was sure that Anna had intuitively sensed his excitement. She was indeed aware that there was something more to the casual conversation that she had just overheard, but was at a loss to think what it could be. She decided that at this stage of their relationship, it would be prudent not to question her guest on such a delicate matter.

On Mathew's return to the Kinloch homestead, he immediately got down to establishing a viable strategy which he hoped would enable him to carry out as many observations on the local chacma baboon population as he could during the final two months of his stay in Inyanga. He was well aware that he would have to spend a considerable amount of time preparing the tutorials that he was scheduled to present at the start of the academic year. Just a few days after his return, he called Mariette so that she could pass on the message that he looked forward to meeting Jan at the Imire Game Farm in eighteen days' time. He was careful to add here that the purpose of his meeting with her sister was so that Jan could personally introduce him to the farm's founder, Norman Travers.

Mathew's second encounter with the baboon family, which he had christened the Appletreewick group, went much better than he expected. While the baboons were crossing one of the park's earthen tracks, they took much longer to scatter than they had done previously when they saw his Land Rover approaching. During the initial days of this study of a family of over thirty individuals, he was intrigued to note that the troop appeared to have no single leader, although a few of the larger dominant males (who were over twice the size of the females) always appeared to be quick-tempered and could be frequently seen chasing the younger members of the troop in order to exert their discipline over them. Although on one occasion, Mathew was amused to see one of the powerful-looking males run for his life from an infuriated mother, whose small infant he had slapped for pulling his tail.

The most recognisable feature of the chacma baboon family, in comparison to members of the guenon monkeys he had previously studied, was their long, square-jawed, dog-like muzzles and the way that the adults communicated with one another through their constant barks and coughs. Mathew had recorded a series of the baboon's grunting sounds that, while feeding, were frequently accompanied by soft chattering noises of pleasure. These contrasted significantly with the frenzied roars, screams and squeals that would erupt whenever one of the sentinels uttered one of their characteristic alarm barks. On these occasions, the barks would not only immediately scatter the rest of the family troop, but would also cause any other animals in the vicinity to be on the alert.

While Mathew started to draw some mugshots for identification purposes, he became only too aware of how intimidating an adult male chacma could be. For whenever he got too close to an individual, they would throw their heads back, grind their teeth, yawn deeply and after raising their eyebrows, give out such a piercing laser-beam warning stare from the black pupils of their deep-set pale brown eyes that only the most foolish of behaviourists would venture any closer. These reactions did not only occur when Mathew looked directly at one of the males during the process of sketching, but also whenever he came too close to one of the pink-faced infants clutching tightly to their mother's chest, or to one of the older infants riding jockey-style on their mother's back.

In comparison to the amount of time Casimir's gorilla family had spent mutual-grooming, Mathew had been surprised at the additional time that his Appletreewick troop of baboons spent in picking the salt out of each others' coats. After their early morning routine of foraging, which he noted included a typical omnivorous diet of wild fruits, roots, bulbs, seeds, birds' eggs, insects, spiders, beetles, and even scorpions, their favourite pastime while relaxing in close physical contact with one another during the heat of the day was to preoccupy themselves with mutual grooming and meticulously attending to each others' coats.

On a number of occasions, Mathew saw younger females waiting for a chance to kidnap an infant from its mother. Such an event would be immediately followed by pandemonium within the troop, with the loud roars and barking of the elders and the squeals of the younger members of the family, who would scamper away from the furor to seek refuge behind a nearby tree or boulder. Mathew found his Appletreewick troop of chacmas to be highly intelligent, social animals who possessed remarkable eyesight and were able to pick out and identify different objects – even quite motionless individuals, which so many other animal species are unable to do. The baboon sentinels always appeared to maintain a high degree of vigilance and a level of watchfulness which contributed so much to their family group's security and welfare.

On Mathew's return to the Kinloch household late on the Friday afternoon, prior to his planned meeting with Jan at Imire the following morning, Miles told him that he'd had a message from a Mrs Smoelke and could he phone her back between eight and nine that evening. Mathew immediately feared the worst; that Jan had contacted her sister to say that after all their planning and hopes, she would be unable to make the Imire rendezvous. After he had taken one more sundowner than usual, he plucked up courage and managed to get through to Macheke on a rather erratic party line to speak to Mariette.

Instead of being told that Jan would be unable to meet him, her sister was calling to say that she was going to be later than expected. 'Normally she drives down on a Friday evening but as Major Bushney isn't due to leave until the Saturday morning, she's going to be delayed and won't get to Imire until just after midday on Saturday. Norman Travers is still expecting you to arrive at the farm at 10.30 a.m. It's a terrible shame but as my husband Willie is away for the weekend on a military exercise – he's in the Terratorials – I won't be able to leave the farm to join you at Imire. But as Macheke was on the way back from Marandellas to Inyanga, I do hope that you'll have time to drop in for tea or a sundowner with myself and Jan? She's told me so much about you.'

'I'm sure there'll be time for that, Mariette. It would be lovely to meet you, too. Well, thanks so much for letting me know, it's very kind of you – I look forward to meeting you then.'

Relieved that his meeting with Jan hadn't been cancelled, Mathew returned to enjoy a nightcap with Miles. He told him that a great friend of Simon and Anna Vaughan-Jones (he carefully avoided mentioning Jan's name) was a friend of Norman Travers and had set up the Saturday morning meeting with him. 'I've been told that Travers has expressed a keenness to discuss topics of mutual interest, in particular with regards to the future of endangered species and animal conservation matters in Rhodesia. I think he'll be a useful contact.'

'I've visited the Imire Game Farm,' said Miles, 'but I haven't had the opportunity to meet Norman Travers personally. I know he's very well respected. I've heard he's done a lot to hold together the farming community of the Wedza district. It's a small, white community which has been under frequent attack from black nationalist guerrillas. He's a brave man, a war hero – he was awarded an M.C. during the Italian campaign and he's recently also been awarded the Meritorious Service Medal. I'm sure it will be a very worthwhile trip.'

As far as Mathew was concerned, it was a lucky coincidence

that Addie wasn't able to come down to Inyanga for the weekend. Michael Lamb had asked her to attend an all-day meeting with Sir Roger and himself on the Saturday, with a couple of diplomats from the British Foreign Office who were due to arrive in Rhodesia on Friday. She had previously told Mathew, in the strictest confidence, that the diplomats were bringing with them proposals for a peaceful settlement from James Callaghan's Labour Government to present to Ian Smith. Although Mathew treasured his friendship with Addie, and held her in very high esteem, he would have hated to have intentionally misguided her as to the main reason behind his visit to Imire. He could justify his secrecy with the thought of how dangerous it would be for Jan if it should become known that they had planned a clandestine meeting.

It took Mathew just under two hours to drive from the Kinlochs' to Imire. He was impressed by his first sight of the Travers' home, with its immaculately kept green lawns and flower beds. Norman Travers was there to greet Mathew as soon as he got out of the Land Rover, grasping his hand and welcoming him enthusiastically to his game farm. During the next hour and a half, while sipping glasses of iced lime juice under the delicate shade of an acacia tree, Travers told Mathew how he – like so many other veterans – had come out to Rhodesia after the war to start a new life, and in 1950 had bought Imire to farm maize and cattle.

'I carried on like that for several years, but in the end I just got bored with commercial farming and decided that what I really wanted to do was to get involved with some of Rhodesia's indigenous animals, so I branched out into game farming. I started off with a number of orphaned impala I had collected together, and then had added duiker, kudu, waterbuck and, more recently, Cape buffalo. What I would really like to do, if and when Rhodesia reaches a satisfactory political settlement and things return to normal, is to establish a wildlife and rhino conservation sanctuary at Imire. We need to take urgent measures for the conservation of the black rhino – its population is in drastic decline throughout the African continent, particularly in Rhodesia.'

Throughout their conversation Mathew found his host to have an encyclopedic knowledge of the animal kingdom and, like so many people who have achieved a great deal in life, was reticent to talk too much about his area of expertise. Instead, Travers showed a great deal of interest in Mathew's field work, past and present. During the course of Travers' many questions, Mathew thought that he had seldom met a person, other than his mentor, Osman Hill, who had shown so much genuine interest in his work with primates. He also seemed very interested to hear about the natural history of the Kahuzi-Biega National Park, the culture of its local Pygmy population and how they interacted with the local African tribes.

When Jan arrived in her Hillman pick-up vehicle just after midday, she looked to Mathew as beautiful as he had ever seen her. Her face was illuminated by a smile that radiated happiness. After Travers greeted her and told her how inspiring and productive their conversation had been, Mathew took Jan's hand and addressed her as formally as possible. The last thing that either of them wished to convey to Norman Travers was that there was anything more to their relationship than that they were both good friends of the Vaughan-Joneses, whom Travers knew well.

'I must apologise for not having the time to give you a tour myself,' said Travers as they had a quick lunch by the swimming pool. 'I've arranged for one of the staff to take you round but before you go, I must show you our herd of Cape buffalo. I'm particularly proud of these animals – the government's local veterinary department has certified that the herd are totally free from foot and mouth and TB. I'm now in the process of building up the herd, as there's already quite a good South African market for these farm-reared animals. As soon as the UN trade sanctions are lifted, I'm confident that there will be a European market too. The African bovids are considered to have lower cholesterol levels than European animals and as a healthy, disease-free herd, they should be in demand. Ah, here's your guide, enjoy the tour and I'll see you back here later.'

During Mathew and Jan's tour of Imire, they were able to talk quite freely to one other and, out of sight of the driver, to hold hands. Apart from being able to see so many of Imire's game species as if they were living totally free in their natural environment, they also saw a good cross-section of the local bird life which ranged from saddle-billed storks, crested cranes, spurwing geese and plum-coloured starlings, to flocks of the ubiquitous helmeted guineafowl.

On the drive back to the Travers' spacious farmhouse, Mathew told Jan that Mariette had suggested he visit her home on the way to Inyanga, and they agreed it would be a delightful end to the day.

'Jan, would you like to come and see Peter now?' said Travers when they got out of the truck. Jan had said over lunch how much she'd enjoyed her first meeting with his tame sub-adult male cheetah, a graceful and affectionate wild animal. 'Oh, yes please! I can't wait to see him again... You should have seen him, Mathew, he was just like an overgrown kitten. He let me scratch him around his neck and stroke him along his back, and he purred louder than anything. I'll never forget it.' After a few minutes of Jan stroking Peter's beautiful silky coat and talking softly to him, he began to purr loudly. She placed her arms around his neck. 'Norman, would you take a photograph of Mathew and me with Peter so I can show it to Simon and Anna? I wish they could see him.'

After that, it was time to head for Mariette's home at

Carnock Farm. It had been an unforgettable afternoon for Jan and Mathew, for reasons other than their host might have imagined. Following Jan's pick-up down to Macheke, Mathew reflected how very impressed he was with Norman Travers' dedication to the cause of conservation, and how very much he hoped that his ambition to create a wildlife and rhino conservation sanctuary in the future would be realised. Just as the brilliant sun started to settle above a mountain range to the west of them, blossoming into one of the eastern district's renowned sunsets, they arrived at the turn-off to Carnock Farm and their vehicles began to bump their way up the stony drive to the Smoelkes' homestead. Mathew found Mariette to be an attractive but older version of Jan, rather plumper and a little dishevelled-looking in comparison to Jan's neatly attired mannequin-like figure. Her barley sugar-coloured hair hung loosely over her shoulders, and her complexion illustrated its regular exposure to the sun while she assisted her husband on the farm.

'It's lovely to meet you, Mathew. Come through, make yourself comfortable,' said Mariette, leading them on to a mosquito-netted veranda with large, comfortable seats. 'I think it's a little late for tea, don't you? Shall we go for a sundowner instead? How about a cold bottle of Castle?'

'I couldn't imagine anything I would like more at this very moment. Thank you, Mariette.'

'Now, Jan, shall we just have a drop of something to keep Mathew company?' said Mariette as she poured two sizeable glasses of South African medium-dry sherry.

As they sipped their sundowners on the veranda, the conversation flowed easily and the situation seemed very natural, despite its strangeness. Although Mathew had every intention of leaving Carnock Farm for Inyanga by sunset, he was so happy to be in Jan's company again and was so much enjoying sharing his thoughts with her, he felt reluctant to leave.

'Look, it's just about suppertime now – why don't you stay a little longer and have a meal with us? It would be lovely to have you here.' Mariette could see how much her sister was enjoying Mathew's company and vice versa; she was correct in her assumption that it would take little persuasion on her part for him to stay. 'Well, I really should get back ... but why not? It's a long way to drive on an empty stomach.'

'That's settled, then. Let me go and have a word with the cook-boy and see what he can rustle up for us.' Mariette went inside the house, tactfully leaving the two of them alone on the veranda.

As soon as Mathew and Jan were alone, Mathew rushed to Jan and lifted her up into his arms, whereupon Jan burst into a flood of tears. As he kissed her moistened cheeks and lips, he felt the pent-up tension of her body start to dissolve in his firm embrace. 'Please Mathew ... don't leave me yet, not until tomorrow. I've waited so long for us to be together.' Jan's sobs wracked her body, making it difficult for her to speak, but once she had managed to regain control of her emotions she said, 'Don't worry, Mariette will be only too happy to arrange a camp bed for you on the veranda. No one else will ever find out that you spent the night here, I promise – Mariette has known about the state of my marriage for a long time.'

'If you're sure Mariette won't mind, of course I'll stay. You know I want to be with you every minute that I can. But I must call Miles Kinloch, he's probably already worried about me and I shouldn't leave it any longer. I'll tell him that I'm staying to attend a dinner party.' Miles was indeed hugely relieved when he answered Mathew's call; there had just been a radio bulletin with news of a terrorist alert in the Rusape area, so it was of the utmost importance for Mathew to stay off the road and remain where he was until the following morning.

SOMEONE WISHES TO SPEAK TO YOU

The three of them shared a very convivial evening, full of laughter and high spirits. Mariette could see how very much in love her younger sister was with this similarly aged, handsome young Englishman, and how well matched they looked. At the same time, she was at a loss to think just how they could possibly ever manage to share a future together, for the odds were so much against her brother-in-law releasing his trophy wife to another mortal; especially to a native of Great Britain.

As the insurgency alert had been announced, Mariette was happy to ask her house-boy to make up a camp bed on the veranda for Mathew, although she was well aware that her sister had every intention of spending the night with him. So after supper, she joined them for an initial Cape brandy and then tactfully left the two of them alone, to finish a second nightcap that Jan had just poured for them both. As soon as Mariette returned to her bedroom, she dropped to her knees by the side of her matrimonial bed and, as a staunch member of the Dutch Reformed Church, she prayed for God's forgiveness for facilitating such an infidelity as was no doubt about to take place under her roof. At the same time, she prayed that Jan and Mathew would have a future together, for she had seldom seen her sister look so happy.

10

A Diversity of Decisions

After a series of prolonged hugs, and a tearful goodbye, Mathew left Jan's room and went to make his camp bed appear as if it had been slept in. He didn't want Mariette's house-boy to think that he had spent the night anywhere but on the veranda. As he negotiated his Land Rover down the farm's rocky drive, his emotions were overwhelmed by leaving Jan. Although he had told her during their night together that he wanted more than anything else in the world to spend the rest of his life with her, he hated the fact that he now had to leave her to return to the misery of life with Major Paddy Bushney. For when they had been so reluctant to separate from each other's arms, he had proposed marriage to her if she could ever manage to secure a divorce from her possessive and domineering husband.

They agreed that it was important they should meet again at Carnock Farm prior to Mathew's flight home to see his parents in mid-September, in just over a month's time. However, they both knew that a meeting would be dependent on Paddy Bushney being away from Salisbury on counter-insurgency operations, as well as Willie Smoelke being absent from his farm while serving with the RLI.

On Mathew's arrival at his Inyanga base, Miles Kinloch came out to greet him, immediately followed by Huggins and Welensky, who did their customary barking and jumping up as soon as his feet touched the ground.

SOMEONE WISHES TO SPEAK TO YOU

'Welcome back, Mathew,' said Miles, patting him on the shoulder. 'I must say I was immensely relieved when you phoned last night to tell me that you'd decided to stay in Macheke. I've just had a call from Jock Whitton saying that there was quite a sizeable insurgency alert just after dark, at a farm north of Rusape.'

'It sounds like I made the right decision. What happened?' Mathew was thankful that Miles did not ask any questions about the supposed dinner party at the Smoelkes' the previous evening.

'The usual, awful sort of thing – they began by setting fire to the wooden outbuildings, then machine-gunned out each of farmhouse's windows, before trying to set the building alight. Fortunately, the farmer and his family managed to avoid being hurt, very much thanks to the rapid response of the security forces. They managed to injure and capture two of the fleeing insurgents, although the third one managed to escape.'

With only four and a half weeks to go before Mathew's trip to the UK, he had to move all his belongings to the Vaughan-Joneses' house in Salisbury as he was due to start his tutorials at the university at the beginning of October, almost immediately after his return to Rhodesia. He was also anxious to carry out some final observations on his Appletreewick chacma baboons, as well as being keen to check on his Castle Beacon Stairs' and vervet monkey groups. To return to the Vumba, he would have to gain the necessary permissions and permits from Jim Prior, who was responsible to the District Commissioner for the overall administration of that area of Manicaland, and from Major Baxter, the officer who had interviewed him on the eve of his departure from the Vumba.

Mathew needed to return to his research site so that he could complete some of his forthcoming tutorials, and also because he had recently received an invitation from the editors of the highly respected scientific publication, *Conservation Biology*, to submit a paper regarding his observations on primate communication through facial images and eye flashes. As with most career academics, it was always important for Mathew to submit the results of his research findings in well peer-reviewed publications at regular intervals.

Ten days after Mathew had made contact with Jim Prior and the major, he received the most welcome news – he had been granted permission to revisit his old study site between the daylight hours of 9 a.m. and 4.30 p.m. providing that he agreed to be accompanied throughout his visit to Castle Beacon by two African askaris, and to return to Umtali by sunset. Although Mathew considered that the presence of two uniformed soldiers could well cause his habituated monkey groups to become more nervous, he was grateful to Jim Prior, who told him later that he had put pressure on an initially reluctant Major Baxter to issue the necessary permits to allow him to pass through the various road blocks. Permission for him to return to his study site had only been granted due to the considerable build-up of security forces in Umtali and the constant military presence within the Vumba Mountains.

A few days before Mathew's trip, Angus Whitton dropped in to enjoy one of his regular sundowners with Miles Kinloch.

'I've just been at the official opening of the Tsango Lodge Rehabilitation Centre in Inyanga for convalescing soldiers – opened by P.K. van der Byl himself, no less. It occurred to me that as most of the young soldiers are getting extremely bored of having to put up with enforced physical inactivity due to their wounds, I wondered if you could spare some time to give a talk one evening at the centre about your field studies in Zaire? It's fascinating stuff, bound to go down well. I thought it would help to take their minds off some of the atrocities they've experienced. Some of the boys in there witnessed the aftermath of the Honde Valley Tea Estate

SOMEONE WISHES TO SPEAK TO YOU

massacre. That's not something they'll be able to forget in a hurry, if ever, but at least if we do something to keep their minds occupied, it might help.'

Mathew was only too happy to agree to Angus's request. He was well aware that if he had been a Rhodesian citizen, he too would have been involved with the country's compulsory military service. He could have been in the same situation as the soldiers at the rehabilitation centre.

When the evening of the talk came, Mathew was accompanied to the Tsango Lodge by Addie and her father. On arrival, Angus introduced Mathew to a Captain Darling of the Medical Corps and as soon as they entered the small assembly hall, the twenty or so patients present started to applaud them enthusiastically. When Mathew looked around the room, he could see that most of the young soldiers in the audience had been maimed in some way. While Angus introduced him, Mathew could not help feeling a great sadness that all such wounds and misery were a result of the disastrous conflict between ZANLA's freedom fighters and Rhodesia's security forces. In his opinion, this conflict was causing needless suffering to the entire population.

After Mathew's talk, illustrated by a series of his mugshot drawings of Casimir's family group and some similar sketches of his Stairs' and vervet monkey subjects, he asked if there were any questions. A young soldier raised his arm immediately with a question about the significance of eye flashes between individual primates, and how much this type of communication could be relevant to the way humans interact with one another. Mathew was hugely gratified that there was an interest in this aspect of his talk. After he had answered the question, the emphasis shifted.

A number of the convalescents were keen to hear about how, as a European, he had been received in the Kivu Province of Zaire, so comparatively soon after the bloodbath resulting from the country's independence from Belgium. And, in

A DIVERSITY OF DECISIONS

particular, due to the way some of the mercenaries in the employ of Patrice Lumumba had been responsible for the killings of so many Africans in the eastern Congo.

Although Mathew could appreciate the degree of the soldiers' concern should their security forces lose the war against ZANLA, he explained that he had always been well received. 'I never experienced any racial problems between the remaining whites, and the indigenous African population in the Bukavu region of Kivu Province. I found the Africans in and around Bukavu to be on the whole very welcoming.' (In this context, he decided not to mention anything about his unfortunate experience with the hostile police sergeant in Goma, who had been scarred while being interrogated by foreign mercenaries.) 'Should a black majority government ever come to power in Rhodesia, I very much hope that in spite of the killings on both sides, as Rhodesia is such a very special country, such political wounds will mend and the harmony that exists between the races in Zaire will soon be achieved.'

Mathew hoped that at least by giving a positive account of his experience, he had expressed his view that peace was not an impossibility.

On his journey down to Umtali on Monday morning to meet Jim Prior for coffee at the sports club, Mathew had to pass through a series of road blocks, heavily manned with BSAP and RLI personnel. After they had inspected the contents of his Land Rover and made a note of his passport and visitor visa numbers, they had all asked him why he wasn't carrying any type of weapon, such as the usual self-repeating pistol, for self-protection. Much to the amusement of those who asked the question, he always responded (untruthfully) that as he had always been such a bad shot, if he were to be confronted by a terrorist he would in all probability shoot himself by mistake.

SOMEONE WISHES TO SPEAK TO YOU

He found Jim Prior was no longer the relaxed District Officer of former times. He had become very pessimistic about the outcome of the Bush War.

'You know Mathew, I'm not at all happy about you going back to the Castle Beacon camp. I want your absolute assurance that in accordance with the permits, you promise to return to the safety of Umtali at least one hour before sunset.'

'Don't worry about me, Jim. Look how long I was there before, day in day out – nothing ever happened to me.'

'You don't understand, it's a whole different ballgame now. You'd be very welcome to stay with me at the flat tonight. It's not safe anymore for Europeans to drive alone out of Umtali during the hours of darkness. There's been quite a number of terrorist attacks on unescorted vehicles in the region.'

After leaving the sports club, Mathew headed off for Castle Beacon and as Jim had said, the two African askaris were waiting for him at the first police road block on his way out of Umtali. They were surprised when he greeted them in the Manyika tongue and how he went on to tell them that during his time in the Vumba, he had made a number of friends amongst their fellow tribesmen, who had taught him the dialect. By the time they arrived at the turn-off to Castle Beacon, it was obvious to Mathew that they had become relaxed in his company and that in all probability they had not had such a friendly conversation with a European before.

On arrival at his campsite, Mathew was disappointed to find little left of the hut that Edgar and Joshua had constructed for him, or much evidence of the two canopy platforms they had made. However, as he had less than six hours to look for his monkeys, he was fortunate to locate the Stairs' group within half an hour of walking up a forest trail to one of their favourite mid-morning resting places, by a small mountain stream. He was delighted by the way they accepted him, as if he'd seen them yesterday, for none of the adult male sentinels uttered any of their usual alarm calls. They appeared to be completely nonchalant about his reappearance.

After Mathew had carefully positioned one of his tape-recorders, he did some mugshots of two of the sub-adults, playing hide-and-seek in the foliage above him. What had been their infant pelage had changed quite dramatically since he had last seen them and he hoped that by doing some sketches, he would have the chance to identify their parentage. In the meantime, he requested his two companions to remain on the path some distance away from the stream, as he was worried that the presence of strangers would cause an unnecessary disturbance within his study group.

Although Mathew was disappointed that none of his vervet monkey group had put in an appearance, he found that his few hours of observations on the Stairs' family had been most worthwhile. In particular when they started to crash through the branches of the forest canopy away from the stream to commence their early afternoon foraging, one of the adult males had spotted the two askari on the path lower down the hill. Immediately, it uttered a series of warning calls alerting the rest of the group to their presence, which turned out to be vocalisations Mathew had not previously recorded. He was also pleased to have updated a number of the mugshots, as some of the sub-adults of the family group had now reached adulthood.

After returning to the remains of his old camp, Mathew enjoyed sharing some sandwiches and a Thermos of locally grown coffee with his two companions. On the drive back to Umtali, he had the opportunity to speak once more in their native tongue. When the two askaris stepped down from the Land Rover at the police roadblock where he had collected them, their African sergeant was surprised to see the warmth in the way that Mathew shook their hands and said goodbye. Without doubt this was the first time that the two soldiers had experienced such an informal meeting with a European, or had conversed with an Englishman who could speak their language.

SOMEONE WISHES TO SPEAK TO YOU

Mathew could well imagine the degree of amusement that would arise when the two of them returned to their barracks and told their comrades-in-arms that they had just spent the day looking after the safety of a British gentleman on a trip to the Vumba. Particularly when they said it was to provide the Britisher who could speak their Manyika dialect with the opportunity to do some drawings of the faces of a family of monkeys, and to take tape-recordings of some of their noises.

Over dinner at Jim Prior's flat that evening, he was pleased to learn how successful the mission had proved to be. He seemed genuinely interested when Mathew showed him some of the sketches he had drawn and played back the adult Stairs' monkey alarm vocalisations. Over a balloon glass of Cape brandy, the conversation reverted to the progress of the Bush War.

'On the international front,' said Jim, 'since the beginning of 1976 the US, in cooperation with the British, have begun to take a more active role in the search for a settlement. The main reason for the general election was the internal political crisis in Ian Smith's party, due to the defection of twelve RF MPs. They were complaining that the government had become too liberal, and was no longer adhering to party principles or election promises. Despite that, Ian Smith's RF has managed to sweep all the seats for his party again. As Rhodesia is currently involved in such difficult negotiations as to its future, it gives the country a more secure footing.'

Mathew was interested to hear Jim talk about the reasons behind the general election and encouraged him to expand on the subject. He explained that the general consensus within the party was that the twelve MPs who defected were reactionaries attempting to put the clock back. Due to the degree of public concern caused by such a sizeable defection, the government wished to clearly establish where it stood with the electorate. Ian Smith reluctantly decided to hold the general election on 31 August.

A DIVERSITY OF DECISIONS

'I heard something very interesting recently – it was strictly confidential but it's recently become declassified,' said Jim. 'The British Government is considering appointing Field Marshall Lord Carver as Britain's Pro-Consul in Salisbury, and if this is the case it will undoubtedly cause the termination of your friend Sir Roger's posting and the Willocks' return to the UK.'

Mathew had not heard any word of this from Addie, although he did recognise that anything to do with her secretarial work for either Sir Roger or Michael Lamb had to be kept strictly confidential. He was very concerned at the thought of his friends' enforced return to the UK.

'Do you know what's behind it? Is it part of wider scheme?'

'On the day after the general election,' said Jim, 'David Owen and the US Ambassador to the UN, Andrew Young, who had previously enthusiastically increased UN sanctions against Rhodesia, arrived in Salisbury and demanded the immediate handover of the security forces to Robert Mugabe's ZANU/PF, and to Joshua Nkomo's ZAPU. Owen is reported to have informed Ian Smith that the British Government wanted Field Marshall Lord Carver brought in to take command and control of all "security matters", as well as stating that they wished to have the Field Marshall appointed as Britain's Commissioner Designate. All the members of Ian Smith's government were taken aback by this, which they considered to be Owen and Young's total rejection of the strong mandate that the election results had provided the RF with. Particularly as the results represented a strong vote of support as a message to both the British and US Governments that the Rhodesian nation is united in its determination to negotiate for a fair and just settlement for the long-term benefit of all Rhodesians.'

'I'm glad to have this insight into the various national and international manoeuvres – I know that when I go back to the UK I'm going to face a barrage of questions about what the real situation is. So many people have friends or relatives in Rhodesia and I know many of them are concerned about the long-term future of the country, for both its black and white populations. All they have to go on are the politically biased and often fabricated reports in the British press... The media there still refer to the country as the "British colony of Southern Rhodesia".'

After Mathew returned to Inyangar, it took him a further ten days to complete writing up his chacma baboon observations and to move his belongings to the Vaughan-Joneses' home. In appreciation for all the hospitality he had received from Miles and Addie over the last eight months, he hosted a farewell dinner at the Rhodes Inyanga Hotel to which he also invited Angus Whitton. During the course of the evening, Mathew could not help teasing Addie by mentioning a few bits of the recently declassified information that Jim Prior had provided him with.

'I was interested to hear, Addie, that the British Government is wishing to appoint Lord Carver as Britain's Commissioner Designate. What will happen to Sir Roger?'

'Mathew, where on earth did you hear that?' whispered Addie, visibly alarmed. 'Please say I didn't tell you.'

Feeling slightly guilty, Mathew said, 'No, don't worry. Your professional confidentiality has remained unbreached. It was a District Officer friend of mine in Umtali. It's no longer confidential, apparently.'

'Just as well!' Addie laughed. 'I don't know what the timescale is but I will miss Sir Roger, I've enjoyed working for him.'

Mariette had contacted Mathew to say that Willie would be away from Carnock Farm at a maize market for the majority of Monday, so he agreed to call in to see her in an attempt

A DIVERSITY OF DECISIONS

to arrange another rendezvous with Jan before leaving for the UK. As they drank some local coffee together on the farmhouse's 'stoep', Mariette asked Mathew a question that had been preying on her mind.

'I want you to tell me the truth. Are you as serious about Jan as she is about you? I would hate to see her suffering from another broken heart. She was so upset when her last English boyfriend left her without any warning, and her feelings for you are so much stronger... I can't bear to think what would happen. I'm putting my neck on the line for you two, imagine what Paddy will do if he finds out – I'm even deceiving my own husband.'

'I promise you Mariette, my chief ambition in life is to secure Jan as my lawful wedded wife at the earliest opportunity.'

'I hope you're telling me the truth. I know how desperately unhappy Jan is married to such a domineering man, he treats her more like some type of war trophy than a sensitive young wife to be adored.'

'As we won't be able to marry until she has divorced Paddy Bushney, there will be difficult times ahead, particularly for Jan. But Mariette, please believe that I love her and whatever we have to go through, it will be worth it in the end. I will do everything in my power to make her happy.'

By the time Mathew left Carnock Farm, Mariette and he had agreed that she would act as a conduit for all future personal communications between Jan and himself. Also, as Jan and Mathew lived in such close proximity to each other at Gunhill and the situation they were about to enter was of the utmost delicacy, it was crucial for them to both always act as formally as possible in order to convey, even to the most suspicious, that there was nothing more to their relationship than both being close friends of Simon and Anna Vaughan-Jones.

They also agreed that providing nothing changed, as neither her husband nor Paddy Bushney were currently at home during weekends, Mathew would do everything possible to come up with some excuse to revisit Imire. The plan was that he would be able to stay at Carnock Farm for twenty-four hours on the Saturday prior to his evening flight to London, two weeks on Monday.

The next ten days passed as agreeably as possible, for both Simon and Anna had gone out of their way to make Mathew feel very much at home. As he had now taken up residence in Salisbury and Sir Roger had heard that he was about to return to England to see his parents, he had invited him and the Vaughan-Joneses to a buffet dinner party. Mathew was later to learn that one of the main reasons for the occasion was to introduce a good cross-section of Rhodesian society to Jeremy Hughes, the British diplomat that Lord Carver had left in the country, and that it was Hughes' task to assess how the RF Government was progressing with its attempts to establish an internal settlement with some of the African politicians.

When Mathew checked his Causeway post office box, he was surprised to see a padded envelope from Antonia Clinton-Kemp, who he had not been in correspondence with for well over a year. It contained a two-page letter and a glossy colour photograph from *Country Life*, wrapped in tissue, of Antonia immaculately dressed in hunting attire standing beside her thoroughbred mare Gillespie, under which was printed:

> Lady Antonia Clinton-Kemp
> Antonia, aged 26, is the eldest daughter of the Earl and Countess of Drysdale of Bardon Towers, Yorkshire. Educated at Cheltenham Ladies' College and Girton College, Cambridge, Antonia is engaged to the Honourable Timothy Ludlow, eldest son of Viscount and Viscountess St Claire of Hexham, Northumberland. The wedding is due to take place at Bolton Abbey in the autumn.

A DIVERSITY OF DECISIONS

Mathew replaced the photo in the tissue paper and picked up Antonia's letter.

Dear Mathew,
I thought I'd better let you know that after finally giving up waiting for you to return to the UK from your seemingly everlasting monkey studies in Africa, I concluded several months ago that our lives had drifted apart too much for me to consider that we could ever have a meaningful future together.

At this year's college party during the university's May Ball, I met Timothy Ludlow – and fell in love with him. Timothy has completed his degree at Cambridge University's Department of History of Art, and has recently started a post-graduate MA degree course at Sotheby's Institute of Art. My mother has just told me that you are about to return to Hartington Hall for several days before you take up a lectureship post at the University of Rhodesia, so I wanted to say how much I would love to introduce you to my fiancé, whom I'm sure you will just adore.

I know you too will have moved on and news of my engagement won't come as a disappointment to you, but I do hope that we can continue to be friends.

With great affection,
Antonia xx

Mathew was initially rather stunned by Antonia's letter, and had to look again at the *Country Life* announcement of her engagement to Timothy Ludlow. Before receiving the letter, he was totally unaware that Antonia, his first teenage infatuation, had become romantically involved with someone who was a stranger to him. He recognised the absurdity of retaining any emotional attachment when he was so much in love with Jan. But through his study of sub-human primates he philosophically put such intimate feelings down to the possessiveness of the male mind. He had often come to the conclusion that monogamy could be a difficult status to come to terms with.

The evening buffet reception at the Willocks' took place on their spacious, well-manicured lawns. On arrival, Sir Roger introduced each person to his guest of honour, Jeremy Hughes, who was immaculately dressed in a light tropical suit and looked the personification of an English gentleman. When he was introduced to Mathew, he told him how much he had heard about his primate studies on Rhodesia's borders with Mozambique, as well as how he very much looked forward to talking to him more personally at a meeting that Sir Roger had told him was to take place later on in the evening.

Mathew was pleased to renew his acquaintance with Michael Lamb and his vivacious wife Denise, and was delighted that Addie was with him for the majority of the evening. She made it her duty to introduce him to as many important Rhodesian citizens as possible, although all of these were representatives of the European community. The only Africans present were either serving the drinks or officiating at the buffet table. During the course of the evening, Professor Tom Martin introduced him to some of his university colleagues, and said how very much he was looking forward to Mathew joining his department. David Montgomery was also there and was extremely interested to hear about Mathew's recent return to the Vumba and the sad state that he had found his Castle Beacon camp to be in.

During his conversation with Montgomery, Mathew noticed out of the corner of his eye how Major Piet Erasmus from the South African Embassy had been negotiating his way slowly through the guests towards them, and was particularly surprised by the way he greeted him, almost like a long-lost friend. Although the major had initially appeared to show considerable interest in how Mathew's primate studies were progressing, it wasn't long before he changed the conversation and began asking him about his involvements with the African communities of Inyanga and the Vumba region. He said that although of course he wanted to know whether they were supportive of ZANLA and its terrorist activities, he had always been keen to hear about the African viewpoint.

What surprised Mathew more than anything else was that it appeared from their conversation that Piet Erasmus knew about his recent visit to Castle Beacon and his meetings with Major Baxter and Jim Prior. Because of this awareness, Mathew could not help wondering to what degree Rhodesia's Central Intelligence Organisation (CIO) was monitoring his movements in the sensitive Bush War regions of Umtali and the Vumba, and how much intelligence-sharing the CIO had with officials at the South African Embassy like Major Erasmus, and with BOSS.

By the time Michael Lamb came to take him into the house for the meeting with the diplomat, Mathew told Simon and Anna that that they should perhaps go home without him. Michael Lamb had arranged for a car to return him to Gunhill later on. Just after eleven o'clock, Mathew remained to have a nightcap with Jeremy Hughes and Sir Roger in his office. (Addie had said that the room had been very carefully checked over by an SAS specialist who had accompanied Lord Carver on his recent visit, and it was totally free of any CIO bugging devices.)

Sir Roger enjoyed a glass of the peaty Islay malt whisky that Hughes had brought out from England with him, before taking leave of his two young countrymen. He knew that his guest wanted the opportunity to talk to Mathew alone and realised that his presence could well handicap the possibility of them speaking freely.

'You know, your parents are looking forward immensely

SOMEONE WISHES TO SPEAK TO YOU

to seeing you again,' said Sir Roger, handing Mathew a letter. 'Could you pass this on to your father? Devra and I are hoping that we will be able to see them before too long, as soon as we return to the UK. I expect it will be quite soon, as James Callaghan's government has already decided to replace me with a British Commissioner Designate of their choice.'

'That will be Rhodesia's loss, but without doubt your British friends will be grateful to have you back in the UK. I know my parents will be thrilled to see you both again, they hold your friendship very dear. I'll pass the letter on.'

'Well, I'll bid you both goodnight. I hope you've enjoyed the evening.'

Once they had recharged their whisky glasses, Hughes got straight to the point.

'The chief objective of my stay in Rhodesia is very much focused on the amount of grass-root support that the African tribal people are likely to have for the RF Government's intention to establish an internal settlement. That is why I've been particularly anxious to speak to you on your own. I've been informed that during your time of primate field observations in Manicaland, you have made many African friends, including such important tribal leaders as Chief Chidzikwee. I need to know as much about these involvements as possible.'

'It's true to say that throughout my time in Rhodesia, I have made many friends within both the African and European communities, but I've always maintained a policy of distancing myself from anything to do with the country's political situation. I greatly admire many of its citizens, black and white, and in some cases I can well appreciate how the often entrenched attitudes on both sides of the political pendulum have come about. As a result of this tragic conflict between the races, there is a huge amount of unnecessary heartbreak and misery throughout the region that I have come to know so well. As far as I'm concerned, the sooner a peaceful settlement can be achieved, either through internal negotiations or from without, the better it will be for what I hope will mature into a truly multi-racial state within the British Commonwealth.'

'Well, as we both wish for the best possible future for Rhodesia, it is important that you share any information that you have gained from your African friends which you consider could in any way assist the peace process. As an Englishman it's your responsibility to provide me, as a diplomat of the British Government, with the type of information that I am seeking. From what I've already been told about your African friendships, I am sure that such an insight into their opinions would represent valuable material for the dossier I am compiling for the British Government and military Chiefs of Staff. I am well aware that you're about to go back to the UK for ten days, but during that time you must consider carefully what has been requested. Soon after your return to Rhodesia, I'll arrange to meet you again.'

Their meeting ended with Mathew rather reluctantly shaking hands with the diplomat and taking the waiting car back to the Vaughan-Joneses'. During the drive to the Gunhill estate, Mathew felt rather compromised in having been asked by an agent of the British Government to break some of the confidentialities that he had shared with his African friends, in particular those of Chief Chidzikwee.

On Mathew's way down to Carnock Farm the following weekend he called in at Imire, as Norman Travers was keen to discuss his plans to change the game farm into a breeding sanctuary for some of Rhodesia's endangered species. Among his ambitions, he wanted to try to breed the critically threatened black rhino. He was also keen to become involved with the rearing of orphaned young elephants and was interested in the domestication of Sable antelope, which he considered could well be of significant benefit to the economics of game farming in southern Africa. On his drive down to Macheke, Mathew could only admire Travers' enthusiasm and dedication to the welfare of Rhodesia's wildlife heritage. Part of him rather wished that he could be more personally involved with such meaningful conservation projects.

Mathew arrived at Carnock Farm mid-afternoon, and when it was only Mariette who came out of the farmhouse to greet him, he immediately feared that after all the careful planning for his meeting with Jan it had been thwarted at the eleventh hour. Mariette put his mind at rest by explaining that she had been delayed as Paddy had returned home unexpectedly to pick something up and then stayed for lunch. He told Jan that during the next twelve hours, he would be leading a major counter-insurgency raid across the border. Jan was now not expected to arrive at the farm much before sundowner time.

When she arrived some five hours later than originally expected, her reunion with Mathew could not have been more rapturous and Mariette rejoiced in seeing her sister looking such a picture of happiness. She very much hoped that her prayers would be answered; that Jan would find a way to escape from her disastrous marriage and that in the not-too-distant future she would be able to marry this handsome and very likeable young British academic. They were obviously very much in love and absolutely made for one another.

'Since Mathew was last here,' Jan told Mariette over dinner, 'we've seen each other on a number of occasions at the Vaughan-Joneses', and once even at a small gathering which Paddy arranged at home. I can't tell you how hard it is for us to keep everything formal – it seems so odd – but we are so prim with one another, I am confident that Paddy is totally unaware about my clandestine extramarital love affair! Do you know, Paddy thinks that in spite of Mathew being a British national, hailing from a country that is currently causing Rhodesia so many problems, he rather likes him! He reminds him of a well-educated ex-Sandhurst British officer whom he shared a billet with during the Malayan Emergency.'

'I find it excruciating to keep up this casual act of indifference toward Jan whenever we met. I just want to wrap her in my arms! On two occasions, we've managed to pass a note to each other without anyone seeing. Oh Mariette, I'm so grateful to you for giving me such a warm welcome to your home, and for providing such an agreeable place for me to spend time with Jan. It's only when we're here that we can discuss finding a way to sort out our future together.'

When the conversation moved on to the increased amount of terrorist attacks in the region, Mathew mentioned his surprise that at the small party Paddy Bushney had recently thrown, some of his brother officers had freely discussed in detail the nature of their past and forthcoming counter-insurgency raids.

After dinner, when Mathew was left in the small sitting room to listen to the BBC World Service News, Mariette had a confession to make to her sister. 'Jan, I have found it impossible to keep your romance with Mathew a secret from Willie, and I've told him in confidence about you both staying here and the depth of your feelings for each other. All he said was that he wishes you every future happiness, but that it's absolutely essential that the four of us make sure no word of your relationship goes any further. Of course, he can see that if Paddy heard even the slightest rumour about your unfaithfulness, the consequences wouldn't bear thinking about.'

'Willie is a good man and I hate to think I've dragged him into this situation... I can understand that you couldn't keep it from him and I'm glad he wasn't angry with you. I don't want to cause trouble between you.'

'Willie and I have never had any secrets between us. He was a little concerned about you and Mathew spending the night in the spare room, although I did say that the camp bed had been made up on the veranda so that for all appearances on the following morning, he had slept there. Willie is a staunch member of the Dutch Reformed Church and the local priest is a close friend of his – he asked me to visit his presbytery and within the confidentiality of the priesthood, to seek his advice and understanding.'

'I can put your mind at rest. We spent the night in each other's arms, but we didn't make love, not in the true sense of the word. So I haven't committed adultery. We agreed before we spent the night together that we would only consummate the relationship once I'm legally separated from Paddy and we can become man and wife.'

'Well if that's the case, I believe you've made the right decision and you'll be glad of it, in the future.'

'You know, Mathew told me recently that through his research for his study of facial images, he found an old Jewish quotation that we both consider to be completely relevant to our relationship, which is "Adultery can be committed with the eyes". Meeting Mathew, I've come to recognise that love is not merely a physical act, but can be blessed by a spiritual wealth as well.'

After Mathew had spent a further blissful night with Jan, and they had experienced another tearful separation, he left Carnock Farm on Sunday morning and drove down to Inyanga to have lunch with the Kinlochs. During the journey, he could not help very much regretting that he had to keep his relationship with Jan a total secret from the outside world. In particular, the degree of deception that he had to adopt when telling not only Simon and Anna, but later Miles and Addie, the conflicting stories as to his exact whereabouts over the weekend. He knew Anna would have warned him of the dangers should the relationship become public knowledge, and how disappointed Addie would be that he had not confided in her about his deep love for Jan. For since his first meeting with Addie soon after his arrival in Rhodesia, they had shared so many personal confidences.

On Monday evening, the South African Airways flight arrived on schedule from Johannesburg at Salisbury airport, prior to its onward night flight to London Heathrow. On clearing immigration, Mathew's entry card was stamped. Since UDI, visitors to Rhodesia had been asked whether they would prefer not to have their passports stamped in case this record of their visit could impede, or even prevent, their entry into another country, especially into another African country that wanted to see Ian Smith's RF Government defeated and brought to its knees.

Mathew's return to Hartington Hall proved on the whole to be most enjoyable, especially as his brother, Sebastian, had managed to arrange a week's leave from his Northern Ireland posting. A number of his relatives and childhood friends, including Antonia, were currently in Yorkshire enjoying some early autumn sunny weather. Mathew did however find it disconcerting to see his father looking considerably older than he had done on his previous visit; he had lost a lot of weight and his complexion was noticeably flushed.

During his time with Sebastian, they enjoyed riding around the estate, visiting some of their favourite old haunts and also sharing a number of confidences – which in Mathew's case he had never discussed with anyone else.

'A British diplomat, Jeremy Hughes, has asked me to divulge all the relevant information I have been given by my African friends, particularly an influential tribal chief. Our conversations have been confidential, but Hughes has told me that it's my duty as a British citizen to tell him as much as I know about the African population's attitude to the Bush War, the movement of Africans from across the Mozambique border and whether they are in favour of the proposed internal settlement. It's not just him, either. The South African Embassy's Military Attaché, Major Piet Erasmus, has also put pressure on me to divulge confidentialities.'

He told Sebastian in the strictest confidence about his intention to marry Jan Bushney, the young wife of the second in command of the Selous Scouts, and that only her sister and brother-in-law were aware of their romance. He explained that as Major Paddy Bushney was playing such a significant part in the Bush War, it may take a number of months before his intended bride would be in a position to start divorce proceedings.

'Back in the carefree days of my youth,' said Mathew, reverting to more lighthearted matters, 'my first infatuation was Antonia. She wrote to me recently to tell me that she's become engaged to a viscount's son, Timothy Ludlow – we'll meet him at Saturday's tennis party at Bardon Towers. It was a long time ago and I've moved on, but I must admit it feels a bit odd that Antonia's marrying someone I've never met. I hope I approve.'

'Well, before the delights of the tennis party at Bardon Towers, Mother wants to see us tomorrow morning while Father is in Skipton with his lawyer,' Sebastian warned Mathew. 'I don't expect it to be good news.'

Lady Sally Duncan sat with her sons in the spacious drawing room of Hartington Hall, just after 10 a.m. on Thursday morning. A maid passed each of them a cup of fine Kenyan coffee from a silver tray and left the room. Then, Sally Duncan dropped what Mathew considered to be almost a bombshell in their midst.

'The family doctor has recently told me that your father is suffering from a serious heart condition, primarily due to high blood pressure which he is trying to bring down by oral medication. In all probability, your father will have to be operated upon in the near future. In the meantime, it's important for as much as possible to be done to relieve him of the current pressures of the running of the Hartington estate. Mathew, you did tell your father that you may be able to take on the management of the estate at some stage – is there any possibility that in the not too distant future, you could give up your academic work in Rhodesia to return home?'

He found her request almost impossible to find an adequate response to, for he knew that before he even thought of leaving Rhodesia, he had to be supportive of Jan as soon as she started her divorce proceedings. 'Of course I'll think very carefully about what you've said, Mother,' said Mathew. 'I don't want to let you and Father down but at the same time, I'm currently under contract to the university and I have some field studies to complete... Perhaps Sebastian and I should talk this over, discuss the possibilities? It might be easier if we can work through some ideas together. Shall we talk again tomorrow?'

'I would very much appreciate that. I know it must have come as a shock to you both, it's come as a shock to all of us, but we do need to somehow take the stress of the estate away from your father. It's a great relief to talk to you about it, but I don't want your father to know I've spoken to you – not until we can give him a solution.'

The next morning, the brothers presented their idea to Lady Sally. 'Mother, Mathew and I have given the matter a great deal of thought and we think we might have a viable plan. Obviously, the priority is for Father to step back from his present role as soon as possible. We suggest that Andrew Higgins is promoted and given a salary increase, in order for him to act as the interim overall manager of the Hartington estate.' Andrew Higgins was the farm manager, much trusted and well liked by Sir Colin. 'Higgins can then act as interim manager until Mathew considers that he is in a position to leave Africa for good.'

'Do you know,' said Lady Sally with a smile of relief, 'I think you've come up with something that your father may well accept. He will be delighted with the thought that one day, Mathew will return to Hartington to take on the duties on behalf of the Duncan family.'

'Timothy, meet Mathew – he was the first love of my life, but soon escaped my clutches and fled to Africa to study monkeys.' Everyone laughed, although Mathew couldn't help blushing slightly at the truth behind Antonia's words. Mathew and Sebastian found Antonia's fiancé, Timothy Ludlow, to be intelligent, down-to-earth and very likeable. After a doubles match on the tennis court, which the Duncan brothers allowed the newly engaged couple to win, Timothy plied Sebastian with questions about the current political situation in Northern Ireland, the ongoing conflict between Republicans and Unionists, and Roman Catholics and Protestants, before switching his attention to Mathew.

'Do you think Ian Smith's regime will ever agree to one man, one vote elections for Rhodesia's black and white citizens?' asked Timothy. 'If so, what do you consider the chances are for the country to achieve a peaceful settlement, and what do you think the timescale will be?'

After Mathew had given his opinions on the political situation in Rhodesia, he was pleased that Timothy began asking him about his primate field studies, which he showed a great deal of interest in. 'While I was in the process of compiling one of the major parts of my MA, I visited the Museo del Prado in Madrid and saw a number of late-sixteenth to mid-seventeenth century paintings of New World primates, which included David Teniers II "Banquet of

A DIVERSITY OF DECISIONS

Monkeys", which depicts marmosets and tamarins. Apparently they were Brazilian golden lion tamarins – quite beautiful, their colour reminded me of barley sugar.'

'I know the painting. It's amazing Teniers could keep the monkeys still for long enough to get an accurate representation.'

'Absolutely. There was an interesting reference at the museum explaining that lion tamarins became all the rage among the aristocracy in Spain and Portugal in the seventeenth century. Apparently, the nobility would pay enormous prices for healthy specimens. What I found particularly amusing was that aristocrats would sometimes present them to their wives and daughters, but more often for some curious sociological reason to their mistresses, who carried them around in their sleeves or other convenient retreats about their raiments.'

Antonia heard them laughing and came to join them. 'What on earth has tickled you two? You're like a pair of giggling schoolboys.'

'Well my dear, I've just been telling Mathew some of the delights of viewing paintings of a diversity of the monkey kingdom within the solace of art galleries, and therefore not having to battle one's way through dense forests and steaming jungles in order to gain just a fleeting glance of one.'

On the morning before Sebastian had to return to Northern Ireland, Sir Colin asked his sons to come to the drawing room for an important discussion with he and Lady Sally.

'I'll be honest with you, boys, the doctor has told me that if I carry on with my present workload and the daily stresses of running the estate, I will in all probability be dead within the year. As a result of this prognosis, I agree with the suggestion that you put forward to your mother, that being to promote Andrew Higgins to the position of the estate's interim managing director. I just want to say how delighted I am to hear that one of my dreams will one day come true, that some time in the future one of my sons, Mathew, will continue with the Duncan family's long-adhered to tradition of being directly involved with the overall management of the Hartington Hall estate.'

On Mathew's return flight to Africa, after a rather sad farewell to his parents, he found himself to be in a sombre state of melancholy. He realised that if he hadn't fallen so deeply in love with Jan, if he didn't have to resolve their future together and if he wasn't so eager to continue with his academic career, it would be his duty to resign from his forthcoming tutorial post at the University of Rhodesia and return to Hartington Hall to take up his responsibilities at the earliest opportunity. Although he was longing to see Jan again, he had recently become increasingly concerned about the meeting that Jeremy Hughes wanted to have with him as soon as he was back in Salisbury. It weighed heavily on his mind.

Simon and Anna were at Salisbury Airport to give him a warm welcome back to Rhodesia and drive him to their home. Over brunch, they were anxious to hear all about Mathew's trip, after which Anna excitedly told him that their co-authored scientific paper about the comparative social behaviour of captive and wild populations of vervet monkeys had been accepted by the editors of the *International Journal of Primatology*.

'That's not all! One of the vervets has had twins!' she told him with a degree of enthusiasm no less than if she had just given birth herself. 'I managed to film the whole thing, and to record some of the calls made by other members of the family group – they make a gentle chattering noise, "yokko-yorgo-yorgo-yok", at the time of the parturition, as if they're supporting the mother. It's quite incredible. I can't wait for you to hear it.'

As Anna was determined to show Mathew her new 'pride

and joy', which Simon referred to as her twin babies, they visited the museum without delay. Mathew was delighted at how relaxed the family group of vervets were, and to see a part of the recording of the birth. After they returned to Simon's office, he handed Mathew two letters marked 'Private and confidential', which had arrived at the museum by recorded delivery on the previous day. Mathew didn't open the envelopes until he returned to the Vaughan-Joneses' home and had taken a shower, prior to joining his hosts for dinner. Their contents almost made him want to get on a plane back to his homeland as quickly as possible. One had come from Jeremy Hughes to inform him that he would be receiving a phone call the following morning; the second was from Piet Erasmus, demanding that they should meet as a matter of great urgency.

11

The Reluctant Informer

Immediately after breakfast the following morning, Mathew decided to drive to the Causeway post office. He thought that should Jeremy Hughes' colleague phone during his absence, he would avoid talking to him and thus put any meeting off for as long as possible. As he hoped, his post box contained a letter from Jan. He couldn't resist tearing it open immediately.

Dear Mathew,
Just to let you know how very much I am missing you and am longing to see you again. I have so much to tell you, and I want to say it when we are together.
When you get back after your trip to the UK, I'll be spending a week staying with my parents in Mazoe, but I very much hope that we can arrange another stay at Carnock Farm at soon as possible. If you suggest a weekend to Mariette when you could get away from your university lectures, I'll see what I can do.
With all my heart,
Jan xxx
P.S. I love you more than words can say.

Buoyed by the warmth of Jan's letter, Mathew drove to the Willocks' home to give Sir Roger a letter his father had asked him to deliver to his old friend. On arrival, he was informed by an armed BSAP African policeman, standing guard by the gate, that Sir Roger and Lady Willock were away and that they would not be back until the following week. Mathew drove on to Michael Lamb's nearby office to leave the letter in his care, and found him to be his normal cheerful self and as friendly as ever. During a mid-morning drink together, Mathew formed the opinion that Lamb was not privy to any aspect of the late-night conversation that he'd had with Jeremy Hughes just before his trip to the UK. Lamb told him that as the Willocks were staying with friends in Bulawayo, and would not be returning from Matabeleland for a week, Addie had taken the opportunity to join her father for a holiday with some of his friends in Durban.

'While you were out, there was a call for you from a woman with quite a strong Afrikaans accent,' Anna told Mathew on his return to Gunhill. 'She left a number for you to ring back at the earliest opportunity. I tried to find out who it belongs to, but the operator said that it was ex-directory.' When Mathew dialled the number, he spoke to a switchboard operator who asked for his name, and was then immediately put through to Major Piet Erasmus.

'Dr Duncan, it is of the utmost importance that I meet you tomorrow. Can we talk over lunch?'

'I have only just returned to Rhodesia and am extremely busy preparing for university tutorials. Couldn't this wait until later on in the month?'

'For your own safety, it's imperative that we meet as soon as possible. I look forward to meeting you in the bar at Meikles Hotel at noon tomorrow.' Their conversation came to an abrupt end, with the operator apologising that the line had gone dead.

Shortly afterwards, Mathew received a phone call from Hughes' colleague.

'As my superior, Mr Hughes, is currently out of the country,' said the diplomat in a clipped English accent, 'I look forward to meeting you very soon. It is essential that we arrange a meeting at the earliest opportunity.'

'I am extremely busy with university matters, and I already have a lunchtime appointment on Thursday.'

'I'm free for lunch on Friday, so I shall reserve a table at Brett's Restaurant in Second Street. I look forward to seeing you there at around twelve-thirty.' His persistency suggested that the diplomat, like Erasmus, was not expecting his luncheon invitation to be turned down. Also like Erasmus, he had been quick to conclude his conversation before Mathew could suggest that they meet at a later date.

So within twenty-four hours of Mathew's return to Rhodesia, he had to battle against the strong desire to drive to where Jan was staying in Mazoe and for them to run away together to the sanctuary of another country. He recognised that such an action would be totally counter-productive for their future together. Instead, he had been pressurised to accept two luncheon dates that he didn't want, with people who had as their main agenda to elicit as much information as possible from him about his contacts with members of the Manyika tribe.

From the previous conversations he'd had with Hughes and Erasmus, he was aware that they were anxious to secure any details that he might have about the locations of cross-border routes taken by Africans in the Vumba region, and whether any such movements involved ANC infiltrators. They were also interested to learn about the attitude of the local Africans to the Bush War, the degree of influence that ZANLA was gaining in the region, and how many members of the Manyika tribe had been recruited by the freedom fighters to become directly involved. In particular, they were keen to hear about Chief Chidzikwee's opinions, and whether he was supportive of Ian Smith's RF Government's intention to arrive at an internal settlement.

Mathew's lunchtime meeting with Piet Erasmus at Meikles Hotel was a considerable shock. After they had at first enjoyed quite a convivial talk about the current pressures on Rhodesia's

THE RELUCTANT INFORMER

wildlife, and Erasmus told him that he had always been a keen ornithologist, he suddenly changed the conversation to explain why he so urgently requested to have the meeting. As Mathew considered that the major's questioning would be confined to his friendships in Manicaland, and whether any of these had ANC connections, he had not in any way been prepared for the bombshell that Erasmus was about to divulge, or the line of questioning that he was to be subjected to. Mathew began by giving the usual disclaimer about his political stance.

'Throughout my time in Rhodesia, I've always considered it important not to become involved in the country's internal politics, but to be as friendly as possible to all of its inhabitants, whether European or African. During my initial time in the Vumba, I decided to take the opportunity to learn the Manyika dialect of Shona, in order to better understand the viewpoints of the indigenous people on many different aspects of their tribal life. During my primate studies at Castle Beacon, I did indeed make a number of African friends and acquaintances, for I believe that through such friendships I became totally trusted by them, and for that reason I am reluctant to breach any confidences that I may have shared with them. I must say that if I had voted at the recent elections, I would in all probability have gone for the NUF.' (The National Unifying Force were a moderate party led by Tim Gibbs, the son of Rhodesia's last governor.)

Erasmus had been toying with a glass of Cape brandy and, as if suddenly tiring of listening to Mathew's answer, he adopted a more authoritarian approach.

'I consider it is very much your responsibility to divulge any information that you think will be of interest to Rhodesia's security forces, particularly about the movement of Africans from across the Mozambique border. Also, although some of your conversations may have been in confidence, including those that you had with Chief Chidzikwee, I consider that it is your duty as a European to provide me with the type of information I'm seeking.'

Mathew got up to leave the table, only for Erasmus to gently reach for his arm and request that he hear him out. 'We have a great deal in common, for all the South African Government want is to help Ian Smith's RF Government reach a satisfactory internal settlement for the future of Rhodesia's black and white communities. I'm sure you will agree that the present conflict between Africans and Europeans should not be allowed to continue. A satisfactory solution could never be realised as a result of the increased warlike terrorist activities being employed by ZANLA and ZIPRA so-called freedom fighters in their conflict with the might of Rhodesia's professionally trained security forces.'

When Mathew sat back on his chair and remained silent, deep in thought, Erasmus adopted a more conciliatory approach.

'I would like to take you into my confidence and to share with you some information that I have recently been given by a colleague in BSAP's Special Branch.' Before Erasmus related the confidence, he ordered another Cape brandy for himself, and a Scotch for Mathew. After the glasses had arrived at the table and they had both taken a tentative sip, Erasmus exploded what seemed to Mathew to be the equivalent of a verbal hand-grenade. 'BSAP's Special Branch has been suspicious for some time that you have been working undercover for British intelligence. At first this was due to your regular visits to the Willocks' household in Salisbury; subsequently it was due to your friendships with the Lambs and with Michael's confidential secretary, Adeline Kinloch. The Rhodesian government already knew that Michael Lamb was directly involved with MI6. For these reasons, Special Branch started to keep an eye on your movements.'

Erasmus paused to take a sip of his brandy. 'During the last year, the degree of surveillance on you has considerably increased because of some evidence that my Special Branch colleague was given by one of his informers. A technician who works in the film processing department at a camera shop in First Street recognised in one of the prints he was developing the young wife of the well-respected second in command of the Selous Scouts, Major Paddy Bushney. A photograph of Jan Bushney had recently appeared in a feature article about her work in tourism and her interest in Rhodesian wildlife in one of the local glossy magazines, prior to her marriage to the major. The print showed Jan Bushney in the company of a handsome young man, both with their arms around the neck of a cheetah. By the way they were looking so lovingly at one another, he sensed that there could well be a degree of intimacy in the couple's relationship that could be of interest to Special Branch. Once it was confirmed that the woman in the photograph was indeed Major Bushney's wife, and at the same time that you were her companion, he decided to upgrade his level of surveillance. This subsequently revealed your quite regular visits to the Causeway post office.'

Mathew was so taken aback at being told about the intensity of Special Branch's interest in him, he found it difficult to concentrate on what Erasmus then went on to say. However, he was able to glean the general gist of how what he considered to be the most important secret that he had ever held in his life had been exposed in such a surreptitious fashion. At first he was unable to respond to what he had been told, but instead took a further sip of his whisky while he attempted to gather his thoughts as to how best to reply. For Erasmus had told him that as his Special Branch colleague had considered that they could well discover some incriminating material about Mathew in his post box, he had managed to gain permission from the RF Government's Minister of the Interior to instruct the postal authorities to give him access to it. As a result, Special Branch had read some of Jan Bushney's love letters to him, including the date and location of a forthcoming rendezvous that was planned at Carnock Farm.

SOMEONE WISHES TO SPEAK TO YOU

'My colleague in Special Branch went down to the BSAP station at Marandellas and under the cloak of a top-secret exercise, was given an African police sergeant and two constables to accompany him on what was referred to as a "security check" on the Smoelke's farm in the middle of the night. My colleague told me that when they got close to the farm, he took the precaution of getting out of the jeep so that he could approach on foot and take up a position with a good view of the veranda, from which all rooms are entered. The police sergeant was instructed to leave the jeep's engine running and its headlights full on, and by doing so to keep the interior of the veranda well illuminated. The sergeant and his two constables then went up to the front door and, as instructed, to ensure that all the occupants would hear, they banged on it as loudly as possible. As a result of this commotion, the veranda lights were switched on and almost immediately Mrs Smoelke was seen coming from her bedroom holding a standard issue PI 9 mm self-loading pistol in her right hand, demanding to know who was at her front door, prior to opening fire.

'After she checked to see that it really was a BSAP police vehicle and three uniformed policemen outside, she opened the door to the sergeant. While she was asking him about the seriousness of the terrorist alert in the Macheke area which he had just told her about, my Special Branch colleague managed to get closer to the house, and then, Mathew, what do you suppose he saw? You and Mrs Bushney came out of the same room together, scantily dressed in your nightclothes. A little incriminating, wouldn't you say?'

Erasmus seemed to savour the moment as he took another slow sip of brandy.

'As a result of my colleague having witnessed the scene first-hand, I know that Special Branch have sufficient information about your romantic involvement with Major Bushney's young wife to pressurise you into becoming an informer. As a consequence, you may be prevailed upon to cooperate not only with myself, but also with other intelligence agencies such as BOSS, that BSAP regularly share such security matters with. It's been through the cooperation of my Special Branch colleague that I have become so directly involved with him on such information-gathering matters, on behalf of the government of the Republic of South Africa.' Erasmus finished his speech with a rather triumphant smile.

Mathew had been stunned into silence. Erasmus went on to give his full assurance that both he and his BSAP Special Branch colleague would maintain the strictest confidence about what they considered to be his philandering with Mrs Bushney, for neither of them had any idea as to the seriousness of their affair. Finally, Mathew agreed to provide him with the type of information that he was seeking. He knew how extremely dangerous it would be if Jan's husband should hear even the slightest whisper of his wife's infidelities.

'Do you give me your word that, if I agree, you will not divulge the source of any information I may give you in the future?'

'You have my word.'

'In that case, I will agree to cooperate with you – but only as you leave me with no other choice. It's not just my own interests I have to consider.'

Mathew was as white as a sheet and utterly dismayed as he rose from his chair and grudgingly shook hands with Erasmus.

'Thank you for giving me your assurance, and that of your Special Branch colleague, that you will keep my relationship with Jan strictly between the three of us. I trust that will continue to be the case, so long as I fulfill my side of the agreement. I will give some serious thought to what you have requested of me, and will phone you at the beginning of next week in order to arrange a further meeting. In the meantime, I will consider the best course of action in order to cooperate with your wishes.'

SOMEONE WISHES TO SPEAK TO YOU

Driving away from Cecil Square, Mathew headed for Salisbury's highly regarded botanical gardens in the hope that he would be able to come to terms with the serious predicament that he was now confronted with. Walking under a canopy of the brilliantly red flamboyant trees in such tranquil surroundings, he was able to acquire a degree of solace and become more resolute in coming to terms with the nightmarish scenario that he was faced with. Instead of returning to Gunhill afterwards, he decided to call in at the museum, where he knew Anna would be with her vervet monkeys. He knew that discussing her various observations would help to take his mind off the acute anxiety that Erasmus had just heaped upon him. Also, he recognised how important it was to take a step back from his present emotional state, and to adopt as pragmatic an approach as possible. As far as he was concerned, no obstacle in the world would be allowed to thwart his objective of gaining Jan as his lawfully wedded wife.

On the Friday morning, Mathew received a phone call from Jeremy Hughes' diplomat friend with the excellent news that he had been suddenly recalled to the UK and would have to cancel his luncheon date at Brett's Restaurant. He was to take part in talks with the team that the potential proconsul Lord Carver had established in Whitehall.

'It is very much my hope that we will have the opportunity to meet in the future,' added the still-unnamed diplomat. 'Although this does depend on whether I am to be included in the squad that the Field Marshall is planning to establish for a British Consulate in Salisbury later on in the year.'

It was only after Mathew had replaced the receiver that he realised the Willocks' time in Rhodesia was soon to come to an end, and how important it was for him to see them before they went. He wondered whether Michael Lamb's appointment would be terminated at the same time and, if it was, whether Addie would be employed by the much talked-about British Consulate – although he feared this would not be the case. However, Mathew was greatly relieved about the cancellation of the lunch. At least he would be spared for the time being from being subjected to any further pressure to divulge precious confidentialities.

'I must say, Mathew, your first two tutorials have gone down extremely well among the students,' said Professor Tom Martin, 'and I think we can safely say that you are already a popular member of the academic team. It's been a good start.'

On Mathew's part, he was delighted by the welcome he received from both the staff and the students themselves, for the latter had shown so much enthusiasm and keenness to learn. He also found the subject matter chosen by the four MSc graduates that he was supervising to be extremely stimulating, although he was realising that he had to put in considerably more time than he had at first expected. Particularly in order to gather sufficient information about the diverse subjects that the graduates had chosen, so that his lectures and supervision of their studies would be as apposite as possible.

Mathew's second meeting with Piet Erasmus also took place over lunch at the Meikles Hotel, and their conversation on the whole was carried out in a businesslike and conciliatory fashion. 'I can guarantee that your affair with Jan Bushney will not be communicated by either myself, or by my BSAP Special Branch colleague, to any other intelligence-gathering operator. I also guarantee that the source of the information you will be giving me will never be revealed to your African friends. As previously agreed, Special Branch have already withdrawn the surveillance that they had been carrying out on your movements.'

After the reiteration of such reassurances, Mathew gave Erasmus the majority of the information he was seeking. This not only included his close relationship with Edgar Chidzikwee and Joshua Dombo, and with some of their fellow tribesmen, but also how much ZANU/PF operatives in the area had been pressurising tribesmen to cross the Mozambique border to join the ZANLA terrorist forces. Also, he told Erasmus about the majority of his two in-depth conversations with Chief Chidzikwee, which provided him with a good first-hand insight into the feelings and attitudes of one of the region's senior tribal leaders.

'I have no hard proof that ZANLA terrorist camps are cooperating with FRELIMO in providing training for ANC activists, although I have heard rumours that this is the case. I've also heard reports that both organisations have aided their ANC colleagues to travel south to the banks of the Limpopo, assisting with their movements across Rhodesia's border and their infiltration into the Republic of South Africa.'

'Well, Mathew, I must say I'm very pleased with the information that you have provided, but in order to complete all aspects of our bargain, should Ian Smith succeed in achieving the internal settlement that his government is currently trying to establish, it may be necessary for you to return to your campsite in the Vumba for a few days in order to glean as much information as possible from the local African population. It might also be beneficial for you to arrange a further meeting with Chief Chidzikwee – I would be particularly interested to learn the chief's views on the sustainability of the potential of an internal settlement should it come under the stewardship of Bishop Abel Muzorewa, as opposed to that of Robert Mugabe or Joshua Nkomo.'

Although Mathew was reluctant to inform on his African friends, he knew only too well that with the knowledge Erasmus and his Special Branch colleague held about his intimate relationship with Jan, he had no alternative but to cooperate fully with whatever was requested of him. Even if this did require him to return to Umtali and the Vumba Mountains.

As Simon and Anna had accepted an invitation to another *braai* at Paddy and Jan Bushney's home, Mathew decided to drive down to Inyanga to stay with Miles Kinloch and Addie for the weekend. Although he too had received an invitation, he knew it would be far less stressful for him to carry on exchanging notes with Jan through the Causeway post office (especially now Erasmus had confirmed that he was no longer under Special Branch surveillance) than having to be in her presence and to act in a formal fashion. During the Saturday evening dinner with the Kinlochs, Addie spoke only a little about the present state of affairs in her Salisbury office, although she mentioned that if Field Marshall Carver were to take over as Britain's Chief Representative, the Willocks and the Lambs would be recalled to the UK. As this was very likely to be the case, she thought that her services would not be required by the new Consulate.

On Mathew's return to Salisbury, Simon told him how the party had developed, with the usual loosening of tongues after some of the major's younger military colleagues had consumed more alcohol than was advisable. First, an enthusiastic young lieutenant from the RLI headquarters at Salisbury's Cranborne Barracks said how much he was looking forward to his participation in a major strike on terrorist camps in Mozambique, which was due to take place later on in the month. He also mentioned how earlier on in the year, General Walls' establishment of Combined Operations (ComOps) had so well streamlined a far more coordinated approach to the fight against ZANLA and its terrorist gangs. It was in connection with this forthcoming ComOps counter-insurgency raid that Paddy Bushney let slip, as if to highlight

SOMEONE WISHES TO SPEAK TO YOU

the independent nature of his regiment, that he was about to take a task force of Selous Scouts to Hot Springs, a settlement just to the north of Birchenough Bridge, in order to undertake some cross-border strikes of their own.

'Jan told me how very sorry she was that you were unable to make the *braai*,' added Anna, 'but she said that she hoped there would be an opportunity to meet up with you again in the not-too-distant future. She always says that she finds you such an interesting person to talk to.' On hearing this, Mathew so very much wished that he could confide in Anna and tell her that Jan and he were lovers, although he did have the feeling that Anna was already aware there was something going on that she couldn't quite put her finger on. At least Mathew was safe in the knowledge that his next meeting with Jan was already arranged to take place at Carnock Farm in just under a month's time; providing of course that there were no unexpected let-ups from Paddy Bushney's counter-insurgency operations, which usually took place over the weekends.

In the latter part of November, it was widely reported by the press that Lord Carver had arrived in Salisbury in his field marshal's uniform, accompanied by the UN-appointed General Prem Chand. According to the *Rhodesia Herald*, by wearing the insignia of a field marshal, Carver had wanted to make the point that he outranked the officer commanding the Rhodesian forces. But as Ian Smith had been pre-warned of Carver's hostility toward his government, he had chosen to ignore the field marshal's presence in the country and had instead spent the day watching a cricket match at the Salisbury Sports Club. Carver and Chand were totally unaware that the mayhem of Operation Dingo was about to be unleashed. It was a raid by Rhodesia's ComOps on two terrorist camps in Mozambique only a few days after their arrival, while they toured the country on a fact-finding mission.

It was subsequently reported that early in the morning of 23 November, Rhodesia's greatest and most successful counter-insurgency attack on ZANLA forces had taken place. The target was Robert Mugabe's headquarters at Chimoio. Two days later, a second ZANLA base to the north, known as Tembué, received a similar devastating onslaught. According to the official reports that followed these two cross-border raids, about ten minutes before the initial air strike a DC-8 airliner was flown over the Chimoio camp as part of a deception plan causing the insurgents to disperse, only to reform on parade a few minutes later, in time for the main air strike. The approach of the RAF's aging Canberra and Hunter aircraft had not caused any undue alarm; the assembled ZANLA forces did not take cover as they assumed it was just the DC-8 returning to fly over them.

In the first pass, the Canberra bombers were reported to have dropped 1,200 Rhodesian-designed anti-personnel fragmentation Alpha bombs. Following the initial devastating air strikes by the Canberras, it was reported that Hunters, FB9s, and ten Alouette III helicopter gunships engaged opportunity targets in allocated areas, which together inflicted the majority of the casualties. The paratroopers and heliborne troops had been deployed on three sides of the camp and were effective in killing large numbers of fleeing ZANLA cadres. Reports stated that Operation Dingo accounted for the deaths of more than 3,000 ZANLA fighters, with an estimated 5,000 wounded.

The Rhodesian forces had withdrawn in good order with only one SAS member being killed at Chimoio, and a Vampire pilot being killed on crash landing after his plane had been damaged by ground fire. Mathew was later told by Jan that on the day after the ComOps raids on Chimoio and Tembué, her husband had led the Selous Scouts' Operation Virile, which successfully destroyed five bridges over the Mozambique border, two of which represented major targets across the

Lusito River. Jan had said how very proud Paddy Bushney had been of the tight-knit troops that had accompanied him, and how highly he spoke of some of the African soldiers involved, who had carried out their duties with the utmost efficiency and professionalism.

Once the death toll of Operation Dingo became public knowledge, the international community was outraged and insisted that the targets had been refugee camps, not ZANLA training bases for terrorist insurgency. Whatever the truth was, Mathew was well aware that there were sure to have been numerous camp followers, women and children. He couldn't help thinking what a tragic new phase the Bush War had entered due to the Rhodesian forces' attempts to put an end to any future insurgency from across its borders. As Operation Dingo had resulted in so much loss of life, Prime Minister Jim Callaghan called for the Rhodesians to be held to account for the slaughter of refugees and vowed to intensify pressure on Ian Smith's government to hold elections at the earliest opportunity, stating that he would not support an internal settlement unless this was achieved on a one man, one vote, basis.

During the university's Christmas break, Mathew spent the majority of the festive season staying with Addie and her father in Inyanga, and even took the opportunity to see how his partly habituated family group of chacma baboons had progressed since his last visit. However, after a flurry of notes through their respective post office boxes, Mathew and Jan arranged their twenty-four hours together at Macheke, without Mathew having aroused any suspicion as to his whereabouts. The Vaughan-Joneses would consider that he had already arrived in Inyanga on the Saturday, whereas the Kinlochs would think that he was still at his adopted home in Salisbury, and was driving down to Inyanga on the Sunday morning.

THE RELUCTANT INFORMER

Their reunion at Carnock Farm was an intensely emotional and joyful occasion, as this was the first time they had been together since Mathew's visit to his family in late September. While they enthusiastically embraced as if nothing in the world could ever separate them, exchanging words of love, their togetherness was only interrupted when Mariette's footsteps were heard on the gravel as she had approached to welcome Mathew back to her home. During their twenty-four hours together, Mathew found it most difficult not to tell Jan about his meetings at Meikles Hotel with Piet Erasmus, or how he had been under surveillance by a member of BSAP's Special Branch for some time so that during their previous stay at Carnock Farm, he had been seen coming out of her bedroom in the middle of the night. Mathew knew how extremely upset she would be to learn that Special Branch were aware of her extramarital relationship, and the great concern and horror she would experience at the thought that her possessive husband could possibly find out.

They talked again about when the best time would be for Jan to file for a divorce, although they both recognised that at the present stage of the Bush War, with the regular news of some of the Selous Scouts' and Major Bushney's successful operations against the insurgents, the break-up would have to be delayed. So they both agreed that until the Bush War came to an end, and a constitutional settlement was arrived at, they would have to continue with a clandestine relationship. While politicians both in and outside the country had been trying to find a satisfactory settlement, the Selous Scouts, with their military associates the SAS and the RLI, were still very much involved with counter-insurgency operations. As Major Bushney was currently one of the country's heroes, they both realised an announcement that Jan had started divorce proceedings against him would appear highly counter-productive, perhaps even unpatriotic.

On 31 December 1977, Mathew listened to Ian Smith's

SOMEONE WISHES TO SPEAK TO YOU

New Year message with Addie and Miles Kinloch, in which he highlighted that, 'The British have been trying to settle the Rhodesian problems in a manner which would best settle their own interests, rather than the interests of Rhodesia.' He had gone on to report that whereas the rest of the world was pursuing a settlement between Nkomo's ZAPU and Mugabe's ZANU/PF, his RF Government were currently negotiating to establish an 'internal settlement', with him becoming joint prime minister with Bishop Abel Muzorewa, the Rev. Ndabaningi Sithole and Senator Chief Chirau, in order for Rhodesia to establish a fifty-fifty black/white transitional government, which he hoped would be fully recognised by the international community. Smith had ended his broadcast by saying, 'Let us hope that with 1978 a new era is about to begin. With goodwill, understanding and courage, we should grasp the opportunities open to us to end our dispute, to the benefit of all of our people.'

The spring term at the university started off well with a good deal of optimism among the students about the country's future. In early February, the Willocks held a small farewell dinner at their residence, which Mathew attended with Michael and Denise Lamb, and Addie. The Lambs were to follow the Willocks back to the UK after a short handover period to the newly arrived staff at the British Consulate. Addie, as expected, was given a month's notice, but Simon Vaughan-Jones managed to find her a job at his Victoria Museum. On 4 March, the fifty-fifty black/white transitional government was sworn in, but this 'internal settlement' was not recognised by the outside world.

In April 1978, ZANLA insurgents killed Lord Richard Cecil, who had been working on a documentary about the Bush War, after he parachuted with the RAR into northeast Rhodesia. Lord Cecil's ancestor had been a notable builder of the British

Empire and Cecil Square in Salisbury had been named after him. Acts of terrorism having increased, including the fatal shootings of two women in their sixties in the dining room of Inyanga's Montclair Hotel; a thirteen-year-old boy being killed as his sixteen-year-old brother fought off a gang of terrorists at their family home in Glendale; and a horrific atrocity on 23 June when eight English missionaries and four children were slaughtered at the Elim Mission, in an isolated mountainous region in the Eastern Highlands. The killers were reported to have dragged black students from their beds and harangued them for paying school fees to a 'racist government', while the whites were removed and butchered elsewhere.

In August, it was reported in the *Rhodesia Mail* that President Samora Machel had admitted holding 20,000 religious dissenters in camps in Mozambique but refused to bow to pressure for their release. On the 29 August, a Viscount carrying fifty-eight passengers was shot down by ZIPRA insurgents with a SAM-7 missile, only a few minutes into its flight from Kariba to Salisbury. After the plane had crash-landed in the Zambezi Escarpment, twelve ZIPRA insurgents arrived at the scene and shot and bayoneted the majority of the survivors, with their commander being reported to have shouted, 'You have stolen our land, you are white, now you must die.' As the country mourned this major atrocity, another mortar and rocket attack was carried out by ZANLA operatives on Umtali. In view of the numerous terrorist attacks that were taking place, Mathew came to the conclusion that neither of the African political parties ZANU/PF or ZAPU would ever recognise the overall authority of the RF's recently established Interim Government.

Soon after Lucienne had joined her husband, Daniel Olingo, at the US Embassy in Lusaka, she wrote to Mathew in the hope that they could arrange to see each other again. They

SOMEONE WISHES TO SPEAK TO YOU

soon arranged to meet at the end of September at the Royal Livingstone Hotel in Zambia, where she would stay with her two children. On the day before their meeting, Mathew flew up to Victoria Falls from Salisbury, via Kariba, and booked in for two nights at the famous Victoria Falls Hotel, sometimes referred to as the 'Gleneagles of Africa'.

As a British citizen and holder of a British passport it had been comparatively easy for him to acquire a day tourist visa to enter Zambia, whereas Lucienne and her children were refused entry into Rhodesia and due to the country's racist policies, would not be allowed in his hotel.

Mathew had been interested to read that in 1855, Dr David Livingstone, the missionary, physician and explorer, was the first European to witness the magnificence of Victoria Falls, which he then named after his sovereign. The natives had called the dramatic phenomenon 'the smoke that thunders', whereas Livingstone had written in his diary '...seems so lovely, must have been gazed upon by angels in their flight'.

As the drive down to Livingstone from Lusaka was expected to take Lucienne in the region of six and a half hours, her chauffeur-driven embassy car was not expected to arrive at the hotel much before 2 p.m. For this reason, after Mathew had eaten an early breakfast he took the opportunity to walk down to the Devil's Cataract, on the western side of the falls. Here, he saw the bronze statue of Dr Livingstone gazing over the savage splendour of the cataract to the magnificence of the main falls, as they crashed down roughly a hundred metres into the roaring cauldron beneath. He walked along a network of paths running parallel to the falls that, at intervals, led to vantage points at the edge of the gorge. In the majority of cases, there were no safety barriers to prevent a slip into the abyss beneath. During his walk to the famous railway bridge that spanned the ravine, linking Southern Rhodesia with Zambia, he encountered small family groups of warthogs, vervet monkeys, chacma baboons and various species of butterflies, which all appeared to be enjoying the coolness of the fine spray. The unspoilt tropical environment greatly helped Mathew to become as relaxed as possible before his reunion with Lucienne; but he still could not help thinking of their dramatic and tearful parting five years previously in Atlanta.

Mathew was interested to see a plaque at the side of the pedestrian pathway which recorded that the bridge had taken fourteen months to construct in 1905 and that it was the brainchild of Cecil Rhodes, a part of his dream for a Cape to Cairo railway. The plaque also stated that this outstanding example of Victorian manufacturing had been forged in England by the Cleveland Bridge and Engineering Company and, in 1904, was shipped to Beira, then transported on the newly constructed railway to Salisbury, via Bulawayo, to Victoria Falls. Rhodes was reported to have instructed the engineers 'to build the bridge across the Zambezi where the trains, as they pass, will catch the spray of the falls'.

Mathew passed through both the heavily fortified border posts without any undue delay, although the weapons loosely carried by the Zambian soldiers had looked particularly threatening. However, after having found a friendly taxi driver to take him to the hotel where he was to meet Lucienne and her two children, the driver soon dispelled any feelings of hostility and apprehension that he may have had by telling him how very much he welcomed him as a tourist to his country, especially during such troubled times.

On the previous evening Mathew had read how in 1911, the British South Africa Company had made the township of Livingstone the capital of the new British colony of Northern Rhodesia. He could see how much Cecil Rhodes' realisation of his dream of a Cape to Cairo railway had made this part of southern central Africa, what the European explorers had initially referred to as 'Darkest Africa', accessible and open to trade with the outside world.

On arrival at the Royal Livingstone Hotel, Mathew tipped

the driver with an over-generous amount of US$ notes, and asked him to return to the hotel by 5 p.m. He had only been able to obtain a one-day visa to Zambia and had to be back at the border crossing half an hour before sunset, prior to the border being closed for the night.

Lucienne arranged for their meeting to take place at a time when Daniel had to return to Washington DC to report to his superiors at the African Section of the States Department, on the increase of the cross-border raids by Rhodesia's security forces into Zambia. Such territorial incursions had greatly increased as a result of ZIPRA's downing of the Viscount in the Zambezi Escarpment, in which 38 were killed in the crash and ten survivors were subsequently massacred.

Apparently Daniel was delighted that while he was in Washington, she was taking the opportunity to visit the falls with their two children and to meet up with one of her old Emory University friends. It was very much due to his pressure of work at the embassy that he had been unable to take his family to see Victoria Falls, acknowledged to be one of the 'Wonders of the World'.

Mathew arrived at the Royal Livingstone just after midday, with plenty of time to spare before Lucienne was due to arrive, and chose a table in a corner of the shaded veranda with a good view of the drive leading up to the main entrance. After ordering a pint of Castle lager and a light snack, he couldn't help reflecting on some of the traumatic times he had experienced during his last few weeks with Lucienne in Atlanta. He had never been able to rid himself of his feeling of guilt after having abandoned her to undergo an abortion in San Diego. Also, for the thousandth time, he tried to reconcile why they had both separately come to accept that due to their very different ethnic and social backgrounds, their intimate relationship could never have developed into a marriage that would be sustainable in the long term.

Almost on the dot of 2 p.m. Mathew saw a smart, black

limousine come slowly down the drive and park under the shaded portals of the hotel's entrance. A uniformed African chauffeur and a plain-clothed US Embassy security man were sitting in the front. As soon as the car stopped, the security man got out and opened the rear door, out of which stepped Lucienne holding the hands of her two excitable young children. Mathew had asked the reception to direct an American lady with her two children as soon as they had arrived to where he would be waiting for them on the veranda. Lucienne was wearing an elegant navy and white outfit, and as they walked towards each other, he recognised her customary broad smile and eyes that appeared to shine like treasured jewels.

'Mathew – you don't look a day older! So good to see you again,' said Lucienne as she gave Mathew a friendly but reserved embrace. 'These are my children, Marcus and Polly.'

'It's lovely to meet you, Marcus and Polly,' said Mathew, smiling at the confident-looking and handsome young boy and the coy but most attractive little girl who stood on either side of their mother.

As they exchanged mutual enthusiasms and Mathew ordered some iced lime juice for them all, Lucienne's face radiated happiness. 'Children, this is the gentleman I told you about who spends most of his time looking at monkeys. We've seen baboons and vervet monkeys crossing the road on our journey down from Lusaka, haven't we? Lots of them!'

'My daddy is a very important man, who works in the US Embassy in Lusaka, in Africa,' said Marcus, unprompted, causing Mathew and Lucienne to laugh at this fine appraisal of his father. 'I'm sure he is, young man,' replied Mathew. 'That sounds very much more important than looking at monkeys, if not as much fun.'

'I promised Daniel we would only travel during daylight hours, so I've booked into the hotel for the night. I suppose you need to return to Rhodesia by sunset?'

'I do – how about to make the most of our time, we walk

to the banks of the Zambezi? I've been reading up on Victoria Falls so I can share the benefit of my wisdom with the children. We may even see some animals on the way.'

'Yes, let's do that. I must warn you that the armed security man has strict instructions to keep us in his sight at all times. It's not as bad as it sounds, we're quite used to it. He won't be intrusive.'

During their walk along an earthen path toward the Zambezi, under the shade of groups of acacia trees, they could hear the massive roar of the waterfall and see the clouds of spray erupting from the top of the eastern cataract and far beyond. When talking to each other, Mathew and Lucienne were careful not to say anything that could be misconstrued as something other than memories of university life, should it be picked up by either of the children and subsequently repeated to their father. Although when they talked about Adrien Deschryver and the eastern lowland gorillas of Kahuzi-Biega, and their mutual friendships with Osman and Yvonne Hill, they managed to convey a great deal to each other through their eyes. At one stage Mathew saw Lucienne become tearful but she quickly wiped them away, telling her children that she sometimes had an allergy to some of the local vegetation.

When they reached the eastern bank of the Zambezi, just above the waterfall's eastern cataract, Lucienne was surprised by the way Marcus quickly released her hand and took Mathew's, as if wishing for his protection from the thunderous noise of the water as it plunged over the rapids into the cauldron below. While Polly hid behind her mother in awe of what was in front of her, Lucienne could see how tightly Marcus held Mathew's hand as he had gazed at the magnificence of the spectacle. Marcus' contact with her former lover almost appeared to represent the start of a natural bonding between son and father.

'Down there at the bottom, children – all that angry water

churning around – it's known as the "Boiling Pot". You wouldn't want to go for a swim in there, would you?'

How Lucienne wished that she could have told Mathew that the hand he was holding so firmly was that of their son, the product of their one-time deep love for one another. But she had agreed with Daniel, whom she loved deeply and was so extremely happily married to, that they would only tell Marcus once he had reached his mid-teens that although she was his real mother, Daniel had adopted him when he was only a few months old, soon after they were married. Lucienne respected her husband very much for never having asked her the identity of Marcus' real father. She had still to make up her mind whether she would ever tell Daniel, or at some time in the future reveal to Mathew that the young boy he had got on so well with when they met in Livingstone was their son.

As they walked back to the hotel, while Marcus and Polly chatted to the security officer, Lucienne said, 'I was very lucky that I met and fell in love with Daniel after you left Atlanta. I am very happily married, and we are fortunate to have two beautiful, healthy children. It's funny – Marcus seems to feel very comfortable with you. Thank you for holding his hand and reassuring him when we were near the rapids.'

'I'm glad it worked out well for you. I've never felt comfortable with my decision to leave Atlanta when I did…' Mathew sensed that Lucienne did not want to talk about the time of their parting, although he could never have guessed the reasons why. 'I do hope I get to meet Daniel one day. I know I can rely on your discretion about this, but I too have found someone I wish to marry… It's a very complicated situation. She's a South African-born Rhodesian woman, married to a considerably older husband who treats her like a war trophy. She wants to divorce him as soon as the right opportunity presents itself.' Mathew avoided giving Lucienne any details about who Jan was, even using a false name. 'If we have the chance to meet up again once Judy and I are married, I'm quite sure that you would approve of her.'

'Mom, I like your friend very much. Can we see him again soon, with Daddy too?' said Marcus when they were back at the hotel and Mathew was just about to get into the waiting taxi. 'And I like you too, Marcus. And Polly. It would be lovely to see you again,' he replied.

'Mom,' continued Marcus, 'why does your English friend look so important, like Dad, when he only watches monkeys in the trees?'

'That is a very good question,' replied Lucienne. 'A few lucky people are born to always look important, and my English friend is one of them.' Mathew put his arm around both the children and gave them a light farewell hug, then kissed Lucienne with the fondest of goodbyes, telling the security man to take extra good care of them. As his taxi sped away towards the border, he found himself submerged under a deluge of reminiscences, mixed with sadness and joy.

Later, as he tried to relax in his room, Mathew tried hard not to dwell upon the unwelcome thought that Jan had spent her short honeymoon with Paddy Bushney at the very same hotel.

12

A Paradox of Valour

'Honestly Mathew, you wouldn't believe how irresponsible they were,' said Anna as she updated Mathew on all the latest news after his return to Salisbury. 'My friend said her husband and one of his colleagues were having dinner in a restaurant, when they heard an Englishmen sitting at the next table say how he had forgotten the name he had used to book into his hotel, and asked his friend whether he could remember what it was. He was completely unguarded. He may as well have gone to the nearest police station and given himself up. My friend's husband and his colleague went over to their table, produced their CIO credentials, and asked the two of them to come to their CIO HQ.'

Anna's friend's husband had not given her any further details about what had occurred immediately after the arrest, although she was told that the two Englishmen were escorted onto a London-bound SAA flight within thirty-six hours of their arrival in Rhodesia.

He had also mentioned that during the latter part of the previous year, the CIO had arrested three CIA agents who had been accused of undermining Bishop Muzorewa's authority. Such an arrest was to cause the US Government considerable embarrassment, by increasing the possibility that the CIA network in southern Africa could be exposed.

* * *

SOMEONE WISHES TO SPEAK TO YOU

During the early part of 1979, Mathew found his tutorials at the university to be both stimulating and exacting, and staying with the Vaughan-Joneses to be most agreeable. However, he found living in such close proximity to Jan and maintaining the pretense of being just casual friends to be increasingly difficult.

At one of the weekends that they managed to be together at Carnock Farm, they had started to see some light at the end of the tunnel.

'I've made up my mind,' said Jan. 'As soon as Rhodesia establishes a Government of National Unity, and the Bush War comes to an end, when the Selous Scouts are sure to be disbanded, I will file for a divorce. After a socially acceptable period of time, we can get married. It makes me so happy when I talk about becoming your wife; it makes it seem real. Once we're married, we can go to England and start a new future together. There, doesn't it sound easy?'

Throughout their relationship, Mathew had never mentioned that his father was a baronet, that he had been brought up in a mansion or that the family had a substantial ancestral estate. He was anxious to keep his family and Hartington Hall as much as of a surprise as possible.

Life went on relatively normally in Salisbury and Bulawayo, although the *Rhodesia Herald* regularly reported the brutal murder of rural people, even though the country's security forces had been continuing to hammer ZANLA and ZIPLA operatives internally as well as in Mozambique and Zambia. However, as the RF Government came to recognise that it required at least one of the hard-line nationalists to authenticate a sustainable settlement for Rhodesia, it had for some time engaged in a love-hate relationship with Joshua Nkomo rather than the more belligerent Robert Mugabe.

By the end of January, the campaign for the referendum on Rhodesia's new constitution came to a climax, with eighty-two per cent of the white electorate having approved it. On 12 February, just when Rhodesians were becoming more confident that a satisfactory settlement for both the black and white communities could soon be achieved, within five months of Mathew's flight to Victoria Falls to meet Lucienne, a second Viscount had been shot down just after it had taken off from the Falls Airport. It was already well known that the Soviet Union had supplied Zambia with SAM missiles for such attacks against Rhodesia, and soon after the downing of the Viscount, Joshua Nkomo and his ZIPRA insurgents triumphantly accepted responsibility for this act of terrorism.

By way of retaliation, RhAF Hawker Hunters of No 1 Squadron attacked ZIPRA bases near Livingstone and, at the same time, four Canberra bombers took off from a runway on the edge of Wankie National Park, crossed Zambia on a 4,000 km round trip to Angola and successfully bombed a garrison of UNITA insurgents. Also, during the confusion caused by the 'overfly', the jittery ZIPRA forces had in a case of mistaken identity downed one of their own Zambian Air Force Macchi jet fighters.

In early March, one of Mathew's greatest fears had come to the fore again, with the return of Jeremy Hughes' colleague. The unnamed diplomat almost immediately made contact with Mathew to reschedule their meeting. He had reserved a table for lunch on the Saturday at Brett's Restaurant, and on Mathew's arrival he was directed to a secluded corner table where a smartly dressed and clean-shaven middle-aged man was waiting for him.

'Dr Duncan, so pleased to meet you at last. My name is Augustus Pitt. Do take a seat.'

Pitt ordered a bottle of South African Sauvignon and exchanged a few short pleasantries before he got straight to the crux of the matter.

'I don't want to waste your time, Dr Duncan. One of my MI6 colleagues has informed me that as a result of the second downing of a Viscount by ZIPLA, and the proven involvement of Joshua Nkomo, the Rhodesian Government have given the Selous Scouts the go-ahead to assassinate Nkomo at the earliest opportunity. As far as the British Government is concerned, it is of the utmost importance that such an assassination attempt is avoided at all costs.' It was another verbal hand grenade, similar to that exploded by Piet Erasmus at Meikles.

As Augustus Pitt had already been told by Hughes that Mathew was the type of person likely to be susceptible to blackmail, he was ready with the ammunition he needed to secure Mathew's cooperation. 'I would like to share some of the considerable amount of confidential information that MI6 has had on their files in London about you for some time. This information not only includes details of Jan Bushney's extramarital relationship with you, which has been provided by MI6 informers working undercover at CIO's HQ in Salisbury, but also some valuable material about your time studying in the Deep South of America.'

'Where on earth did you get that?'

'I contacted one of my colleagues working at the CIA Langley HQ in Washington DC to carry out an information-gathering exercise on any significant movements during your time at Emory University.'

As was the case when Erasmus had informed him about the extent of the surveillance that the CIO had carried out, Mathew was totally taken aback by the involvement of the CIA.

'They provided us with some information about your time at Scaife University in Mississippi, your membership of Tupelo's Civil Rights Movement and participation in one of its protest marches, and also details of your time in Atlanta studying for your doctorship. Their documentation included a copy of an unpublished article written by an investigatory journalist from Macon's local press agency. You may remember the title,

'*In flagrante delicto* – Son of British noble engaged in immoral behaviour with black girl ends up with an assault charge'.
Mathew was stunned that the CIA could possibly hold such a file.

'Believe me, Mathew, the last thing I want to do is release any of the information in this dossier to the press, but taking into consideration your close relationship with Major Bushney's wife, I expect you to cooperate with me.' Pitt concluded in a matter of fact tone, as if asking for the merest favour. 'I want you to find out as much as possible about the Selous Scouts' operations, in particular about their plans to assassinate Joshua Nkomo.' Mathew had no alternative but to comply.

'As soon as I find anything out that I consider to be of significance, I'll call you.'

Mathew shook hands brusquely and left the restaurant, his head spinning. After driving to his office at the university, he wrote a note to Jan to ask that should Paddy be away during the course of the following week, it was important for them to meet at the earliest opportunity. He suggested that they could meet in the early evening at the botanical gardens and said that he would check his post office box daily for her response. On his way back to the Vaughan-Joneses', he dropped the note into her Causeway box number and dreamt of the day when he would be able to rid himself of the degrees of blackmail that the intelligence agencies were subjecting him to. Mathew couldn't help wondering whether there was anything else that he had done in his life that was not already known to either national or international intelligence agencies. He could not help dwelling on the horrific thought that as Daniel Olingo in his post as Cultural Attaché was a CIA operative, he may be aware of the dossier about him. If so, did he realise that the black girl referred to in the scandalous headline from Macon was indeed Lucienne? He just had to pray that the CIA file had not been copied to Daniel.

Mathew and Jan arranged to meet on the Wednesday

evening just after 6 p.m. To any onlooker, it would have appeared that they had just bumped into each other by chance while walking through the gardens. They even refrained from giving each other a welcoming kiss. As they did not want to risk being seen together for any longer than was necessary, Mathew came straight to the point.

'It's very important that this goes no further, but I have to tell you something urgently. I've just been approached by a well-connected British diplomat who has been informed by MI6 that the Selous Scouts have the government's go-ahead to assassinate Joshua Nkomo. As the British Government consider that the assassination would be totally counter-productive to arriving at a satisfactory future political settlement, it is imperative that any attempt on Nkomo's life is thwarted or, at least, that he is given prior warning.'

Jan had to suppress her disgust, and whispered, 'I can't believe the Selous Scouts have agreed to assassinate Nkomo... It can only make things worse. It will set back any settlement and cause more fighting and bloodshed – of course I'll do what I can to find out if Paddy is already involved. I'll be in touch as soon as I have anything to tell you.' They shook hands and waved goodbye to each other nonchalantly, as if they were the most casual of friends.

While Jan walked back to one of the side entrances to the gardens, Mathew returned to the main gates and drove to the home of David Montgomery for a sundowner and an early dinner. The evening gave the two friends a chance to relax and reminisce about the happy times they had spent together in the Vumba, which helped to distract Mathew's thoughts from the increasing amount of pressure being forced upon him.

Shortly afterwards, while her husband was attending a regimental dinner at his Inkomo Barracks, Jan took a considerable risk by entering his normally 'out of bounds' office at their home and unlocking the draws of his desk, for she had always known where he hid the keys. In one of the top draws she found a file labelled 'Top Secret/Restricted' which contained a copy of an action plan entitled Operation Dodo.

The plan gave details of how a radio-detonated car bomb had been selected as an appropriate device for the assassination of Joshua Nkomo, and that the vehicle carrying the bomb was to be driven via Botswana to Lusaka by a captain of the Selous Scouts. Wearing civilian clothes, the captain was to be given a South African passport and impeccable documentation to describe him as a commercial traveller for a pharmaceutical firm with its headquarters in Johannesburg. At the same time, one of the Scouts' undercover agents, already operating in Lusaka, would maintain surveillance on Nkomo's movements.

As a bug had been recently found on the phone of the Scouts' Commanding Officer, Reid-Daly, and it was expected that a foreign power had a mule in the CIO, Jan had taken the precaution of wearing gloves throughout her time in her husband's office, as well as being as quiet as possible prior to returning the keys to exactly the same position she had taken them from. She was aware that all of her husband's telecommunication equipment was routinely security-checked by one of his trusted warrant officers, including the positioning of a sensitive tape recorder; she had worn slippers and opened the draws as silently as possible to avoid making any noise.

Jan had the opportunity to tell Mathew the details of what she had uncovered when they met at Carnock Farm, two weeks after their meeting in the botanical gardens. Mathew in turn passed it on to Augustus Pitt at the earliest opportunity.

Pitt was delighted, but told Mathew it was crucial that he should be kept abreast of any further information about the assassination attempt. Pitt had also been told by an MI6 colleague, but not Michael Lamb, that a ComOps communication had been intercepted, stating that if 'one man, one vote' elections were to take place, and if Robert Mugabe were to run for presidency, there would also be an attempt on his life. According to the document, the assassination would be scheduled for when Mugabe was electioneering in the southern Beitbridge district of Rhodesia. This, too, would have to be prevented.

In mid-April it was reported that with a high degree of precision Rhodesia's SAS, and not the Selous Scouts, landed several Land Rovers on the Zambian side of the Zambezi and drove brazenly into Lusaka. They attacked Nkomo's house so ferociously it was almost demolished, and a large number of ZIPRA personnel were killed. According to a subsequent CIO report, Nkomo had not been at home as he had been tipped-off beforehand by British intelligence sources. The incident caused Zambia's President Kenneth Kaunda considerable embarrassment, for he had been hosting an OAU conference in Lusaka at the time of the attack.

Some time later, Jan told Mathew that the Selous Scouts had made three attempts to infiltrate a small assault team into position for the proposed attack on Nkomo's house in Lusaka, but all of these were abandoned due to mechanical failures, bad weather conditions, or to the lack of sufficient financial resources. The operation had also left one of their officers in an infamous Zambian prison. Because of the Selous Scouts' failure to successfully execute the mission, ComOps had decided to transfer the job to the SAS. This greatly wounded the pride of the Selous Scouts, and demoralised Major Paddy Bushney, whose moods became even more unpredictable. Mathew and Jan were never to know whether the information that they gave to Augustus Pitt had resulted in Joshua Nkomo being constantly on the alert for an attempt on his life, and as a result escaping the SAS attack on his home.

On 31 May, Ian Smith concluded his last day of office. The following day, Bishop Abel Muzorewa, after a seventy per cent electoral turnout, took office as prime minister and head of the new Government of National Unity, but it was only South Africa who was to recognise the new government of their neighbour.

Soon afterwards, Paddy Bushney had a *braai* at his home to celebrate the outcome of the court martial of the commanding officer, Reid Daly, which he had accepted an invitation to attend. Although the court had declared, 'While having regard to the tenets of military discipline that a guilty verdict had to be returned', he had simply been sentenced to a reprimand. The court martial was the consequence of an incident that took place at a reunion dinner hosted by the RLI at its Cranborne barracks on 31 December 1978, to mark the regiment's seventeenth anniversary. Reid Daly gave an impromptu speech during which he thanked the army commander, Brigadier General John Hickman, for bugging his phone and remarked that if he ever saw Hickman again, it would be too soon.

According to reports, within minutes the two were in heated arguments and had to be pulled apart by colleagues, with Hickman demanding that Reid-Daly be arrested for insubordination.

The Vaughan-Jones and Mathew had been also invited to the *braai*, and Mathew was surprised at how amicable Bushney was towards him. He told Mathew that he had read his article in *Rhodesia Science* about the pros and cons of the Zoological Society of Rhodesia's proposal for a zoo at the Graniteside site, although he did add rather sarcasticly that if a zoo was to be established, the Selous Scouts had a number of humans that they would like to put into it. After asking Mathew how his lecturing at the university was progressing, and whether he was still studying monkeys, Bushney had introduced him to the guest of honour Reid-Daly, about whom Mathew had heard so much.

* * *

SOMEONE WISHES TO SPEAK TO YOU

During the university's summer break, Piet Erasmus made contact with Mathew and requested him to return to the Vumba and to see Chief Chidzikwee, as soon as a meeting could be arranged. Erasmus said that the South African Government were keen to learn as much as possible about the Manyika tribespeople's attitude toward Rhodesia's newly elected government. In particular, whether the chief was likely to change his political support of the current Zimbabwe-Rhodesia Government of National Unity led by Bishop Muzorewa, or did he think that the Lancaster House Conference, which was due to take place in London in just under three months time, should instead favour the Patriotic Front (ZANU & ZAPU), headed by Robert Mugabe.

Although Mathew said he was reluctant to return to the Vumba because of the danger involved, he knew only too well that he would have to comply. Since his last visit to Umtali and the Vumba at the beginning of the previous year, he had met up twice with his D.O. friend, Jim Prior, in Salisbury. Prior had told him how fortunate he had been to escape the sustained terrorist attack on Umtali on 17 October, ten months previously, a barrage of rocket and mortar fire had descended on the city; some fifty shells had landed over an area of a square kilometre injuring five people, including one of his office staff.

Making contact with Chief Chidzikwee proved to be far more difficult than on previous occasions, and at one stage Mathew considered that the chief was reluctant to see him again. It was only due to the help of his good friend Edgar Chidzikwee that the meeting was eventually arranged. Edgar stressed that it should be completely confidential and told him that due to an increased amount of intimidation being carried out on his fellow tribesmen by ZANU/PF activists, his father wished to be seen as being as open-minded on the political situation as possible, until a final settlement resulting from a nationwide election of one man, one vote could be achieved.

A PARADOX OF VALOUR

* * *

The weekend prior to Mathew's planned meeting with the chief, he stayed with Jan at Carnock Farm and met her brother-in-law, Willie Smoelke, for the first time. Willie was very welcoming to Mathew and seemed genuinely pleased by his relationship with Jan. He said that he had never liked the way Major Bushney treated his sister-in-law and although like the majority of his military colleagues he greatly admired Bushney's leadership skills, he had never enjoyed being in the major's company.

On Sunday, Mathew headed to Inyanga to see the Kinlochs. Addie was staying with her father for a few days, taking a break from her new job at the Victoria Museum, which she was enjoying greatly. Angus Whitton had also been invited to Sunday lunch, although the news he had to share with them was not good. He explained that there had been a considerable increase in terrorist activities in the Inyanga region, and described the events of the Elim Mission massacre that had taken place in the Eastern Highlands, close to the border with Mozambique, just over a year ago. From everything that Mathew had been told about the bravery of Inyanga's residents, in spite of the constant terrorist threat to their personal safety, he could only be greatly impressed by the stoicism of the farmers and their families. They stood fast with their refusal to give up so much of what they had managed to create, rejecting the suggestion they should vacate their properties and go to the safety of Salisbury or across the border to South Africa.

Before his meeting with the chief, Mathew spent the night at Jim Prior's flat in Umtali. Jim explained that he'd been surprised when informed by an unspecified 'higher authority' in Salisbury that Mathew had been given clearance to visit the Vumba region again. He had been given instructions that Mathew had to be accompanied by an armed plain-clothes

Special Branch African marksman, who would be waiting for him at his D.O.'s office at 8 a.m. the following morning. Mathew accepted an invitation to stay at the flat again on the Wednesday, after his return from the Vumba. It was obvious from Jim Prior's conversation that he was unaware of the forthcoming meeting with Chief Chidzikwee, and for the chief's sake Mathew decided not to mention it. However, it was later established that Mathew's return to Umtali, and his forthcoming visit to the Vumba, was already known to ZANLA. A ZANU/PF informer who worked in the D.O.'s office had passed on the information that he was to visit his old camp at Castle Beacon, as well as to rendezvous with Edgar Chidzikwee who was to take him to a meeting with his father, although it was not known where this was to take place.

The next morning, Mathew collected the plain-clothes policeman from the D.O.'s office just after eight-thirty, and drove to the meeting place that Edgar had described to him in such precise detail. Just two thirds of the way up into the Vumba Mountains, and not too far away from the still-closed Leopard Rock Hotel, he had been directed to turn off onto a rough track where, round a corner, he would soon come across a small forest clearing on the right, where Edgar would meet him soon after 10 a.m. When Edgar arrived in an old borrowed Ford pick-up, much to the surprise of the man from Special Branch, the two men greeted each other like long-lost friends. After which it had taken them some time to persuade the policeman that his duty was to guard Mathew's Land Rover, as opposed to accompanying them to the rendezvous with Edgar's father, whom they had been careful not to identify.

Twenty minutes later, Edgar had driven into a small settlement consisting of no more than five *rondavels*, and after scattering the usual ubiquitous assortment of hens he parked his pick-up behind another vehicle under the shade of a sizeable fig tree. On entering the hut, the tall figure of Chief Chidzikwee rose from a stool in the dimly lit shadows, greeting Mathew with his customary firm handshake. At first, Mathew found the chief to be very reserved. It took almost an hour of general conversation before he managed to gently move on to Rhodesia's future. Mathew had one particular question that he needed to ask.

'Chief Chidzikwee, are you supportive of Bishop Muzorewa's Government of National Unity, or is the Manyika tribe more in favour of a Patriotic Front government under the Shona leadership of Robert Mugabe, should the outcome of the forthcoming Lancaster House Conference suggest that after a free election, such a government could be formed?'

'I'm not ready to answer that question, but I will say that myself and my tribe have been subjected to a great deal of pressure by ZANU/PF activists to ensure that when free elections do take place, we will vote for Mugabe and a ZANU/PF government. In the meantime, I have had to allow the ZANU/PF activists the freedom to distribute their propaganda leaflets within our tribal lands, without any interference.'

When the time came for Mathew to leave, he said, 'I must tell you that my time in Rhodesia is drawing to a close. Not only is my contract with the university soon to be completed, but also by the end of the year I will have to return to Great Britain. My father is very old and I need to take over the management of our family estate in the north of England. I just want to say goodbye, and thank you.' The two men stood up to shake hands with genuine warmth and affection. They both knew that this would be their final parting.

As Edgar drove back to the Land Rover, both men were quite subdued at the realisation that they too would be unlikely see each other again. On arrival at the forest clearing, they found an extremely relieved-looking marksman from Special Branch, who had locked himself into the vehicle. Before Edgar left, he said, 'Perhaps one day I shall be able to visit you in

SOMEONE WISHES TO SPEAK TO YOU

your country, and be able to make some more canopy platforms for you to observe your country's monkeys from.' Mathew hadn't got the heart to say that England had never had wild primates living in its forests, but told Edgar how important it was for him to always take care of his country's valuable wildlife heritage.

As Mathew already knew that there was little or no evidence of there ever having been a hut at Castle Beacon, he had through David Montgomery been granted permission by the National Parks Department to spend a night at its headquarters in the Vumba Botanical Gardens. On their arrival at Montgomery's former home, it looked like a mere apology to the pristine residence that it once was. But Mathew was pleased to renew his acquaintance with Joshua Dombo, who after Montgomery's departure had been given a small wage to act as caretaker to the property.

During their conversation over a meal of rice and goat meat, washed down by some bottles of Castle lager which Mathew had sensibly brought with him, the policeman was surprised at Mathew's command of the Manyika dialect. During their lively conversation, both the policeman and Joshua gave Mathew a good insight into the thoughts of the local community about its level of support for Muzorewa's Government of National Unity. They both reiterated how much the political activists of ZAPU/PF were continuously bullying people to support their party.

After an uncomfortable night on a mattressless bed, Mathew was up and shaved by dawn, in a similar fashion to the timetable that he had always adhered to while carrying out his primate field studies. As he knew that he had to be back in Umtali well before sunset, he thanked Joshua for the breakfast of eggs and goat milk, gave him some banknotes, and wished him well for the future. Mathew and his armed escort then drove to the nearby village, where he had visited Edgar and Joshua quite regularly during his time in the

Vumba. Although it had been over four years since his last visit he was surprised to find how descrtcd it was, but he did meet a few of the inhabitants that still remembered him. The village headman, Edgar's distant cousin, Kingstone Chimuka, asked him into his *kraal* to have a lunch of mealies with him, while the Special Branch man was left rather unceremoniously to guard the Land Rover to prevent an assortment of scantily dressed children from climbing all over it. Gabriel provided Mathew with some valuable additional information about what had occurred in the Vumba region since ZANLA's rocket attack on the Leopard Rock Hotel.

'After the hotel was closed and taken over as a billet by the security forces, the majority of the European community in the Vumba left their properties for safer parts, which caused a considerable amount of unemployment among the villagers. Some of them went to Umtali in search of work, while others gave in to ZANU/PF's propaganda and crossed the border to join ZANLA.' The remainder of Gabriel's account was much the same as Mathew had heard from his previous day's conversations with the chief, Edgar, Joshua and the policeman.

When Mathew sought his views on the future of Bishop Muzorewa's new Government of National Unity, Gabriel just sighed and smiled, saying, 'Only time will tell. It will be the African people of Zimbabwe who will ultimately decide on the country's future, and not the European.' A sentiment that Mathew was happy to agree with. However, when he asked Gabriel whether he considered Robert Mugabe would one day take control of the Patriotic Front and become Zimbabwe's president, he had smiled again and said, 'Robert Mugabe has his own ways of achieving his ambitions, some of which I would prefer not to speak about. The country's major Shona majority will always favour having Mugabe as their president, as opposed to Joshua Nkomo and his MDC party taking control of a future Zimbabwe.'

'Thank you so much for your hosptitality,' said Mathew,

SOMEONE WISHES TO SPEAK TO YOU

getting ready to leave. 'I need to be back in Umtali by sunset but before that, I plan to make a brief visit to my old campsite in the hope of seeing some of the monkeys. I miss their company.' After shaking hands with what seemed like the majority of the remaining villagers, he drove slowly back to the turn-off to Castle Beacon. Mathew noticed that his Special Branch companion had started to look decidedly more relaxed in the knowledge that it would not be too long before he was back in Umtali with his companions, his bodyguard duties safely completed.

Mathew parked the Land Rover in the shade of the familiar clump of fig trees at Castle Beacon. 'I won't be long, you stay here while I take a short walk up the forest trail to see whether I can find any of the monkeys that I used to know so well.'

'Dr Duncan, the instructions I have been given by the inspector made it quite clear that I am not to allow you out of my sight.'

'Don't worry about me, I know it very well around here. The problem is that if I were to approach the monkeys with a stranger, they will disappear almost immediately.'

So, once again, the policeman locked himself into the vehicle to wait for the return of his charge.

Mathew had walked only a short distance up the forest path when he caught a glimpse of some Stairs' monkeys, crashing through the forest canopy to the left of him. On one occasion, when two adults had detached themselves from the rest of the family group to forage quite close to where he was standing, he was almost certain that they recognised him. On his part, he had certainly identified them as two of the group's senior alpha males.

The next thing Mathew was aware of was waking up from a semi-conscious state, lying on some damp sacking on the wooden floor of an almost pitch-black hut. His head ached as if it had been hit by a sledgehammer, and his hair was matted with congealed blood. The cell-like dwelling was stiflingly hot and his mouth felt as parched as a piece of sandpaper. Mathew's body was weak and dehydrated; he found it difficult to move onto his side or to raise himself. As he tried to collect his thoughts, the door of the hut was kicked open and for a moment the massive image of an African man in military fatigues was framed in the doorway. The figure approached him. Mathew attempted to raise his head and feebly utter the Shona greeting '*Mangwanani*', to which the man's only response was to grunt and kick him forcibly in the groin. After which, he threw a bucket of water over Mathew, laughed, and then left the hut as quickly as he had entered. The only consolation of the visit was that Mathew was able to scoop some small amounts of water from the bucket, which had been left on its side near to where he was lying, and to lick some moisture from his bare arms. He then slipped back into a semi-conscious state, in which he was to remain for some time.

When Mathew had not returned to Jim Prior's home by sunset, the D.O. immediately got in touch with BSAP H.Q. to enquire whether they had received any reports from Special Branch as to the whereabouts of their man. When this drew a blank, alarm bells immediately started to ring and wireless contact was made with BSAP and RLI units stationed in the Vumba region. They in turn were quick to organise search parties for Mathew's Land Rover in the locations he had told Jim Prior that he planned to visit. As this included his old campsite, a detachment of RLI was sent to Castle Beacon. In the early hours of the morning, the RLI search party located the Land Rover and found locked securely inside it a very frightened-looking officer from Special Branch. They subsequently failed to find any evidence of Mathew's presence within the forest clearing.

Just after first light, a team of highly skilled SAS African trackers who had been rushed to the scene found a site where there had obviously had been a skirmish and traces of blood could be seen on the ground. The trackers told their lieutenant that the deep spoor they had found in the peaty ground had been left by two men and that in all probability they had been carrying something heavy, like a body. The conclusion was that Mathew had been kidnapped and carried away. The close mesh pattern of the composite rubber soles of the boots was identified as those warn by ZANLA and ZIPLA insurgents; it was believed that Mathew had been snatched by activists from the former. On receiving this information, the SAS lieutenant rapidly signalled it to his H.Q. adding that his trackers were continuing to follow the spoor and that he would signal again as soon as he had anything more to report.

News of Dr Mathew Duncan's kidnap by ZANLA insurgents soon reached Rhodesia's press and made the front page in the majority of the newspapers. The Thursday morning issue of the *Rhodesia Herald* used the headline 'Dead or Alive? Popular English University Lecturer Kidnapped by Terrorists in the Vumba Mountains', and the Reuter News Agency was quick to issue a press release about the kidnap. The first time Sir Colin learned about the disappearance of his son in Africa was at the breakfast table on the Friday, when a solemn-looking Sid Stockdale handed him a copy of the *Daily Telegraph* and pointed to the relevant piece. This was almost immediately followed by a phone call from Sebastian in Northern Ireland, who had just been told of the news by one of his brother officers. Numerous other calls were soon received from family and friends. Both the *Ilkley Gazette* and Skipton's *Craven Herald News* carried double-page spreads about the kidnap of Sir Colin and Lady Sally Duncan's youngest son.

It was fortunate that Paddy Bushney was away from home when Jan received the news, for she was unable to contain her grief and ran upstairs to collapse on her bed in floods of tears. After Anna had gone round to her home to see whether she had heard the news and how she was, Jan managed to begin to come to terms with what was happening.

A PARADOX OF VALOUR

Although Jan had never told her friend anything about her relationship with Mathew, Anna had been aware for quite some time that there was a potent chemistry between them. The looks that passed between them were far more than casual glances.

At the University of Rhodesia, Professor Martin had launched a publicity campaign to highlight Mathew's liberal credentials, not only including his activities within the Civil Rights Movement while he was at Scaife University in Tupelo, but also emphasising that Mathew was an ardent supporter of the forthcoming one man, one vote, elections. At the same time as the professor's publicity campaign and the gathering of signatures to present to the offices of ZANU/PF, the commanding officer of ComOps, Lieutenant General Peter Walls, held a series of meetings with senior service personnel at Military HQ, King George VI Barracks. Before long, the SAS trackers reported that they had followed the spoor of the kidnappers to a small, earthen track, where it looked as if Mathew had been loaded on to a vehicle which was then driven speedily away to the south. Regrettably they had been unable to trace the tyre prints beyond a flooded part of the track, although they had managed to establish that the vehicle had headed south toward the Mozambique border.

Among the many messages that General Walls received with regards to Mathew's possible whereabouts, there was one from David Montgomery. Montgomery reminded the general how they had first met just over five years ago at Plumtree School, when he was the guest of honour at their old school's seventieth anniversary. He said that as he knew the Vumba area and its tribespeople extremely well, he would like to help to try and locate his close friend. The retired Lt General Keith Coster had also contacted General Walls in order to tell him that he knew Mathew personally, and that everything should be done to rescue him, providing his ZANLA kidnappers had not already ended his young life.

SOMEONE WISHES TO SPEAK TO YOU

As ComOps had acknowledged that the Selous Scouts' specialist Reconnaissance Troop represented the most ideal unit to infiltrate some of their Portuguese-speaking 'turned-terrorists' to carry out the surveillance required across the border, they had been directed to immediately undertake such a mission in the hope of finding Mathew alive. If this proved to be the case, a rescue operation was to be put into operation at the earliest opportunity. In spite of P.K. Van de Byl having been constantly approached by both the national and international press media as to whether there had been any news about Mathew's fate, a total news blackout had been adhered to.

The Selous Scouts' infiltrators, in the disguise of ZANLA operatives, had taken five days to locate where Mathew was being held in a small forester's hut, in a clearing quite close to the border to the west of Bandula in Mozambique. Once ComOps had received confirmation that Mathew was alive, they immediately assembled a task force of specialists from the SAS, Selous Scouts and RhAF, in order to arrive at a rescue plan that could be implemented as quickly as possible. They were all aware from previous ZANLA kidnappings of those they considered could provide them with valuable information that after interrogation, which usually involved torture, the victims were murdered.

Therefore, within twenty-four hours a plan of action code-named Operation Primate was agreed upon. After Paddy Bushney informed General Walls that he knew the Bandula region well and was a personal friend of Mathew Duncan, he was appointed to lead a small group of Selous Scouts disguised as ZANLA operatives across the border to Bandula. The chief objective of Bushney's mission was to cause a diversionary action to draw away any serious military attention that a rescue party may encounter and, during the distraction caused, a volunteer SAS assault team was to be flown to a bush landing strip within striking distance of the hut where

A PARADOX OF VALOUR

Mathew was being held. A territorial Flight Lieutenant, Chris Falla, had made his privately owned de Havilland DHC-2 Beaver available for the mission. This type of aircraft was considered to be the most ideal to land and take off from such rough terrain. On landing, the SAS team was to be guided by one of the Selous Scouts Portuguese-speaking African soldiers to Mathew's hut. ComOps had given Operation Primate the go-ahead to take place on the Wednesday night, exactly a week after the kidnap.

Paddy Bushney told Jan in the strictest confidence that their mutual friend Mathew had been located and was alive, and that it was hoped an assault team of the security forces would be able to rescue him. Bushney refrained from telling her that he would be personally involved in the attempt to secure his freedom, although he had said that he expected to be away during the course of the next five to seven days on a major counter-insurgency operation. He also mentioned that during his absence, he would be happy for her to go down to Macheke to spend some more time with her sister. Jan was so overjoyed to learn that Mathew was still alive that she surprised her husband by spontaneously kissing him; he couldn't recall when she had last acted in such an affectionate manner.

It was later established from information gathered by the Selous Scouts specialist reconnaissance troop that it was a senior general in Robert Mugabe's ZANLA guerrilla force, Solomon Mujuru, under his *nom de guerre*, Rex Nhongo, who had implemented Mathew's kidnap. The general had known for some time about Mathew's friendship with Chief Chidzikwee. Due to the chief's popularity within his Manyika tribe, and as he had yet to speak out in support of Robert Mugabe and ZANU/PF, Mujuru was keen to incriminate him by producing evidence that throughout the Bush War he had been an agent of Rhodesia's security forces and, as such, had acted as a traitor to ZANLA's war of independence. Mujuru's plan was to have Mathew kidnapped and, in whatever way may be necessary, for him to be made to sign a document to implement Chief Chidzikwee for having been an agent of Rhodesia's security forces throughout the Bush War.

Chris Falla landed his single-crop Beaver aircraft on the landing strip with the proficiency of the expert bush pilot that he was. Each of the three European and two African SAS task force members, armed with 9 mm calibre Sterling machine guns, a weapon designed specifically for close-quarter encounters with a high rate of fire, were all as tense as any rescue force on such a mission could have been. As the Selous Scout soldier started to guide the SAS men toward their quarry, they heard an explosion to the west of them, where Bushney and his men had successfully blown up one of the road bridges near to a ZANLA encampment.

Twenty minutes later, the SAS team arrived at the clearing where Mathew was imprisoned, but just before they reached it they were almost detected by the headlights of a vehicle, emblazoned with FRELIMO markings, that was speeding down a dirt track in the direction of the explosion. Soon after this, the second member of the Selous Scouts reconnaissance team joined the SAS men and informed them that there were now only three ZANLA soldiers left guarding Mathew. After a further ten minutes, when the lieutenant in charge had carefully assessed the exact whereabouts of the soldiers, he caused a distraction by throwing a stick grenade into the nearby forest. Two of the ZANLA soldiers rushed to take cover, but were immediately dispatched by a burst of SAS machine-gun fire. After the lieutenant had shone a spotlight on the door of the hut, and the Selous Scout Portuguese-speaking soldier shouted for the third terrorist to surrender, a terrified ZANLA operative meekly came out of the hut with his hands in the air.

Inside the hut, the lieutenant found Mathew gagged, unshaven and tied to a chair, with blood stains on his face, his torn shirt and his trousers. After the bindings were untied, Mathew attempted to stand, but immediately collapsed. The SAS team were prepared for this and had a canvas stretcher on which to carry Mathew back to the bush landing strip, with their securely handcuffed ZANLA prisoner being dragged behind them. Chris Falla had his Beaver aircraft in full readiness and after they managed to carefully load Mathew's stretcher on to it, the overloaded aircraft managed to taxi along the bush clearing, make a perfect take-off and fly low over the border to the safety of Umtali's RhAF base.

As far as Mathew's rescue was concerned, Operation Primate proved to be a highly successful operation. If the rescue attempt had failed, he would undoubtedly have ended up being murdered by his ZANLA captors. But the ultimate irony was the bittersweet ending of the whole operation, which culminated in the tragic death of Major Paddy Bushney. After his task force had successfully blown up the road bridge to draw FRELIMO and ZANLA military operatives away from where Mathew was being held, he had been killed when he went back to rescue one of his badly injured African Selous Scouts. A counter attack by his men had managed to retrieve the wounded soldier, as well as the body of their leader. At much the same time that Bushney had been shot and killed, Falla landed his DHC-2 Beaver at the RhAF base in Umtali.

After an army doctor had climbed on board the aircraft to examine Mathew, he found him to be suffering from chronic dehydration and due to the condition of both of his feet, as he was unable to place any weight on them, the stretcher had to be carried to a military ambulance that was waiting for him. Once transferred to a small military hospital for treatment, Mathew was immediately put on a saline/glucose drip, after which the doctor was able to carry out a thorough examination. He found that the soles of his feet had been quite badly lacerated, which as Mathew later told both the doctor and Special Branch was due to frequent beatings by one of his ZANLA captors, using a bamboo stick. This was because he repeatedly refused to sign a document that his captors had presented to him in order to incriminate Chief Chidzikwee as being a long-term informer for the security forces, reporting on ZANU/PF activities. By doing so, they wanted to portray the chief to his people as a traitor to his Manyika/Shona tribe, and to ZANLA's fight for freedom from the yoke of the Europeans.

The torture went further than the soles of his feet and the many cigarette burns on his chest. Mathew told a senior Special Branch officer that on one occasion he was blindfolded, tied to a tree, and told that unless he put his signature to the document he would be shot. The person who they had referred to as their leader, General Nhongo, told them that he would have all three of the interrogators severely punished should they fail in their attempt to get their captive to sign the document concerned. Although Mathew had been left out in the scorching sun for some time, and occasionally punched in the stomach, he had steadfastly refused to sign the incriminating notice and, having fainted, he had only come round again when a bucket of water was thrown over him after being returned to the hut.

Perhaps the stoic way that Mathew had managed to deal with the extreme pain that the interrogator had inflicted upon him had, to some degree, resulted from his time at Wellington College. For in those days, whenever a boy received a caning and no matter how severe it had been, it was considered 'bad form' to betray either the person administering the beating, or afterwards to his peers how much the experience had hurt.

Soon after the news of the death of Major Paddy Bushney had been released to the press, and his body taken to the small chapel at Inkomo Barracks, P.K. Van der Byl announced that the major was to be the second person to be posthumously awarded Rhodesia's Grand Cross of Valour, the country's highest military decoration for conspicuous bravery by a member of the security forces. Ten days later, a memorial service was held at Salisbury's Anglican Cathedral of St Mary Magdalene. This was attended by Ian Smith, senior politicians, the majority of the senior officers connected with ComOps, Lieutenant Colonel Reid-Daly and other members of his Selous Scout regiment, including European and African soldiers who had served under his command.

Jan was dressed in a smart, well-tailored black suit, with a matching hat fitted with a thin veil, from which a lock of blond hair had escaped to fall over the collar of her outfit. As she walked slowly behind the pall-bearers carrying her husband's coffin, all eyes were upon her and those sitting on either side of the aisle could see that she had been weeping. It was not, as they would have assumed, due to the sudden loss of her husband but rather because she was burdened by an intense feeling of guilt.

The coffin was draped with the regimental flag, and on either side of a large wreath of white lilies had been placed the khaki jungle hat that Bushney had been wearing at the time of his death and his array of dress medals, including the scarlet-ribboned Grand Cross of Valour. Piet Erasmus was seated at the back of the congregation when Colonel Reid-Daly gave the eulogy. He couldn't help feeling a degree of responsibility. If he had not insisted that Mathew, under the pressure of blackmail, must return to the Vumba region to meet Chief Chidzikwee again, his kidnap would not have taken place. Without him, Mathew wouldn't have experienced such harsh brutality from his ZANLA interrogators and one of Rhodesia's Bush War heroes would not have been killed.

Mathew was unable to attend the service as he was still hospitalised, recovering from the severity of the wounds to the soles of his feet, which took some time to heal before he could place any weight on them. Due to the severity of the dehydration he had been suffering from at the time of his rescue, he remained in quite a weak condition, as well as frequently experiencing nightmares about his time in terrorist hands. When Reid-Daly referred to Mathew in his eulogy, Jan was relieved to consider that the tears which had started to trickle over her cheeks would have been seen by her parents, sitting on either side of her, to be a sign that she was no longer able to control her grief over the death of her husband.

At the beginning of September, just before the start of the Lancaster House Conference in London, Mathew and Jan started to be seen together in public. Soon afterwards they told the Vaughan-Joneses and the Kinlochs that they intended to get married. In late October, six months after Paddy's death, Jan and Mathew's wedding took place at the Dutch Reformed Church in Marandellas, followed by a reception of family and close friends at the Ruwa Country Club. Sebastian had flown out from England to be his younger brother's best man and Mariette was the maid of honour. Other guests at the small reception included Jan's parents, the Labuschagnes; Willie Smoelke; the Kinlochs; the Vaughan-Joneses; Jim Prior; David Montgomery; Angus Whitton; Tom Martin, who had been accompanied by three of Mathew's university colleagues and a number of Jan's friends from her school days and the time that she had worked in tourism before her first marriage.

After a short honeymoon in the Moremi Game Reserve in the Okavango Swamps, northern Botswana, they returned from Maun on a morning flight to Salisbury. After a farewell luncheon party at Simon and Anna's home, at which Jan's parents and sister had joined them, they all accompanied the newlyweds to the airport in time for them to catch the SAA overnight flight to the UK. It was a very emotional farewell for all concerned, in particular for Jan who was not only

A PARADOX OF VALOUR

leaving Rhodesia and going overseas for the first time to live in a foreign country, but also saying goodbye to her parents and to her closest friends, Mariette and Anna.

To some degree, Mathew was also sad to be leaving his friends and the country where he had spent so many constructive, meaningful and enjoyable years. At the same time, he couldn't help reflecting on how fortunate he was to have been rescued before his ZANLA kidnappers murdered him. In spite of the tragic death of Paddy Bushney, an irony that doubtless would haunt him for the rest of his life, he knew how very lucky he was to have married a person whom he loved so profoundly, a woman for whose companionship he had yearned for so long.

After clearing customs and immigration, a SAA steward approached them. 'Dr and Mrs Duncan, would you like to come with me?' he said, leading them towards the executive lounge. Jan gripped tightly to Mathew's arm, wondering what was coming next. When they entered the lounge, the airline staff and the other passengers began to clap.

'SAA would like to say how proud we are to have you flying with us today,' said the steward, 'and also that we wish you both every possible future happiness. Please ask if there's anything at all we can do for you.' Most of them had read about Mathew's much-publicised rescue by the SAS and some were aware of his recent marriage to the widow of Major Paddy Bushney, one of Rhodesia's most highly respected Bush War heroes and the recipient of the Grand Cross of Valour. As a token of goodwill, SAA had upgraded them to premier class for their overnight flight to London Heathrow and once on board, the couple were treated with every possible courtesy. 'This is wonderful, Mathew,' said Jan, reclining in her spacious seat and accepting a glass of champagne from the passing hostess. 'I could get used to this, let's hope it's a sign of things to come.'

They landed at Heathrow, enveloped in the fog of an

SOMEONE WISHES TO SPEAK TO YOU

autumnal day, and soon caught the onward British Midland Airways flight to Leeds-Bradford Airport.

Mathew explained that he had arranged for a car to take them to his parents' house, though he was careful not to tell her that the driver, Sid Stockdale, had been a family retainer for many years. For, from the start, he had wanted to keep everything about Hartington Hall as a surprise. He had sent a message via his parents to Stockdale to ask that he act as if they were total strangers. Addie Kinloch had always been aware that he was the son of a baronet, but he had asked her to keep it to herself. During his time in Rhodesia, Mathew had managed to keep his 'landed gentry' background secret from both Simon and Anna and, most importantly, from his new bride.

As Stockdale loaded their luggage into Sir Colin's black Daimler, he acted his role as a hired limousine chauffeur most professionally.

'Welcome to Yorkshire, Mrs Duncan – have you ever visited the county before?' said Stockdale, holding the rear door open for Jan.

'Thank you. No, I've never been to Britain, although my husband has told me that Yorkshire is particularly beautiful, of course.'

On their way through the Dales into Wharfedale, through Ilkley to Bolton Abbey, Mathew said, 'There's a hunting lodge close to the abbey that belongs to a Duke. I'll show you when we get near it.'

'I suppose hunting on the Yorkshire moors is rather different to the big game shooting in the Zambezi Valley... Is that the abbey?' Jan was startled by the sight of the sombre ruins. She found it difficult to understand how such a one-time stately edifice could have been allowed to fall into such a sad state of disrepair.

'I ought to explain that in England, you will see many such ruins. In the sixteenth century, many significant buildings were destroyed for no other reason than that King Henry VIII was unable to persuade the Pope to sanction an annulment of his first marriage to Catherine of Aragon. It was called the Dissolution of the Monasteries – Henry was destroying the might of the church to exert his own power.'

'I see I have a lot to learn.'

'After severing his links with the Catholic Church, destroying the monasteries and founding the Church of England, he made the most of it by marrying another four wives.' He thought it prudent to leave out the more gruesome fact that Henry had some of them beheaded for supposedly conducting extramarital affairs. It may have been a little too close to home.

The greenness of the fields, the late autumnal colours of the trees on the banks of the slow-running River Wharfe and the carpets of heather that blanketed the surrounding moors could not have formed more of a contrast to the environment Jan had been brought up in and had always felt so much at home in, during her formative years in the Northern Transvaal and the bushveldt. As the Daimler passed over the attractively arched five-span bridge at Burnsall and they drew close to Hartington Hall, Mathew couldn't help feeling a strong sense of excitement, although at the same time he had a degree of apprehension as to how Jan would react to seeing the magnificence of her new home.

Prior to the Daimler reaching the ornate gates of one of the hall's four drives, as Mathew was anxious to give Jan as much of a surprise as possible, he had pre-planned with Stockdale to carry out a detour of deception. 'I've asked the driver to take the turning into the drive by the lodge here, as I want to show you an excellent example of Britain's glorious heritage before we meet my parents. It's an eighteenth-century Queen Anne mansion.' As they drove slowly up Hartington Hall's mile-long south drive, between the metal railings to the north of the Home Park, Jan was completely mesmerised by the overall beauty and tranquility of the surroundings. The peaceful environment could not have been a more welcome contrast to all the horrors, tragedies and traumas that they both had to experience over the course of the last six months.

'This is just so beautiful. It's better than I could ever have imagined. I can't tell you how happy I am to be Mrs Duncan and to be here, to start a new life together.' Just as Mathew was about to respond, Stockdale drove slowly around the small copse of beech trees, and brought the Daimler to a halt in order for Jan to gain her first view of the fine south elevation of Hartington Hall, bathed in golden sunshine.

Jan was almost spellbound by being for the first time in such close proximity to the grandeur of one of England's stately homes. 'Is this a National Trust mansion? I've seen pictures of places like this in *Country Life*, back in Rhodesia.'

Mathew simply leant over to gently kiss her lips and said, 'Darling, let's just call it home.'

Postscript; 'A Sadness to Behold'

Eastern Lowland Gorillas

Conservateur Adrien Deschryver communicating with the silverback eastern lowland gorilla, Casimir, in the Kahuzi-Biega National Park, Zaire, October 1974 (see Chapter 2). © Jeremy Mallinson

SOMEONE WISHES TO SPEAK TO YOU

Since Mathew Duncan's field work in the Kahuzi-Biega National Park during the winter of 1973 and 1974, the current situation for the species could not be more serious. For during the mid-1990s there were around 17,000 eastern lowland gorillas in the wild, but today it is estimated that as few as 2,000 of these shy and majestic creatures remain. They have been pushed to the brink of extinction.

In order to combat such a critical situation in the Democratic Republic of the Congo (DRC), Fauna & Flora International (FFI) aim to build on initial population surveys by pushing ahead with full and comprehensive follow-up surveys and monitoring of the region that the eastern lowland gorilla is known to inhabit.

FFI's initiative represents essential work in the first step of implementing the IUCN Conservation Action Plan (CAP) to save the eastern lowland gorilla. FFI has highlighted how vital it is to understanding the surviving population of gorillas, to establish the threats they face and – crucially – the steps that need to be taken to protect them.

The vice-president of FFI, Sir David Attenborough, has recently stated, 'The Maiko and Kahuzi-Biega National Parks in DRC are home to some of the most endangered species in Africa, including the endangered eastern lowland gorilla. However, as human populations in the region expand, so too does the risk of habitat loss. A participatory form of conservation is giving these communities a means to exist and is helping the eastern lowland gorilla and other wildlife. Time is short and I urge supporters of FFI to quickly back this vital work that is crucial to the survival of the eastern lowland gorilla.'

In order for FFI, through the IUCN's CAP, to create a safe and secure future for this endangered species, the organisation requires as much public help as possible in support of its efforts to secure the species' survival for future generations.

Donations can be sent to:

POSTSCRIPT; 'A SADNESS TO BEHOLD'

'FFI – Eastern Lowland Gorilla Appeal'
Fauna & Flora International
4th Floor, Jupiter House,
Station Road
Cambridge CB1 2JD,
United Kingdom

ZANE: Zimbabwe A National Emergency

It had been soon after the newly married Mathew and Jan Duncan had left Rhodesia in October 1979 that as a result of the Lancaster House Conference, which had taken place in London under the chairmanship of Lord Carrington, Lord Soames was installed as governor of what the British Government still referred to as the Colony of Southern Rhodesia.

After a general election (one man, one vote) marred by gross intimidation, Robert Mugabe was declared winner, and on 17 April 1980 Zimbabwe became an independent state with Mugabe as its prime minister and the Reverend Canaan Banana as president. After an initial positive start as an independent self-governing state, the country was soon to witness dramatic ethnic cleansing. ZANU dealt with what they referred to as the 'Ndebele problem', which resulted in a genocide involving an estimated 20-25,000 tribal people in rural Matabeleland.

When Robert Mugabe lost a referendum in 2000 which would have given him dictatorial powers, he played his political trump card and commenced the seizure of 4,000 commercial white-owned farms that had provided the economic mainstay of the country. The Zimbabwean economy soon became the fastest collapsing in history with at least four million citizens, both white and black, fleeing the country. Those who remained were at that time condemned to a life of abject poverty, with the country becoming effectively a failed state.

SOMEONE WISHES TO SPEAK TO YOU

Prompted by the murders of a number of white farmers, in 2003 Mr Tom Benyon OBE founded ZANE, a charity that has helped over 1,800 elderly people, including about 600 ex-servicemen and their wives and widows who receive no pensions or state support. ZANE employs an amazingly brave, skilled and dedicated team of thirty-three workers in Zimbabwe who get to know everyone that they help, as well as always ensuring that donor money goes to those whom they know face the most hardship. For the key strength of the charity is its responsiveness, flexibility and lack of bureaucracy, and operationally ZANE is frugal, focused and effective in delivering aid directly to the most needy.

When the Zimbabwe currency collapsed and switched to US dollars in 2008, it resulted in huge price rises. Essential foods, medicines and utilities now cost about 600 per cent more. As a consequence, ZANE has had to raise substantial funds just to stand still, yet there are still many, many more people awaiting their support. However, the charity prides itself in never having lost any donor money to corrupt officials; it represents the only organisation operating in Zimbabwe which supplies aid to all communities, and is the largest supplier of financial grants to the country's pensioner community.

Deborah Bronnert CMG, the current (2014) UK Ambassador to Zimbabwe, has recently stated, 'ZANE's work in Zimbabwe quite simply provides a lifeline to those who are least able to help themselves. Their committed, inspirational team works hard to ensure that every penny raised goes to where it is needed most.'

Donations in support of ZANE can be sent to:

ZANE
PO Box 451
Witney OX28 9FY
United Kingdom

A Selected Chronology of African Events

With Special Reference to the Evolution of Rhodesia – Zimbabwe

1889 – a) Cecil J. Rhodes secured a Royal Charter from Queen Victoria to establish the British South Africa Company, to explore and exploit the land north of the Limpopo River.
b) The company's British South Africa Police (BSAP) formed.

1890 – 5 July; the Pioneer Column raised the Union Flag at Fort Salisbury, which had been named after the British prime minister, Lord Salisbury.

1893 – Chief Lobengula's impis (regiments) were conquered in Matabeleland.

1896 – March; Matabele rebellion broke out which was soon followed by an uprising in Mashonaland.

1897 – a) Dominican nuns opened the first school in Rhodesia.
b) Rail link from Beira to Salisbury started.

1902 – a) 26 March; Cecil Rhodes died (born 5 July 1853).
b) The planned 'Cape to Cairo' railway reached Salisbury from Bulawayo, and represented a through link of over 2,000 miles connecting Cape Town with Beira on the east coast of Africa.

1923 – a) 1 October; settlers in Rhodesia were conferred 'self-

SOMEONE WISHES TO SPEAK TO YOU

government' by London after white voters chose home rule over union with South Africa.
b) British South Africa Company turned over administrative control of the country to the settler representatives, under the 'Southern Rhodesia Constitution Letters of Patent'.
c) A sum of £2,000,000 was paid to the Imperial British Government in return for the new government obtaining 'all the unalienated lands' in Southern Rhodesia, other than native reserves.

1953 – Federation of Rhodesia and Nyasaland was formed by the British Government, as it had been convinced that such a federation between Southern Rhodesia, Northern Rhodesia and Nyasaland was the only practical means by which the central African territories could achieve security for the future and ensure the well-being of all their peoples.

1957 – 6 March; Ghana became the first African country to gain independence from European colonial rule. Kwame Nkrumah was soon to establish a one-party dictatorship.

1960 – a) 3 February; Harold Macmillan gave his African 'Wind of Change' speech in Cape Town: 'The wind of change is blowing through this continent and whether we like it or not, this growth of national consciousness is a political fact. We must all accept it as a fact, and our national policies must take account of it.'
b) 30 June; the Belgian Government gave independence to the Congo, which caused a sudden influx of refugees into Rhodesia.
c) October; the Monckton Commission suggested the component territories of the Federation of Rhodesia and Nyasaland be allowed to secede as a prelude to gaining independence.

1961 – a) February; Rhodesia was administered under a new constitution with a revised electoral formula, together with a Bill of Rights. The publication of the Commons' White Paper on the Rhodesian Constitution increased the power of the Crown, granting it a veto over all legislation.
b) 1 May; Tanganyika became Tanzania under Julius Nyerere, and immediately adopted Leninism and a one-party state embracing laws suppressing basic human rights.

1962 – a) Summer; Sir Roy Wellensky dissolved the Federal Parliament, leading to the break-up of the federation.

A SELECTED CHRONOLOGY OF AFRICAN EVENTS

b) December; Rhodesian prime minister, Edgar Whitehead lost the general election to the Rhodesian Front (RF) party.
c) 9 October; Uganda became independent under Milton Obote.
d) Britain agreed the secession of Nyasaland and Northern Rhodesia. The fate of Southern Rhodesia left in limbo.

1963 – a) 1 February; Dr Hastings Banda returned home to Nyasaland to lead the country to its independence.
b) August; Ndsbaningi Sithole formed the Zimbabwe African National Union (ZANU).
c) Internecine fighting broke out in Rhodesia's African townships.
d) 1 November; a new constitution for Southern Rhodesia came into force.
e) 10 December; Zanzibar gained independence under the constitutional monarchy of the sultan.
f) 12 December; Kenya gained independence under President Jomo Kenyatta.
g) 31 December; Federation of Rhodesia and Nyasaland was dissolved.

1964 – a) 12 January; after an uprising in Zanzibar which overthrew the sultan and his mainly Arab government, Abeid Karume became president and head of state.
b) 13 April; Ian Smith became Rhodesia's prime minister, charged with securing independence as well as with restoring order in the African townships.
c) Robert Mugabe and Joshua Nkomo jailed for being identified as the primary source of the troubles.
d) Ian Smith insisted that the 1961 constitution must be the basis for any settlement, and not London's preference for immediate black rule.
e) Labour won the general election in the UK and Harold Wilson said he desired an amicable settlement in Rhodesia, but majority rule was non-negotiable.
f) Rhodesians were warned, should a Unilateral Declaration of Independence (UDI) be declared, to expect sanctions, abandonment, citizenship-stripping, non-recognition and expulsion from the Commonwealth.
g) 6 July; Nyasaland gained independence and Dr Hastings Banda became president.
h) 24 October; Northern Rhodesia became Zambia and Kenneth Kaunda became president.

SOMEONE WISHES TO SPEAK TO YOU

1965 – a) Nine heavily armed Zimbabwe African People's Union (ZAPU) saboteurs, under direction from Lusaka, were arrested in the south-east part of Rhodesia from information supplied by local Africans.
b) 11 November; Ian Smith declared UDI. Governor Humphrey Gibbs went through the motions of dismissing Smith and his Cabinet, which was predictably ignored, and Harold Wilson recalled London's high commissioner.
c) More than ninety per cent of Rhodesia's white electorate supported the government, and prepared to take up arms.
d) Harold Wilson had the BBC install a broadcasting post in the neighbouring Bechuanaland Protectorate.
e) In the Congo, General Joseph-Désiré Mobutu forcibly removed President Kasavubu and began to rule by decree.
f) After a coup in the Central African Republic, Jean-Bedel Bokassa came to power. Bokassa, having been fascinated by Napoleon, went on to declare himself 'Emperor' and establish one of Africa's most brutal regimes.

1966 – a) 7 February; twenty-four Moscow-trained ZAPU terrorists were brought before the Salisbury High Court, charged with sabotage and attempting to overthrow the government.
b) 10 April; Britain received UN permission to enforce sanctions and to forcibly intercept vessels suspected of violating sanctions. At the same time, the UN surprisingly declared Rhodesia 'A threat to world peace'.
c) 30 September; the British Bechuanaland Protectorate gained independence. Sir Seretse Khama became Botswana's first president.
d) December; Harold Wilson invited Ian Smith to hold 'talks about talks' aboard the cruiser HMS *Tiger* off Gibraltar.

1967 – a) 30 May; the oil-rich Nigerian state of Biafra seconded from Nigeria's ruling junta in Lagos.
b) September; retrieved documents identified African National Congress (ANC) operatives in Rhodesia linking them with South Africa. The news alarmed South African intelligence and they began to deploy police on its borders with Rhodesia.
c) An international incident was narrowly averted off the coast of Beira, when a Royal Navy frigate fired warning shots at a French tanker making for port in violation of the British blockade.

1968 – a) 6 March; three Africans were hanged at Salisbury's

A SELECTED CHRONOLOGY OF AFRICAN EVENTS

Central Prison. Two had been convicted of the political murder of an unarmed white farmer.
b) The movement of hundreds of terrorists was detected in the Chewore Wilderness Area in the Zambezi Valley. No previous incursion of this magnitude had taken place. Troops from the Special Air Service (SAS), Rhodesian Light Infantry (RLI), and the Rhodesian African Rifles (RAR) were immediately mobilised. The terrorist camp was located, and for the most part successfully liquidated.
c) April; Kenneth Kaunda commenced seizure of white-owned farms and businesses in Zambia.
d) October; renewed settlement efforts between Harold Wilson with four days of talks aboard HMS *Fearless* at Gibraltar, with the British insisting that Rhodesia renounce its current constitution and abandon power.
e) Suspected influx of British intelligence agents in Rhodesia.

1970 – 2 March; Rhodesia became a republic.

1971 – a) January; General Idi Amin toppled the Ugandan government of Milton Obote.
b) 21 November; an agreement was signed between Britain's foreign secretary, Alec Home, and Ian Smith that included an immediate increase in black representation in Parliament, and the principle of majority rule was enshrined with safeguards ensuring that there could be no legislation which could impede this.
c) Enoch Powell warned that uncontrolled immigration into the UK would lead to conflict and 'rivers of blood'. Resulting from this statement, he was promptly sacked from government by Britain's new prime minister, Edward Heath.

1972 – a) 12 March; The Pearce Commission, formed to carry out the test of acceptability of the agreement of both the African and European communities, completed its work. When the report was published in May, it recorded that while the majority of Europeans were in favour of the proposals, most of the African people were not.
b) Fighting by insurgents in Rhodesia intensified when tactics changed, moving the majority of forces from the Zambezi Valley east to Mozambique to give them easier access into Rhodesia.
c) Samora Machel's Mozambique Liberation Front (FRELIMO) welcomed the new combatants, whilst fighting their own liberation war.

d) December; two white-owned farmhouses were attacked by rockets and machine-gun fire in the Centenary district of north-east Rhodesia. The farmhouse was damaged, a farmer and his two children were wounded and a RLI trooper who had gone to their aid was killed by a land mine.

1973 – While war in the east of the country was escalating, tragedy struck at Victoria Falls with the murder of two Canadian girls on holiday, when they were shot by drunken Zambian soldiers firing across the river.

1974 – After South Africa's President Vorster stopped a shipment of munitions and supplies going to Rhodesia, Ian Smith reluctantly agreed to an immediate ceasefire and to the release of political detainees, including Robert Mugabe. The *quid pro quo* guaranteed by Vorster was to be that Zambia and Mozambique would bring to an end their armed incursions. But this undertaking was never honoured, and the incursions were to continue.

1975 – a) 25 June; Mozambique given independence by Portugal and immediately proclaimed a republic by President Samora Machel's Marxist regime, with houses and businesses declared state-owned.
b) 11 November; Angola achieved its independence from Portugal and Agostinho Neto (MPLA) became the country's first Marxist president. Just prior to this, over 300,000 people left Angola after having experienced the devastation of the civil war between UNITPA and MPLA (1961-1975), which claimed millions of lives.

1976 – a) In Mozambique, an estimated 50,000 inmates filled concentration camps. The Roman Catholic Church was driven underground and baptism was banned. The country's legal code was abolished and replaced by military tribunals.
b) 3 March; the British Government gave £15 million aid to Mozambique, which was followed almost immediately by Samora Machel declaring his country on a war footing with Rhodesia.
c) Mozambique deported an estimated 28,000 Portuguese residents and incarcerated 150 Catholic priests in concentration camps.
d) 27 April; Ian Smith announced the inclusion of black ministers in the Rhodesian Government.
e) 16 June; an estimated 20,000 students staged an uprising in

A SELECTED CHRONOLOGY OF AFRICAN EVENTS

Soweto, South Africa, for better education. The police responded with tear gas and live bullets, killing 176 rioters.

f) Rhodesia's Selous Scouts carried out a raid, disguised as FRELIMO, on a camp in central Mozambique, killing an estimated 2000 insurgents.

g) December; a large group of African workers at the Honde Valley Tea Estate in Rhodesia's Eastern Highlands were brutally shot and bayoneted in front of their families. They were told it was their punishment for working for the white man and that their wages were so low, they were better off dead.

1977 – a) In March, Cuban troops marched into Zaire's (Congo) Katanga Province, having previously fought UNITA forces in Angola.

b) In Uganda, a British newspaper reported more than 90,000 dead in ongoing genocide with Idi Amin directing and participating personally in the slaughter.

c) 31 August; Ian Smith went back to the polls, once more sweeping all seats for his RF party.

d) The British Government demanded the immediate handover of the Rhodesian security forces to the Patriotic Front, and wanted a British Field Marshall to take command of all 'security matters'.

e) 23 November; Rhodesia's Combined Operations undertook two huge strikes in Mozambique. Two hundred soldiers attacked a ZANLA base and two days later, hit a secret terrorist camp, with approximately 3,000 insurgents killed and a few thousand wounded.

1978 – a) 4 March; the 50-50 black/white transitional government was sworn in with Ian Smith becoming joint prime minister with Sithole, Muzorewa and Senator Chief Chirau.

b) 23 June; eight English missionaries and four children were slaughtered at Elim Mission in the Eastern Highlands, close to the Mozambique border.

c) 14 August; Ian Smith held meetings with Kenneth Kaunda, Joshua Nkomo, the Nigerian foreign minister and others in Lusaka. Smith returned to Rhodesia with a feeling of optimism but a few days later, Tanzania's president, Julius Nyerere, vetoed the budding plan by repeating his 'absolute prerequisite' that the Rhodesian Army be disbanded prior to any further talks.

d) In August, Samora Machel admitted holding 20,000 religious

dissenters in camps in Mozambique but refused to bow to pressure for their release.
e) 29 August; grand-scale terror came to Rhodesia with the downing of Viscount passenger plane by a SAM-7 missile. Of the fifty-six who started the flight from Kariba, only eighteen survived. Twelve ZIPRA insurgents soon arrived at the scene and shot and bayoneted the majority of the survivors, with the commander shouting, 'You have stolen our land, you are white, now you must die'. While the country mourned, another mortar and rocket attack took place on the eastern border town of Umtali.
f) P.W. Botha replaced John Vorster as South Africa's prime minister. At the same time, Rhodesia's CIO arrested three American CIA agents accused of counter-intelligence activities and of undermining Bishop Muzorewa.

1979 – a) January; a 'bug' was discovered on the phone of the officer commander of the Selous Scouts.
b) Eighty-five per cent of the white electorate approved Rhodesia's new constitution.
c) 12 February; a second Viscount was shot down after leaving Victoria Falls. Joshua Nkomo triumphantly accepted responsibility.
d) 12 April; a company of the Rhodesian SAS drove brazenly into Lusaka and attacked Nkomo's home, which caused considerable embarrassment to Kenneth Kaunda who was hosting an OAU conference in Lusaka at the time.
e) 26 February; Rhodesian Air Force Hawker Hunters carried out a retaliatory strike on a ZIPRA base near Livingstone. At the same time four Canberra bombers hit a garrison of ZIPRA forces in Angola.
f) Soon after the raids, Abel Muzorewa was elected in a seventy per cent turnout.
g) 31 May; Ian Smith finished his last day in office.
h) 1 June; Bishop Muzorewa became prime minister in Rhodesia's Government of National Unity, but only South Africa was to recognise the new government.
i) 10 September; the Lancaster House Conference took place in London under the chairmanship of Lord Carrington, with the Rhodesian delegation led by Bishop Muzorewa and a delegation from ZANU/ZAPU headed by Robert Mugabe.
j) 12 December; Lord Soames was installed as governor, with the

A SELECTED CHRONOLOGY OF AFRICAN EVENTS

British Government still technically referring to Rhodesia as the Colony of Southern Rhodesia.

1980 – a) 27 February; voting (one man, one vote) commenced.
b) 4 March; after an election marred by gross intimidation, Robert Mugabe was declared winner.
c) 17 April; Zimbabwe became an independent state with Mugabe as prime minister and Canaan Banana as president.

1982 – a) July; South African Special Forces raided Zimbabwe's Thornhill Air Base in Gweru. Thirty Zimbabwe white air force officers were immediately arrested on suspicion of conspiring. All were brutally treated while in detention.
b) December; Mugabe formally presented Colonel Perence Shiri with the colours of the North Korean-trained 5th Brigade with the task of resolving the 'Ndebele problem', which resulted in the deaths of 20,000-25,000 tribespeople in rural Matabeleland. (A record of this ethnic cleansing was to be later recorded at the Kigali Genocide Memorial Centre, Rwanda.)
c) Joshua Nkomo fled the country and two former ZIPRA generals were both arrested and detained without trial.

1987 – Unity Agreement to merge ZANU and ZAPU, and Zimbabwe effectively became a one-party state with Nkomo as Mubabe's vice president.

1989 – 18 January; F.W. de Klerk became President of South Africa.

1990 – Nelson Mandela was released from prison on Robben Island and the journey to majority rule in South Africa commenced.

1993 – The dreaded process of eviction of white farmers began. At the same time, a parliamentary report indicated that 'corruption was so pervasive and civil servants so venal' that virtually no service was now provided without a bribe.

1994 – 10 May; Nelson Mandela became President of South Africa.

2000 – Robert Mugabe lost a referendum that would have given him dictatorial powers. Furious at its failure, he played his political trump card and commenced the seizure of 4,000 commercial white-owned farms that had provided the economic mainstay of the country. The Zimbabwean economy became the fastest collapsing in history with at least four million citizens fleeing the country. Those that remain seem to be condemned to a life of abject poverty, with the country being effectively a failed state.

2008 – Results of the country's general election were subsequently found by the team of election monitors to not represent the wishes of the people. ZANU/PF intimidation was rife, with over 200 murders having taken place. Although after the disputed results of the election, a coalition between ZANU/PF and the MDC was established with MDC's leader, Morgan Tsvangirai, becoming Zimbabwe's prime minister. During the following years there have been many incidences of political corruption, human tragedies and economic catastrophes.

2013 – a) April; Britain's Ambassador to Zimbabwe reported that there were now some general grounds for optimism, with the coalition government having had in some instances achieved success. For since 2008, when life expectancy was less than forty years, it had now risen to an average of forty-eight, and the coalition has established a Commission on Human Rights. Also, it announced that free and fair elections were soon to take place on a referendum for a new constitution, which both ZANU/PF and MDC have agreed upon.

b) 27 May; South Africa's *Sunday Independent* recorded that Robert Mugabe considered that Nelson Mandela had been 'Too soft on whites' and had been 'Too saintly, too good, and too much of a saint'. It was also reported that at a rally, he had referred to Mandela as a 'coward and an idiot'.

c) 15 June; President Robert Mugabe unilaterally set 31 July as the date of the general election, a move which directly violated the new constitution and a requirement of the Global Political Agreement.

d) 8 August; eighty-nine year-old Robert Mugabe hailed his re-election as Zimbabwe's president as a victory over the 'British and their Allies', although the Zimbabwe Electoral Commission admitted that 350,000 voters had been turned away from polling stations apparently because their names had not appeared on the roll. It also disclosed that 207,000 people had been 'assisted' to cast their votes – which represented another mechanism for rigging the final outcome of the election.

e) 10 August; the leader of the opposition, Morgan Tsvangirai, and his MDC party, filed a legal challenge urging the Constitutional Court in Harare to overturn Mugabe's victory and to order a re-run.

A SELECTED CHRONOLOGY OF AFRICAN EVENTS

As all the judges had been appointed by Robert Mugabe, few people expected the judges to defy him, regardless of the evidence presented.
f) 16 August; Morgan Tsvangirai, who was no longer the country's prime minister, and the MDC withdrew their legal action against the results of the election. For Tsvangirai had concluded that the outcome of the proceedings would be sufficiently biased not to come out in its favour.

On 7 December 2013, the ninety-five year-old Nelson Mandela, South Africa's first democratically elected black president, and one of the world's greatest statesmen, the symbol of forgiveness and reconciliation, died at his home in Johannesburg. World leaders were quick to send their condolences to the government and people of South Africa, with Barack Obama saying, 'We have lost one of the most influential, courageous and profoundly good human beings that any of us could share time with on this earth,' and that, 'He no longer belongs to us, he belongs to the ages, and he will be remembered as the last great liberator of the twentieth century.'

Well after the news of Nelson Mandela's death had been announced, Robert Mugabe issued a written statement which, in comparison to some of his previously reported negative comments about Mandela, represented a politically correct and positive appraisal of his lifetime achievements. For Mugabe's statement described him as, 'A champion of the oppressed whose commitment to liberation would always be cherished by Zimbabwe,' and that he was, 'Not only a great champion of the emancipation of the oppressed, but also a humble and compassionate leader who had showed selfless dedication to the service of his people.'

On 10 December, ninety-one heads of state and world leaders gathered to celebrate the life of Nelson Mandela at a memorial service held at the 95,000-seater FNB Stadium in Soweto. Barack Obama was introduced as 'A son of the African soil' and in his impressive speech he praised Mandela as the embodiment of the African ideal of unity, '*Ubuntu*'. He was also inspired to lecture some of the other world leaders sitting around him (viz. China, Iran, Zimbabwe – Robert Mugabe) by stating, 'There are too many leaders who claim solidarity with Nelson Mandela's struggle for freedom, but do not tolerate dissent from their own people,' and 'It took a man like Mandela to liberate not only the prisoner, but the jailer as well.'

Glossary

ANC African National Congress
BOSS Bureau of State Security – South Africa
BSAC British South Africa Company – Rhodesia/South Africa
BSAP British South Africa Police – Rhodesia
CIA Central Intelligence Agency – USA
CIO Central Intelligence Organisation – Rhodesia
ComOps Combined Operations – Rhodesia
FBI Federal Bureau of Investigation – USA
FRELIMO Mozambique Liberation Front
FR&N Federation of Rhodesia and Nyasaland
IRSAC Institut pour La Reserche Scientifique en Afrique Central
KAR King's African Rifles (1st/2nd Battalions) – Nyasaland
MI5 British Security Service
MI6 British Secret Intelligence Service (SIS, 'The Firm')
MDC Movement for Democratic Change – Rhodesia
MPLA People's Movement for the Liberation of Angola
NDP National Democratic Party – Rhodesia
NRR Northern Rhodesia Regiment
NUF National Unifying Force – Rhodesia
OAU Organisation of African Unity
PEA Portuguese East Africa – Mozambique
PF Patriotic Front – Rhodesia
PSYAC Psychological Action Group – Rhodesia
RAR Rhodesian African Rifles
RF Rhodesian Front
RLI Rhodesian Light Infantry
R&NSC Rhodesia and Nyasaland Staff Corps
SAS Special Air Service – Rhodesia

SOMEONE WISHES TO SPEAK TO YOU

SASO Senior Air Staff Officer – RAF
SIS Secret Intelligence Service (MI6) – UK
TTLs Tribal Trust Lands – Rhodesia
UDI Unilateral Declaration of Independence – Rhodesia
UFP United Federal Party – Rhodesia
UNITA National Union for the Total Independence of Angola
ZANLA Zimbabwe African National Liberation Army
ZANU/PF Zimbabwe African National Union – Patriotic Front
ZAPU Zimbabwe African People's Union
ZIPRA Zimbabwe People's Revolutionary Army

Bibliography

Politics and Patriotism:

Adams, M. & Cocks, C. *Africa's Commandos: The Rhodesian Light Infantry* (Johannesburg: 30 Degrees South Publishers [Pty] Ltd. 2006)

Andrew, C. *The Defence of the Realm: The Authorized History of MI5* (London: Allen Lane/Penguin, 2009)

Baxter, P. *Selous Scouts: Rhodesian Counter-Insurgency Specialists*, Africa@War Series, Vol. 4. (Solihull: Hellon & Compay Ltd. & 30 Degrees South Publishers [Pty] Ltd. 2011)

Clarke, R. *Ian Smith – A Bit of a Rebel*, DVD (London: Fine Claret Media, 2009)

Corera, G. *MI6 Life and Death in the British Secret Service* (London: Phoenix, 2011)

Davies, P.H.J. *MI6 and the Machinery of Spying* (London: Frank Cass Publishers, 2004)

Deacon, R. *A History of British Secret Service* (London: Frederick Muller Ltd. 1969)

DiPerna, A.P. *A Right to be Proud* (Salisbury: Books of Rhodesia, 1978)

Ellert, H. *The Rhodesian Front War* (Gweru: Mambo Press, Zimbabwe, 1989)

Flint, J. E. *Cecil Rhodes* (London: Hutchinson, 1974)

Godwin, P. *Mukiwa: A White Boy in Africa* (London: Picador, 1996)

Hall, R. *Great Zimbabwe: Mashonaland, Rhodesia* (London: Methuen & Co. 1905)

Lamb, C. *The Africa House* (London: Viking, 1999)

Lamb, C. *House of Stone: The True Story of a Family Divided in War-Torn Zimbabwe* (London: Harper Perennial, 2007)

Lee, C. *This Sceptred Isle: Twentieth Century* (London: BBC, 1990)

Macmillan, H. *At the End of the Day 1961-1963* (London: Macmillan Ltd. 1973)

Mechener, J.A. *The Covenant: The Nations of South Africa and Surrounding Lands* (New York: Random House, 1980)

Muller, C.F.J. (ed) *Five Hundred Years: A History of South Africa* (Pretoria: H. & R. Academica, 1969)

National Archives, *The Cabinet Papers 1915-1980 [Keyword] Military Intervention in Rhodesia 1965* (London: The National Archives, 1981)

Pringle, I. *Dingo Firestorm: The Greatest Battle of the Rhodesian War* (Cape Town: Random House Struik, 2012)

Rogers, D. *The Last Resort: A Memoir of Zimbabwe* (Johannesburg: Jonathan Ball Publishers, 2009)

Roth, A. *Sir Harold Wilson: Yorkshire Walter Mitty* (London: Macdonald & Jane's, 1977)

Rothberg, R.I. *The Rise of Nationalism in Central Africa* (Cambridge: University Press, 1965)

Smith, I.D. *The Great Betrayal: The Memoirs of Ian Douglas Smith* (London: Blake Publishing Ltd. 1997)

Stapleton, T. *Police and Soldiers in Colonial Zimbabwe 1923-80* (New York: University of Rochester Press, 2011)

Tabor, G. *The Cape to Cairo Railway & River Routes* (London: Genta Publications, 2003)

Thornycroft, P. 'Zimbabwe's White Farmers Manage One Last Smile Before they leave for Good' (London: the *Daily Telegraph*, 7 August 2002)

Todd, Garfield, J. *Through the Darkness: A Life in Zimbabwe* (Cape Town: Zebra Press, 2007)

Trento, J.J. *The Secret History of the CIA* (New York: Carroll & Graf Publishers, 2001)

United States Congress *Civil Rights Act, July 2nd* (Washington DC: US House of Representatives and Senate, 1964)

United States Congress, *Abortion Act, Roe v. Wade, January 22nd* (Washington, DC: U.S. Supreme Court, 1973)

Walker, P. *Towards Independence in Africa: A District Officer in Uganda at the End of Empire* (London: The Radcliffe Press, 1999)

BIBLIOGRAPHY

Wellensky, R. *Wellensky's 4000 Days: The Life and Death of the Federation of Rhodesia and Nyasaland* (London: Collins, 1964)
Wessels, H. P.K. *Van Der Byl: African Statesman* (Johannesburg: 30 Degree South Publishing [Pty] Ltd. 2010)
West, M. *Catching the Bag: Who'd be a Woman Diplomat?* (Edinburgh: The Pentland Press Ltd. 2000)
Wikipedia, *Wikipedia – The Free Encylopedia* (California: Googleplex, Google Inc. 2011-2013)
Wilson, H. *Final Term: The Labour Government 1974-1976* (London: Weidenfeld and Nicholson and Michael Joseph, 1979)

Natural History:

Candland, D.K. *Feral Children & Clever Animals – Reflections on Human Nature* (Oxford: Oxford University Press, 1993)
Chaillu, du P. *Explorations & Adventures in Equatorial Africa* (London: John Murray, 1861)
Durrell, G. *The Stationary Ark* (London: Collins, 1976)
Fossey, D. *Gorillas in the Mist* (London: Hodder and Stroughton, 1983)
Goodall, A. *The Wandering Gorillas* (London: Collins, 1979)
Hill, Osman, W.C. *Primates, Comparative Anatomy and Taxonomy Vol. IV* (Edinburgh: The University Press, 1960)
Hill, Osman, W.C. *Primates, Comparative Anatomy and Taxonomy Vol. VII.* (Edinburgh: The University Press, 1966)
Kingdon, J. *The Kingdon Field Guide to African Mammals* (London: Academic Press Ltd. 1997)
Lawick-Goodall, J. *In the Shadow of Man* (London: Collins, 1971)
Mallinson, J.J.C. 'The modern role of zoological institutions', *Rhodesia Science News*, 5 (2) (1971) 42–44
Mallinson, J.J.C. 'Observations on the reproduction and development of vervet monkey with special reference to intersubspecific hybridisation (*Cercopithecus pygerythrus*)', Cuvier, 1821. *J. Mammalia, Tome* 35 (4) (1974) 590-609
Mallinson, J.J.C. 'Wildlife studies on the Zaire River expedition with special reference to the mountain gorilla of Kahuzi-Biega', *Jersey Wildlife Preservation Trust Annual Report* 11 (1974) 16-23

Napier, J.R. & Napier, P.H. *A Handbook of Living Primates: Morthology, Ecology and Behaviour of Nonhuman Primates* (London: Academic Press, 1967)

Roberts, A. *The Birds of South Africa* (London: H.F. & G. Witherby Ltd. 1940)

Schaller, G.B. *The Year of the Gorilla* (London: Collins, 1965)

Selous, F.C. *African Nature Notes and Reminiscences* (London: Macmillan & Co., Ltd. 1908)

Smithers, R.H.N. *The Mammals of Rhodesia, Zambia and Malawi* (London: Collins, 1966)

Smithers, R.H.N. *The Mammals of the Southern African Subregion* (Pretoria: University of Pretoria, 1983)

Williams, J.G. & Arlott, N. *A Field Guide to the Birds of East Africa* (London: Collins, 1980)

Yerkes, R.W. & Yerkes, A.W. *The Great Apes* (New Haven: Yale University Press, 1929)